1795

THE ORDER OF THE FURIES

A NOVEL

Niklas Natt och Dag

Translated by Ian Giles

ATRIA PAPERBACK

New York Amsterdam/Antwerp London Toronto Sydney New Delhi

ATRIA
PAPERBACK

An Imprint of Simon & Schuster, LLC
1230 Avenue of the Americas
New York, NY 10020

Copyright © 2021 by Niklas Natt och Dag
English language translation copyright © 2023 by Ian Giles
Originally published in Sweden in 2021 by Bokförlaget Forum as *1795*
Published by agreement with Salomonsson Agency

First Atria Paperback edition March 2025

ATRIA PAPERBACK and colophon are trademarks of Simon & Schuster, LLC

For information about special discounts for bulk purchases, please contact Simon & Schuster Special Sales at 1-866-506-1949 or business@simonandschuster.com.

The Simon & Schuster Speakers Bureau can bring authors to your live event. For more information or to book an event, contact the Simon & Schuster Speakers Bureau at 1-866-248-3049 or visit our website at www.simonspeakers.com.

Manufactured in the United States of America

1   3   5   7   9   10   8   6   4   2

Library of Congress Cataloging-in-Publication Data has been applied for.

ISBN 978-1-9821-4597-2
ISBN 978-1-9821-4598-9 (pbk)
ISBN 978-1-9821-4599-6 (ebook)

Who spins the yarn that leads our way
through the obscure labyrinth of our desires?
—Donatien Alphonse François, Marquis de Sade, 1795

Cast of Characters

Tycho Ceton: defector from the Order of the Furies; former slave owner in the Swedish West Indies, and patron of an orphanage, following his return to Sweden in order to conceal his crimes with charity. The vicarious killer, via his agents, of Erik Three Roses's wife, and the architect of his misfortune. Since a fire at the Horn Hill orphanage, he has been destitute and defenseless.

Jean Michael Cardell: known as "Mickel," formerly a sergeant in the Artillery; after losing his left arm at Svensksund, employed by the Stockholm Watch. His momentary inattention led to the fire at Horn Hill in which Anna Stina Knapp's twins were burned alive, and he holds himself responsible for their deaths. Badly burned, although his conscience stings more than his scars.

Cecil Winge: lawyer, temporary appointee to the Chamber of Police; a model of rationality. Now dead and buried.

Emil Winge: Cecil's younger brother. Perpetual student at Uppsala University in revolt against his father's demands and expectations; thrust into the shoes of his late brother by Cardell—with fateful consequences. Once a drunkard in order to alleviate his delusions, latterly sober.

Anna Stina Knapp: escaped workhouse inmate. Widowed and now childless, she was tasked by human trafficker Dülitz to seek out her fellow prisoner at the workhouse on the Island of Scar, Magdalena Rudenschöld (convicted of high treason), who entrusted her with a letter bearing the names of those who allied themselves with Armfelt against the regency.

Maja and Karl: Anna Stina Knapp's twins, burned to ashes at Horn Hill before their first birthday.

Erik Three Roses: a young man of noble descent who once languished at the Dane's Bay Hospital asylum, later trepanned. Deceived by Ceton, he burned down the orphanage in revenge. Furiously slain by Cardell in the flickers cast by the flames of the burning orphanage.

Lisa Forlorn: a vagrant girl who lives in the Great Shade in summer; the assistant, on one tender occasion, to Anna Stina, she fled south last autumn to shirk responsibility and remain faithful to her name.

Petter Pettersson: custodian at the workhouse on the Island of Scar; having set Anna Stina free on a promise she later broke, he now retains Rudenschöld's letter as evidence of that broken pledge.

Isak Reinhold Blom: secretary to the Stockholm Chamber of Police; a poet of limited talent. Once Cecil Winge's colleague, latterly Emil Winge's champion.

Dülitz: once a Polish refugee; now a merchant-trader in people's lives.

Miranda Ceton: wife of Tycho; paralyzed and bedridden; kept alive by her husband against her will; assisted Emil Winge and Mickel Cardell in the pursuit of Tycho Ceton, albeit for her own ends.

Gustav III: by the Grace of God, the King of Sweden; shot at the Opera, succumbing to his wounds in March 1792.

Gustav Adolf Reuterholm: the strongman of the regency; dubbed the "Grand Vizier"; effectively the ruler of the kingdom; irritable, vain, and resolutely determined to eradicate the remaining loyalists in the country.

Duke Karl: the younger brother of the late King Gustav; governing as regent until the king reaches the age of majority on his eighteenth birthday. Uninterested in politics; Reuterholm's willing hunting dog.

Duke Fredrik Adolf: youngest brother of Gustav III; a superfluous prince; a debauchee.

Gustav Adolf: the only son of Gustav III; the nominal King of Sweden; still a minor, subject to guardianship.

Gustaf Mauritz Armfelt: the favorite of the late King Gustav; fled the country into exile after being unmasked as the principal conspirator against the regency.

Magdalena Rudenschöld: formerly a lady of the court; the lover of Gustaf Mauritz Armfelt and his coconspirator; held captive on the Island of Scar.

Johan Erik Edman: Keeper of the Records for the Department of Justice; Baron Reuterholm's enterprising and ruthless henchman; preoccupied with the hunt for Gustavians.

Magnus Ullholm: Stockholm's chief of police; former embezzler from the ministers' widows' fund; a cunning devil.

The Furies: A fraternal order in which powerful men derive pleasure under the pretense of charity.

Prologue

AUTUMN 1794

I

Gone is the blessed melody of string and bow that until recently filled his world and made him forget all else. Instead, the bells ring out from the tower into the autumn night, their timbre the toll of tentacles seeking him and no one else, singing out his vulnerability for all to hear. Tycho Ceton hunches his shoulders up towards his ears and crouches as he emerges from the cover of the alleys and hastens towards the thunder of Polhem's Lock. A pothole where a broken cobblestone has disintegrated twists the buckle off his left shoe, but he does not stop for its sake, instead adjusting his gait to keep the leather on his foot. He is alone—Jarrick is no longer by his side, having vanished down a side alley without a word with the coin he demanded in exchange for his final message. Ceton isn't surprised. He expected no better. He is exposed—there will be a queue of buyers once his life is offered for sale. Better to part ways now than see those ties formed by avarice tested to breaking point later. What trust remained would only be deferred by treachery.

The waves in the bay are crested with white as far out as visibility permits in the starlight. While crossing the drawbridge he must support himself on the railing to remain upright on the slippery boards beneath his feet. The wind is dashing the waters of Malar Lake between the stones with violent force, and the din of the breakers rises through every crack between the timbers. A malicious whisper as the foam caresses the wall says: *The bears are at your heels. All your debts have become due, and the blood in your veins is the only coin that will suffice for payment.* Once on the other side, he soon finds a carriage. The coachman has dozed off on the bench, his hands tucked in his armpits and his chin on his breast. Tycho Ceton crouches behind glass obscured by cracks and dirt as the hooves find their pace.

The leaves shed by the roses lie trapped in the shelter of the wall, whipped into swirls every time the squalls gust through. He knocks on the door and wheezes his name at the maid before wrenching the candlestick from her hand. She is sharp enough to scamper quickly out of his way as soon as the door is opened. He can already scent the inner room from the hall, and that which perfume can no longer conceal. Outside her door he raises his perfumed silk handkerchief to cover his nose, but changes his mind and presses it back into his pocket again, reluctant to show that anything about her can force a reaction from him, even if only disgust. The brass of the handle is cool as his hand hesitates against it for a moment. He twists it, opens the door, and steps into the darkness of the bedchamber.

The stench that awaits him beyond the threshold gives the very darkness shape, as if it were mist or smoke. The light he carries dazzles rather than illuminates as he crosses the floor. He sets down the gilded candlestick on a table by the wall and stands for a while in the deep shadow cast by the canopy bed. Veils of gauze conceal its owner. Tycho waits out his own heartbeats, and once they lessen their pace he hears her breathing calmly and warily; it is not the snoring of someone asleep. Resentment fills him. He's already the underdog. She lies there like a viper in her nest, contemplating him with all the patience she has acquired over the years—a patience that he can never hope to match.

"Dear Tycho. You've kept me waiting."

Her voice makes Ceton shudder—he knows which shapes the sound belies. She may have departed utterly from her original form in her paralysis, but her voice remains that which once emanated from a young girl's delicate breast. Her pangs must be terrible, but in her words there is an audible satisfaction, as if she is savoring them like the sweetness in a glass of wine. Sweat prickles beneath his shirt as he squeezes a reply past his lips.

"Miranda."

She bursts into laughter at her own name. Tycho can feel his tongue swelling in his mouth, his thoughts becoming immediately sluggish and unwilling, and he can do nothing other than wait for her to take the initiative that has slipped between his fingers.

"Oh, Tycho. Your voice. How it trembles! And before your own wife . . . But the credit for your shame is not mine alone. The church bells have been tolling for hours. I sent little Gustava up to check. She tells me it is the King's Isle that is in flames, and here you come hot on the heels of that news, and in quite a state at that. You've sweated right through your shirt and coat, and your anxious thoughts put my own tainted leg to shame. Come, come, what is the matter, my darling?"

Her tongue is always a whiplash to his most tender points, to her own undoing. The mockery sears with every word. Indignation devastates any hope of eloquence and he speaks freely in an incensed whisper.

"How much of this is your doing, Miranda?"

"Now then, Tycho, as you understand, such matters are not easily accomplished for one who cannot even lift a fingertip from her sheets. But I sincerely hope that the disaster has not befallen you entirely without my influence, for I have contributed as best I can."

She moves her head on the pillow, the small bell jingling.

"I had visitors, Tycho, ones that I had long awaited in vain, and I must confess that initially the visit did not meet the expectations woven by my daydreams. A big one and a little one. The big one so exhausted and worse for wear that he barely resembled a human being, not to mention the missing arm. The little one . . . he wasn't quite right. That much was clear. I was left in no doubt that the case they had taken upon themselves was hopeless. Who would take riffraff like that at their word, even if they had both a confession and evidence to hand? But the one-armed one . . . There was such anger smoldering in him. Rage of the kind that almost made the paper curl and peel off from the walls. I wonder what lies you've fed him, given how you've crowed about your foul deeds. Nevertheless, I dispatched him to the anatomical theater in the hope that he would slay you on the spot in his fury, but I must have underestimated the fellow's powers of self-restraint."

"Is that all?"

"Naturally I also spoke of you, dear Tycho, and your many embarrassments. But not everything."

"Why not?"

"Terror has constipated your head. You know why. Of course, I never believed they had any great chance of success—not in the one matter nor the other. But even if that odd couple doesn't return with more inquiring minds, others soon will. Then I'll tell all, unless you give me what I have so long desired."

He awaits her elaboration as the pulse throbs ever more rapidly across his temples.

"You must set me free now, Tycho. I've left you with no other choice. I know you are accustomed to letting others carry out such tasks while you watch. No, don't glance around looking for Gustava. She's gone. I advised her to flee and never look back once she had opened the door to you. Tonight, for once, the duty falls upon your shoulders. As you do so, and for as long as you manage to prolong your pitiful life which no longer has any worth, you should hold this thought in your head: Tycho, I have won. The final battle between us is mine, and all the years I have spent in this bed—every hour and every minute—are rewarded to their fullest when I see you in your misery. Do you remember the day I married you? I found you fair then—before I became better acquainted with you. But now you are a thousand times more beautiful than I, as afraid and degraded as you are. Well then, hurry, my darling, for your whereabouts are known and your enemies long for retribution. This loss will hardly be your last. Who do you think will get to you first? The one-armed watchman and the meager lunatic? Your former fraternal brothers? Any one of the many gentlemen whose favor you have contrived to bestow upon yourself? I wonder whose hands are to prepare you for the worst fate? If there is a God then He can hardly refuse me a glimpse, even if it is from the depths of my own hell. But those are the concerns of others. Now do as you're told before time grows too short."

He knows she has spoken the truth. Yet he hesitates, vainly trying to twist and turn the problem, akin to the loser who must suspiciously study the board from all angles to assure himself that he is in checkmate. As if in a nightmare, he moves closer to the bed, step by step, until her swollen form is visible under the quilt, to his disgust. Powerful inhalations fill his lungs with putrid air, and he gulps heavily to ensure he does not bring up the contents of his stomach. She chuckles with quiet satisfaction.

"My Tycho. It's like seeing a timid schoolboy facing his first bedding."

He snatches the pillow from beneath her head and with quivering hands he places it across her face. His arms straight, he presses down, but his strength is not enough and time congeals to molasses in his hourglass. He is obliged to sink down and apply the full weight of his torso across her in an obscene parody of an embrace, and he shakes with repugnance when her loose flesh wobbles under him. And yet for a long, long time—muffled by the feather down and silk—he hears her triumphant laughter and a bell that continues its muted jingle.

....

On his way out, Tycho Ceton supports himself against the wall. He has gathered the few valuables and coins that remain of his fortune, but he has not even been able to take all of that, forgetting many a hiding place as panic deadlocked his mind. She lies dead in her chamber, but her eyes are open and their mocking gaze follows him through the walls. He has filled a small cloth bag—that is all. Back in the yard, the night still reigns, but it is different from before, and something forces him to stop by the gate as surely as if it were an arch with its portcullis lowered. It is the horror: the one he has always harbored in the innermost chamber of his heart—a kernel worn smooth and safely brooded upon, if not forgotten then at least hidden away from the world. But now it has broken free from its shackles and taken possession of the earth. It is all around him. He swallows a cry and flees like a hare from a wind carrying the scent of dogs.

II

Dülitz smells a rat the moment he hears the knock on the door. He is accustomed to the petitioners' unobtrusive supplications—an apology for the inconvenience implied by the scraping of fingernails on the planks. Now, instead, there are hard raps from a cane—a rhythmic salvo from someone who knows they will not have to answer for the dents left in the woodwork by the silver handle. The hour is late, but he can still see well enough between the curtains of his second-floor window, careful not to allow the shadow of his figure to be cast against the glass. Two men incognito, their brimmed hats pulled down across their brows. That much he is accustomed to. Few visitors boast of his company. Behind them on the slope towards Serpent Salter Alley there are two others waiting under orders to maintain their distance, their backs stooped to protect their necks from the pouring rain, steady men whose coats conceal the fabric of uniforms. Across the roof ridges beyond Polhem's Lock the lamps of the alleys and the illuminated windows glimmer in the City-between-the-Bridges, shrouded in veils of rain, a many-eyed beast that seems to watch with tender disinterest, tender malice. Many a time Dülitz has surveyed the vista of Stockholm, still unfamiliar after all these years, and been filled with the foreboding that she will one day mark the grave that he has dug for himself.

Dülitz knows immediately what the visit concerns—but he is still baffled, despite expecting it. Yet, faced with the fact, he cannot help but question the choices that have brought him to this cul-de-sac. Perhaps there is a time in every man's life when the fallow field of habit is spurred to risk, and when the life whose weight has tipped the scale of the future to the past has no way to remember its youth other than by foolhardiness. He ought to have declined the commission imposed on him, but he paid no heed to the voice of reason that advised against it. It was the girl— Anna Stina Knapp. Without her, no danger would have sought out his door on a night such as this. Her arrival was opportune and she had what sufficed—a rare coincidence. Perhaps he was beguiled by compassion, perhaps it was infatuation. He dismisses the self-reproach from his mind, for whatever use that may once have served is now gone. His door is used as a drum yet again. Newly awoken and hungover, Ottoson gives him a look filled with questions and misgivings from down the hall, but Dülitz waves his servant aside and unbolts the door in the knowledge that a die is being thrown and that its number will determine his fate.

....

The stove is newly lit but as yet the warmth of the flames has not spread through the tiled surround, and Chief of Police Ullholm sees fit to keep his gloves on when he grasps the goblet of wine handed to him by Ottoson, whose arm is trembling. The two guests have each been shown to a chair.

"You perhaps know my companion by sight?"

Dülitz lights the candles in the candelabra, one after another, nodding, satisfied in spite of it all that his own hands betray his emotions to a lesser extent than those of his man.

"Keeper of the Records Edman is preceded by his reputation."

Johan Erik Edman must be at least fifteen years the chief of police's junior, his eyes anxious above a swollen, runny nose that he is obliged to blow repeatedly. Ullholm savors the wine.

"Good. A man in your line is wise to be well-informed. In that case you know that Mr. Edman is the spider in the web spun by the Crown's informants—our lion in the pursuit of the Gustavians. It is his toil we have to thank for the fact that the traitor Armfelt fled the kingdom with his tail between his legs."

Dülitz inclines his countenance.

"Mr. Edman is also esteemed in shadier circles for his unforgiving nature and his brilliant methods for coaxing confessions even from those whose guilt is so well concealed that they have altogether forgotten it themselves."

A wheezing sound emanates from Edman's throat, perhaps intended as a laugh, but he soon begins to cough instead, worse and worse, until he must cover his face with his handkerchief. Ullholm thumps him on the back as respectfully as he can, to little avail.

"Mr. Edman has unfortunately lost the power of speech on this particular day. Health has always been his Achilles heel and his enemies' foremost ally, and the many bitter trials this autumn and the constantly pouring rain have deprived him entirely of his voice—let us hope only temporarily. His zeal permits him no rest, and he has thus entrusted me to speak on his behalf during this visit."

Dülitz allows the silence to urge the chief of police to continue.

"Well: as you know, Ehrenström was pilloried in the New Square just the other week, his guilt in the Armfelt conspiracy having been proven in the Court of Appeal. All this as a result of Edman's efforts. Ehrenström was spared the sword to his neck on the block, and was instead dispatched to languish at Karlsten fortress. He had scarcely laid eyes on the wooden bunk and the stone walls of his new home before the absence of feather beds and gilded leather became too much for him, and the willingness to cooperate that had been so neglected before the prosecutor was recovered as if by a stroke of magic."

Ullholm lets the cane roll in a tight circuit he has formed between his thumb and middle finger.

"As you know, Ehrenström was a diplomat—held in high esteem at court in Petersburg. A cunning man who understood not to place all his eggs in one basket. He knows that his life sentence may be exchanged for honors two years hence when the king comes of age and Reuterholm is but a memory, but he is reluctant to await clemency under any and all conditions, and in exchange for greater comfort he has consented to make certain admissions without betraying his coconspirators more than he deems necessary."

Edman's eyes are gleaming maliciously, now that the crux of the matter promises to manifest itself. Ullholm leans forward.

"Here is the burden of the song that Ehrenström sang: an intermediary whose name we have agreed to overlook for the time being came to your door last autumn. Money changed hands and you were tasked with finding a way for Magdalena Rudenschöld to connect with her former allies. The idea was that she would compose a register of all the plotters whose names were not even known to each other in order that the conspiracy might reach a new unity and that the Gustavian revolution might once again be given hope."

Ullholm, his throat dry from speaking, takes more wine and swallows. Having set down his goblet, he gropes for a while for the dropped thread, scratching under the edge of his wig in irritation until Edman draws his attention by clearing his throat. For a moment, the chief of police watches in perplexity as Edman performs a rhythmic, stamping movement with his foot and seems to balance something invisible between his two hands. Eventually, the meaning of the gestures becomes clear.

"Rudenschöld was in with the whores on the Island of Scar, lodged in borrowed chambers while iron was being forged to bar the windows of a more suitable place of confinement. The workhouse is a particularly poorly managed place, which made her sojourn there your best possible opportunity to fulfil your obligations. Having interrogated several of the watchmen, we believe that this came to pass, but they are a rabble of drunkards and those who have guile enough to lie are hardly preferable to those too stupid or intoxicated to note with reliability what is taking place under their own noses."

Johan Edman leans forward to nudge the candelabra close enough for the light to fall more clearly on Dülitz's face ahead of the question that Ullholm has come to ask.

"So, Dülitz. Where is Rudenschöld's letter with the names of the plotters?"

It is Dülitz's turn to fill his glass and drink, mostly to play for time, but no final vestige of cunning can be induced to emerge from the haze of his mind, and he can taste nothing of the flavor of the wine.

"All that you say is true. I have no cause to deny it. But something has gone awry."

Ullholm and Edman exchange glances, and Edman makes a gesture that encourages him to continue.

"I found a girl—Anna Stina Knapp—as if by chance, who to my knowledge is the only person alive familiar with a secret way into the workhouse on the Island of Scar—a tunnel under the wall, once intended to dry out the foundations and then forgotten, and so hidden as to defy almost all discovery. It was by that route that she evaded her own punishment in the summer of last year. I commissioned her to use the same route back inside. Since then, I have waited in vain for word."

"What makes you believe that she even carried out her task?"

Dülitz has already asked himself the same question many times.

"She gave me her word. I'm surrounded by liars day in, day out, and yet I believed her. She was in a tight corner, and my offer was her only way out. The girl is no longer on Scar—that much I know for certain. If any such letter was written, then its whereabouts are unknown to me."

Edman's eyes seek out his gaze; he is used to chasing the shadow of untruth in those he is examining. Ullholm's fingers brush across the table in irritation.

"Your own activities hardly inspire confidence."

Dülitz, his eyes still locked on Edman, leans across the table.

"If the letter was in my custody then I would already have embarked upon negotiations with you for its price—at a rate that if no higher than that offered by the original associate would have been discounted in exchange for the goodwill of the Chamber of Police. And if I had already completed my undertaking and passed on the letter to my client, whose name I do not know, then surely Mr. Edman's informants ought already to have noticed the shifts among the ranks of the revolutionaries?"

Edman ponders for a moment before he once again leans back in his chair, the corner of his mouth taut as if to confirm the logic, and he nods curtly to Ullholm. The chief of police sighs and stands up, brushing his coattails as if he had been sitting in ashes.

"Well, it would seem we have been wasting our time. Find that girl, Dülitz. She's the key. This letter, whose whereabouts are known only to her, constitutes the most important document in the kingdom."

"Let me assure you that my efforts have already been considerable— to no avail."

Edman extends his left hand before him in a gesture worthy of a Roman emperor passing judgment on a defeated gladiator, forms a pair of tongs with his right hand, and pinches his outstretched thumb. Ullholm yawns into the back of his glove.

"What my colleague wishes to impress upon you, Dülitz, is that some further tenacity on your part would be favored, now that the stakes have changed somewhat. Our thumbscrews may be antique, but they're in perfect working order, and with a dash of oil to the threads are like new.

When the shafts of the bone begin to crunch, even the most hardened sing their aria *molto vivace* to be rid of the agony as quickly as possible, and we are happy to loosen the screws to be rid of the racket. But you? Mr. Edman would lock you up in the vault and only come back to see if you were still screaming at the end of the century."

III

The shadows creep over the city's households as soon as the fading glow of their hearths allows them to, before being chased away again into hiding by the dawn. Down by the charred ruins of Horn Hill, the men call out to each other, tired and sooty, their cries free of desperation now, for they know that their work has borne fruit. The fire has made its retreat. The hoses relieve each other as they water the smoking meadows, and with each steed that draws its burden close enough for the leather hoses to reach its previously blazing terrain, the fire shrinks. Thick smoke belches from the retreating boundary, where the living stamp out the devastation of the dead, and only with vain hissing do the final flames assert their rights. The grave of a hundred children. Two figures are standing, as if turned to stone, a little way up the hill, concealed among the trees and mist, surveying the blackened bones that poke up above the red cauldron before them. The sun has conquered the horizon, but the fog still shrouds it.

....

Emil Winge clutches Cardell's hand and feels it tremble with each hoarse breath that bestows the strength to endure the pain. Yet it is with less violence than before. No tears remain to moisten the smarting cheeks. The departing darkness took the bull's head with it, and the watchman's countenance is his own again, albeit cast in new forms by heat and flame. Hair gone, blisters all over, blood and soot intermingled.

"Come with me, Jean Michael."

Freshly settled scabs crackle and burst as Cardell twists his neck to see him better. Squeezed between swollen bags of flesh, the glint of his eyes is barely perceptible. Out of the pain arises a question Emil needn't hear in order to answer.

"Support yourself on my shoulder. We can't stay. If we're caught here it will make bad worse."

As if noticing for the first time, Cardell twists his single hand in amazement that another's is there. He shakes his head.

"I have never slain before. Not like this. Under orders, I have loaded shot and powder and taken aim as best I could towards the spot where the damage promised to be worst. In brawls, too, I have prevailed, giving change for cuts and blows in the same coinage till the debt was repaid with interest on the interest. But never have I extinguished a life in such a way. Three Roses had nothing to put up in response. In that moment he was innocent. I shall remain here to await justice."

Emil peers over his shoulder. No shiny sergeants' insignia can yet be seen glinting in the first rays of the sun. No one other than those damping down the ground is visible, except for those peasants hurrying from elsewhere on the island, eager to assist in the protection of their own land and to share the glory that may now be won with little risk. It cannot be long until the men of the Chamber of Police drag themselves out of their beds to ask questions about the cause of the devastation.

"Justice? I fear your wait will be both long and fruitless. You know that better than anyone. Whatever justice we seek we must help upon its way."

Emil's gaze flickers down to the deceased. The water is red and cloudy. Three Roses's slender calves are all that mark his grave.

"His death shouldn't burden our conscience unduly after this night's work, especially among so many others. Erik Three Roses may have set the fire, but we passed him the match and Tycho Ceton lit the kindling. All you did was assist Erik in accomplishing what he had resolved to do. His death was already certain, and the sooner it came the happier he was. Erik Three Roses burned Ceton's protection in order to give us an opening. If you feel guilt, then you will do best to see his last will fulfilled. Otherwise this would all be for nothing."

"After this there is no struggle worthy of the price."

"Perhaps the loss can be mitigated. We must seek out those victories that remain to be won."

Emil tugs him by the arm. He might as well have tried to move a statue of a man. Cardell coughs, his voice lowered to a mere whisper.

"Why would you help me now—you of all people? I was given the choice between you and another, and I chose her."

"I know that. And I know why."

"I roasted her children with my kindness. Hers and that of a hundred others."

Emil's gaze turns down to the glowing household hearths where he saw the girl with his own eyes less than an hour ago. She is gone now.

"Only half the responsibility is yours to claim. The rest belongs to me. But I cannot make your choice for you. Do you recall my first day sober? You gave me the freedom to choose. I shall return the favor to you. But if you follow me, then you must give me your word. Swear it. To those victories that remain to be won."

Silence settles for a while, and Emil Winge holds his breath until the answer comes.

"Yes. My word. For those victories that remain to be won."

"No price is too high."

"None."

He takes Cardell by the arm.

"Come with me now."

His tug dislodges the burnt statue, with one staggering step and then another. Emil grips Cardell by the elbow to steer him the right way, wending up the hill. On the far side of the crest, the road towards the City-between-the-Bridges begins. Cardell stops at the top of the hill, and his limp arm, suddenly stiffening, stops Emil as if it were a bolt of oak.

"This road leads only to hell. You know that, don't you? Do you really want to follow it with a cripple who has betrayed you before?"

The sound Emil makes isn't a laugh, isn't a lamentation.

"Is your position any more enviable, Jean Michael? You are being supported by one who consults with the dead and cannot distinguish poetry from reality. But if another course remains open to us, say which it be. If this is not our desire, then let it be our punishment. Hope is no longer the shackle that fetters us to life. Now it is guilt."

"And will we then be friends during our time together?"

Emil shakes his head, incapable of lying and bitter in tone.

"No, Jean Michael. Never again shall we be friends. And I do have one request: set your affairs in order with the girl Anna Stina first. Before that is done you are of no help to me. Come to me then."

"And you? What shall you do?"

"I will go to the Chamber of Police, and to Isak Blom, to do every-thing in my power to renew our mandate. It will not be easy, given how we parted. Then I shall begin to seek out the scent we are to follow. Be ready when the hunt begins."

Cardell takes his first step unaided and each movement elicits a groan. Emil turns his back on the smoking pillar of devastation. Not only life and property have been lost here—he is no longer the same either. For as long as he can remember, he has nourished the anger within, but that which was previously a solitary flame is now a bonfire, and it burns even more strongly from the fuel of his impotence. He is captive, snared, like a netted fish or a moth pinned beneath a glass dome. What has happened cannot be undone, but invisible restraints require responsibility. He volunteered his assistance before, but now there is only coercion. He must do what he can. Until then, the City-between-the-Bridges will remain his cage.

Fear was always the companion of rage. He tries in vain to take solace: he has been face-to-face with the Minotaur, he has braved the darkness at the heart of the labyrinth, he has heard the children screaming their anguish in their final hour. He has seen the worst—can there be anything worse to come?

PART ONE

The Hunting Dogs
SPRING AND SUMMER 1795

All blazed, for all burns. What had happened?
The flame was at last extinguished, and it was
only ash they both held in their hands.
                              —Carl Gustaf af Leopold, 1795

1

Autumn becomes winter and the year turns. Winter becomes spring and a fairy tale is told in the City-between-the-Bridges—one of the cautionary variety, although it is not children that it frightens, but grown men. Among the alleys by night wanders a phantom figure, and if sinners of a certain kind cross its path then things do not end well. As to its appearance, testimonies vary. It is big—that all agree on—and ugly, its face not that of a human, its skull scarred and bald but for odd wisps of hair. Some know more of it, and they say that its one hand is as scorched earth and that all hope is lost for any who venture within its reach. As for its origins, a fog of guesses and rumors arises. It is said that it burned down the Horn Hill orphanage but was itself caught in the flames. Hell hath denied it entry, and this lost soul seeks out its old haunts. A crime has been committed for which it has been sentenced to atone. Now it is a symbol of all that is pitiable.

....

The yard slopes, and that has never bothered Frans Gry when sober, but when drunk the angle constantly baffles him. No matter how hard he tries to navigate the straight route from door to privy, it begins to wind; he drifts off down the hill, and those damned nettles find gaps and holes in his stockings as if that is all they are good for. His revenge is always the same: one step backwards, breeches down and shirt up, piss on them; to hell with the fly-ridden privy. Intoxication protects him from the evening chill. He grunts and strains to piss. With each passing year, he must go more often, although it becomes ever more difficult to pass water. The nettles are likely still damp from his last visit, but then again there are plenty of others that may benefit from his efforts. After shaking off and tucking away, Frans stands for a while, looking around. The stone hovels are already past their best—it's hard to believe that they're just a few decades old, their foundations laid on the hill cleared by the Great Fire of 1759. Somewhere down in the gap behind the bottommost building is the Golden Bay, the City-between-the-Bridges in its center. He wishes the whole island would go straight to the seabed under the weight of the palaces of the rich. They swagger about by day uselessly lisping away in court French, while he can barely afford to buy wine so sour that the corners of his mouth convulse with every sip. In his mind's eye, he sees the slops rising and foaming their way up the ornate staircases—the latrine barrels discharged straight into the lake have dispatched a brown fleet to storm and soil such opulence. Bewigged bitches choking on the sewage into which they have slipped, their chevalier menfolk howling in nasal soprano as they cling to the branches of the crystal chandeliers. Come to think of it, the Great Flood needn't stop there. The tide is most welcome to make its way up his own slope too, just as long as the waves stay below his own floor. Farewell, loafers, whores, and beggars! He lets out a sigh that begins in longing and ends in resignation, because the dream is just as fleeting as it is beautiful. The mills grind on—a damned racket, all creaking and pounding. Yet that is better than the racket inside the houses—children running all over the place, one indistinguishable from another. If you take up the chase, then you need only turn a corner and—hey presto!—you have no idea which of the little bastards is which. You just have to grab the most obvious child by the collar and rap its jaw as a warning to the others. He wishes everything to hell and staggers back to his room; his wife is out gadding about somewhere, and while she will be given a hiding upon her return, just to be sure, he is content to drink on in peace, without nagging, without the usual gibes about rent and food.

He sits there rocking, with the bottle in his hand, his thoughts dwelling on bygone days. With the inertia of inebriation, he arranges every word in the defense he has assembled to explain the adversities he has met in life—a task that has been going on for years, performed with as much zeal as if he were some priest's son reciting the catechism to him. Momentarily satisfied, his mind wanders to more agreeable things: to life as it should have been if his qualities had been appreciated; toasts of Rhenish wine from glasses of crystal, oysters, raisins and waffles, a beautiful girl in his arms. And retribution over all those who have wronged him—his detractors cudgelled, the lot of them, their limbs broken on the wheel, and braided around its spokes, in full sight from where he sits at his feast.

A knock on the door. Damn them all—what good has ever come of such a thing? He leaves the discordant sound unanswered and returns to his own preoccupations. And now the door flies off its frame, kicked to splinters, and someone grabs him by the scruff of the neck and tosses him down the stairs, his limp inebriation the only thing saving him from broken arms, legs, or back. He rolls from kick after kick to his buttocks and thighs, the threshold striking his forehead, then out into the stinging wind of the spring night and into the shelter of the wet nettles, where he lies still and dazed for a while, hoping that his misfortune will disappear as quickly as it arrived. Then a popping sound echoes between the house fronts—one as familiar to him as his own voice: the cork of the bottle from which he's just drunk. There is so much one can tolerate, but there are limits. Frans rises on shaky legs again, and feels the air whistling as the bottle passes a hair's breadth from his ear and bids the cruel world farewell in a crash against the wall behind him. Soon he feels a fist in his hair with a grasp hard enough to knock him off his feet and drag him onto bare ground, where he lies gasping for air, every breath a reminder of blossoming bruises. Someone paces back and forth before him, only their contours shown by the failing light, the neck thrust forward on broad shoulders, arms thick and brutish. Life has not so blocked Frans Gry's nose for danger that he cannot sense that worse looms. Pent-up wrath lingers in the air like thunder, the figure before him tense as anchor ropes in the frames of a ropery. In a panic, Frans seeks a reason and finds too many from which readily to choose. He begins at the mildest end, in the hope of haggling down the sum total.

"I know the walls are thin, and I'm told I snore badly . . ."

"Hold your tongue."

Gry counts his sleeping dogs and chooses one at random.

"Unless I am mistaken, I returned every penny that I owed Jan Faithless at the Last Farthing long ago. He was so drunk when the loan was made that I'm amazed he remembered it at all."

"Shut up."

The voice is deep but hoarse at the same time, as if it springs from a throat unused to human speech. Only now does Gry remember the fairy tales he has heard, and he puts two and two together. The monster has come; he himself is its prey. He does as he has been told.

"The woman whose bed you share has a daughter of her own. Lotta Erika. Thirteen this year."

He nods reluctantly.

"You sought her out beneath her sheets. She clawed at your eyes. You chased her out of the house."

Frans Gry's jaw drops, as if of its own volition, but he has sobered up enough to stifle his excuses.

"Tomorrow she returns home. The next finger you lay upon her I shall feed to the pigs."

The figure approaches, crouching an arm's length away, and Frans Gry locks his gaze onto his own stained knees to spare himself the nightmare of looking at its face. A rap across his shin makes him cry out, because the hand that strikes him is as hard as a cudgel.

"Ideally, I would render you harmless forever. Break arms and break legs. There is but one reason why I do not: you must keep the girl in food and shelter. Be the stepfather she would wish for herself. As if she were your own. As if you wanted nothing but the best for her. Solely for her sake do you leave here of your own volition. She can easily find me. If I hear otherwise, you shall see me again. Is that understood?"

"But I . . ."

"There is work, albeit of the kind you consider yourself too good for. Carrying pig iron to the scales. Clearing dung from the barns. Turning dunghills. Good men find occupation. You, however, are all but worthless."

The words awaken a vague recollection, one that stifles the final glow of intoxication. Frans Gry flips through his memories, seeking a hole where it all fits: the voice, the body. As he sits quietly, the monster rises, turns on its heel, and begins to move towards the place where the houses thin out and the road makes off towards Polhem's Lock. Gry holds his breath until he is alone, and there, in the void of his thoughts, the images he has sought emerge. A face and a name.

"Cardell! Mickel Cardell! You were on the *Ingeborg*! I was on the *Alexander*! We were at anchor off Crow Island when the *Stedink* fired and the *Prince Nassau* responded as best he could. I saw you burn and sink."

Context begins to solidify around the figure: he tenses his brow as if to force his brain into obedience, and grimaces with distaste as his memories arm him.

"They say you were there when Horn Hill burned down. They say it was your fault. They call you a child killer."

Rarely has he thought so clearly. Hatred and humiliation harry the conclusions straight into his arms.

"You're here for the sake of your own conscience, not Lotta's, you selfish bastard."

He's on his feet now, and staggers a few steps towards Cardell's departing shape, raising his voice to a wheezing roar.

"She'll always get her bread, of that you can be sure, but welcoming little ones into the sunshine opens no graves. Do you think you're better than me, Cardell? You're not. You're worse. Worse! Beside you, I am a saint. There is no blood on my hands."

His own words startle him and he hurries across the yard, across the threshold, and up the stairs, letting out a pained whine at the door—now smashed to splinters, no longer affording any protection. He does what he can to piece the largest parts back together, and keeps them in place with his back as he sits on the floor, alone again, shaking with relief, with terror, with triumph.

....

Cardell has stopped around the corner out of sight, and there he allows his panting breaths to quieten. He wishes he had made it out of earshot, but every word is like the lash of a whip. For a long time he stands still, seeking comfort in the fact that he has at least helped the girl Lotta Erika to something better. She is not the girl he was seeking, but still . . .

....

He finds them all over in his search—these distressed little red herrings, and he helps them whenever he can. Sometimes they help him in return. The street girls are many—their hearing is good, their eyes keener. In their innocence, they gain easy entrance to where he himself is barred.

2

There is a knock on the door of his room and Cardell blinks the grit from his eyes, rising dressed from the bench in a cloud of his own exhaled mist. He shakes off the cold, turns the key in the lock, and finds a pale face with a shawl pulled close around it. One of the many of whom he has lent his fists in defense, in some mêlée he can no longer recall. She curtsies and lowers her gaze, whatever gratitude remaining shrouded in shyness. He has come to learn that they only look him in the face once, then never again. They do this partly out of consideration, but for Cardell it is merely a reminder of how badly burnt he is.

"The fisherfolk are back by Klara Lake. You can see the smoke from their fires. You asked me to keep an eye out, sir, if you remember."

He can't recall her name, but the context grows clearer. She is in the service of a merchant over by the Russian Yard—one who used to be pre-disposed to miscounting on payday and offered the warmth of his own bed by way of compensation. He gives her a nod.

"Thank you."

She curtsies again, taught that subservience is desirable in any given situation.

"Is all well otherwise? Have you had anything to eat yet?"

He is grateful for her nod, for the crust that remains in the bread tin is hard enough to give even his practiced jaws a trial and it would be shameful to offer it to a guest. He nods awkwardly, and with a third curtsy she takes her leave, departing quickly on soundless feet. He does what he can with the bread before enveloping himself in the coat that he has turned inside out in order to wear down the reverse side. The material is worn down to a gauze at the elbows. The care required to avoid further tearing the wool with his wooden fist makes Cardell grunt. Had they cut off his left arm higher up then at least he would only have worn it down on one side.

....

The ice on the lake has broken up. Distended by meltwater, the current is an irate muscle hectoring white floes forward, floes at times so big that they get stuck crossways between the pillars of the North Bridge. More ice gathers at the barrier, forming a white wall against the stones of the bridge. Pent-up force intensifies like the anger before battle, all the more threatening in its weight, and those people who have dared cross the bridge hurry for land. If they don't remember themselves how the spring flood tore at the bridge abutments some fifteen years ago, then there are others who will gladly tell them. Then the core breaks with a crunching crack and the ice rumbles beneath the bridge, free to scourge the anchored hulls in the Salt Sea.

Cardell hurries over, passing the Red Sheds, where people are teeming about with the sort of purpose that only the cold can encourage. Spring is approaching and the darkness is giving way—they must sweep and tidy and prepare as best as they can for the season of commerce. Where the promontory sharpens into a tip, the bridge crosses Klara Lake—it is longer and more exposed than the one across the Stream but better protected from the rapids. He nevertheless grasps the rope strung to the railing with his good hand, scanning about him to verify that the girl was right: the fisherfolk from the lake are finally here, their boats pulled onto the shore. Smoke rises from their camp.

The path along the shore of the bay is uncertain. The ground frost underfoot is treacherous; it may crack at any moment, sinking a whole boot into chilly mud, and the pebbles dislodged by the ice are loose and unreliable. Cardell limps forward at an uneven pace, rarely without a curse upon his lips. He reaches their camp without any major incident. The nets hang in rows between hooks on wooden poles, while women and children are occupied mending holes in the meshes with string. The menfolk are preoccupied with their boats, doing all manner of things beyond Cardell's ken. He stands there, perplexed and disregarded, until he catches someone's eye and turns his feet in its direction. It is a man with a beard and tousled hair, seated on a stool in front of the fish smokers lined up in a row, and Cardell cannot determine whether the soot has soiled his white hair, or whether dark strands are intermingled with those that have faded. The man is the firewatcher, surely, given his age. Cardell senses a single, squinting eye taking the measure of his being, noticing his official boots and the white belt beneath his coat, lingering on his burnt face. He clears his throat awkwardly.

"Good catch?"

The man shrugs noncommittally, and nods at Cardell's midriff.

"Got tobacco?"

The voice is as bright as that of a woman, yet feeble and fragile like an old man's, as if deprived of the power of the lungs and with only the shallow oral cavity to launch itself from. The pouch that Cardell wears at his belt speaks a universal language, and Cardell unties it and passes it over. The man cuts himself a plug using a small knife that appears so quickly in his hand it might have been there already, and then he begins to chew, spitting when the juices fill his cheek to bursting. Cardell finds an adjacent flat rock and sinks down on it, half-crouching, half-sitting, knowing that he has paid for something; he waits for the silence to end. The man chews for a long time before considering himself satisfied.

"So?"

"I'm looking for someone, and have been doing so since last winter. I've spoken to the people up on the King's Isle, but every trail ends down here at Klara Lake. I was sick for a long time, and was unable to reach you before the ice came. I've been awaiting your return ever since."

The man nods curtly, as if the news were no surprise, but offers no reply. Cardell has no choice but to continue.

"A girl with light hair and sooty clothes. Soot from the big fire over at Horn Hill last autumn. Her name is Anna Stina."

The man spits and coughs his throat clear.

"I'm of an age. God knows how. The sea took my father, the shivers took my mother, and had we been born in the same year I would have survived them both. Now I'm good for little more than guarding the embers. But I've time enough and then some for pondering."

For the first time, the man turns towards Cardell, opening the eye that has only so far been glimpsed, and Cardell sees a white spot where the pupil should be black, like a marble at the bottom of a hole.

"There is a spot that grows bigger in my bad eye. It is black and awful. If I have both my eyes open, then it is as if I see it amid trees and people, on the scales and in the sails. I dare say it is death's shadow itself. He grows closer and closer to me with every passing day. I think on him a lot. He comes to everyone, and it is never good to know when."

He twitches his chin towards the children patching the net.

"Big and small alike. One wrong step by the rail and it is all over. For some of us, at least, it is given to await his arrival as if he were a guest travelling on the road, always keeping the table laid and the hearth warm. I'm no more afraid than I ought to be. It is not good to know what awaits us. On the water, we are never called to mass and I haven't heard the Gospel in a long while, but I have talked enough foolishness about the dead in my time to understand that no one should take their debts with them to the grave. I think a lot about putting my affairs in order as best I can, while there is time. You want to have everything arranged."

The wind is rising from the bay, and the man draws his blanket around his shoulders for better protection.

"I can conceive of many a reason why a man would seek out a girl. Not all of them good."

The rising blood stings Cardell's face.

"I mean her no harm."

He feels his heart pounding and his throat tightening, his vision clouding. He reaches for a fistful of the wet snow that still lies in slowly thawing drifts, and lets it cool his brow and throat. Only when he feels that his lungs are slowing and his voice is capable of carrying does he open his mouth again, turning to meet the gaze that has never left him.

"If you are in debt, then you are not the only one."

The old man sits quietly for a while before nodding briefly and resuming his former thread.

"I believe I remember the girl. I wish I could have helped her then, but I couldn't. It has gnawed away at me, but I could not do otherwise. We've mouths enough to feed and we rarely have more food than we need. Everyone must do their bit, otherwise it won't go around. I will soon no longer be of use, and I would rather walk into the lake than burden the very air around me. But I'm glad you came—for the sake of my conscience. Perhaps I may help her, now at least."

The chewing tobacco is used up, the final flakes leaving with the man's next mouthful of spittle. Cardell passes him the pouch again.

"It was the day after the fire. The bells were ringing in the city all night long—we saw the glow of the flames on the mainland, but their troubles are not ours. When morning came and the smoke began to settle, she was sitting on the shore over there, just as you describe. Light hair, sooty clothes."

The old man nods at a willow that has dipped its crown into the bay some distance away.

"She was sitting quite still, not moving. When she was still there the next morning, some of the children went to see what was amiss, but she neither replied nor made any gesture. After that, they left her in peace and didn't mention her again, and slept with iron under their pillows—because it is never good to know what is wrong with those who no longer see, and it is best to keep away. But I sat where I sit before you now, and for three days I saw her sit still on the shore without raising a finger. She had two white streaks on her face. There had been tears in the soot—many enough to see from here."

"And then?"

"A lad came on the afternoon of the third day. He spoke to her. Sat down beside her. I saw him coming, saw how he behaved, and I thought he knew her from somewhere. Whether she answered, I don't know. He took her by the hand and raised her to her feet. It was a clear day. He supported her across the bridge. I lost sight of them on the other side, but their direction was unmistakable."

He points towards the City-between-the-Bridges, pitiful from this point on its islet where the jagged floes have stormed the ramparts, its church spires the drowning hands of those seeking rescue.

"Now you know what I know. Leave me to guard the embers. It is an undertaking as important as any other. Although anyone can see that you know that better than most."

3

Emil Winge is woken early from uneasy sleep by a runner from the Indebetou, the bastard child of some police constable or some other urchin thankful to have found favor. Dirty blond mop of hair, clothes far too thin, snot dripping from his nose, simply happy to have a task where the double-quick turnaround helps him keep the cold at bay. Arriving at Emil's threshold, he jumps up and down on the spot to prevent the sweat from freezing.

"They're asking for you at Axesmith's Alley."

"Give me a moment."

The light in his room is very dim and he is obliged to angle his Beurling pocket watch to capture what illumination there is to be found in the rose-cut diamonds to check the time. Just after five on a wet spring morning that sanctifies the memory of winter all too well. He wraps his coat around his body and descends the stairs. The boy is already gone—he must have taken Winge's words as a dismissal. Outside, the night still holds sway and the lamps that have been lit have greedily drunk their oil to the dregs. Winge straightens his collar to better protect his neck, and tries to bring to mind the route to the address he has been given. The City-between-the-Bridges still confuses him. Although he is growing better acquainted with its alleys with each passing day, he still hesitates at crossroads, chooses incorrectly, and is forced into detours. The street is towards the Flies' Meet, that much he is certain of. He has found that the vast dungheap beside the Grain Harbor helps him to navigate. If there is a southerly wind, then its direction is unmistakable, and if there is no stench then the wind is blowing from the north. The morning frustrates him: the wind of the night has died down. Instead, he follows the hill downwards, hoping for the best.

A sergeant and two constables await him farther down, in Axesmith's Alley. Emil knows the officer in command by sight, as indeed he does one of the other two men, but he cannot recall their names. His face betrays his ignorance even at first glance.

"Johansson. Mårten."

The sergeant alone steps forward to greet him. The constables keep their distance, although both take care to nod respectfully at him. He heard them whispering and tattling from a distance. They have nicknamed him "the Little Ghost," and they treat him with reserved reverence, as if he were a creditor newly infected by the plague. Some malevolent gust of wind carries a whiff of spirits from them: that they have drunk their breakfast is evident from their rosy cheeks. Emil feels the old sinking feeling in his stomach, a feeling that is never distant—the stab of jealousy at the inebriation they may enjoy while he cannot. He blinks and swallows, turning back to the officer in charge for a report. A finger is pointed towards a recumbent figure, a draped jacket concealing the face.

"This fellow took a blow to the head hard enough to crack his skull. Sigvard and Benjamin have asked around on the stairs. No one saw or heard it, which is strange if there was a scuffle here. A row outside the window is the best entertainment the people around here can afford. Without any witnesses, this looks particularly hopeless. Normally I would have sent word to the gravediggers and settled for that, but you have a reputation for seeing what others miss."

"Who found him?"

"A fellow watchman was doing his round here and close enough tripped right over the body an hour ago."

"Was he lying like that when you arrived?"

"More or less. We've just lifted him out of the way—a couple of arm's lengths to the right."

He doesn't have to request to be allowed to work undisturbed. They back away, give him space, take turns to try to light their pipes. He can feel their gazes and he hesitates. What he is doing is a performance for them, and they are mumbling in low voices among themselves.

The deceased is lying stretched out on his back. Winge raises the jacket that has covered him, nodding to the police constable who is shivering in just his shirt that it has fulfilled its duty. He exposes a man in his fifties staring up pop-eyed, his jaw slack beneath his open mouth. The bare head is almost bald, and those few tufts of hair that remain do little to obscure the dented fontanelle. The crater is in shades of black and blue, the blood of the wound largely caught inside the skin in bulging blisters that have been worn into death like a blackened skullcap, a cauterized tonsure.

Cecil says to check his pockets. A tobacco pouch in the coat, so poorly knotted that the pocket is full of shreds. The fob watch is where it should be, but no longer ticks—the hands are crooked beneath the cracked glass. In the waistband of the trousers, against the protective folds of the belly, there is a purse attached with a pin. Its coins jingle. Cecil says this was no robbery. Cecil says that such men as the deceased rarely quarrel— witness his age, witness his attire, he lacks neither home nor coin, and would no more present assiduous resistance as initiate an assault on another. Emil surveys the stretch of ground up the hill, and the filth covering its cobblestones.

"Was it raining when you arrived?"

"As if God himself had chosen Stockholm as his potty."

Cecil says to take a closer look, and Emil crouches to scrape in the mud while clumsily gathering the folds of his coat around him to avoid soaking the hem. He hears the men whispering. Thus far he has not disappointed them. When they fall silent, one of them begins to whistle a simple melody that Emil has heard sung before by drinkers and tavern companions: a droll biblical travesty about Noah. It may be that the whistler has been spurred on by his comrade's simile. A little way up the hill, a few steps lead up to a door. Cecil says that is where he was sitting. Cecil says to search the ground, to search towards the wall. They are not easy to discern, but the pitched timber of the door has stains fresh enough to color his fingertips red when the crust is broken, as if he has just crushed some ladybirds there. The stone steps bear the same traces where the rain has not reached to scour them clean. Emil probes the surrounding ground. Cecil says to look to the left; the man wears his rings on his right hand, the one he uses least. Atop the dirt are white shards of burnt clay. Cecil says to look in his mouth, and Emil trudges back to the body; he reluctantly uses his little finger to part the folds of the cheeks for a better view, to little avail: it is as dark as the grave, and he has to probe and feel for himself. Afterwards, he wipes his hand on the deceased's waistcoat, turns around, and squints into the night sky, raising his voice to his companions.

"Can you open the door?"

They oblige him. A constable taps on the nearest window and waves his insignia around until a sleepy hag stumbles out of bed and unlocks the door for them. Winge climbs the stairs to the very top until his way is blocked by the door to the attic. He places his ear against it and hears what he expected. Scratching sounds. Rats in their hundreds. Weary neighbors know all about a merchant who rents the room as a grain store, but before they get any farther the sergeant nods meaningfully at the man who has accompanied them upstairs and who is leaning heavily enough against the door to make the lock give way. A wet, rancid smell permeates the air. The rats' small bodies are visible everywhere, oily patches of more compact gray in the shadows cast by the beams and slanting roof. They are clambering over the sacks covering the floor, making the material bulge and billow. The bounty they have found is too precious for them to be scared off by humans. One of the men stamps his foot on the floor and claps his hands, but only the vermin within his reach pay any heed, and barely even then.

Emil leaves them be. He draws a fistful of oats from one of the sacks, feels its damp heaviness, smelling the mold. Above them, the leaking roof is dripping. Behind the rows of sacks, a two-part hatch opens into nothingness—four storeys above the cobbles of the alley. He moves the bolt to one side, pushes until one half of the hatch has swung far enough on its hinges for the incline of the roof to catch it and keep it open. A beam extends out just above his head, tacked with sheet metal, well supported and with a bracket at the far end to hoist goods and furniture. At its end there is an empty hook. He turns on his heel and goes all the way back down again, into the alley and past the spot where the body lies and farther down the hill. He searches the gutter where the slope flattens until he finds what he seeks—a chunk of stained wood that has slid down the greasy cobbles until it has fetched up against a heap of rubbish that has avoided the winter bonfire. He can picture it now as the circumstances coalesce around this death, and inside himself the hope he always harbors is extinguished—that shameful hope that he will one day be summoned to the pool of blood from which he distinguishes Tycho Ceton's fleeing footsteps. Instead, he waves over the sergeant, who is unable to prevent his men from following to listen.

"This is no murder, but an accident, albeit a strange one."

The men exchange glances and the sergeant holds his hands out as if urging explanation. Winge points to the stairs.

"He was sitting there. Likely on his way home from the inn or Bagge's Row or from whatever other nightly spot he haunted. He decided to smoke a pipe. Perhaps he happened to fall asleep with it hanging from his lips—his mouth is certainly full of shards of clay, and the rest of them are beside the steps. The grain in the attic has been rotten for a long time, the layer of dust on the floorboards is years thick, and the beam up there can hardly have held any weight since last year. If you interrogate the landlord, I believe you will find that the tenant has abandoned his wares—spoilt as they are—and since the roof has leaked, there is probably a dispute as to indemnification and unpaid rent. There may even be proceedings. It was a windy night—that much I heard before I went to bed. The block was attached with a loop of rope that rubbed against the hook until only strands remained. The storm of last night put it out of its misery. The block fell, struck the man grievously on the head, and bounced down the cobblestones. The block is to be found down there, bloodied and hideous. I dare say it cannot weigh less than half a lispund—had he not been sitting in the way it would have cracked the stone step. He may have rolled to where he lies now, or he got to his feet and staggered a few paces before his body admitted death. All sorts of peculiar tremors may occur following trauma to the head."

He pauses before a flash of memory: Erik Three Roses swaying on a chair without a bottom, his forehead covered in bloody bandages, gushing into the chamber pot below. He trembles, and the police constables have time to exchange knowing looks before he masters himself.

"The block must have crushed the skull, but it barely broke his skin, which is why he did not bleed all that profusely. There is some blood spatter still discernible in the mud. Had it not been raining, you would have seen it for yourselves."

The sergeant whistles and allows his gaze to wander past all that Emil has identified.

"Well I'll be damned. What are the odds?"

Cecil says that it is beyond the reach of mathematics. Emil settles for a shrug of the shoulders.

"The world wouldn't be such a strange place if strange things weren't constantly happening."

"And the burden of guilt?"

Cecil says it's a hopeless affair. The cocksure voice of the crown attorney.

"If you are so inclined, then you might attempt to divide culpability between the merchant and the landlord, but I don't believe anything good will come of it. Both are likely to adopt defensible positions. More than anything, chance is to blame. The next of kin will make themselves known in due course. If you want, you can tell them everything so that they may take the case to the courts if they believe it worthwhile."

The sergeant rubs his stubbly chin without committing one way or the other.

"Oh. Well then. Thank you for your help."

Emil nods in reply and turns to leave. The trio follow him with their eyes, but cannot bring themselves to wait until the corner has hidden him from view before erupting into eager conversation. As he turns right, he sees coins change hands from the constable he hadn't recognized to the one he had seen before. He feels nothing but irritation, as if having been prompted through a performance where the lines were delivered in a language he did not fully understand.

In his absence, the men from the Indebetou breathe a sigh of relief.

"He gives me the cold shivers, does that one."

"Yes. But if you are intent on a life of crime you would be wise to wait until they have put him in the asylum."

4

They never meet at Indebetou House for fear that Ullholm himself might come by on some errand. Emil Winge is handicapped by his face: he is far too like his brother, who was once Ullholm's nemesis. The worry that his own part in the collaboration will come to light has given Isak Reinhold Blom many a sleepless night, and by day it is a constant thorn in his side. He shakes himself to ward off his difficulties together with the cold of this damp spring day. The means may be questionable, but the ends speak for themselves.

In the quarter between Grill's House and the Scorched Plot, they have chosen a nook beneath a protruding roof, concealed by day, sheltered from the wind and protected from precipitation. Some hundred door numbers are crowded into this area, just a stone's throw from the Indebetou but still somewhere that no one visits unnecessarily. Blom wonders if it is he who is early or Winge who is late, but he can do nothing but wait. His pocket watch has given up and the clockface on the tower at Saint Nikolai is too blurry to make out, no matter how much he squints and screws up his eyes. The ground frost has thawed, the melting blanket of snow revealing the rubbish no one bothered to sweep up last autumn. Noisome topsoil squelches as he stamps his feet to urge blood into his frozen toes, splatters to his stockings his only reward. Here comes Winge, and he ceases his attempts to rub his shins clean. He has a headache to boot.

"Emil. I gather you've been on your feet for a long time. Johansson felt that congratulations were in order for a job well done—others would probably have advocated a witch burning had you not been on the right side."

He's a strange one, is Emil Winge. The resemblance to Cecil is no longer limited to just the facial features. At times, he seems to adopt the same mannerisms that Isak Blom remembers well from his early years in the Chamber of Police when he made the acquaintance of the brother. In such moments, he finds it increasingly difficult to separate them—it demands constant attention not to attach memories to Emil that in fact belong to Cecil. It seems to him that Emil has increasingly begun to speak like his brother, and he walks with his arms behind his back in the same way. At other times it is not at all the case, and Emil is more reminiscent of the anxious and perpetual student who in the autumn of last year barged into Blom's office, babbling a lot of twaddle. Winge stands beside him, sheltered from the wind, and Blom inserts his hands into his coat pockets.

"Blom. All well?"

"You haven't heard? The Academy has been terminated. The idiots gave Reuterholm a pretext and the vizier by no means missed his chance."

"What happened?"

"Old Count von Fersen died in the spring of last year and left the seventh seat empty. Silfverstolpe was elected as his replacement, and seized the opportunity to ingratiate himself with the regime by declaring the late king an autocrat. The salute backfired with a vengeance: the poor sod was practically accused of lèse-majesté, and the whole Academy was accused of holding revolutionary intentions and has been set aside. Silfverstolpe had to resign from court service too—he's penniless. Rosenstein's secretarial position was withdrawn immediately, but he managed to save himself as the prince's informant with a distress call."

"I've rarely seen a heart bleed so much for others in someone who had no stake in their misfortune."

"And that's true too. I'm doing well for myself in that regard, Emil, albeit nowhere else. Have I not mimicked Leopold's verses to such an extent that tributes to me are the closest he can come to paying homage to himself? I received the Academy's double prize just the other year— two times twenty-six ducats. The Lundblad Prize last year—fifty daler straight into the stock market. That's better than a poke in the eye for one who must make their way as a lackey in the Chamber of Police. Now, damn it, now I just have another year of drudgery to look forward to. One in an endless row."

Winge slaps his own shoulders with the palms of his hands, whipping up the blood to bring warmth. His carousing has left visible traces on him that he will never be rid of, no matter how sober he remains.

"And what news from the Indebetou?"

"Larks and devilry are playing tag. The regime sees spies in every corner. Just the other day their eye was drawn to a teacher of Italian who they imagined had plans to bring the Duke back to life. Edman himself ordered Ullholm to personally detain the man and convey him to the right side of the border. Thus far you might think it was foolish enough, but the fellow was commonly known as a meek man who preferred to open a window than kill a fly. But no! Ullholm, that ass, got the wrong door in the stairwell and chased a surprised Finnish officer out of the arms of his sweetheart with stabs and blows. Only when the poor Italian stuck his nose round his bedroom door to timidly ask whether he could be of service in any way did the misunderstanding come to light. Thanks to his thoughtfulness, they bundled him away and put him on the first boat home to Rimini. Naturally all without any due process before the law. Who needs that kind of thing when we have the arbitrariness of the regime? The Finn was promoted for his pain and suffering. This misrule is beginning to stick in people's craws, you mark my words."

"Well."

Emil Winge shrugs his slender shoulders. His attitude betrays neither surprise nor particular interest. Blom clears his throat and changes tack, cursing himself because irritation with the country's situation in general and his own in particular has now made him hesitate in the small speech he spent the morning preparing. He gropes in his coat pocket for what he seeks.

"But not everything is doom and gloom. I have a spare theater ticket for you. Indeed, for a premiere. *The Reconciled Father* at the Arsenal on the final Saturday in May. The author's first play was a success, and expectations are high for this one too. What do you say? It would do you good to see something other than bloodstains and grotesquerie. Let's go together. Naturally we'll have a box so there will be no rubbing shoulders with every Tom, Dick, and Harry."

Winge glances at him coldly.

"Why such courtesy? It's unlike you, Isak. And I have little interest in such things."

Blom sighs, unsurprised that his hopes for a more gracious reply have been dashed, and returns the theater ticket he has just brandished to his coat pocket.

"When you came to me, it went against the grain for me to take pity on you—I'll willingly admit that, and I don't think you can blame me. Since then, you've proven your value in the service of the police. You've been of assistance to us on cases great and small in the months since last autumn, so much so that I struggle to recall it all. The hunt for Ruuth's missing receipts; the body in the locked room. Anyone who has dealt with legal matters knows that when a woman is killed her husband is as likely guilty as they are to sing amen in the church, but you found the exception to the rule, and without you that poor journeyman would have lost his head and the murderer would have gone free. Without your input, the misappropriated Fahnehjelm press would still be minting false coins."

"Like the theater ticket, I assume that this flattery has its reason."

Blom throws up his hands in capitulation.

"You're a strange bird, Emil, but there is a future for you with us, if you want it. Not even Ullholm's grudge against Cecil would stand in your way any longer, given your exploits."

Winge doesn't like eye contact, but he stings Blom with a sharp glance before resuming his survey of the mire before them. "You know my answer."

Blom has been holding his breath and now he exhales a belching cloud through both nostrils.

"Yes. Yes, I do. But it would be a disservice to all if I didn't ask the question yet again."

Winge sighs. He looks tired, exhausted, and freezing cold, and younger than he ought to—albeit experienced. He would give a lot for a drink.

"Every time Father received word of one of Cecil's successes, he was happy for a time, bounding up and down the stairs and waving the letter about like a banner. Once again, reality had confirmed his views on how his offspring should be raised. He had created a genius; here was the evidence. Yet another twig for the laurel wreath of reason. Then he would catch sight of me sitting in my nook by the pulpit as usual, defeated by the unseen shackles of childhood. He would glance over my shoulder at all the blots I had left on the paper, at all the things I pretended not to understand, and at all the answers I had zealously got wrong in the way that I knew would most draw his ire. I could feel his anger rising like a fever until he could no longer contain himself, instead seizing me by the neck with one hand and screwing up the paper in the other, rubbing it across my eyes until my nose bled. Other times, he would play chess and move the pieces so badly that it was a challenge to put myself in check. Rare was the night that did not end in a sound beating from one of those hazel switches he cut anew each Sunday to ensure that desiccation would not deprive them of weight and flexibility. I still bear the marks. My back is as striped as a wildcat's and shall likely remain so for as long as I live."

It is Blom's turn to look away, averting his gaze into the mud to give Emil consideration in his confidence. He senses where this is going.

"Can you comprehend, Blom, how badly those old scars sting simply because they are forced to wear Cecil's shirt?"

Blom replies with a blush, turning his face towards the wind to cool the cheek that is heated.

"You may be able to guess why the question has come now."

"Because the terms of our agreement are to be fulfilled."

"In some part, yes. I've done as you told me. You asked me to make inquiries into the origins of one Tycho Ceton. The answer has been delayed because the winter makes the post so uncertain, but I have it now."

Anticipation ignites in Winge's eyes, hunger so naked that Blom loses his thread.

"And?"

"An old passport suggests that Ceton passed the Cat's Rump tollgate for the first time upon entry in the year seventy-nine, and that he sailed south that same year. As to his return, I have hitherto found no details. The archives are as usual a morass. He has not allowed himself to be admitted to any congregation as far as I have seen."

"And the place of departure?"

"Is listed as Saxnäs. A hamlet in the parish of Hällbo, if my geography is not much mistaken. Bergslagen way."

Winge pulls his pocket watch from his waistcoat, one foot already turned towards the path that will take him away. Blom shakes his head.

"I must admit that I don't fully understand what joy that knowledge brings you. As far as we know, Ceton remains in Stockholm. All customs officers have been notified. If he corresponds to your description then he may as well have his name written across his face."

"When did you last spend any time on a tollgate, Isak? Not infrequently have I encountered customs officers who are either drunk or preoccupied by cards, and even less infrequently have I encountered those who hold the affairs of the Chamber of Police in higher esteem than their own. I have done everything in my power to uncover his hiding place, to no avail. Either he is better hidden than I could have imagined, or he has departed. He cannot have much money left, and what refuge does one in such extremity have other than among those who will feed him out of the obligations of blood ties?"

"But is the journey worth a straw?"

"Ever since last year, I have been singing the same song to you, Isak: you are underestimating this man. You don't understand what he is capable of. You never saw Erik Three Roses loose-limbed on his chamber pot, his skull trepanned. You never saw a bridal chamber's chandelier spattered with blood. You know nothing of the fragrance of flowers grown on brimming graves. You never saw him steer another to insert a blade into fresh meat. Worse is to come. I have no doubt of it. Unless we get to him first. If Jean Michael and I were able to get more help, things would be different. Yet again, I implore you to make this a priority for the Chamber of Police."

Blom shakes his head.

"Impossible. The reasons are the same as before. Benefactors flocked to the orphanage at Horn Hill. If word spread that its founder was suspected of such a thing, powerful men would demand Ullholm's head on a platter. It would be an altogether different matter if you had evidence. That, or a sure chance of apprehending the man yourselves in order to hold an interrogation. But he cannot be the subject of a search."

"I hope I am never tempted to remind you of my warning, Isak. I shudder to think what he may be doing, and the atrocities are never worse than when committed against the defenseless. He has a way of gaining trust, and if he is let close enough he strikes like a snake wherever life is at its weakest. I go while there is still time."

Blom holds out his hands, exhibiting equal parts powerlessness and frustration. And then Emil has gone, leaving Blom alone to deliver his farewell to an empty yard and the silent rain that has just begun to fall.

"It's as damnable as if the Ghost of the Indebetou were in charge, speaking through your mouth."

5

There is a tiny flicker in the corner of his eye, no more. The shift of light in a space, undulating as if over sun-warmed earth. The hint of movement. Emil closes his eyes. In the darkness that is his solitude, he does not need sight to know its shape.

"Let me be. You are nothing. You are just my mania clad in memories. One drink and you'd be gone—drowned like a cat in a single cup of spirit. If the price weren't higher than I am willing to pay I would not hesitate."

In his mind, he sees not the Cecil who was waiting for him in the alley last year, not a corpse screaming out the desecration of death, but the brother he remembers from their last year together, the brilliant student returned to the parental home as a guest to celebrate the weekend, in the bloom of his life and with his future ahead of him; half his nearest sibling, half someone he no longer knows.

"All this is the afterbirth of your work. You are like a sore whose rot not even death can cleanse. Had you not asked Jean Michael for assistance two years ago, none of this would have happened. But no, you needed his help. To secure it, you gave him a purpose, and what else could he do after your death than try his best in a situation far beyond his skill? He knew as much himself, and you had taught him what to do in such a situation. When it happened to you, you sought out a helper, and he did the same. He chose badly. I can't find fault with him in any respect except for my own shortcomings. After all, Jean Michael means well. But that isn't enough. It cost the lives of one hundred children."

The weather must have shifted yet again; the wind is just a foretaste of a storm from the archipelago in the east. A sudden shiver brings Emil to his feet to rub warmth into his upper arms with the palms of his hands.

"I go north now. Blom has found Ceton's place of birth. I cannot be certain what awaits me, but may luck stand by my side in my encounters! There is not much else to be done, and being in Stockholm sticks in my craw. How you chose to work here is beyond my understanding."

He surveys his possessions and finds few that are worthy of a place in his portmanteau.

"The girl, Anna Stina, will leave Jean Michael no peace of mind, even though she is nowhere to be found. A conclusion must be found, of whatever kind."

He begins to fill the bag pell-mell. It is big enough to accommodate everything and more.

"It is most definitely love of a sort. I don't envy him. If she rejected him before, what wouldn't she do now? His guilt is great, and to the extent that his exterior was ever attractive, now he is badly burnt by the flames."

Emil shakes his head.

"But I don't owe him anything. He has no right to expect further support from me. When the time comes, I shall let him do his part. That is enough—then we shall be free to go our separate ways."

Cecil's golden pocket watch ticks in the silence. Emil remembers how Cecil looked when his logical reasoning encountered emotional arguments: offended and compassionate, all at once. The memory makes him angry, incapable of keeping his voice subdued and steady. He looks at himself in the mirror as he speaks. It's easiest that way, after all. They were always similar, he and Cecil. So similar that it might now be his brother he was addressing.

"My whole life, everyone has wanted me to be like you. Only now, after they have had their way, do I know how little their appreciation means. Deceit and lies, rooms splattered in red. I want nothing more than to turn my back on them. I want to leave here, the sooner the better. As soon as that which must be done is done. My whole life has been squandered, locked up—by Father, by my siblings, by spirits, by myself. But nothing new will germinate until the old has been cleared away. That is what I am doing—nothing more. I want to live too—like others do. Most of all, as far from here as the roads will take me. I don't want to be you, Cecil. I want to be myself, to be *enough*. To be in a place where the doings of others are all one."

He leans closer. His brother's gaze meets his in the mirror.

"And soon you'll be gone, Cecil. You're nothing more than a delusion. When this is over, you'll no longer serve any purpose. Know that each step in this search is in the footsteps of Cain, as far as I'm concerned. With Stockholm behind me, I shall forget you."

Someone screeches a song out in the street, already drunk. Emil can practically feel it in his throat—the hot caress of the spirit, its passage down his throat, deep inside him like a white-hot pill come to spread light in the dark nooks and crannies and offer them blessed emptiness. A relief he is deprived of and misses, never more so than in moments such as these. He closes his eyes and lowers his voice to a whisper.

"I'll prove you both wrong. You and Father. I'll show that the paths you took weren't the only ones possible. The coming conclusion will be on my own terms."

6

He sees her face everywhere, but it is never her, and it is never as clear as in the dream. So he shuns sleep. During the winter months, his vigil was easier, because no matter how Cardell lay, it hurt, and when he lay pressed against a blanket and straw mattress, it was as if flames had once again been ignited against his skin. The sweat was trapped in distended blisters, incapable of escape, and it was best to remain still. Now he misses those pustules, because they no longer keep him awake. The skin has healed as best it can—old wounds have become angry red patches that have spread their pattern all across him; at their worst they are as lumpy as hardened wax on a candle that has burned unevenly. They howl at the touch, are a source of constant discomfort, but Cardell pays little heed. The costume of pain he once wore is gone, unabated only in the stump of his left arm. It is as if that were still in the trough where Erik Three Roses met his demise. Cardell applied all his weight to give the wooden fist the power it needed—enough that he himself cried out, he who had simply gritted his teeth even when the field surgeon had blunted the bone shaft with a rasp.

He cannot remain awake forever. Sleep eventually lays an ambush, drawing him in as he relaxes his guard. In the dream, he is running through fire, Karl and Maja in his arms, small fragile bodies. He runs towards the stairs, he falls, he drops his burden. With smoldering hair, he tries to take up once more what has been lost. His helping hand brings ruin to all it touches; it brings forth flames from his head, he is driven to flight, nothing is extinguished by his tears. Her children are dead, the fault his. He sees her as she must have been, outside, beyond the inferno, the disaster even worse than the one written on her face, and he realizes that her life too has been lost from his faltering grip. She is breathing, she is moving, but that is not life. Time and time again, he begs her forgiveness, but it is as if he speaks a language she no longer understands, and no matter what he says he cannot reach her. She is deadened by a sadness so great that it shrinks him to nothing but an inconsequential murmur, a meaningless buzzing in her ears.

But for now, the victory is his. All day he has tramped the city's streets on the same old errand; soon evening will fall, and with that he will return to the streets again, always anxious that the hour he forsakes the cobblestones will be the one when she passes. The words of the fisherfolk watchman echo in his mind: a lad took her by the hand and led her back to the City-between-the-Bridges. The mischief he suspects is like a wound in his side.

....

There is a knock at the door, a sound so unusual that he waits until it recurs to assure himself that it is not one of the other doors in the stair that was intended. He rises, opening the door for someone who now hesitates to cross the threshold.

"Emil. Well, well."

He waves his guest in.

"You're lucky to catch me. If lucky is the right word. I was just about to leave."

Cardell lifts his wooden fist off the floor, its timber blackened by the bite of the fire. With practiced effort, he begins to lay the straps out correctly so that he may attach them to his own flesh. Time and time again, they elude him, slipping from his grip and forcing him to start again. Winge can only turn away, neither asked for assistance nor keen to offer it.

"Blom has managed to discover Ceton's hometown. I'm going."

Cardell nods.

"Is that all?"

"For now. If he shows himself in the city then we'll have him. The Chamber of Police have been notified through Blom, albeit discreetly. If anything happens then I shall know."

"You've been around and about."

"I've done what I must, no more."

The question of guilt joins them, as always, uninvited by both of them but never distant. The cold silence of burnt children. Cardell shrugs and the movement makes the straps slip out of position yet again.

"It was not meant as a gibe. I wish I had accomplished nearly as much."

"No joy yet?"

The watchman shakes his head as he threads leather through buckles and seeks the right hole.

"It is as if she has been swallowed by the earth. Perhaps that is just what has happened. Perhaps I am searching for a grave. It changes nothing."

Winge looks around the room, which is more neglected than ever.

"Are you short of anything? Money?"

Cardell snorts.

"I have enough to get by. I want for little."

Winge receives this information without surprise.

"Well. If you need me, seek out Blom. Should my journey meet with any success then we'll soon be in touch. It should take a few weeks. Perhaps I'll return with the warm weather."

He lingers at the threshold, something else weighing at his heart. Cardell cannot imagine what, but he is patient.

"You seem to be healing well, given the circumstances."

Cardell grunts in response.

"I've heard that Sergel wants to carve the Farnese Hercules from marble and is accepting nearby gentlemen for nude modeling at the horse-breaking track. I often pass by there. Each time I think that today is the day they will call me in, but thus far I have remained disappointed."

"I don't know what method you are using in your search, Jean Michael . . ."

Cardell interrupts him, already exhausted—exhausted by the way that Emil's presence makes his conscience pain him more than usual, exhausted by the realization of how much he could do with the help of someone with greater acuity, and how little he deserves it.

"I trudge up and down the street every waking moment. I ask for her, to little avail. Far too many fit the same description. At times, I let myself be led astray when I feel I am left with no choice."

"Were Cecil still among us, he would advise you to go back to basics, over and over again if necessary: begin with what you definitely know until you find something there, and then take it further."

Cardell seeks out Winge's gaze and holds it for a while for the first time since he crossed the threshold.

"But he isn't, Emil. Is he?"

7

The month of May is nigh and yet the lingering freshness of spring is putting up a good fight against the promised summer. Although the final night of frost bade farewell to the year in mid-April, the chill refuses to depart. A few days' warmth brings hope, only to be replaced by cold showers. For Cardell and many others, this weather is the worst that Stockholm can muster, hardly better in spring than in autumn. The City-between-the-Bridges is squeezed between the sea and lake, prey to the whims of the wind. It doesn't get cold enough to repress the damp—in frost and snow you can dress according to judgment and retain warmth, but nothing helps against this suffocating, overcast weather. If there isn't a downpour, then it's drizzling. The moisture seems to penetrate the skin, cooling the marrow and bones, saturating one's clothes until they hang around the neck like the embrace of the drowned. Everything is shrouded in gray, as if every color has leached out of the world, as if the weather gods have decided to show Reuterholm half-measure in his Ordinance of Abundance, to the detriment of the Baron himself and inflicting suffering on his subjects. The weather affects temperament, making men peevish and sullen, taciturn and withdrawn. Those who can, stay inside. Tirelessly, Cardell mortifies his sodden soles against the cobblestones and muddy quagmire of the streets.

It will be some time before he acts upon the advice he has been given, but as soon as the meaning of the words has sunk in, it seems that the habit of obedience remains within him: so much of his prime has been spent with field ushers, warrant officers, and staff sergeants bellowing into his face, that he need only close his eyes and dream himself away to the past for a panoramic vision of standing at the bowsprit in the face of an oncoming gale. To those who learn to master such an onslaught, the point of doing so will often reveal itself amid the profanities expended in the effort. He turns his steps towards the Great Shade on a day when the clouds are rushing across the sky to further tax the poverty of the rays of sun, making for the clearing where she summoned him last summer to play childminder.

He makes his way north until he discerns the stale headwind of the Bog in his nostrils, and then he turns up towards Lill-Jans. Some cows are grazing in their pasture close to the Bay of Wells. A beggarman is sitting by the roadside holding his cap out before him in short-lived hopefulness. Two stone towers flank the barrier, but he passes without any passport other than his articles of uniform after a collegial nod from the constables. Behind this is the Customs House itself—a single storey under a roof covered in cracked tiles. A road extends in both directions alongside the customs fence whose neglected maintenance has left gaps big enough to welcome all who prefer to visit the city incognito on Shanks's pony; given the rate of decay it is only a matter of time before someone attempts a customs-free entry to the city by horse and cart. Beyond the ditch on the northern side of the road the trees take over, first offering a barricade of thickets and shrubs, a scourge to unprotected legs. A little farther in, the terrain unfolds. High galleries stretch in every direction, oaks mastering the earth by virtue of the shade cast by their crowns, in which all life is quelled. He last set foot here in winter—and at regular intervals at that—but he never found any trace of a human being, the one he sought least of all. They had parted ways; Anna Stina had forsaken her burrow and never returned. The snow had been falling, making it even easier to prove the matter. No new footprints ever crossed those left by himself.

It takes him a moment to get his bearings. The forest is a living and changing thing, and if you lack the good fortune to catch sight of a known hillock or the right boulder, the way ahead becomes uncertain. The snow that has thawed has left new windfall and revealed a floor of decaying leaves from the preceding year. Those new leaves that have emerged are damp in the raw air, everything shrouded in the earthy haze of spring where whatever is to grow must feast on what was felled last autumn. He wanders around for a good while before an animal trail sets him on the right track.

The burrow is not as it was. There are traces to be read here. The branches that once formed a door are broken and dispersed. A human legacy if ever he saw one. The ground is dank and full of impressions. Anxious not to spoil anything before he has had time to draw his conclusions, he settles down on a fallen log from which he has an overview. His heart is pounding, because the clearest traces are small and recent. He tries to recall when rain last fell. Yesterday? Yes. No precipitation has blunted the edges of the imprints. By the circle of stones forming the hearth, there are more of the same, and beneath a broken spruce branch he finds a hide containing a dented frying pan and a few other items wrapped in cloth. It's hard to say how long they have been there.

He reads the tracks as best he can, following them as far as they can be made out and then choosing the path of least resistance, going along a trail that at times loses itself in empty scrub, but resumes its course where the rows of trunks allow.

A meadow opens up on the forest hill, clad in splintered brown straws that the wind has erected after the snow kept them retracted. It takes a while before he spots her back, bent over a spot on the ground, wrapped in a faded blanket and initially hard to distinguish from a lone deer's coat. She is nimble in flight: for far too long he stands there powerless to break the spell of the reunion until she feels the weight of his gaze. With a silent curse, he sets off after her.

Elusive as a siren of the woods, she is gone. The best he can do is to run a while before stopping and listening as he forces his heaving lungs to hold their breath, choosing the direction where her course through the forest is betrayed by dry twigs and disturbed branches. He clumsily hurls himself forward with the wooden fist before him to protect his face. In spite of it, the branches whip his throat and neck with fiery lashes. When he realizes that the chase is lost, he stops to catch his breath, bent forward on stinging thighs with the taste of blood in his mouth. The noise is distant now, but the direction has changed, and all of a sudden he remembers the bundle by the fire, uses the incline of the ground as a waymarker and sets off on the most direct route, whence he came.

Panting, he thunders into the camp, coming to a halt in time to avoid blurring new tracks. The cupped coniferous fist of the pine branch is lying undisturbed above its treasure. He is the first to return, but as his pounding heart is stilled in his ears, all that awaits is the whisper of the forest. Perhaps he was mistaken: either the bundle is not hers, or she preferred to sacrifice her possessions rather than be intercepted. He lurches back up the hill towards the burrow. Water is purling out of the ground at the point where the forest stream breaks forth, but not loudly enough to conceal her breathing, as quiet as it is, and he carefully leans closer.

She is standing as upright as the low ceiling allows, her back against the packed earth that serves as a rear wall. In front of her she clutches a knife, so small and worse for wear that it is better suited for use as cutlery than as a weapon. As soon as she sees that her hide has been found, she pushes back the material that has served as her hood, as if it would help her to expose herself. It takes a moment to come to terms with what he sees and relinquish the shadows and illusions, but once that is done Cardell lowers his tensed shoulders in resignation. The girl is another, now as always. From a hidden source beneath a tangled shock of hair a port-wine stain runs down over her forehead and across the meager girl's face. Angry and red, it is borne to the left by the eyebrow, darkening one eye and rendering its blue twinkle terrifying in its intensity. Disappointment and relief in turn drain the life out of him, and he seeks out a fallen log to spare his swollen feet his weight.

"Why don't you come out? I mistook you for another. I mean you no harm. You have my word."

"If I were in the habit of taking strangers at their word then my life would have been even shorter than it has been."

"My name is Mickel Cardell."

One at a time, he lifts his heavy legs over the log, trying to show her the side of himself that others usually appreciate the most.

"So please be so good as to not stab me in the back with your sewing needle."

He gives her time to retreat. He silently, slowly, counts to twenty, before turning his head and finding her standing outside the opening of the burrow, the knife still in her fist but now lowered.

"You're still here."

"My things are still down the hill. You're sitting in my way."

He grunts irritably, too tired and despondent to move. The sweat has begun to congeal beneath his shirt; his mouth is full of the taste of iron brought on by his brisk march.

"Well go round then."

When he hears her steps, he thinks that is just what she is doing, but instead she finds space on the same log as him, albeit far enough away to be out of reach.

"I was burned in my mother's belly. But the fire seems to have caught you too."

"They say the Red Hare seeks out all that is beautiful. The flames left me alone as soon as they realized I wasn't much in the way of prey."

"You and I both."

He takes these words as a pretext to scrutinize her, and finds that she speaks untruths. Her features are pure: high cheekbones and angled eyes of the kind that remind him of the landscapes on the far side of the Baltic, although nothing in her speech sings that song. The red stain is of the kind that turns gazes away, but for those that linger, it quickly loses its power.

"I can offer no sop to the self-esteem of a homeless lass from the alms-house, but don't bloody sit there and provoke me with that remark. Surely you understand that you are fortunate? With that face unmarked, the world would have shown you even less mercy."

She sits quietly for a moment before changing the subject.

"I've heard your name before."

"Admittedly, I'm not unknown in the City-between-the-Bridges, but I would never have imagined that my notoriety had spread beyond the city gates."

"Anna Stina whispered it in her sleep sometimes."

His throat tightens at every possible answer, his breath clogged as if by an insidious blow to the pit of his stomach. The girl does him the kindness of waiting, occupying herself with something hanging from her waist as he collects himself.

"Would you like some tobacco? I've saved a little for bartering."

Cardell has seen enough of the girl's possessions to appreciate the value of the offer—far too great to decline, even if he had the ability to do so. She passes him a cloth pouch with a hand slender as a defoliated twig, and he takes as little as he dares, without hurting her. The cut leaves are dry and old, crumbling to grains in his fingers but they still find their place inside his cheek after he has been chewing for a while.

"So you know my name already. Then what might be yours?"

"Lisa."

"It's a pleasure."

His tongue already feels swollen in his mouth, sluggish and unwilling, and his stomach is fluttering for fear of an ill-chosen word, a misplaced question, anything that may corrupt this fragile calm. Instead, she is the one who leads, and he follows.

"Karl and Maja. They're dead now, aren't they?"

He would have preferred to take her knife in a soft part of his body. He cannot answer other than with a curt nod, and she echoes the same gesture in resignation at expectation met.

"I've already mourned for them all winter long. Ever since we parted ways. I saw it in my leaves, although you need hardly have second sight to foretell the death of a child."

The pain is a cartridge detonating in his breast. The confession wants to burst out with the eagerness of a white-hot bullet.

"The blame is mine."

Lisa looks away for the sake of his dignity.

"Move over beneath the yoke. It is not yours alone. I betrayed them first. When they most needed me, I packed my bundle and disappeared into the night along paths they could not follow. You know, I was god-mother to them, for want of better. Their first swaddling was my ragged shirt. They saw the light of day down the hill beside the stone hearth."

He sees his shame mirrored in her, but she wears it far better. Her eyes tell of waking nights haunted by the agonies of a merciless conscience; nevertheless she manages to keep her voice level, tamed by a strength that all but frightens Cardell.

"Where did she go?"

"I'd hardly be here if I knew. She left me without saying where she was going or why. I was here searching in the winter to no avail. Now I'm back yet again, hoping for new traces. What about you? Do you know anything?"

Lisa points to the broken and discarded branches around the burrow.
"No. But others have searched here, perhaps for the same reason."
For the first time, he hears hesitation in her voice.
"Why . . ."
The words fail her, and she tries again.
"Why are you searching for her now?"
When he cannot answer, she catches his gaze and holds it firmly, and Cardell finds that he couldn't turn his neck even if he wanted to. It is as if he were naked, incapable of covering himself, and the blood rises to his face until even his ears are on fire. Only when Lisa directs her gaze down is the spell broken.

"She talked in her sleep. I think she forged her plans in her dreams. There was another name alongside yours. More alien."

She tries the syllables over and over again, and Cardell searches his memory for what is missing, going back through a two-year-old labyrinth of memories. Anna Stina Knapp, the workhouse, the Scapegrace, Kristofer Blix's demise on the day-old ice of the Golden Bay. The lad's unsent letter. Cecil Winge's red smile at Cellar Hamburg. In the end, he has to give up. He is lost, unable to find what he seeks. In frustration, he sighs at a feeling closely related to one with which he is even more familiar: when the itch takes hold in a limb that is no longer there to be scratched. A strong gust of wind rakes the crowns of the trees, dives through the branchwork, and drives fallen leaves before it down the hill. They sit together for a time before he follows them away.

8

The road is not long when seen in terms of distance, but there are other ways to count, and it is with ill-concealed irritation that Magnus Ullholm hastens as quickly as dignity allows across Castle Hill and through the arch into the inner courtyard. Since his appointment at the beginning of last year, the Chamber of Police premises have filled Ullholm with hopelessness of a particular kind, but the Castle has its very own variation on the same theme. There has always been a lingering sense that Indebetou House came with a lifetime tenancy in the grounds—a manifestation of the stepmotherly treatment that his authority has always received. The Castle in turn is a model of the kingdom at large: stateliness in decay, confusion, stupidity immortalized in stone, all solidified into a block housing a maze of passages and rooms, each regulated by rank and routine. He feels out of place: even though he pays careful attention to the corridors and stairs, he could swear that the offices change places with one another from month to month. Chief of police though he be, on this occasion he must suffer the amused contempt on the face of a porter before being pointed in the right direction. He knocks on the door and with a sigh of relief he is shown into Johan Erik Edman's office. Farther down the corridor he hears Chancellor of Justice Lode ranting and raving in dictation to a secretary who promptly closes the door when he becomes aware of the visitor. Ullholm also closes the door behind him—the more doors there are between him and Lode, the better.

"How are you, Mr. Keeper of the Records?"

Edman gestures at a desk filled with papers and writing materials of every kind.

"We're beheading the Gustavians one by one. Count Ruuth is due before the bar by month's end. We're prosecuting him for embezzlement."

"Is he guilty?"

Edman laughs.

"What does it matter? Anyone asking such a question has misunderstood the priorities. But he has undeniably made matters easier for us by misplacing the late king's old receipts. Ruuth was ultimately responsible for the finances of the kingdom, and without proof of where the money has gone he may as well have put it in his own pocket. If he can't repay then he will have to make amends in the fortress. Regardless, he will be a broken man. Assuming, that is, that I ever finish writing this speech."

In response to Edman's raised eyebrows, Ullholm adds a folded letter to the stack on the desk and sinks into the armchair intended for passing visitors.

"A dispatch from Dülitz. A runner just arrived, sweat pouring. One of his henchmen says he has caught sight of the Knapp girl."

Edman allows his gaze to flicker across the sheet, but he quickly loses patience and turns back to Ullholm.

"Why didn't he arrest her on the spot?"

"The fellow took a bayonet to the hollow of the knee at Uttismalm and since then has become accustomed to being outrun by most folk. But he had her in his sights for a good while inside the theater, drawing for his own amusement and capturing her portrait in charcoal on the back of a newspaper, alongside her chaperone."

"So where does that leave us?"

"Dülitz is no fool. As soon as he got word, he deployed people to scout the bridges. Knapp is still in the city. I'll task people with duplicating the drawing and ensure that it is posted in the customs booths and the city guard barracks. Every man will learn to recognize her."

Edman rises and goes over to the tall window with its view across the Islet of the Holy Ghost and the Stream, its flood still wild as if sent by spring to storm the bones of the bridge's structure, now held together by slippery planks.

"If she still has Rudenschöld's letter in her possession then it would bring me joy. If old Ruuth's name isn't there to be read I shall eat my shoes. The trial could be curtailed by weeks and his cronies put under lock and key without delay. The Gustavian conspiracy exposed in its entirety overnight."

A knock on the door: a servant.

"Gentlemen, forgive my intrusion, but Mr. Edman has himself insisted many a time that he is to be kept fully abreast of developments. It is said that Copenhagen is in flames."

9

From inn to inn, on the journey goes. A little over a mile beyond the city, the road remains wide enough to allow carriages to pass each other without trouble, but it soon narrows to a meager track scarred by heavy hooves and wagon wheels, muddy and waterlogged. He's lucky if he sees a milestone once every two hours. His coachman is a slow fellow who hums monotonously in time with his horse's hooves. Time and again they encounter travelers bound south, in places where the road is narrower than two axle-widths. Someone must back down, and yet more time is wasted in halfhearted quarrels over who has right of way. Emil Winge can do nothing but impotently gaze upon the scene and wrap what habiliments he owns around himself as best as he can, thankful at least that this first carriage affords him a roof to shield him from the drizzle, and hangings of brittle leather to fasten to the windows when the wind is up. Among his fellow passengers are those who are more choleric in inclination, checking their restlessness by entering the arguments and thereby further slowing the journey.

He spends the first night at an inn halfway to Uppsala. The passport procured by Blom stipulates the authorities' permission for free lodgings, but farther inland he soon becomes aware that the long arm of the law is shorter than it ought to be. Many an innkeeper shakes his head, and the grounds for squeezing him for hard cash are many and well rehearsed. Such papers have been forged in the past, and without the attestation of the district police superintendent himself they cannot defray the cost based on good faith alone. Some base their rejections on a lack of literacy. Time and again, Emil is faced with the choice of sleeping in the hayloft or paying in coin, and after standing his ground as a matter of principle once, he realizes the hopelessness of the struggle and allows himself instead to be fleeced. Part of him has a hard time blaming them. He knows that his very appearance invites doubt. They see his eyes wander to the barrel of spirits—they know his sort.

Each day takes him farther north. The carriages vary from one parish to another, as do the inns. Horses are often missing. They must be sent for from sulky farmers who hand over beasts of burden who have worn themselves to a lather in forest and field. He grows accustomed to waiting hours, leaning against the plaster stove surround barely warmed by the fires dutifully laid with as few logs as shame permits. They are generally open carriages, but sometimes he himself rides on horseback, straddling a pack saddle bulging with sacks and packages. He is horrified by the height of such creatures—more than enough to break the neck of any who falls, especially since the rhythm of their dreary jog-trot is a siren song that constantly threatens to lull him to sleep.

He is entering a foreign country, even if the language is the same. Out here, people have taken root; they live and they die on the same patch of land that is then dug up to be used as their final resting place. Travelers like him are seen as impious and infamous, even if the coins he offers are always accepted by outstretched hands. He introduces himself as courtesy dictates, but what is that name worth when it cannot be tied to a place, put in context, secured with the ties of blood? Nought but a sound, devoid of meaning. He is a stranger, unpopular. This is the realm of the kelpie, the mermaid, the will-o'-the-wisp, and beasts of the bog, the domain of decay and the siren of the woods. Here they leave iron on their threshold in the hope that they will sleep soundly, and make up the cot with a catechism under the pillow to scare off trolls. At first, Emil is horrified, but it is hard to remain impervious to the world around him, and the forest is big and dark. Not even the sun at its highest is able to dispel its shadows. At night, it is filled with alien sounds and shapes. He cannot safely attribute them to foxes or roebucks.

Pathfinding is a task reserved for those who can be spared. The crippled or young, girls and boys too feeble for heavier work, in pairs if he is fortunate, since gates must constantly be opened and closed to allow passage through the pastures. Otherwise he must climb down from his seat to wrestle the long stakes out of their mounts and return them afterwards. Where land has been cleared for fields, the road is diverted, forced into a winding course that testifies to sullen neighborly feuds. They have failed to break down the rocks, and the substrate has been left at the mercy of horses' hooves and carts' wheels. Where the ground has become marshy, if they are lucky, slippery pines have sometimes been laid down as a gangway.

One stage he completes on foot as the day seems long before him and no horse is to be found. He soon has cause for regret. The wet spring, distended by the thaw, leaves the road brimming with purling meltwater, and each attempt to stumble forward dryshod along the verge creates a risk of tripping and falling headlong into the mud. Behind him in the place he has just left after the promise of yet another delay, the farmfolk have gathered, united in their schadenfreude and with cries that accompany his every balancing act. He chooses to wade rather than offer them any further spectacle, sullied up to his breeches before he has even gone one hundred yards along the road.

Along its sides, the roundpole fences darken in deep puddles, like felled masts from a fleet foundered in its line of battle. By the time he reaches an almost dry hill up into the forest, noon has passed and the sun is beginning to slowly dip towards evening. Rising worry paints the hour as later than it is, making him doubt the testimony of his pocket watch, and within Emil there germinates a fear of the kind he has forgotten, distinct from that which he knows far better. He is a being accustomed to the proximity of others and the protection of walls, but the forest is wild and ruthless, and the rising darkness saturates it with ancient terror.

Cecil says not to make a fool of himself. His brother's tone is masterful but inspires no confidence. Dusk threatens to make the path indistinguishable from the ground around it, and the inky firs marking his course grow increasingly gray. Now and then, the light is caught in a pond or a marsh that glitters between the trunks. The water lies red in its sinks—open wounds in the hull of moss. Were he to go astray here, he would be lost. The prospect of being forced to spend the night beneath the trees terrifies him into a chafing quick march.

He feels the smoke of the fire stinging his nostrils before his goal comes into sight around a bend—a dilapidated dwelling place decked out in moss, with stables and outbuildings, the gaps between the cluster of half-timbered buildings clogged with fences containing a sloping courtyard. He gratefully comes under cover to dry his sodden clothes, still agitated but now equipped with sufficient patience to await horses and guides, and with a new understanding of the tariff demanded of him. In the morning, a skinny lad is waiting for him, and they make an early start—one of many that lie ahead.

10

Noise from downstairs, the kind that evokes bad memories: Poland, his youth, persecution, and for a few anguished, disoriented moments Dülitz is an adolescent again, ensnared in wet sheets, his heart in his mouth. His senses, as they return, do not bode much better. Aging bodies make themselves felt in the worst of ways. The old man's body still earns its keep, but it complains more and more. The most insignificant things leave ailments in their wake; his neck is stiff and his lumbar area refuses to flex. Now the din has spread into the street, and as Dülitz kneads life back into the arm that has fallen asleep beneath him, he staggers to the window in time to see Ottoson, fleet-footed as ever, one hand covering a bloodied nose, heading inwards at such a pace that each new step threatens to end in a tumble. Dülitz wonders which reckoning has arrived, closes his eyes, and wills his heart to slow before he dons his coat over his nightshirt, draws back the bolt, and begins to descend the stairs. He hears Ehrling moaning in the hall; he rubs the last of the sleep from his eyes and he steps through the door. Morning is near—the dawn light is sufficient to illuminate the beginning of the working day for the industrious. Nevertheless, he requires a moment to take in the tableau.

Ehrling is lying by the wall, as small as a big man can make himself, panting like a trapped animal, his broken arm hugged to his chest. The scuffle cannot have lasted long, but it has dealt the furniture some heavy blows: a table overturned and left toppled, splatters of blood on the wallpaper, chairs destroyed and thrown aside. One of them, however, is still standing—a throne for the victor, who now makes himself known.

"Jean Michael Cardell! It took me longer than I wish to admit to recall your name, but now I'm here."

The man is breathless and exuding a torrent of sweat, and it gives Dülitz some cold comfort that his staff did not come off altogether badly in their humiliation.

"And your own name—is it one I ought to be familiar with?"

"What about Anna Stina Knapp? Or Blix, depending on how she introduced herself."

Dülitz nods his assent to this watchword. The figure before him slowly becomes visible in the early light, and nods morosely in response to his gesture towards one of the fallen chairs. The first that he picks up rocks unevenly on broken legs. But he has better luck with the second and sits down opposite the newcomer. The face before him would put more hardened men than himself on their guard. Hair burnt off, skin scarred and scorched, and he is shuddering with the agony that those injuries entail.

"Won't you let go of my man so we can talk undisturbed? If there were any reinforcements to summon, Ottoson would have done so already. I myself am old and well within your power."

He gets a grunt in response and can do nothing but interpret it as assent. Ehrling needs no further instruction, promptly wriggling across the threshold with wheezing breaths, while Dülitz seizes the opportunity to assess his options for negotiation.

"So you want to get hold of the girl. You may be aware that you are in good company?"

A reaction: astonishment, mastered too late. Dülitz is accustomed to reading others, and knows at once that he has struck the bull's-eye.

"Last autumn I was visited by the chief of police, with none other than Johan Erik Edman at his heels, both on the same matter. I have been searching for her since then with little success."

"Start from the beginning and take it slowly. I'm no more quick-witted than I am beautiful."

"I take it that Kristofer Blix is familiar to you?"

"Yes."

"Well. The girl came to me because she needed money. She called herself his widow. She had a single, rare commodity that she could offer for sale: the preceding year she had escaped from the workhouse on the Island of Scar through a hole in the wall that had been forgotten after being made to drain water from the ground. Last year the workhouse hosted a renowned guest for just a few short days, and on behalf of a client I tasked the girl with making her way inside by the same route she had once used to escape. She crawled in under cover of darkness when there was a new moon."

The man on the chair shifts his left arm, and only now does Dülitz see that something is not right. The fist is scorched to charcoal, the wrist straight and rigid. Both bear fresh stains in memory of his henchmen. It is not a living arm, and a superstitious horror of that which is not human makes Dülitz fall silent.

"So you sent her to the workhouse. For that alone I could slay you on the spot."

"I can very well hear how it sounds in this room as I sit here and you sit there, but I swear that I meant her no harm. Most people I associate with founder through self-inflicted distress, not least her husband, but she came to me of her own accord and asked for help. She wanted two hundred daler for the sake of her children. For pennies like that, my clients buy curved ivory rods to scratch their backs with, and they would willingly have paid double or more. I offered to negotiate the sum up on her behalf, but she refused."

"How much were you intending to keep for yourself?"

He opts for the truth, taking a risk to gain in trust what he is losing to contempt.

"One-tenth. From others I would have taken half or more. But I suppose there was something about her."

"And for all you know, she is still lying under the wall, wedged into her grave?"

Dülitz shakes his head.

"No."

"How can you know?"

"My people have been to the workhouse. With some trouble, we found a watchman who was present when they found the girl in the yard during the morning assembly. By degrees we were able to make him more anxious of our displeasure than that of Pettersson the custodian's, whose trust he was reluctant to betray. Petter Pettersson dealt with her himself, and after they had spoken he led her out of the gate and let her flee. Since that same watchman has sworn that he knows the girl's face well, I have ordered him to keep his eyes open and he says he has seen her once since then, in company that became aware of his recognition and smuggled her away quick as a flash."

"Where? When?"

"They staged the premiere of Lindegren's *The Reconciled Father*, if you follow the theatrical season. On the thirtieth of May. He saw them among the groundlings in the pit."

Dülitz sees the disfigured man is lost in his thoughts, his gaze flickering as he chews on a fingernail and spits pieces onto the floor. He spies his opportunity, places his hands on his lap, and remains in that position, still.

"Let me simply say that I carry a poignard in my coat pocket. Damascus steel, mother-of-pearl handle. It's always there, just in case. My field can entail risk, and I live by the motto that it is better to carry a weapon and not need it than the reverse. It's not big, but it is quite sharp. I may not be a worthy opponent in a duel, old and weak as I have become, but as a boy I sometimes played at knife wrestling, and I dare say I might do some harm, perhaps bad enough to delay you in your search for the girl—a task you share with others."

"So?"

"I have certain thoughts on what has happened. I imagine they may be of benefit to you. I would happily share these with anyone whose benevolence I can count upon, especially if they subsequently show me a little consideration and leave me to oversee the cleaning of my miserable abode."

For a second time, Dülitz chooses to take the maintained silence as assent, and he leans closer to emphasize the value of what has been said.

"The girl was sent in to smuggle out a letter from Magdalena Rudenschöld on one of the few nights she was housed in the workhouse before they moved her to a more secure lockup. Undoubtedly with a message intended for Armfelt's coconspirators. Perhaps the girl never achieved her goal, perhaps the letter has been lost since then, but none of us can afford to take that risk. Everyone is looking for her: the conspirators who first gave me my contract, as well as Reuterholm's men. They are all looking for a letter that will be a tinderbox for the very kingdom itself. They're getting desperate. Every week, there are rumors about attempts on the Duke's life: the conspirators want him out of the way. Him and Reuterholm and the whole regency. How the girl managed to evade such interest is beyond me. Why she chooses to stand stock-still between devil and the deep blue sea as well . . . If she wanted, she could set a price of her own. Something must have happened to her."

Dülitz's final guess is worse than any threat, and it drains Cardell of what bloodlust had endured. Everything that can be won here has been won this night. He rises and wipes the wooden fist on a tapestry, tainting a pastoral idyll with rusty streaks.

"When we next meet I may be more inclined to check your pocket."

"Well, until then."

And then Dülitz is alone again, and old and tired, and to his surprise he notices his hands shaking atop his thighs as he lowers his guard and gives free rein to his emotions. It is late in life for new enemies. His pocket is empty, but he realizes that this is the last time this side of the grave that it will be, and while a knife does not weigh much he finds the burden considerable.

11

"High above our heads there hang scales, boy. Any day now, one of them will sink lower than the other, but soon the balance will shift and when the board is tallied it must always be even."

Emil has to make an effort to decipher the old woman's words, distorted by her northern speech, crowded with expressions that sound foreign to his ear. Her age is impossible to guess. She looks as old as time itself, small and hunched and toothless, every wrinkle blackened with soot. Eyes so deeply set that their presence is only betrayed by a glint when some stray ray of light penetrates through the folds of skin. Emil still can't say with certainty whether she is in her second childhood, or whether she merely prefers to respond to his questions in her own way. Practical matters demand patience.

"Don't sit there."

When the rain begins to whisper around their surroundings, he understands why. It is barely more than a hut she has, the roof leaky and the walls leaning against a long-suffering chimney shedding what little plaster remains on it. She feeds her fire with crow's wood, one twig at a time, while she speaks to the flames rather than to her guest.

....

Saxnäs is beautifully situated, cramped inside an S between watercourses. The village surrounds its square, the church nearby. Nevertheless, he has been unlucky. Few have been able to answer his questions, not through unwillingness but from ignorance. Stuttering, he tries to understand why, but they don't make it easy for him. Good things rarely come of southern strangers' curiosity, that much is known of old. The only time any interest is paid to the villages of the north is when they are suspected of wealth worth bleeding under the threat of bailiffs. The priest is abroad in the parish, and between the housemaid's stiffness and Emil's timidity, he turned on his heel at the door without asking for the guest room that she so clearly begrudged him. The inn brings shame on the name: a frozen cottage with wooden benches for beds and the option to buy milk and pork next door. On his way there, he sighted the old woman, like a spirit of the woods in flight towards her forest burrow, and it struck him that she was the only old person he had seen since he arrived here.

Carefully, she removes the snare from the claw of a sparrow with a broken neck and begins to pluck feathers from the small body. The bird lies naked in her hands, alien to Emil without its plumage. He is fascinated by how little flesh it has concealed beneath its vestments: a mouthful or two, no more. She gropes at the side of the hearth for a spit to thread it onto. She patiently turns the stick to roast the meat evenly, and when she is satisfied she proffers the stick to Emil. He meets her gaze and finds it both steady and unfathomable, but he senses that he is being tested. He carefully takes the bird, tears loose a tender wing, and inserts it into his mouth. She does the same with the other.

"You were asking about the village. I was a girl the first time it happened—barely old enough to make the goats listen. Mother and Father had sent me to the shieling for the summer together with some of the older girls. A man came. He was weak and warm. We gave him a bed where he lay and raved. After a few days came the eruptions—terrible blisters everywhere. A man brought us food a few days later, saw how it was, dropped everything in his hands, and ran back the way he had come. The stranger got worse. The next day, they came from the village and spoke to us from the edge of the forest. We were to stay. They left us a shovel. We didn't understand what for until our guest died. Then Kerstin had the shivers, then Elsa. When autumn came, it was only me and the goats left. Afterwards, I was told that our sacrifice had saved the village. That we had been brave. Thanks to us, they had time to lift away the gangways across the stream and no one else brought the pox to Saxnäs. Only afterwards did a girl I knew blab that the well-to-do farmers had put a man down on the marsh armed with a burning torch in case my friends and I had proven not to be quite so bold and had come stumbling home to our mothers. Everyone knew. No one objected."

Emil feels the wing crunch between his teeth, chewing quickly so that he can swallow and harry the spoilt flavor of game from his mouth, all the time hoping that his distaste is not too visible.

"You may barely see them among my wrinkles, boy, but my cheeks are full of healed wounds. You only get them once, you know. When the pox came here next, the village was more poorly equipped and the infection crept from farm to farm quicker than it could be stopped. Those who thought themselves still healthy fled north, straight into the arms of a contagion whose cloven hooves run faster than human beings. Each and every person has their own interests at heart—had self-love not weighed most heavily then surely no plague would have spread. But the old dean was a good man. He alone went in to see the sick and did what he could, humbled by the fate his God had meted out to him. Made sure the dead were put in the ground, read the right words of farewell. Had more people paid what we owed the first time, fewer would have been infected the next. Of that Saxnäs there is nothing left. The cottages may still stand as they did, but the people are different. Outsiders, the lot of them. Only I remember. The priest died himself, with the boils all over his cheeks, but with a smile that he had fulfilled his calling to the Lord's satisfaction and bought his patch of land in the meadows of heaven."

She sighs at the recollection.

"Those plague sores are dreadful. They show a person in their true color. Some say that the infection spreads on the wind, others that it wanders from skin to skin. Everyone finds their own way to protect themselves. You shun old friends, reject water from your well, refuse to unnecessarily help those who might just as well give up before the sun next rises. Some resort to the dark arts, give themselves to the devil just as long as they may live."

Of the bird, all that remains are the bones the old woman has removed from the corner of her mouth and stacked on the edge of the stove.

"I remember little Tycho. That was the priest's boy. Always at his father's skirts, ready to do as he was told wherever he could, even if you could tell how afraid he was. And who am I to blame him? He must have helped to dig half the graves up at the church. But he had to leave his father's pit to others. Tycho fell sick and had the chills for a long time. But the pox spared him, and if I thought the world a better place then I would imagine he was being shown compassion on merit. By the time he was back on his feet, old Pastor Ceton had fallen and left the church to its fate. He cried and cried, but never did I see anyone at death's door without the lad standing at their side, the only company they had, for that was a place shunned by all. The blight moved on eventually, the boy on its heels. Where he went next I know not. He inherited and disappeared. I hope he made the most of the life he was allowed to keep."

12

Dawn, smoldering summer heat in the making. Cardell climbs the stairs. Someone has been at his chamber door and has left their mark with the help of a piece of coal. *12 The Ship's Bridge*, today's date and signed with a *W*. So Winge is back. The meeting place matches, as does the initial. The Ship's Bridge has always been a refuge for him, albeit no longer for conversation with his dead sister but for the sake of the setting, for the open sky, for the constant din of all manner of folk passing through this place between places on their way somewhere else. It is early morning and Cardell tugs off his coat and shirt, pours water from the jug into the basin, and washes his face and neck until clean, wiping himself on the shirt and hanging it up to dry. He has kept the window wide for the last week or so, having wedged it open with a sharpened stick, grateful for every breeze that is lured in. The bunk draws him in as does a cowpat a fly, and he knows that if he answers its siren call then he will miss his meeting. Instead, he remains standing, chewing his lower lip. His thoughts are never far away from her; she is more exposed than he could have imagined, hunted by others. His own search has been transformed into a race. Yet she is still missing. If they too have lost track of the quarry—they whose resources are far greater than his—what does that say about her fate? What arms he has he uses to beat the stinging worry in his diaphragm. His mind seeks out all the secluded nooks and crannies of the city where a body might lie forgotten for years, to the deep holes beneath the dam and the rat-filled cellar vaults. His eyelids flutter; sleep will not be denied. Only there does he find her, but only as a will-o'-the-wisp, and he wakes to equal parts relief and disappointment. He'd prefer to return to the street.

....

Cardell is early, but Winge is already there, pacing back and forth, deep in his own thoughts, unaware of Cardell until they are within each other's reach.

"Ah. I wasn't expecting you for another quarter of an hour."

Cardell shrugs. The breeze pauses before whimsically deciding to set off in a new direction, and Cardell senses something new.

"You smell different."

"How so?"

He has to think in order to answer.

"Fir needles, resin, pitchwood. Mud of a kind kneaded without help from the nightly chamber pots. Not like the city."

"I'll take it as a compliment in that case. The road was long. I dare say the scent shall pass soon."

"You've been gone for a long time. Midsummer is already two weeks' past."

"Do not tempt me to begin cursing the horse-drawn carriages, for if I do then we shall be here until next Midsummer. What news is there in Stockholm?"

"Not much. Copenhagen burned for weeks, but perhaps you have already heard that? The fire came up from the harbor. A thousand homes are gone, the palace is burnt to ashes, and thousands of homeless have set up camp amid its ruins. What of Bergslagen?"

"No Ceton, at any rate. But still something. I spoke to someone who remembered him as a child."

"That sounds worthwhile. Was our Tycho an agreeable little lad? Rosy-cheeked, nimble-legged, kind to the elderly and infirm?"

"You know others as you know yourself, so they say. I've had many an hour in the carriages to ponder to what extent my own childhood has molded me into who I am, who I could have been if things had unfolded differently. What about you, Jean Michael?"

Cardell turns away, standing in silence for a while before he finds the words.

"I became a burnt cripple on my own merits."

Winge offers Cardell a seat on a stack of logs, while he himself goes over to some seamen sharing a pipe on their own gangway, dangling their legs as the wood rises and falls at the discretion of the waves. On language they are unable to agree, but the matter is easily clarified through gestures, and in return for a pinch of tobacco one of the seamen puffs on the embers until Emil is able to ignite a stick and can inherit the fire. Cardell has seen him smoking more and more often this year. That is a new development. But he remains sober, and perhaps this balances matters out. With the shaft of the fragile clay pipe resting between thumb and forefinger, he sits down. A warm wind blows indolently off the water. The acrid scent of simmering tar is borne over from Pitch Islet. Emil is restless, seemingly struggling to find a comfortable position, and Cardell wonders whether he is trying to buy more thinking time, now that his guest has arrived early. In the end, Emil blows smoke out of the corner of his mouth and plucks up courage.

"There's something I want to ask you, Jean Michael. We've rarely spoken of our evening in the anatomical theater. Ceton was more than happy to brag of his atrocities, but only there did we have our fill of them. You, more accurately. I did what I could to keep you down, but not altogether successfully. What was it you saw?"

"The whole thing. Ceton himself, the wretched creature, and the woman on his bunk."

"Ceton—what did he look like?"

"As ever. An evil-looking devil with his scarred cheek, dressed like a peacock in ruffles and expensive boots."

"That's not what I mean. His face and his temperament. Did he enjoy the spectacle?"

Cardell shakes his head.

"I think he was putting it on for the student. What I saw on his face was something else. The man appeared to be terrified. It's hard to say when he is or isn't sneering at the best of times, and for a long time I thought I'd been mistaken then too, but I threw the same words in his face when I was bargaining with him, and a boy caught with his fist in the pralines couldn't have looked more guilty."

Winge adds more tobacco on top of that which is already glowing, blowing into the pipe bowl to better ignite it.

"In light of what you saw, Jean Michael, what do you make of the stories he told us?"

"I'm in no doubt that he is guilty of every damned thing."

"But his role in them may not be entirely the one that he painted?"

"Perhaps not."

Emil leans his head back thoughtfully and releases the smoke to join the clouds wafting past in the sky above. Cardell is back on his feet, still tired after the night just gone and thoroughly tired of being addressed in riddles. Winge is awakened from his thoughts and blinks drowsily.

"Forgive me, Jean Michael. I see you have new wounds. How goes your search?"

"Badly, albeit slightly better than before. Your advice stood me in good stead."

"Do you want to accompany me to Hammarby tomorrow? Let us speak afterwards, if you wish."

"To Gallows Hill—on a Saturday? Why the hell then? I have seen enough of that diversion for this lifetime and several more to boot."

"Your eyes need not be on the gallows. On the contrary. Maybe luck will be on our side."

"You think Ceton will be there? Why would someone in hiding attend such a spectacle?"

"There was something I heard in Bergslagen. If he is still in Stockholm then he will be there. I don't believe he has any choice in the matter."

13

Back at his chamber, sleep claims Cardell where he sits, his head hanging against his breast and his body slumping backwards. The dream is different from the one he feared: it is a memory of a bygone time, every detail as clear as when it happened.

He is a boy again, of some thirteen years or so, but already well grown and capable of doing a day's work alongside his father, a tall fellow with long arms and hands like barrel lids, his face locked in phlegmatic dissatisfaction from a life of toil for little recompense. Their smallholding was one of the farthest flung, adjacent to the forest whose far border none had seen, and from which any who went astray never returned. The cottage was a cross-timbered hut with moss-covered roof logs, the floor fir twigs atop flattened earth. A cleared hill full of stones was his father's lot, and there he spent his days fighting roots and rocks. Even as a child, it was clear to Cardell that the stone was a living thing of a singular kind—an opposite to mankind that lived its life in another way. With infinite patience, it strove towards the face of the earth from the tomb of its birth. Only then did it come to rest, never to move again. What else could explain the fact that their field gave more stones than grain in its annual harvest? If there had been ore in the growing cairns, they would have been rich. The pebbles were one thing, but with each year that the frost left the ground and the soil could be plowed, they found a new boulder as big as a man, which his father had to root up with stakes and levers before work could continue. Such effort can hardly meet with anything but disappointment.

Cardell longs for the day when he is strong enough to meet his father's fists with anything other than snot and tears. Thus he helps willingly in the field, trying his strength every day alongside his father, seeing the difference shrink year by year. Their mother is inside. He doesn't know how old she is, but she looks older than the hags with grandchildren, aged before her time by beatings and miscarriages. In church, she is ashamed of her lameness and black eyes, more often than not concealed by a veil.

One day he answers back, a day like any other. The light is fading and the work is close to its end. He is tired and his gaze is black, and his father strikes him on the back of the head when he slips and drops the spade. When Cardell picks it up again it is not to cut another sod but to throw it as far as he can across the furrowed mud. He has been beaten before, and often too, for the father takes his son's shortcomings personally, every disappointment yet another grain of salt strewn over the wound that is life itself. Little Mickel, who so struggles to read the catechism because the letters dance around each other; Mickel, who is never strong enough or quick enough to please, not with his arms and hardly with his thoughts. Stupid as they come, he is. Now he rises to his full height, expands the chest that has grown wide where his father's has shrunk, and out come the words that he has long pared down to the fewest possible.

"You will never touch me again, and don't touch Mother either."

As if they were both prepared for this, they step onto firmer ground and stand there a while. He sees something in his father's eyes he has never seen before—fear diluted with shame, calculating the sum of all the blows that have mapped out his failure as a father and a husband, a realization of how vast that debt has grown, now that it is being called in. But the flush of anger still triumphs, and they come together and exchange blows without a thought of the morrow. Afterwards, Cardell crawls towards the forest, only able to get to his feet with the aid of a fir tree. In the field, his father remains upright, albeit bent double and bleeding. Then he rises and stands. As the victor, he gives his son a final look, and Cardell spits and feels his parting words stinging his cracked ribs.

"I'll be back."

Then he staggers in among the trees, taking support against one and pissing red, carries on, vowing to the silent forest that he has lost his last fight.

On the day he fulfilled his promise to return, it was in the guise of the

Crown, a grown man arriving by carriage. Too late. Mother gone, Father alone, a sinewy little man with a warped back and narrow shoulders. The patch of field shrunken when the nosebag was adjusted for fewer muzzles, the forest creeping ever closer in a patient siege. Beating him to death would have been merciful. They exchanged glances, then Cardell turned on his heel at the door. He imagines that a sob followed him out, but he never turned to see, the shame of having waited too long adding to the shame of his escape.

....

Slowly he wakes up, lost for a while, and he finds that the dreamed memory has dragged up old emotions into the present. Disappointment, anger at himself and others, doubts about the freedom bought at the price of a guilty conscience. One form of servitude exchanged for another. He can't fathom the angle of the light until he leans out of the window to glimpse the church tower and finds that it is the early dawn. Saturday already.

14

"The weather is siding with the administration of justice."

....

The day is hot, the sun alone in the blue sky, and many have felt the urge to take an outing. Cardell allows his gaze to survey the gathering. The same mix one might have expected—a cross section of the city with a preponderance towards the poor and recent arrivals. Prisoners of higher standing are pilloried in the squares, here in faraway Hammarby, so as to spare the well-to-do any stains on their stockings. Cardell has no desire to see anyone hanged. He has seen it before, and the spectacle offers few surprises. He holds the gallows in the corner of his eye. Emil points vaguely at the crowd with the stem of his pipe.

"He'll do his best to remain incognito."

"Then how are we supposed to find him?"

"I don't believe he'll be expecting us to be here. It won't be a pleasant surprise for him. Look for someone self-consciously incognito. Who turns quickly to beat a hasty retreat."

They scout together for a while in silence. Up by the gallows, the priest says his piece. Soon their chance will be over.

"Jean Michael—your arm. Are you able to take it off and sling it over your shoulder? It would make us more eye-catching."

"Mutilation really is a gift that never stops giving."

Cardell does as he's asked, cautiously gripping each buckle to avoid waking the slumbering pain. Behind them, the hangman's rope creaks in a glissando of death by strangulation. Winge shifts restlessly beside him, craning his own neck for all he is worth.

"Nothing? Still nothing?"

Perhaps. A man in a coat and hat, bearded, who with a sudden jerk turns on his heel and disappears into the crowd. Cardell squints and points.

"There. Over by the gallows. Did you see?"

"Ceton?"

"Maybe, maybe not."

"Come on then. No harm in troubling an innocent man."

They hasten as best they can through the sea of bodies, Cardell carving the way like a plow through loose soil. Even though Cardell has trudged farther this spring than he has since his military days, this forced march is something else. Rarely deployed muscles protest, back and thighs make their dissatisfaction known. He picks up the pace through the thinning crowd, and soon he has gained the hill where fewer people obscure the view. Eyes streaming from dust and haste, he sees his prey lunging down the hill, and he follows, his soles thumping on the ground, each jarring step a blow to his knee. If it is Ceton, then he is running as if his life depended on it—his lead is still pronounced, but it is shrinking with every step, and Cardell's panting mouth cracks into a wolf's grin when he realizes that the race is his for the taking. They aren't far from the redoubt, its customs barrier raised to mark the day for as long as the raised scaffold offers amusement, and behind it a scattering of houses and an unobstructed view across open ground. The stitch in his side and the taste of blood in his mouth be damned—he picks up the pace, egged on by the promise of sweet victory.

Perhaps it will come sooner than expected: Ceton has given up at the barrier and is standing next to the watchmen ordered there for extra duties, pointing in his direction. Cardell glances over his shoulder and sees that Winge is no more than a dot on Hammarby Hill, swears an oath, and closes the distance. The city watch are everywhere, in his way, gloved fists brandished in placatory menace. His heart is in his throat and the blood is rushing in his ears; he is unable to make himself understood, and when the words come off badly and he tries to push past, they're on him, locking down his arms and legs, grabbing his neck and weighing him down until he falls to his knees. Anger and disappointment give him new strength, and they are soon nothing but a single pile of fighting limbs, locked in a furious tangle. Winge finally arrives, just as breathless, and it takes him some time to pour oil onto troubled waters, separating the men with conciliatory words, explaining who is who and who has right on his side. Eyes black, the soldiers adjust their rumpled uniforms and Cardell glowers furiously. Of the quarry there is nothing to be seen.

"Was it him, Jean Michael?"

"As sure as damnation. He may have left his razor to rust, but his hat flew off as he ran. Shit. Bloody fucking shit."

Emil opens his mouth but closes it again when Cardell gives him a defiant look.

"Shit. God damn fucking shit."

Winge nods piously. Cardell brushes gravel off his thighs.

"There, I'm done for now."

They begin to walk back towards the city at a slower pace. Winge nervously twists the chain of his pocket watch between his fingers.

"This doubles our misfortune, Jean Michael. Not only did Ceton slip through our grasp, but he has also been warned of our efforts. But I fear it is worse than that. Now all we can do is wait."

"For what?"

"He'll never return to Gallows Hill. I don't think we've left him any choice other than to find what he seeks elsewhere. It is only a matter of time before he leaves a body in our path that bears his mark. It's bad, Jean Michael. Bad. With mistakes like that, we're reprising the debacle of last year."

Winge kicks a stone across Postmaster's Hill.

"Damn it."

Cardell fumbles with his hand at his waist, making sure that his tobacco pouch is still there.

"You're learning."

15

It is Sunday, never a day to the benefit of Petter Pettersson's temperament. The church bells summon all to mass, and the peals rolling across the bay and from within the city are echoed by the workhouse chapel's own crude little bell. It is yet another piece of mockery to add to the burden that existence seems to heap upon him at every juncture. It is the sound of other people's hypocrisy, intended to give him a guilty conscience that he cannot ward off. In his head, the peals take on words: *You are inferior to others, Petter. You're going to hell, Petter, and contempt will be your legacy. Not even by the yardstick you have carved for yourself are you anything to be reckoned with, Petter.*

It is the latter that stings the most, a thunderclap of truth in the darkness of the mind. He sits up heavily on the bed, feeling his head swim, and the hangover is given fresh fuel as he staggers across the floor towards the basin. He bumps into it and dips his face into the water, holding it below the surface until his lungs burn, and then scooping cool handfuls over his scalp and neck. Between his thighs, his member is chafing, throbbing, and hard as a broomstick. It hurts when he touches it, and he knows from experience that self-abuse is not an option. It makes his shame all too clear. Only by night does he find relief, in fever dreams where he wakes with his heart in his mouth and his stomach sticky, like a child who has not learned to find the chamber pot.

The fault lies with her: the girl, Knapp. She gave him her word and then she broke it. She lied to his face, left him there like a jilted bridegroom, his gullibility a simple prey to female cunning. A hundred laps, she said. She never had a thought of doing so. She lured him into a trap. Fuck. The betrayal gives him no peace, its machinations disturbing him.

Drowsy with sleep and with dark bags beneath his eyes, he inspects the starving workhouse hands each day, forced to rub his eyes each time he confuses someone's face with hers. Then up to the custodian's office, where sleep only comes in fits, saturated with mocking dreams of what might have been.

He tries to find others. God have mercy on anyone who resembles her in the slightest way. Anyone coming from the city who is flaxen blond with a glimmer of fire hidden in her downcast eyes will meet with unwelcome treatment before she sees the end of her first day. But to little avail. There is no stamina in them—they barely take a single stroke before they turn on the waterworks, and shortly thereafter they are worn out, and he must lumber away, not even once out of breath, while they are dragged off to lie in their sickbed. Pettersson knows he ought to restrain himself. He goes too hard. Concealing his urges under the pretext of punishment was never truly convincing, but what was once an open secret is no longer a secret at all. He quietly curses the economy, damns Reuterholm and whichever gentlemen are charged with the abacuses of the kingdom's finances. Had they managed the taxes better to begin with, then his situation would also be different—but suddenly everything must be counted again, and the workhouse's quotas are no exception. The ledgers are being scrutinized, and the spun yarn measured by the yard. Krook himself, Inspector Björkman's replacement who is into his second year in post, previously allowed activities to depend on the favor of the city's coterie, but now he is venturing into the domains of the watchmen and giving Pettersson and his colleagues a good dressing-down in his fiery Finnish accent, his face red as a freshly cooked crayfish and irate as a watchdog. They're not spinning enough. Quotas must go up. No one who knows the reasons for the deficit says anything—they fear Pettersson too much to do so, but even the slowest of his watchmen grasps that the quota will never increase if Pettersson dispatches yet another workhouse hand to the cottage hospital every second day; its walls are already groaning from the burden, and the food they have to offer is hardly nutritious enough to allow wounds to heal.

He is trying to cultivate other vices to alleviate his anguish. He takes spirits in his custodian's office, packs his cheek full of tobacco until his heart is galloping, but it does little to help. On the contrary: inebriation blunts his judgment, and when one of the girls slips with the spinning-fork or is kept in bed by fever, his emotions defy all mastery. As if of his own volition, Master Erik comes to mind, the dance begins, and the gravel is splattered. As always, he counts the laps. They are always so few. A hundred laps. A hundred laps. That was what he was promised. But he has been deceived. The bells are still ringing—they can go to hell.

At the mirror, the decision he has been dwelling upon for a week or more takes solid form: he has to put his back into it for a few weeks, try to lick the house into shape, review the quotas, and leave the hands to spin in peace. Just for this summer. In the autumn, new strokes: his time will come again. He brushes his uniform and he rubs at the many dark stains with soap as best he can. In future, dancing only on Sundays at noon, as custom dictates. With some measure of newfound confidence, he strops the knife to scrape his cheeks rosy and smooth.

He wipes his freshly shaved cheeks and runs his fingers over the skin. A knock on the door.

"Pettersson? Visitor."

Hybinette's voice. Is it old Krook again, come in his dancing shoes with new reproaches? He wipes the knife clean against the towel and sets it aside.

"Who?"

"Cardell. You remember. The idler. I hope your stomach is strong enough to keep your breakfast down—he looks fucking awful."

....

Hybinette may be prone to exaggeration, but this time he has done reality justice. Pettersson's eyes tear up at the sight. Cardell is waiting for him outside the workhouse gate, not moving at all, and Pettersson steps out to meet him.

"Twenty-Four Cardell, isn't it? You look like someone has jabbed a wick through your scalp and left it burning overnight."

Cardell jerks his neck, and together they walk a little distance down the road, away from curious ears. Pettersson senses his errand, his heart beating like a fist against his ribs and his patience quickly faltering.

"The last time you came lumbering in it was about the Knapp girl."

"She was here last autumn. You let her go."

Pettersson cocks his head to one side, expectantly.

"Perhaps."

"Why? And what happened next?"

Pettersson's anger can no longer be contained—not now that it has been given an outlet. He pictures her before him in her feigned sincerity, freckles and blue eyes and flaxen blond hair, innocence itself in human form. The words that have resounded within him for half a year want to pour out, just as quickly as his lips will allow.

"That little whore deceived me. She swore she'd come back. That was the only reason she was allowed to go. I waited a week—that was how long was agreed. I touched no one else, remained chaste for her sake. Then I waited another week. Then another. For that long I thought the best of her—she had looked me straight in the eyes and sworn on the life of her children."

He spits in front of himself and Cardell hisses in reply.

"What was it she promised you?"

"A hundred laps."

"What?"

"A hundred laps around the well taking turns with me and Master Erik. After that, I could have died happy instead of languishing in my office."

"I'll help you to new quarters—smaller but quieter, earth floor, and a six-foot ceiling."

Cardell has stepped closer, his feet suddenly spread wide, his left hand ready to strike, and Pettersson shakes his head to force his mind back to clarity. Then his face cracks into a broad smile. He stretches and puffs out his chest to maximize his size.

"You, alone, against me? Maybe in your prime. If that. But it'll take more than a freshly grilled cripple to take down Petter Pettersson."

The wooden fist comes at him and Pettersson leans back, two rapid fists catching it in the air between them, and Cardell uses his right arm, shifts his weight, presses the stump forward as if against a wall of pain, and beneath Pettersson the gravel crunches as the custodian is pressed backwards on unmoving feet. Pettersson leans forward to better brace himself, and they stand there completely still, locked against each other like two lads in a wrestling match where neither is capable of gaining the upper hand. Pettersson is the first to speak, the words affected as effortless even though Cardell can see the veins pulsing in his bull's neck.

"Not here, Twenty-Four Cardell, and not now. I'm too concerned about my own position to slay watchmen on my own doorstep."

He cocks his head towards the water.

"But you needn't remain unslain for long. There's a beach down by the Golden Bay, right next door. Supposing we were to agree to meet there in the hour of the wolf, when the moon is full, so that we can see properly? Not the coming one, but the one after that. I'm busy working. Have patience and bring your sooty wooden block and whatever else you believe may help. I'll bring Master Erik. He rarely drinks the blood of men, but doubtless it always tastes the same, and you can surely be tempted to dance. You, like all others."

The straps cut into old scars. Cardell breathes hard to keep the pain out of his voice. The effort makes his vision darken, but he still pushes a hair's breadth closer, close enough to see a grubby sheet of paper protruding where Pettersson's jacket has slipped open.

"A pledge. Surely she must have left you a pledge."

Pettersson changes the direction of his thrust and breaks the embrace. He stands at a distance panting as he collects himself, tucking his shirt back into his trousers and smoothing cloth that has been rumpled.

"A letter."

Pettersson smirks at Cardell's expression.

"For her it was worth two hundred daler. When she didn't come back, I felt like the worst cuckold the world has ever seen. That was until people came and started asking after it and I put two and two together. I can tell that you have done the same. It was written by Rudenschöld. It's worth half the kingdom. But what difference does that make to us, Cardell? To us, it's worth far more. It's the princess we want."

He spits into his hand and brushes a tuft of hair away from his temple.

"She carried it hidden in her blouse, against her bare skin. I still hold it under my nose when I retire to enjoy it, and I imagine that it still smells of her bosom. Tell me, wouldn't you do the same?"

"Bring it to the dance floor so that I can pluck it from your cold body."

16

Frans Gry has been in the Last Farthing from early morning until noon with nothing but his bitter desire for revenge for company. It ruined his night's sleep, forcing him to dwell on wasted opportunities: if he hadn't been so drunk he wouldn't have allowed himself to be flogged; had he understood who it was who had set about him he would have defended himself better; had he had anything within reach he would have given back as good as he got. And as of a few weeks ago, Lotta Erika has returned—a constant reminder of his shame.

Ever since the spring he has sought out inns of the kind he previously avoided: the places where old soldiers gather, men marked by battle badly enough to be rendered unusable for anything else, and whose only comfort is the haze of inebriation as they scrutinize memories for meaning. Before, they always depressed him and he regarded them with horror and contempt, retreating from them as the only way to confirm that he was not one of them. Now he is on the fringes of their company, close enough to listen for the name he wants to hear most of all—the one that he dwells upon more and more the drunker he becomes. Tonight, he finally does.

"And what about Cardell! Do you remember him? A scoundrel if ever I met one."

Gry vaguely knows the speaker by sight, and eventually the name comes to him. Although he has seen the fellow off and on over recent years, he has never given Kreutz more than a fleeting look, and now as he examines the former warrant officer he marvels that he is even capable of naming him. The man he once knew has been hidden beneath the mask of age. Kreutz walks straight-backed like a plumb line, and soon Gry sees that this is because something has stiffened and will not slacken, and it forces Kreutz to stagger about on faltering legs and flat feet. Gry has never learned what his forename is. They know each other in the way of soldiers.

At first, Gry doesn't know how best to rekindle their acquaintance. The round pieces in his pocket are probably enough for a few drinks or for supper, not both, and his equivocation makes the choice for him. The drink tastes bad—no better than fox piss. But the price is also cheap enough to stifle all complaints, and once you've forced a mouthful past your throat it spreads its warmth just as well as better goods. As Gry hopes, intoxication kindles courage within his breast, and when the rest of the company slips out he plunges down onto the rough bench alongside Kreutz with renewed confidence.

"Clear the decks!"

Kreutz squints at him for a while without answering. In his furrowed face, Gry can see all the emotions he has just experienced, and he is forced to admit that he is no longer a model of youth and beauty either. Age and debauchery have further tanned the skin that war has weathered.

"Gry, right? From the *Alexander*?"

"One and the same."

He offers Kreutz a drink, and it takes no more than that. In the manner of old soldiers, they are soon lost in memories: flatulence like cannon shots in their hammocks below deck, the Battle of Viborg Bay, the whore dressed as a cabin boy, the cabin boy mistaken for the whore and who screamed in vain. Kreutz now works for small change in the cheap tobacco shop and he spits into the shavings on the floor at the mere thought of it.

"The manager is a swine who makes Captain Risberg seem a miracle of benevolence. When a cannon struck down our mast, I took a fistful of wooden splinters in my back don't you know, and I can't bloody bend over. If anyone asks for things from low down I have to get on my knees and grope blindly. A few brats have become aware of this debility and make it their business to visit the shop because of it, and when I have fought my way back up again they are gone. That's the thanks we get for defending the kingdom."

"Oh well. We were the ones who attacked."

"Cold comfort."

Kreutz leans in conspiratorially towards Gry's ear.

"You know, I pass by the church on the Knights' Isle every weekend to piss on the wall. The king lies there in his coffin with his big Svensksund medal on his chest—the one he cast himself and hung around his neck on a gold chain. If but a few drops seep into the crypt I shall die more contented. Not infrequently I encounter others who have limped there for the same purpose."

Gry takes a deep breath and makes an effort to get to the point. More and more people have begun to gather under the sooty beams, and the hubbub is beginning to trouble his ears, which howl constantly since the rumbling guns have left him hard of hearing.

"I heard you mention a familiar name earlier. Cardell?"

Kreutz pauses for a beat before the memory animates his wrinkles.

"Yes, that bastard. I met him awhile ago when he was at Cellar Hamburg, shirking his duty. We exchanged a few words. Misanthropic like almost no one else, but he's always been a bit superior. I had money in my pocket for a change, a few coins from an uncle whose quill must have slipped writing his will. As soon as Cardell caught sight of the purse his bark took on a different tone—we were brothers in a flash, and after we'd drunk together awhile he wanted to borrow money. Stupid and gullible as I am, I agreed against the promise that it would all be repaid by the weekend, but damn it if I couldn't find the promissory note when I woke the morning after. And what do you think that devil said on the Saturday when I came to explain my predicament?"

"What?"

"He refused to acknowledge either the loan or the promissory note. Sat there smirking in newly waxed boots. That was the thanks I got from an old shipmate. We were both on *The Fatherland* at the Battle of Hogland. She had sixty cannon, and now that counts for nought."

"What kind of fellow was he back then?"

Kreutz eyes his empty goblet with disappointment. Gry silently curses his anxious tone, which has betrayed his question as more than mere curiosity. Now Kreutz sets the price. Gry can do nothing more than ask the host to cover him, albeit on credit. He takes one for himself too, even though he ought not, but seeing others drinking while remaining sober has never suited him. Kreutz smacks his lips, pleased.

"Well, there are sergeants and sergeants. You know that too. There are those who strive upwards for their own sake and become little despots who do well as long as they don't give their hectored men the opportunity to accidentally shoot them in the back. Cardell was of the other ilk—a regular soldier promoted more or less against his will. Ill-suited for the post. Treated his men as if they were his younger brothers, coddling them in his foolishness. That sort rarely grow old. Lead or steel is usually the reward they receive for their efforts."

"And then what?"

"Fools of that type fare worse in peace than in war. The biggest mercy of all would be to die a man's death. If nothing else does it, their conscience kills them. The *Ingeborg* went down with almost all hands—Cardell was one of the few to save his skin. I got the impression that he saw it as a punishment rather than good fortune."

Frans Gry trips over his words now that conversation has made space for his own business.

"I'm not going to hide that I have a grudge against the man—just like you do. Perhaps we ought to help relieve his anguish—for good. You wouldn't happen to know where his haunt is?"

Kreutz contemplates him for a moment before lowering his voice and leaning closer.

"No. But there are bound to be others who do. I can make inquiries. Discreetly. It would be a good deed for him and others."

Kreutz doesn't need Gry's help to wave for refills, and now the bellowing begins around them. A cantor is summoned onto a bench, clears his throat, and taps out his own tempo, which spreads from foot to foot until the floor is heaving. The man sings the alternating verses in a clear, pure voice, while the men sing the chorus, making the melancholy theirs—the drunkest watering their beards with tears.

"On blackest waves, the darkest main, there the mad storm roars . . ."

"Young as we are, we pledge our lives to these thin barrel-boards . . ."

"And so to seek t'outlive the waves, we'll take almighty care . . ."

"Or see our coffins' flags and colors flutt'ring in the air."

17

"Mickel!"

At first he wonders whether someone else by the same name is being called, but when he turns a girl waves to him and detaches herself from a group of friends. They are all basket girls, densely massed by the wall of the house, each dressed in the traditional delicate hues of gray, scarves over their hair. Lotta Erika crosses the cobblestones, empty basket in hand. They meet halfway, stepping into the shadow of the columns of the Stock Exchange to avoid the sun in their eyes. The summer is hot, bursting with eagerness to make up for all the cold spring has begrudged them. He gives her a nod.

"Lotta. How are you doing?"

She shrugs, but he can already read the answer. No marks of the kind attracted by those who must sleep outside besmirch her. Her arms are free from bruises left by the grip of firm hands. Her body is healthy and her gaze self-assured.

"Oh yes."

"And at home?"

She looks away, spitting over her shoulder as if to ward off evil harbingers.

"You should see Frans staring, Mickel. His eyes are sheer lust every time he sees me. I only dare wash when he is out; otherwise it would be as certain as an amen in church that he would happen to be passing in the hope of seeing more than he ought. But he doesn't touch me, and he does as he's told."

"You're saving well?"

"All that I can. And if I find service somewhere, then I suppose I will get a new bed too."

"Well."

He looks restlessly at the pump, waiting for her to get to the point. The jaws of the stone lions spew water into pail after pail. In the queue, words are being bandied over the ways of the heart; a boy in rags challenged over his place entertains the encircling group of scolds with colorful words of persuasion that testify to the excellent skills of his teacher.

"There are three things, Mickel. I believe Frans is plotting revenge. How, I know not. He mutters your name when he drinks; his eyes become dark."

"I've contended with worse than Frans Gry in my time."

"He's an evil bastard, and worse sober than drunk. Now you know."

"And what else?"

"You said you were looking for a man keeping his head down. I've spread word among the girls."

She waves to one of the others, who nods shyly and hurries over, curtsying before Cardell, who nods in reply.

"This is Lisabet. Lisabet, tell Mickel what you told me."

The girl is short and stocky, and appears to be perhaps a year younger than Lotta. "Lisabet is the little sister of a girl I know who carries her basket around Saint Gertrud's. Go on, Lisa."

"There's a man who lives in Cassiopeia, very close to us. He arrived last autumn and didn't stick his nose outside even once all winter. My cousin brought him firewood and food for a few pennies."

"Oh?"

"He has a beard now. But when he arrived he did not. Then, he had a terrible wound on his cheek."

"Which side?"

Using her finger, she extends the left corner of her mouth.

"Would you show me where?"

Before they leave, Lotta delays him with her third matter. Another girl is waved over, the face still marked with fading bruises that intensify when the color rises to her cheeks. She clasps her hands behind her back and proffers her gift only once she is right before him. The girls maintain a breathless silence, and Cardell extends his sole hand to receive what is offered: a pink braid in which clock-shaped flowers have been linked together by green stalks tied in patterns about each other. Their pleasant scent wafts over the stench of the square.

"We were all the way out by the tollgate when we found them."

Cardell clutches the braid in his hand, unsure what to make of it. The giver timidly slips back to her own flock, and when they disperse he remains standing there for a while with the flowers in his grasp. It seems to him as if they are already wilting more than before. He tucks the braid into his belt and follows the girl who has been waiting towards the Cassiopeia quarter.

18

They are waiting in the chamber together. Posted farther up the stairwell is a borrowed police constable ready to bar the escape route should the command be shouted. The man does what he can to remain incognito, coat over his uniform jacket and badge tucked under his collar. The room is small but drafty, the wind entering through the cracks in the floorboards and the gaps where the window timbers and stone wall are joined by the conventions of mutual reluctance, a room of the kind where not even a roaring fire in a tiled fireplace would be able to keep the winter cold at bay. The draft is of an evil sort—it does little to air the room, and hot vapors emerge like heavy sighs from the gaps every time the night breeze picks up. The windowpanes are sooty and obscure the light, dirt and dust cover the floor, the bunk is an unruly nest of abandoned blanket rags. The bedbugs linger in shameless clusters, tame and patient. It has a very particular scent—one that Cardell recognizes as that of confinement. This is the smell of a room in which a person has remained for far too long, whether it be at Dane's Bay, at Kastenhof, belowdecks on the *Ingeborg*, in military barracks, in the vaults beneath Indebetou House. Not unlike his own rented nook in the winter of last year. Cardell shakes himself like a wet dog to ward off the memories.

"If this is Ceton's den, then he must have fewer means than we thought. Stockholm's landlords may be profiteers with their own special place reserved for them in hell, but not even they are likely to charge much in return for lousy digs such as these."

"This is good, Jean Michael. Better than we could have hoped for. Had he gained the goodwill of his former brothers of the fraternity, he would have been better accommodated."

Emil holds up a book between his thumb and forefinger, having recently removed it from the floor beneath the bed. The title page means nothing to Cardell. His guess is to play the safest card he knows.

"French?"

Winge nods.

"One of the titles that Three Roses mentioned in his writings, lent to pass the time on the journey home. I doubt he read it."

At the bottom of a chest there is a bundle wrapped in oilcloth, and after angling it against the light Cardell passes it to Winge with a triumphant smile.

"I'm no expert on heraldry, but if that isn't Three Roses's coat of arms then I either don't know what a rose looks like or I can't count to three."

Winge too seeks out the light, an inlaid stock and tempered barrel balanced in eager fingers.

"Erik's pistol, monogram and all. The one that Schildt had with him. This means we have him, Jean Michael. Now we can tie him to a crime with more than just his own tall stories and our own testimony."

Nothing else of value is to be found.

"Any valuables that he may have brought with him are sold, and if he has any coins upon his person there cannot be many."

Cardell nods.

"Yes. Can't you tell from the smell? It's in the walls."

"What?"

"Desperation."

Next to the window is a chair, positioned to take advantage of what little light the pane admits. Cardell wipes the seat and back clean and offers it to Winge, who sits down for a while before rising to his feet again, restlessly crossing the floor. He settles on the chest lid. The timbered vault groans under his weight.

"Sit down and light your pipe. You can't be seen in the window, and smoldering tobacco is preferable to Tycho Ceton's ingrained dirt. All we can do is wait, and hope that the bedbugs will see fit to leave us with at least a drop of blood for the time being."

His body is already crawling. Halfheartedly, he slaps his neck and shirt, knowing that all such efforts are in vain. He moves the chest away from the wall to improve his chances, waiting for the tinderbox to stop clacking and for the spice of the embers to spread their scent.

"It would be good to seize the bastard now."

Winge raises an eyebrow in silent question.

"I agreed to a duel two weeks since. Petter Pettersson, custodian of the workhouse. If it transpires as planned, then two shall arrive but only one shall leave."

"Are you sure it will be you?"

Cardell stretches.

"He is well grown, that much I'll give him. But what does such a one know of pain other than that meted out by himself? In that regard I am better off."

"For Anna Stina's sake?"

"Hers and others. The man flogs girls for his own pleasure. He is just as ignorant of where she is as anyone else, but I believe that he is also searching and if he finds her, then it will not end well. In any case, that neck has gone unbroken for too long."

"Is this really wise, Jean Michael?"

"You see to your own business and I mine. Wasn't it you who asked me to settle my affairs with the girl first?"

The smoke does little to purify the chamber. Cardell detaches the braid of flowers and holds it under his nose, turning away to avoid Winge's question before it can be asked.

....

Winge quietly smokes his pipe as the light fails. Only the glow of the pipe chases the shadows across the walls each time he puts the stem to his lips. After smoking it to the bottom, he remains still and lets the clay cool, fidgeting, impatient again, and casting yet another fruitless glance down into the cluttered courtyard that is already in the bosom of evening. A sow snores in her pen.

"Things are moving towards a close, Jean Michael. This year is Reuter-holm's last. Soon we shall have a king again."

"Do you think it will make any difference?"

"The misrule has been bad. At times downright farcical. One folly has superseded another, all with the worst possible outcomes. Young Gustav has been able to watch the spectacle from the front row. He has been afforded every opportunity to learn from the mistakes of others."

Cardell snorts so hard the tobacco crackles.

"Were mankind so constituted, then each year of misfortune would mark the beginning of a golden age of peace and benevolence."

Winge shrugs.

"A lot of good has been done this century. Ideas have been conceived that promise a brighter future."

"I dare say that the future is somewhat akin to the view of the City-between-the-Bridges from Hangman's Hill. It may look beautiful from a distance, but when you actually get there it is mostly filled with shit."

"What have we but hope?"

He abandons the subject and stands up to look out of the window.

"What will you do next, Jean Michael?"

"What do you mean by that?"

"Say that we soon hear Ceton's footsteps climbing the stairs and we are able—as you said—to seize the bastard on his own doorstep shortly thereafter. The law will do its part. He will be held accountable for his crimes and convicted. Then what? For you?"

"That depends."

"On the girl?"

Cardell nods sullenly.

"And if you don't find her?"

"Then I'll continue searching."

"But . . ."

Emil Winge stops, allowing the question to die unsaid on his lips, as he seeks a better way of expressing himself.

"I wish you luck. What I want to say is that everyone seems to constantly underestimate you. Don't take their misconceptions for insight and make the same mistake yourself. For as long as your mind remains clear, you have many opportunities left to you."

Cardell replaces his quid of tobacco and shakes himself.

"What of you, Emil?"

"I cannot give you any certain answer. I shall not continue with this, at any rate. I promise to tell you when I know."

"Enough philosophizing. The thought seems to torment you men of letters as the sniffles do common folk. All I have to offer up in response is a dose of common wisdom: don't sell the skin before the bear has been shot."

Winge sighs and nods his agreement.

"And that's true too. Let's wait and see."

Down in the alley by the edge of the courtyard is the girl—the one who led Cardell to Cassiopeia. Her face darkens with effort as she applies all her weight to the broomstick she is using as a lever. The timber bows and creaks, a barrel is dislodged and overturns, and its contents pour into the alley, greasing the cobblestones. With her duty accomplished, she finds a shadow big enough to welcome her and there she too waits.

....

With the dawn, the hunting dogs return home with empty mouths. The long vigil has done nothing more than turn the day on its head. No one comes to the chamber. They must settle for warning the landlord that he should send word if his tenant is seen again—though without much hope of his doing so. In the narrow close leading from the courtyard is enough foulness to add humiliation to failure. Once home, the stench obliges Cardell to leave his boots in the stairwell.

19

Tonight the drinks are on Kreutz. He refills once again for Frans Gry, even though his thirst was long since quenched for the evening. But there are few who decline a drink—if you're drunk enough for the night then perhaps you'll have the good fortune to wake up drunk tomorrow too. Such miracles do happen from time to time. Kreutz has allowed Gry to revile Cardell for several hours as loudly as his voice will carry. By now there must be folk down by the Iron Lock who are aware of his grudge. Now Gry has begun to lose all power of speech in his inebriation, words becoming gurgles and animal noises. Kreutz is more cautious than that. He needs just enough drink to instill courage, but not so much that his judgment is clouded and his fist misses. Affairs such as these are like running the gauntlet, where better men than he have come off worse. He is yet more concerned about the two roughs he has left by the door, each with just a jug of double beer to water their patience. The taproom is roaring, hours have flashed past, everyone is shedding tears in the stinging smoke, and it is high time to come to the point. He's taken his place on the bench alongside Gry, grasping him round the neck with a bandaged arm.

"I came not only to dwell on old memories tonight, Frans. I've made my inquiries. There are others apart from us whose toes Mickel Cardell has trodden on."

Kreutz leans in closer, lowering his voice.

"What's more, I know where the swine's sty is. What do you say, Frans? Why don't we prowl over to Cutter's Alley before the night is past and see whether the odds can be evened?"

Gry is not in need of much pressing, more certain than ever of his capacity for battle even though he cannot stand up straight unless held by the elbow. Kreutz nods to his party to break up, briefly inspecting them on the way out. No, not too drunk. Well then. Two steady lads from the east that he found here in the town, willing to listen to all proposals where money is mentioned, and unshakably spirited about the prospect of hiring themselves out for assassination rather than a dalliance behind the privy. Each carries a knife that looks just the way anyone would want: plenty of signs of use, the steel cloudy from the whetstone. Forward march. He leaves Gry's unruly weight to the sailors, who each seize him with a practiced arm. The fact that he gets no response in a language he understands does not trouble Frans in the slightest. Kreutz himself takes up the vanguard, leading the way along the quay and across the Stream into the City-between-the-Bridges.

Once down in Cutter's Alley, Gry's pugnacious falsetto becomes an annoyance, and he is in no state to take orders either. The walk has been delayed considerably; the clockface high up in the German Tower is visible to the naked eye and it is closer to dawn than to midnight. Even the Easterners are beginning to lose patience, betraying their irritation with rolled eyes and hissed profanities. The door is easily forced, they drag their burden up the stairs, and Kreutz ties a handkerchief around his chin. Gry tries to keep in step with the stairs beneath him—in vain—his boots clattering and slipping on their edges. Once outside the correct chamber, they regroup with difficulty in the cramped space: Kreutz takes Gry in his arms, his hired men drawing their weapons and awaiting commands. With an effort, Kreutz spins Gry half a turn, finds a grip where he can hold the left arm under the armpit with his hand over the mouth, draws his own knife from the sheath with a strained sound, and takes his time to find the right spot on Gry's back. Then he applies all his weight behind the tip, pressing the blade as far in as he can, and feels the warmth spread down through Gry's shirt and trousers until his shoes are brimming and Kreutz has to be careful not to misstep and slip down the stairs.

"You'll excuse me, Frans, but we want you left in the stairs for the sake of credibility. Don't take it personally, and don't make this harder than it has to be for any of us."

Frans Gry is a feeble figure in death as in life, to the surprise of no one: a few astonished groans and a teardrop or two of delayed insight before

Kreutz's point finds his heart between recalcitrant ribs, the life goes out of him, his knees give way, and Gry hurries to his forefathers, pale and wretched. Kreutz nods and the Russians force the door as if it were made from braided straw.

....

The first of them tumbles headlong over a chest left in the way and barely has his face struck the floorboards before there is a heavy heel on the back of his head. The second gets a small cask hurled into his eyes, the knife is knocked out of his grasp, and he is evicted headfirst down the stairs. A rough bass voice echoes after him.

"Run, you bastards."

Cardell follows to discourage any attempt at regrouping and sees another lurking outside, and before he has time to fend them off he feels a sharp pain in his good arm, gone as quickly as it came, washed away in the warm wetness that drenches his shirt sleeve. He twists around and extends his left arm straight into the path of danger. The stump burns when he encounters resistance: hard and mute, and with a whine in response. Beyond him, the vanguard crawls out and casts himself down the steps, whimpering for his mother with the words that seem to be the same in every tongue, and leaving a trail of blood and teeth. The distraction saves the ambushed man—they all flee headlong. On the stairs, the sound of soles slapping on stone can be heard. Cardell thinks himself alone on the landing until he stumbles across the dead man.

20

Cardell shimmers through the thin mist of his sleepy eyes. Winge barely has time to emerge from his door before they widen. The watchman is sitting on the floor with his back to the stone pillar that forms the center of the stairs. The morning light filters through a gap farther up on the half-landing, curved into an arc by the rounding of the wall.

"Well, good morning."

"Jean Michael. You scared me."

"I had visitors last night. Rowdy guests. They departed in such haste they never had time to tell me their reason for calling. Since they didn't give any details, I merely wanted to assure myself that nothing similar was going on around here."

"Have you been sitting here all night?"

Cardell stretches and shakes his head.

"Only for a while. Honestly, I had hoped to get out of here before you found me. This hovel is so deserted not even the rats can be bothered. It's been dead calm here ever since I arrived, and I've maintained my vigil for nothing. I must have nodded off in the early morning."

Cardell's blue jacket is darker in shade than usual over the arm, and the glimpse of the hem of the shirt underneath is red.

"You're bleeding."

Cardell moves his arm to his side, out of sight.

"Just a scratch. The knife caught flesh and skin. Nothing to be proud of."

He rises quickly enough to his feet.

"Who were they?"

"I've shaken one wasps' nest after another of late. If you do that, then you risk being stung sooner or later."

"So what happened?"

"I had only just returned home. I hadn't had time to settle when I heard a racket in the street and clattering in the stairwell. In laying a trap they might have been more discreet, but on the other hand I suppose they counted on me sleeping like a log. After a while, two lads came through my door. By then it was no surprise. I've made my living as one who throws things out, as you know. And out they were thrown. They left a stiff in their wake, altogether without my involvement. I knew him. An old battle comrade whose acquaintance I had the misfortune to rekindle in the spring. To refer to our dealings as friendly would be an exaggeration."

"And his body?"

"I carried it some way towards the street and left it in a corner. I woke the old woman in the back building to clean up. She owes me that favor. She also knows how to stay quiet."

"Why would they kill one of their own?"

"Hell knows. He stank as if it were spirit rather than blood they'd drained from his body. If his cronies came from the same place, it is not impossible that a combination of overeagerness and poor visibility stung him by accident."

"Is that what you think?"

Cardell shakes his head.

"No. Had I thought that, I would have rested in a more comfortable bed. But now I don't know."

Winge steps out, locks the door behind him, and pockets the key.

"Well. I shall go to Blom to inquire whether the night has turned up any dead. At any rate, at least I now know that the body in Cutter's Alley isn't on Ceton's conscience."

Cardell follows him down, pale in the light, and on to the end of the alley, where their paths diverge.

"Jean Michael, have someone dress that wound."

21

The routine is the same every morning, unchanged in summer from when the year was still young. Emil Winge goes to the meeting place in Cepheus to await word. If the night has been uneventful, then no one comes. If Isak Blom has anything on his mind, then the secretary comes himself; if it is something trivial, he prefers to send a messenger familiar with the reports left by the night watch when the shifts change at daybreak. The material is rarely good—either an oral report passed from the dead tired to the recently woken, or a few scant words scribbled in the ledger. Blots of ink and dreadful spelling testify to the Chamber of Police's problems with drunkenness and inadequate education. The best thing Emil can do with the information that reaches him through these Chinese whispers is to note which congregations have been decimated, and then make his own trip from crypt to crypt to carry out his own inspections. By now, the gravediggers know him as well as one of their own. Some shun him, especially now in the summer months when the dead turn bad quickly and any delay of their burial is an invitation to flies and vermin. Others care less, happy for every reprieve from their shovel and lumbago. He feels a tingle in his stomach when he spots that Blom is already there, impatiently watching the sunlight already slowly moving down the yellow plaster on the building walls. As Emil approaches, the short, plump secretary gives him a quizzical look.

"I spoke to the night watch this morning. A body has been found. I believe it may be of interest."

"Where?"

"Jakob."

The twinkle in Blom's eye and that single word of guidance are enough. Emil turns on his heel in that same instant.

"Emil? Expect crowds on the bridge."

"Why?"

"They've gathered the officers there—more or less every uniform the city can muster. I dare say it's one of Reuterholm's machinations to win the goodwill of the people. All summer it has been written in the newspapers that the city is swarming with the loose and idle, and I suspect the Baron intends to do something about it. If I were you, I would stick to the other side of the bridges until evening falls, just to be safe. I have apprehensions, and it would not surprise me if the gutters are painted red before the day is over."

....

It has been hot for several weeks now, and today the heat wave seems ready to be celebrated with a thunderous salute. Ever since first light, flashes of lightning have been perceptible over the islands and sea. Black clouds are emerging from the red dawn. A storm is approaching, and dusty as his path is now, it will be as muddy on the return. At the stables on the Islet of the Holy Ghost an irritable captain of the guard is inspecting his shabby men, the constables in one corner and the Stockholm Watch loosely grouped together. He rants and raves, pointing his saber at the watchmen and encouraging his men in the taunts. Winge passes unnoticed, traverses Slaughterhouse Bridge, passes the bridge under construction seemingly doomed to remain incomplete, passes the Opera and the Court, and soon he is knocking on the door of the church. A sleepy tower watchman gives Emil the news he has been expecting: yes, they found a dead man in the Royal Garden during the night, but they sent the corpse to Johannes instead. That is how they conduct their affairs in Jakob for the most part—they consider themselves superior to others, and if they find dead bodies whose origins are unknown, then they are dispatched on a cart outwards, away, and they buy themselves time for more dignified matters.

He trudges on while the wind from the east chases the last of the heat away. Above him, the sky darkens, and over his shoulder the rumbles of thunder grow ever stronger. Sweat is pouring off him, and his wet stockings rub against damp shoe leather with each step. Soon the hills begin and he must climb up the ridge himself before he reaches the Johannes burial ground, just as beautiful in its setting as it is awful in its form. Here, as elsewhere, the aftermath of all the grand plans abandoned for good when King Gustav gave up the ghost is still visible. For years, the pastor hoped to have the old wooden church demolished and replaced by a new one, but the domed cruciform church agreed upon was rejected in a momentary whim: Gustav had returned home from abroad and decided that all was to be Italian. Plans for a windowless pagan temple with Doric columns and capital, friezes and tiered crepidoma, were quickly drawn up, but even the king was discouraged by the sight of the drawings, and after all, there was more fun to be had with the pennies elsewhere. They let it all rest. The wooden church still stands, its ugliness faded, mocked by a circle of abandoned building blocks.

The gravediggers have gathered in a group above David Baker's Alley, among the houses that constitute their informal guild cottages. Raised voices. Emil Winge is surprised to see them gathered at such a time. Perhaps they are celebrating some holiday or other, or perhaps there are men to be elevated in status and admitted to the fraternity. Neither, it turns out, once he gets close enough. They are standing there, pale and timid, their voices newly silenced, unwilling to spread confidences outside their own circle. To a man, they watch him approaching; just one goes to meet him. Emil knows him of old and knows he is the one who oversees all the graves here; he is a bearded man, his arms now crossed. Jan something. The last name escapes him.

"You've come to see the corpse."

"Yes."

"Best you hurry up. I've done what I can to swear everyone to silence, but I know from experience that gossip makes it across the bridges as quickly as legs can carry it."

"What's the matter?"

The gravedigger scratches his beard and leads the way to his shed.

"Depends on who you ask. Hence our little discord. Best you see for yourself and choose a side accordingly. In you go. I'll mind the door so as you're not disturbed."

As if secrecy were of the utmost importance, the door is nudged ajar and Winge is shooed inside; he just has time to see the gravedigger's back diminishing as the door is closed and he takes up his post outside. Beneath the roof, there are flies buzzing. No room is safe from them when there is the temptation of decay. It takes a minute or so for his eyes to forget the light of day and grow accustomed to the semidarkness. The body on its stretcher is uncooled, its shroud on the stone below, dropped there and forgotten. Time and time again he has to wave the flies away to get a clear view. Little creatures strike his fingers, and they keep coming back, slaves to bloodlust, crawling over every wound and drop.

The corpse is naked and glimmers in a coating of oil—oil that now attracts dirt and soil to the skin. Emil stands still for a long time with an open mind to take in what he is seeing. Satisfied, he begins to walk in circles around the stretcher, at times a few steps away, at times close enough to observe some detail. He raises a cold hand, the arm resisting due to its stiffened muscles, as if the body were reluctant to reveal its secrets. Missing dressings reveal bloody stripes. The palm of the hand bears a wound.

Cecil says they cut, then stemmed. Cecil says the wounds are superficial. Cecil says this has been done for show. The other hand is the same, so are the feet.

The arm won't shift any farther, and rather than force it he crouches to examine its underside. He presses it upwards to catch a glimpse of the skin below where the blood that has coagulated in the veins has thickened. Cecil says it's still red, not blue. Cecil says death came last night. Cecil says look at the forehead, and Emil does as he is told. The head is marked across its circumference, the locks of hair stiff and red.

Emil stops on the right-hand side of the corpse. There is a gaping wound. Its blue edge forms a border around the darkness within. It seems more heinous than the others—this hole that was prevented from closing and leaves the most sacred thing exposed to the world, defenseless. Emil tries to imagine the tool that could accomplish something like this, to no avail. Cecil says that this is where death gained access. The mortal wound. Cecil says to plumb its depth, to scrape its boundary, and Emil looks around for a tool that might aid him. He has to settle for breaking off a splinter from the edge of the stretcher, one long enough for the task, and then he pulls it out and contemplates its sticky nib with a shiver. A drop of fat, akin to a melting pearl. Something else catches the light at the edge of the wound. On the crown of the head he finds more of the same, caught among tangled locks.

He wraps a handkerchief around his findings and puts them in his pocket. Once done, he taps on the door and Jan steps aside to let him out.

"Make sure someone comes to scour and wrap him. The sooner the corpse is in the ground, the better. And best to mark the grave for the time being, so that only you know where it is. I see what you have seen; redouble your efforts to insist on silence."

Jan nods his understanding, and as Emil turns to leave: "Do you always talk to the dead?"

His gestured reply is half valediction, half dismissal. Jan raises his voice to reach him as he departs.

"My most humble greetings and thanks for my daily bread."

22

The light pierces Cardell's eyes. That's how it starts. He squints, dazzled, obliged to keep his arm against his brow to shield his face, even though he is keeping to the side of the gutter left in shadow by the sun. Next, his hearing falters. Out of the city's constant rumble, the sound suddenly moves onto a higher plane: a wagon wheel screams on its dry axle, an iron nail is dropped onto the cobblestones, a girl's shrill cry of unseen joy or distress is heard. They make him take fright as he walks—he cannot defend himself, jumps as if terrified, has to accept glances of the kind usually reserved for drunks and fools. Never have such things bothered him before. He seeks the shelter of his room, lugging a jug of water in, rolling up his shirtsleeve to examine the wound.

The injury isn't pretty, but nor does it bring particular shame upon its kin. Neither big nor deep, milder than others he has suffered on countless occasions when it fell to his lot to show unwelcome guests the door. A red line chalked with nascent scabs, small enough to conceal under the palm of a hand if he had one to spare—merely the latest scratch on an arm so marked that you would be able to use it for a game of faro if you played with a smaller deck. The wound is not leaking pus, it does not smell rotten, the adjacent skin is no more swollen or tender than it ought to be. No gangrene in the offing—at least not of the kind he has seen before. Yet something is wrong. Outside, the distant rumbles of the night have come closer to Stockholm, and it grows worse and worse the longer the day persists. He thinks he hears shouts and voices among the thunderclaps, as if Thor himself has come with all his ghostly legions in tow. Rain has poured down as the day has suffered on, in noisy abundance.

His attempt to sleep off his affliction goes badly. When he wakes, he struggles to swallow and time and again there is something that spasms in his jaw, pressing his mouth together until his teeth clench. His digs his fingers as deep into the tensed muscles as his strength allows, and gradually they give way, but he doesn't know whether the credit is due to him or the flareups are anyway brief. He drinks water, struggles to chew, prefers hunger. The next day finds him even worse. The cramps have taken possession of his entire face, and when they begin there is nothing he can do. They pull the corners of his mouth apart until his teeth are bared in a rictus of insanity, and his face remains locked like that for minutes at a time. He slaps himself in the hope that the shock will dislodge the stiffness. Sometimes it helps. Usually not.

Cardell wishes he could sate the hunger of the crescent moon, but each night it grows bigger than before, and soon the full moon is above him. That which is slowly taking possession of his body spreads further, and increasingly often he is woken by his right arm trembling, tense as a mooring cable, folded against his breast as if to protect his body, his wrist curved and his fingers clenched under whitening knuckles. Worse still is the stump where the unattached muscles meander beneath scar tissue and bruised skin, the invisible arm beset by cramps in its own phantom world.

....

Emil Winge comes to him at a favorable hour, fortunately. Tendons taut as harp strings have just tuned down, the most recent attack is past, and Cardell rubs the sweat from his face with a fistful of water, pushing aside the shattered door he has as yet been unable to bring himself to hang back on its hinges.

"It's beginning, Jean Michael."

"A body has been found?"

"Yes. Last night, close to morning, in the Royal Garden."

"Ceton's doing?"

"I think so. It's not what I expected, but deep down I sensed that he might try to outdo himself. I need your help now, and your undivided attention. Are you ready?"

Cardell takes a deep breath and responds with a look of resignation.

"I have my rendezvous tomorrow. Let me resolve that and then I am yours."

Winge remains silent until his searching gaze brings Cardell out in goose pimples. "So what do we have to go on?"

"The usual, to begin with. We'll have to ask around. The scene of the act itself is unclear, and we'd be wise to find it quickly. And then there are these."

Emil pulls his handkerchief out of his pocket. Of the small gate-leg table belonging to the room there remain only splinters, so Emil holds his find in his hand to allow Cardell to look. Reflections from the sun hurry across the walls and ceiling.

"What is it?"

"Shards of a mirror."

23

Evening is coming, inexorably. The circle of the moon becomes whole on the night when one week ends and another begins. It seems to him that the bells have been tolling mass for hours. He awaits the next cramp with forced patience. The face contorts first, and with teeth bared each attack begins. The neck, shoulders, and arms follow next, like a tangled rope slowly contracting into a single knot, making the back arch until the vertebrae creak and his chest stiffens so that every breath is a shallow sigh, his big thigh muscles locked. It comes and it goes. He measures the time as best as he can, counting for himself from the moment that the big bell at Nikolai strikes. He has time to get to a thousand before the small bell chimes for the first quarter.

He knows that a fight can be settled as quickly as a blow is landed, especially if he deals it with his left hand, but also that the blow that hits its target is often the gift of good luck. Cardell knows that Petter Pettersson will be prepared. If only the cramps will spare him for long enough. He counts one and a half hours without anything occurring, but the next attack comes quicker, just after eight hundred. All he can do is wait.

....

Cardell begins his ramble in good time to allow him to inspect the battlefield, counting as before, allowing his feet to maintain pace. He persuades himself that the walk may do him good: the night air is cool after the fallen rain now that the sun has drawn the lingering heat of the day away with it like a bride's train. Near Ansgar's Mound, his body locks up and forces him to stop and wait for mercy. Eight hundred and fifty. Better now than later. All he can hope is that he is spared the cramps when he needs his limbs most, that the attack will subside and leave him with an hour or so of respite. He starts counting from one again as soon as he can move, shaking loose his stiffened muscles.

Two hundred. He is the first to arrive. The evening is well chosen, the place too: an open strip of land against whose edge the bay laps, the ground free from obstacles and depressions. An expanse of black water extends away towards the City-between-the-Bridges. The water is uneasy although the breeze is gentle, bobbing waves careening as if to shake off the reflection of the starry sky. High above him, the August moon wanders among the ragged clouds, big and rose-red, its beams strong enough to cast shadows. He becomes aware of other figures in the distance on the way towards the same shore. Pettersson must have spilled the beans: here comes the crowd. Four hundred.

Cardell tightens the straps holding the wooden fist fast as tight as he can without obstructing mobility. That bastard is late. Six hundred already. A sound from behind gives his opponent away. Petter Pettersson is strolling with a cane under his arm towards a battle that Cardell would have been certain of leaving as victor on any night except this. As Pettersson gets closer to him, the custodian stops midstep.

"Well I'll be damned, Cardell. Are you that happy to see me?"

PART TWO

Ceton's Masquerade
SPRING AND SUMMER 1795

Many a mother will warn of the threat
That may stalk her innocent child:
Foul as a nightmare, pale as a ghost,
Bane as soon seen as reviled.

The lad listens, he plans and he ponders
How best such grim flags to outsail,
Before being stung by a vicious troll's tongue
Beneath perfume, pomade, rouge and veil.

—Anna Maria Lenngren, 1795

24

Proud city! Once his Garden of Eden, his playground, but she is a deceitful lover, is Stockholm. Her tender feelings are past. Now she suffers his presence only from pity. She is recast into a labyrinth of horror where the Minotaur strides in pursuit, one-armed and indefatigable. Tycho Ceton tests the cobblestones only rarely, and he always has his hat pulled low across his brow, and a scarf wrapped over the beard that has grown wild over the winter. An outsized coat envelops him, the collar turned up and the frayed hem almost dragging along the cobbles, salvaged from the heirs of a giant or pawned when hunger became worse than the cold. His own mother would not recognize him. Yet he hastens along the walls in the rats' quarters, dodging from corner to corner, always maintaining a watchful gaze to see who is coming in the opposite direction. One unfortunate encounter and his fairy tale would be over. He knows the city's tides, daring to show himself beneath the fragments of sky that the edges of the roofs have carved in the peaks and valleys of the flow: when the riffraff provide him with cover, or when the streets are deserted and dark. Saturdays are worst: all the way across the water and beyond the Southern Isle to Hammarby. But he must go. An invisible rein leads him, and man does not live by bread alone.

Occasionally he sees windows illuminated high above the street, in the palace where the opulence continues without him, where the long tables are soon to be pushed aside to allow for dancing. He remembers how palaces and residences rose over clustered quarters that have never before been permitted to sully his soles. There the sky was wider, the light different. There were halls and state rooms with lofty ceilings with cherubs floating naked in painted space, where gold leaf and silk shimmered together under the caress of the candlelight. The Stockholm into which he has fallen is the domain of the louse and the rat, ceilings so low that the beams stamp bruises onto inattentive foreheads, where tallow and rapeseed oil spread more stink than light. The constant semidarkness suffocates what colors the riffraff dare to dress in and subsumes every minor rebellion against the sumptuary laws in the same gray mist. The irregularities that cause him to falter in his step seem to him to be an invitation to the type of dance befitting a shackled bear; the putrid miasma from down where the crown of the Flies' Meet competes against the ridges of Skinner's Cove is little better than the stifling cell that is his chamber. Worse than ever now that the shit has been exposed anew beneath thawed drifts and cracked ice. He slips along the facades by the Scorched Plot to see the carriages stop to drop off folk from the country whose dreams of something bigger and better have led them here, and who are welcomed by street urchins politely bowing and offering to help with their heavy chests and trunks. Laughing, the boys run off with their booty, quick and knowledgeable of all the passages and vaults that will lead the pursuer astray.

The rain falls often in this cold spring. Stockholm is rinsed by showers, sometimes persistent enough to bind the whole day together, sometimes with dry spells where the damp seems to saturate the very air itself, and where anyone who does not cower beside the warmth of a hearth soon finds his clothes hanging in wet slabs. Under whatever protection they can find, the pigeons sit tight, their plumage ruffled, quiet and patient, until hunger lures them out one by one and the alley echoes to the crashing of wings. The sun makes its trek shrouded in clouds, low and gray, that filter the light stingily and tax the warmth promised by the season. Cloudy water seeps down the gutters running from the square in a constant flow. Wherever it finds resistance, a pond forms, and where the puddles remain, the midges breed by the thousand. Such is Stockholm's kiss for him now—a token from the City-between-the-Bridges, marking him with blisters and demonstrating that he is no longer worth anything.

It may happen that he lingers in the warmth of a doorway or beneath the light of a window, on the boundary of people's noise and gossip. Much of what is spoken of is old; other things are new. The assault of change adds grist to the mill of all. A dissolute future offers all manner of promises that it is unlikely to fulfil. In the south, a bad harvest is once more a fact this year. It is worse than before: famine is rampant. The regency is approaching its final year, but few dare wager their pennies on there being any kingdom left for the young king to rule over. The gentlemen of the kingdom appear to be increasingly small-minded and short-tempered with each passing year, and any heavy sigh at the misrule might have become a roar of laughter had the farce of it not been so real.

Nonetheless, the party continues. Spirits flow along the rim of the abyss. The fact that the morrow is uncertain does not make the intoxication of today any less pressing. Impending apocalypse does not deprive the pleasures of the moment of their value. On the contrary: cause and effect are eliminated, and although the pale rider may be unwelcome, he also promises to write off all debts. The dance across soiled boards is wild, a desperate rejoicing. Colorful notes flutter down onto the card tables like never before, and breathtaking sums change hands as the rich man becomes insolvent and he who was begging bread yesterday can now stand drinks for all. It is as if there is a fever in the city.

Tonight, Ceton is on a special errand. He is running low on money, every item of any value pawned, his rent soon to be prohibitive. Before month's end he will be evicted from his lair, and he will be unable to hide on the street for long. He needs help, and there is but one straw left to grasp at. He awaits evening, listening for those sounds that indicate the time more clearly than any clock.

At ten o'clock each evening, the drummer passes on his rounds through the alleys, called upon to summon the constables with a roll outside any and all inns that remain open. The innkeepers slip him his long-established tariff to keep the peace, and readily pour him a drink or two for the sake of goodwill. Two blocks from the North Bridge, the man is so drunk that he seeks all possible assistance from the walls to remain on his feet, and some attentive devil has taken the opportunity to stick a fork through the drum skin to ensure value for money.

Tycho Ceton pulls his coat over his shoulders and his hat down his forehead. He strokes the beard that he has assumed. He often finds his hand by his cheek when his thoughts wander, as if to make sure that the rag is able to cover the mouth that sets him apart. The fingers sting the edges of the wound, and each time he notices what he is doing he wrenches away his fingers and returns his hand to his coat pocket. But the hand has a will of its own and soon seeks its way back, restless and anxious, a spider in an alien web. A glance over each shoulder, and so away.

25

The misery of winter chafes in recent memory as he makes his way through the alleys. Week in, week out, in the rented darkness of the room, his chest puckered with goose pimples despite pressing his shoulder blades against the tiled stove, rheumy-eyed from the soot of the whale-oil lamp, with the landlord's boy his only visitor, a knock on the door twice a week to deliver a sledload of firewood and to deposit a few volumes from the book box, randomly chosen from those newly procured by the hawker in some clearance sale. Food from the inn downstairs, the same turbid stew renamed with each passing day. The ingenuity of the lice is endless, despite the day offering few occupations other than squeezing them to death between fingers dented by the task. The madness pent up in languishing silence, the more excruciating with each passing day. The purse slowly bled dry to the absolute minimum necessary to remain among the living.

The people he meets disgust him. They seem to him akin to ugly children, aimlessly staggering through existence without a single sensible thought. Those who can, enjoy the flesh that all too soon will betray them; those who suffer already numb the pain with spirits. The effort with which they cling on to lives that seem worthless horrifies him. The shoemaker's apprentice with scabbed fists, the secretary who squints at him cross-eyed through scratched lenses on skew-whiff frames, the foppish dandy showing off clothes he has been swindled into overpaying for with the promise of the admiration they will win from all those around him, the girl walking bent double over her bulging belly of shame. They take their places slowly, docile components of a context too great for them to see and too intricate for them to grasp. Its purpose remains a mystery to them from cradle to grave. He makes for the Ship's Bridge, allowing the incline to hurry his steps. Beyond the final houses, the waves sigh, anchor ropes creaking in time to the play of the water. At Stockholm's border with the outside world, a blend of foreign languages of every kind forms an incomprehensible hubbub.

....

They keep him waiting for a long time after he knocks on the right door. The same constable who took his report shows his haughty face fully thirty minutes later, eyebrows raised by a hair's breadth as if in surprise that someone would condescend to such patience, even though every moment of delay measures the difference in rank between host and supplicant.

"The gentleman will see you now."

As Ceton takes a step forward, the constable remains at the threshold, expressionless.

"Not here. Please go around to the back."

Ceton is obliged to force his way between the houses and into the courtyard. Oozing matter from the rubbish outside the house saturates his shoe leather, and rough walls scrape his shoulder and elbow each time he attempts to swerve round the worst of this soiled trench, usually the preserve of the nightsoil wagons and the lowest of the house. Humiliated, he staggers into the courtyard where the constable is at least waiting for him at an open door and spares him the need to knock again. He is shown in and up to a beautiful office adorned with a desk surrounded by nothing but beautiful things: a covered cage where songbirds rest in their captivity; a bureau with ornate inlaid woodwork, whose many drawers promise every manner of curiosity; bookshelves weighed down by handsomely bound volumes arranged by size, folios at the bottom and octavos at the top. Along one wall stand three cabinets arranged in a group, each one crowned with a glazed cube in which butterflies of all varieties are pinned onto angular surfaces clad in silk. No chair awaits him. He must remain standing before the seated host, like a schoolboy receiving a scolding from the master.

The man behind the desk is thin and bald, his cheeks pocked by small-pox scars. He is informally clad in his waistcoat, his shirtsleeves rolled up to his elbows and his cravat loose. With an expression of distaste, his scrutinizing gaze inspects Ceton up and down—from the wooden buckles of his shoes, the stains and dirt on his much-too-large coat, to the disorder of his beard and the lank sheepskin wig. Ceton has made no effort to present his worn appearance in a better light, certain that to do so would make no difference. Instead, he stands up straight in his squalor, a concession to whatever dignity remains to him. The voice that addresses him is nasal, and its owner makes little effort to conceal his feelings.

"Tycho Ceton. How low have the mighty fallen! I hardly thought you would darken my door again."

Ceton clears his throat, the better to allow his voice to be heard.

"Bolin, of all fraternal brothers, you are the one I have always felt closest to . . ."

"Is that the best compliment you can offer? Don't waste our time on flattery or familiarity."

Ostentatiously, his host takes his watch from his waistcoat pocket, detaches the gold chain from the buttonhole, and places it between them on the table, the resonant surface making the ticking piece sound louder.

"I'll give you five minutes, and not a moment more. I advise you to get to the point quickly."

"Due to unfavorable circumstances, I have come to grief. The guilt is not my own: this may happen to anyone, regardless of merit. We both know that the Furies have not always looked kindly upon the liberties I have taken . . ."

Bolin audibly snorts at the understatement. The whiff of pent-up winter that Ceton has brought with him has spread throughout the office, and his host waves his pouncet-box beneath his nostrils.

"Nevertheless, I choose to believe that last summer's gift of reconciliation was the beginning of a new mutual understanding."

Bolin lets the fingers of one hand dance across the desk.

"Divert me with your troubles, Tycho. As briefly as possible."

"I have been robbed of the fortune I managed to accumulate, despite the considerable difficulties. Soon my final pennies will be gone."

Bolin raises a skeptical eyebrow.

"And what else?"

"I am being baselessly persecuted. By two rabid hunting dogs, for whom I appear to have become an entirely irrational obsession. I have reason to believe that I am charged with things of which they are themselves guilty. So far as can be judged, they harass me with the sanction of Indebetou House."

Bolin shifts position in his chair, and rises painstakingly with the support of an ivory cane. He is obliged to lift one foot from a stool covered in a soft pillow; he limps across the floor in his stockinged feet and stands one-legged in front of one of his glass-fronted cabinets, where he allows his practiced connoisseur's gaze to inspect the petrified wings bursting with color and shape. With a sigh, he rubs his face.

"I wonder, Tycho, whether you even know why you have caused such bad blood among the brothers?"

He takes a step back to give Ceton space.

"Come and see. In the middle of the second row from the top you will see two butterflies alongside one another."

"Two of the same kind."

"Only to a layman's eyes. They are, admittedly, both *Lepidoptera*. Pieter Cramer brought them back to Amsterdam from the New World the year before he was torn from this life. Cramer was the first to sort butterflies according to Linnaeus's system, and when he placed these two side by side beneath his convex glass, he noted that every similarity between them was confined to the surface. The right-hand one has learned to fly under the same flag as its neighbor, for the left-hand one is bitter in taste. Those birds that seek out prey have learned that this is the case, and wherever they see white spots on a fiery yellow base they keep their beaks closed and move on for better prey elsewhere. The right-hand one tastes excellent, but thanks to its analogous costume it is also permitted to remain uneaten."

"How can you be so sure?"

"Thus far it is merely my guess. But I have proved it to my entire satisfaction."

"How?"

Bolin bares his teeth in a grin, sharp and vigorous despite his age.

"By tasting them both, of course. Regardless, it was not my intent to teach the science of nature but to make a parable."

Bolin turns around, making a laborious lap on a radius around his bad leg, and does not bother to await further questions.

"The problem with you is not your thoughtlessness, your excesses, or your incapacity to follow the edicts of our statutes demanding discretion. Good God, if those were grounds for grudges within our brotherhood then the halls would echo empty at our gatherings. *Così fan tutto*. No."

He moves closer, but stops himself with a grimace when the stench overpowers him.

"You're not one of us, Tycho. You just look like us. How a man otherwise so quick-witted thought he could conceal that from others is beyond my comprehension."

"I protest that this is not the case."

Bolin snorts.

"If only you could see yourself when the bacchanal rages at its worst. You can't. But I have done, and others too. Your face stiffens as if in horror, your trousers dutifully at your knees, flaccid member in a still fist while others let themselves go. You shun the proximity of others. What true libertine would conduct himself in that manner? The City-between-the-Bridges is small, Sweden is no longer great, and even from faraway Saint Barthélemy the newspapers find their way home. We hear the cock and bull you share about your adventures, the exaggerations you have concocted. For those of us who know you better, it chimes badly with the testimony of our own eyes. You do not offer sacrifice at Freyja's grove like we do, you do not worship our own Venus. No. Your inducements are of a different kind. You have in vain sought to conceal them from us behind rhymes and spectacle, and with lines borrowed from books you do not fully comprehend. There are certainly crossroads at which our interests intersect, but no one will place their trust in one such as you in the long term."

The words resound in Ceton's ears as if they were blows to his temples. He has no answer to give; the mere effort of keeping his heart pumping seems overwhelming in the moment. Bolin gives him another wry smile, almost in pity, before his host limps over to the window, which he nudges ajar in the hope that the breeze off the sea will have made its way in among the alleys.

"I declare you smell worse than the gutter, and that is no mean feat in a month such as ours."

Anselm Bolin inhales air between his teeth as he changes his position and stumbles. He has entered his tenth year as secretary to the Furies, and in this moment that has enticed him to attempt to summarize the society's essence, he feels paralyzing exhaustion. Age has crept up on him, a disaster so easily foreseen, but previously only something that has afflicted others. Too late to avert now. In his youth he felt immortal, that feeling now a bittersweet memory at times regarded with longing and at others with contempt. He won't keep damned minutes of the brothers' coterie. Dry rituals where rank is elevated and feasts celebrated. Everything in dissension, constant intrigue, endless politics, even in a group whose members share so much in common. Power can always be quarrelled over—money, order of priority and rank too. Factions are pitted against each other, loyalties swing overnight, the knife stuck through your own back is one you will gladly stick in another's tomorrow as if in a relay of betrayal. When the time comes to vote for the next president, the underhand dealings reach fever pitch, and the inner circle are forced into threats and bribes to secure a favorable outcome. This year the mandate is to be renewed, in the new year elections. He is tired, and can generally only passively watch a game intended for younger men. To hell with them. His mood shifts.

"Even if you are merely a *Limenitis* disguised as a *Danaus*, there are those among the brothers who still speak positively of how weddings are celebrated at the Three Roses estate."

Bolin taps snuff into the fold of his thumb from a turtleshell box, inhales the grains, and smothers the sneeze with his forearm.

"Had you come as anything other than a simple beggar, you would have made it harder for me to show you the door."

Ceton gropes for a moment in the dark, reaching for the spark that has been thrown out.

"Perhaps there is something I can offer in return for the goodwill of the brothers? A performance of the same variety?"

Bolin blows his nose in an embroidered handkerchief.

"The gods know that there is great melancholy at the moment, and with that comes tension. A diversion would be most welcome. But it must be one in a class of its own. Expectations are low at a farmer's wedding, but here in the city sophistication is called for. Give it some thought, Tycho, and send me word when you know."

Ceton's throat is too dry to allow his vocal cords to vibrate, and he must clear his throat and cough before he can produce a word.

"When?"

Bolin contemplates him for a while, and Tycho stifles a shiver at the enjoyment the approval bestows upon him.

"We await your inspiration. But don't linger for too long."

Bolin once again hooks the watch chain to his buttonhole, slips the timepiece into his waistcoat, but stops himself in the middle of the ritual of dismissal.

"By the way, Tycho, you'll find a bundle of tickets given to me on the secretaire. Yes, there. Under the lion. Take one on the way out. I'm too old for such things myself, but perhaps the performance will give you in-spiration."

Ceton does as he is told, removing a theater ticket from the stack held in place by a stone lion's carved front paws. Then he is shown the door.

"At any rate the beard is an improvement, Tycho."

On his way out, Ceton recalls something that the lad Three Roses con-fided in him on their long journey over the sea, a few words that Samuel Fahlberg had given to the lad in warning, but without arousing his under-standing: this is not the first time Ceton has been compared to a creature shrouded in the likeness of another. But that time the reasons given were of another hue. He wonders who has come closest to the truth.

26

The name legible on the ticket is one he has heard spoken of before: young Lindegren, the Uppsala lad who composed so many audacious drinking songs and has now written a new play—the one who came from nowhere and had a great success with *The Blind Lover*. The new play has been assessed and approved, and voices from the theater assert that a good run is expected. Tickets for the premiere have long since sold out, and those who took the opportunity to buy when they were available may be persuaded to sell for twice the value. He could sell Bolin's gift dearly, but he refrains. Tycho Ceton refuses to line his pocket like a common tradesman. In the past he often frequented such spectacles, but now it is Bolin who has issued him with a challenge. Perhaps the old man will hobble his way there after all to see whether he accepts it.

On the day, rain falls but the sky clears as the afternoon progresses. Evening comes—the one everyone has been waiting for—and Ceton joins those crossing the bridge towards the Northern Isle and walks along the quay past the Opera. There she still stands, she who was once called the Nonpareil, and still merits the name. A fairy-tale palace between the Royal Garden and the water, sleek and ornate, while Tessin's coarse royal castle broods heavy and flat with its odd proportions, its breadth seemingly robbing its height of all impressiveness. The Nonpareil stands as a monument to the century itself: erected in honor of its commissioner, lost to the state when money was exhausted, made into an arsenal for King Gustav's Russian war, and now the final bullet has been squandered, residence only to vanity and imagination.

Even though it is the final Saturday in May, it is cold for the season.

That suits Ceton: all parties come heavily dressed, many with winter shawls wound high around their necks. He takes the stairs like before, but finds his path barred by an outstretched arm.

"Pray may I see your ticket first?"

The liveried guard shakes his head and smacks his tongue as Ceton passes him the paper, as if satisfied his suspicions have been fulfilled.

"Groundlings go in last. It's no good trying to sneak in ahead of your betters."

Ceton is shown to one side before he can bring himself to protest. He borrows light from an illuminated window to read, and only now does he become aware of what Bolin's gift is worth. A place standing on the parterre to jostle for a glimpse of the stage among the riffraff. Never before has he conceived of anything other than the dress circle or a box, and now it is too late to do anything other than curse his gullibility.

The damp and cold make themselves felt despite the fact that he is wearing every garment he owns. The impatience makes it worse. They are finally admitted only after the guards make an elaborate show of keeping the stairs free and looking out for late arrivals. He is shoved forward in the flood of people, each step curtailed by striking the heels of another. There are profanities and quarrels, the women as foul-mouthed as the men in the press of people. The guards keep letting them in until there is no room for a single more patron in the parterre. Full of regret, Ceton seeks out the exit with his gaze, always sensitive to the touch of others, but that path is already blocked by all those pushing in the opposite direction, leaning forward in the hope of being borne closer to the stage. The curtain has barely waited for the rabble. Its red sheet is drawn apart to reveal what appears to represent a painter's studio.

He can barely hear a word of the actors' affected lines. His attention is fully occupied elsewhere. Sweat is pouring where recently there were goose pimples; he can barely move. The crowd is like an ocean churned up by invisible currents: he is pushed back and forth, powerless to do anything other than sway along. Putrid breaths from the mouths of others waft into his face, and he feels as if he can see the fleas jumping from shoulder to shoulder as people shout and laugh in a deafening outcry. A pungent stench and a wet warmth through his soles are attributable to a drunk man's expression of blissful relief. Ceton's skin crawls with repugnance, but no one can see or hear him.

Above them, the seated patrons rise in three galleries. The fine folk are standing on the balconies with clean air and a clear line of sight, with plenty of space to swing their lorgnettes to better see who else has come and how they have dressed to mark the occasion. They are offered snuff from silver tins, their mechanism chiming through the noise like the bells of angels. Many contemplate the disorder on the parterre with smiles, pointing out things to their neighbor that are worthy of particular ridicule. The crowd below makes their own space pleasurable by comparison— Ceton is himself a performer in the drama they have come to see.

Thus he is forced to endure three acts and an interlude in which the dancers disguise their clumsiness by showing more of their legs than they ought. At the end of the performance, he is obliged to wait at length before the doors are opened—first the stalls must empty, and no one is inclined towards urgency, each departure taking its time. Once outside, he gasps in the night air as if to clean his lungs out, hiding his tear-filled eyes in the creases of his coat sleeve. He wants to vomit but all that comes out is bile. Out on the Stream, the shards of the moon float disparately on the tops of the waves. Behind him, the spires of the Nonpareil point heavenwards, their indifference a mockery. He wends his way from whence he came, back to a room too poor for light, warmed only by his loathing, which neither his powerlessness nor his dread can assuage.

27

"Copenhagen is in flames."

People swarm in the alleys below his room. Din and gossip. A spark in the drought has devastated the Danish capital—all that remains of Christiansborg Palace are sooty mounds of stone. A harbinger, crow the prophets of doom. When shall Stockholm next burn, in spite of its stone houses? The elderly who remember know that winter warmth and freshly baked bread cost more than most people think: the Red Hare demands recompense for service when least expected. Ceton knows this more than anyone. From him it has already taken everything.

Summer draws near, and the rising heat makes his chamber even more excruciating than the winter chill. During the winter, he could retreat under a blanket, but there is no escape from the heat. The air is sultry and reeky, his body demanding through thirst what it loses in sweat. What itching he has becomes worse, ravaging the skin as well as the inner man. Tycho Ceton has lost count of the days. When the clanging from the brass chimes of Saint Gertrud's shakes the quarter, he has to count six days and nights to know that it is Saturday, the day that constitutes his only fixed routine.

He reads the placard by the pump. They have invited a thief to dance a jig in the air at Hammarby. Finally. The gallows have been neglected for weeks on end. Now that performances have resumed, it has been women condemned for feticide, and they are no longer hanged—to the disappointment of the street urchins who crowd under the scaffold to catch a glimpse between the floundering legs under the skirts. Instead, the block is dragged out and put to use on the open ground. The executioner's blow with a broad axe interests Ceton far less than the noose.

He follows the others past the redoubt and climbs the hill. The mood is one of mirth, and it is a clear summer's day with the sun free to wander across the sky without the interference of clouds. Once there, he reluctantly pushes his way as close as he can, spots a group where he does not look out of place, and joins the fringe of it. Soon the cart arrives to the accompaniment of the driver cursing his horse, and profanities from the hands called upon to push when the wheels lose their grip in the dust. The condemned man is led out of the cart in shackles—he is a young man with red hair and a good-natured face. His expression is initially one of surprise, but then elation, as if he is flattered by the crowd's attendance just for his sake. His rosy face lights up each time he is led past someone he recognizes; he smiles and calls out a greeting. The base of the gallows is round and walled off, with a simple opening where a staircase leads to the platform. On the scaffold, beams form a triangle between stone pillars, each one with four loops to bear the strain of the rope raising its burden. Even though the condemned man has the hand of the priest on his shoulder and walks in shackles, he seems more impressed by the view he is afforded—seduced by the attention. When the sentence is read, he cannot help taking a few dance steps and miming the words, and he barely reacts when one of the men slaps him on the back of the head. Only during the silence afterwards does it seem as if the seriousness of the situation asserts itself. The noose is hung around his neck, and he shakes his head as if it is only now striking him that the men surrounding him are there to take his life.

"Wait, wait . . ."

The same man who just boxed his ears hushes him and pats him on the shoulders, calming him, offering the caress of consolation. The knot is tightened, the extension of the rope checked, and the nod that governs life and death passes from the vice governor to the executioner to the men.

"Wait. Wait, wait."

The men know not to wait until panic makes cries of the whispers, and they engage in a tug of war, lifting the man off his feet and tying a knot to hold him there before they wipe their hands against their trousers as if to wipe the manslaughter off. The condemned man's expression still manages to convey his confusion. The lips turning blue and swelling up are still moving in a silent prayer for reprieve, and his gaze flickers back and forth without finding anything to settle on. Feet stretching in vain towards the solid surface of the boards, he arches his back and tenses every muscle to try to break the bonds that hold him. Then he begins to run in the air, quicker and quicker, like a decapitated hen whose convulsions allow it to flee headless from the clutches of its mistress. Each movement allows the snare to tighten even more. The bulging tongue no longer fits in the mouth. Ceton's wide eyes take in the spectacle, eager not to miss a thing while the goose pimples swell across him like a breeze on still water. Horror overwhelms him, but he cannot look away, cannot blink, even though his eyes have filled with tears from the effort. He seeks out the gaze of the dying man, pop-eyed with bloodshot whites; his tie to this world already seems forfeit. Those eyes are staring into eternity, and Ceton seeks a sign, a shift in focus for him to interpret, a hint that they see something reserved for them alone, but the moment is too brief, always too brief when it comes, no matter how long the path to that point has been. What was recently a living man stiffens from his final tremors. Whatever made the man human is gone. That which is swaying on the end of the rope is something else now.

Ceton has to make an effort to calm his breathing as he allows his gaze to wander across the crowd who are now turning one by one and beginning to trudge back to the city in happy spirits. Ceton wonders how they are able to see death solely as the due of the hanged. All of them wear their own nooses around their necks, and that rope leads them step by step to gallows constructed in a thousand different guises for them. They don't see them, but Tycho does. How he wishes that he could be as carefree as they.

Then he stiffens, for among those gathered are two people he recognizes. Cardell, the one-armed one, with his wooden stump still charred and its straps passing over his shoulder, and alongside him Winge, absolutely still with a pipe in the corner of his mouth and his hands clasped behind his back. Both are searching the crowd with their gazes; Cardell makes a gesture in his direction and Winge's head swivels on his neck to see who has been singled out. Ceton crouches behind the backs of others and rushes to where the crowd is at its densest, forcing his legs to obey, even though his entire body is shaking. He scuttles bent double behind the ranks of the masses until he puts the crest of the hill between himself and the place where he saw them. The ground here slopes steeply down to the redoubt.

He indulgently pauses for breath and a glance over his shoulder. This alerts him that he has not been quick enough. They are both after him. Cardell's advance is distinguishable by profanities, exclamations, and an undulating movement as if the people were still water into which a boy had just cast his stone: the watchman hurls himself forward without discernment, dispersing all in his path. Ceton's heart thuds as if trying to flee the bars of his rib cage as he casts himself down the hill so quickly that he loses his grip and has to slide on his soles across the crust of the earth. The blood is howling in his ears along with the headwind that tugs the hat off his head when he increases the pace. His legs stagger under him, having atrophied in the chamber over winter, and his side throbs as if someone has stabbed a needle into his flesh. At the tollgate, the city watch are loosely grouped. Beyond the barrier the road continues, utterly exposed, and Ceton can already feel his strength wearing thin. He has to think, has to find a solution, but fear makes ideas slow to come. A glance backwards: Cardell is so close he can distinguish the shifts in color where the cloth of his coat has been worn unevenly.

He quickly bends forward, obscured from the customs booth by a horse and cart. He takes a few handfuls of the dry earth to smear over his clothes—new dirt to conceal the old—and rubbing his hand across half his face. He tears open his waistcoat, making a few buttons burst. Then he dashes towards the men, doing what he can to catch his breath.

"Captain! I say! Captain!"

The men interrupt their conversation and open their circle to witness his arrival. Ceton raises his voice an octave higher than usual to find the right tone: a wronged man of noble birth aware of his dignity even though his throat is choked with sobs. He addresses the men with appropriate flourishes.

"Captain, a hand has been laid upon my person. I am in service with the governor and was at Hammarby to make a record of rightful justice being served, but as soon as I turned homeward, a hooligan struck my hat off and pushed me so that I flew into a ditch, and then he kicked my writing implements away down the hill. The man is drunk, but made himself well enough understood that I realized he is the brother-in-law of the hanged man."

The blush of effort upon his cheeks is easily mistaken for that of vexation, and when the men are unable to contain their smirks, he extends himself to his full height and begins to fumble with his ragged waistcoat as if to regain some of the honor that has been lost. He tenses the corners of his mouth into a trembling conceit and lets his voice crack.

"Far be it from me to exaggerate my own importance, but I must remind you gentlemen that every attack upon servants of the Crown is an attack upon the Crown itself. When misbehavior such as this is permitted to continue, the revolution cannot be far behind."

Without waiting for a retort, Ceton points back up the hill. Cardell is still some distance away.

"There he comes. Before I was forced to flee, I warned him firmly that I would find rescue nearby from our *corps de garde* and his reproach . . . No, it goes against the grain to even voice the words."

The watchmen exchange glances, and the captain raises an eyebrow at him just as one of the subordinates gives voice to their desire.

"Say it."

Ceton is poised for a moment before shaking his head in capitulation, lowering his voice to a horrified theatrical whisper and putting a hand to his cheek as if to hide his lips from sensitive eyes.

"He said that he had no fear of a run-in with the constables for the only way a city watchman would emerge victorious would be if he competed in fellatio."

A younger man whose accent betrays southern origins looks from one to the other in open bafflement.

"In what?"

The captain removes his saber from its sheath as he begins to gather his muttering troops to offer a welcome.

"Perhaps one of you society gentlemen would interpret for Jansson's benefit."

Several respond in chorus.

"Cock-sucking."

28

Day torments him. The sun patrols the rooftops, burning off mist and shadow, leaving no hiding place untouched. Around Ceton, it is as if the drought is shrinking the walls themselves, incarcerated as he is within an ever-worsening stench of dirt and dusty pine. The lassitude forces him to pace across the floor from the window to the stove and back, over and over again. Every loud noise from the courtyard below sends him running for cover. He is dwelling on his dilemma, can hear Bolin's sly voice in his ear. In the midday heat, the dry boards around him creak as if someone has tapped on his cage to amuse themselves—to scare the tame animal back onto its feet.

By night, the lamps remain extinguished in the City-between-the-Bridges. The sun completes its lap just below the horizon line, close enough for the sky to retain a blueness that only the brightest of stars can challenge. Only with the approach of autumn's darkness will the alleys see the lamps lit again, brittle spots of light showing the way from quarter to quarter, with the whispers of crackling wicks and the sharp scent of rapeseed oil. Until August, only the faded roundel of the summer sky is illuminated, underpinned by the glow from tavern doors left ajar.

Tycho only ventures out after the sun has set and the darkness has lowered a veil over every face. Boredom and a corrosive desperation smoke him out. He grants himself a miserable leave in the evening, watchful of whom he meets. The sounds of the city are many but muted as the dusk forces the vigilant to seek sanctuary by the light of hearth and tallow candle. Children cry in cradles where sickness has taken hold. From the palace emerge the bass notes of the violoncello accompanying the contre-danse, from the square the shouts and cries and sounds of scuffles, from

Bagge's Row the choir of lust, from inns and cellars a bellowing where the mood has given rise to singsongs. The pickpockets and miscreants who lurk in passages and doorways allow Tycho to pass unmolested: they are familiar with both the eager footsteps of their prey and the state of the dead drunk, and see neither in him, just another wretch seeking out the dark like themselves. Rather than run the risk of the unknown, they turn away as if he were beset by contagion.

There is a flaming torch in the square by the well, and Tycho has seen it before on many successive nights. It draws him ever closer with each passing evening, as it does others. The people who hurry across the cobbles are drawn to the light like swarms of midges, a motley crowd surrounding the flame and casting unsteady shadows. The gathering never remains for long before the light also attracts the constables, whose harsh barks dispel the assembled throng. The next evening the same thing, curiosity drawing him still closer. They keep irregular hours, doubtless to ensure they don't become part of the night watch's routine, and some evenings Ceton has to stand and wait for a long time at the corner of the Stock Exchange or by the pump in the square.

They are neither Jacobins nor Gustavians. What he hears is something else. The man standing in the center of the circle points up over the rooftop of the Stock Exchange towards the cathedral spire.

"It is said that the church is spacious—big enough for all. But that is not true. It is cramped, my brothers and sisters. Far too cramped. And where the crowd is too big and there is not enough space for all is a place where the Lord would not set foot."

Ceton takes a few steps closer. Diagonally in front of the man speaking is a woman clutching her torch to bathe him in light. He is a rough fellow, with a salt-and-pepper beard, strands of white spreading among the brown, bareheaded and clutching his hat in his hand.

"Why would the Lord choose to speak to His flock through rigid ceremony and the recital of the same old words? No, my brothers and sisters, the Lord comes to each of us, and speaks as if He were your dearest friend. When your life is at its darkest, you need only pray with the strength of a new fervor and He shall come to you, alone in your chamber, naked and bloodied with a crown of thorns on His head and a lance in his side, and He shall envelop you in His arms and make you aware of your grace. Come to us, listen to those who have received His calling and now share their testimony, and your eyes, too, shall be opened."

Many who have gathered out of curiosity begin to move away when they realize they are listening to the sermon of a Dissenter. Ceton too turns to leave, disappointed, but stops when he realizes that the man's voice is now aimed at him alone.

"Brother! Wait. Don't go. I have seen you, as has the Lord. He has not sent you here in vain, but to extend a hand to you in your time of need. Lars Svala is my name. Won't you follow us?"

Ceton hesitates, turning his head away as if to repel a street juggler, and continues on his way across the square. The man steps close enough to him to obstruct his path and meet his gaze.

"My eyes are keen, and the Lord lets them see more than most. Sometimes you have come close enough to allow your face to be reached by the light of our torch. The emotions that you suffer are greater than you can conceal. Your anguish and pain are a beacon in the night. Help is at hand. It is providence itself that has brought our paths together."

Rather than pushing his way past, Ceton turns and walks in the other direction. Svala extends his arms as if in confirmation of his thesis, and his voice contains a note of triumph.

"See! You have no destination. Every course is as good as the other; you are a leaf in a capricious wind."

Ceton hastens away and, ever the practiced speaker, Svala raises his voice to ensure that no words are lost in the parting—now in deadly earnest.

"Far too many live their lives as if they were a dream where nothing is at stake. But after death eternity awaits. I have kept vigil at far too many deathbeds and have seen the realization creep in only in the final hour of life, and the regret it causes. I have looked into the eyes of the dying just as they have had their first glimpse of what they have bought in exchange for their disobedience. Don't become one of them."

Ceton stops and stands still for a moment before turning around. Lars Svala is smiling beneath eyes that have filled with tears at the germination of a promise to pilot yet another soul to the kingdom of heaven.

29

The congregation of Dissenters has its abode in better premises than Ceton would have guessed, just beyond the walls of the Royal Garden, whose open iron gates afford him a glimpse of the unkempt box-hedge maze and the yellow walls of the orangery. Towards Cat's Bay there is a residence bounded by a large garden where an extension has been erected as a prayer hall. It is Sunday—the very day and time that the church bells call their flocks to prayer. In the sunshine, the cocks and crosses crowning the spires are ablaze, and the chimes seem to fall straight from the blue sky. A plain farmyard bell rings out above the residence in reply, shrill and brittle in tone, and a trickle of Dissenters make their way towards it, some hunched as if ashamed of their worship, others straight-backed and determined to show by their expressions both pride and contempt for what they have gladly rejected. It is a small crowd—some thirty perhaps—and all offer their greeting at the door before entering. The hall is chilly at first, warmed only by the bodies of those gathered there and illuminated by its windows. The panes are soon obscured by condensation. Ceton takes his place at the end of one of the benches positioned in a semicircle in front of a table, covered in an embroidered cloth, that serves as an altar.

Beyond that hangs Jesus Christ on the cross in front of a sheet that has been suspended there as a backdrop, but it is a Savior of a kind Ceton has never seen before. He is practically life-sized, although his bare legs are very thin. The carved timber likeness is coarse and unfinished, still marked by the edges of the tools, but whoever wielded the chisel must have gained inspiration and skill from his faith, because no details of the Savior's suffering has been omitted. The image radiates pain. The head droops over arms and shoulders where every tendon is as taut as a violin string. Where the crown of thorns has broken the skin, blood has splattered over the brow and face, and the hole in the right-hand side of the rib cage has been carefully carved to maintain the shape of the recently withdrawn spear. The skin is painted pale and transparent, but every wound and every drop of blood glitters bright red in the light cast by the coarse wax candle on the altar. Lars Svala—the man who invited Ceton here—is standing in seemingly silent prayer, his eyes shut. The hall quietens into the closest it can come to silence, given the congregation's irregular breathing, the rustling of their clothing, and the scraping of their feet on the floor as bodies shift. Ceton lets his gaze wander from one person to another. It is a motley gathering. The worn rags of vagabonds mingle with the stouter garments of the burghers; the old sit elbow to elbow with the young, women alongside men. Only in their eager faces does a sense of community appear. Lars concludes his own silent prayer, opens his eyes, and lets his gaze sweep across the congregation before his lips crack into a gentle smile.

"Brothers and sisters, we are gathered on this Sunday not to hear what has been scribbled by the dead, but to listen to those who have themselves met the Savior. Which of you wishes to speak?"

A woman of about fifty begins to restlessly sway from foot to foot until Svala reaches out towards her with his hand and invites her to the altar.

"Elsa Gustava."

Her legs shaking, she staggers forward through the rows that open up to let her pass, and for a while she stands champing her toothless jaws. Then she takes a sobbing breath and begins.

"As a little girl I was most committed to Christianity, but there was something missing and prayer was not for me. I asked my mother for advice, but all she could do was show me the words written by others, and urge me to learn them by heart and speak them every evening before bed. Later I was sent to Stockholm to find service, and then it was as if the voice of heaven completely disappeared from my life, and I was led by desire and pleasure. Then one night, as I lay tossing and turning with regret at all the things I could not undo, Jesus Christ came and stood right beside my bed, naked and bloodied, as if He had just descended from the cross."

The woman is so agitated she has begun to cry, and as she continues to speak she stares across the heads of the congregation as if picturing all over again everything she describes, racked, now, with ecstatic sobs.

"I lay completely still, barely daring to move, until He raised his arm and showed me His flank with the wound shining red, and He let me kiss it and I tasted His sacred blood, and the salty edges of the wound were a greater joy to me than all those lips I have put to my own in lechery. Then He wrapped me in His arms and swore that He would be my bridegroom henceforth, and the strongest pleasure I have ever felt passed through my body like a howling wind."

....

Later, after Ceton has endured the singing of the congregation, the men's diffident basses merging with the women's shriller tones, and after the distribution of the sacrament, Lars Svala waves Ceton to one side in an empty corner of the hall.

"You're skeptical."

Ceton lets the silence plead his cause. Svala nods.

"If not Our Lord, then who was it who came to our sister's bed in her time of need?"

"Some skinny drunkard or other who got the wrong door, his hands bloody after falling on them into the gravel once too often, and hair tangled with twigs after a nap in a ditch."

"Ah, raillery! If that is your own balm of choice for your suffering, then I do not begrudge you it. But won't you give me your earnest opinion too?"

"Voltaire said it best, although he was getting at something else: if God did not exist, it would be necessary to invent Him. Your Elsa Gustava's imagination came to her rescue. When fools see visions, we lock them up. When the pious do it, we call it religion."

Svala responds to him with a gentle smile, and in his reply there is no hint of offense.

"Our Savior comes in as many guises as the souls that He comes to redeem. Among us there are simple folk, and perhaps they require a simple Savior. For you He will take on a different shape."

"And for you?"

Svala frowns.

"I am still waiting for the day when He comes to me in the flesh and lets me taste the Blood of the Lamb from His own skin. But long ago I was on my deathbed, overcome by chills that offered no respite, trembling with terror at the seemingly inescapable end. My sins were many, a vast load, one that had cost me my friends and family and what fortune I'd once had. The church priest sat by my bed and mumbled prayers, all the while leaning to one side in the hope of spying the tower clock through the window, eager to rush on elsewhere. Then it struck me: What are his followers' dogmas other than obstacles laid in the path of faith, tollgates at the boundaries of heaven whose guardians enrich themselves with tariffs? Afterwards, I dreamed, and that dream was a promise from a God of another sort, and a view towards the meadows of the beatified. I quietly renounced my old faith and gave myself unto this new one, and at that the fever retreated. It was not long before I found others who felt like me."

Svala makes to put his hand on Ceton's shoulder, but he flattens the palm of his hand into an apologetic gesture when Ceton takes a step back to evade its reach.

"As the shepherd of this flock, I have learned to love my neighbor. Many people come here, both high and low, and their paths are all different. But you—there is something special about you, a pain of a kind I have rarely seen before, and the length of your suffering is made clear by the fact of its practiced suppression from your countenance. Only when your thoughts are roaming does it briefly emerge. It is a terrible grimace. I wonder if you have seen it yourself? I also sense that you are not a God-fearing man. But know that sinners such as you are those that our Savior takes the greatest honor in rescuing from the flames. When you doubt, look in your heart for the desire you have for that which is sacred, and know that this is the very proof of the Lord's existence—a seed sown by the Savior with His own hands."

"Is every urge harbored in my heart divinely ordained?"

Svala shakes his head with a smile.

"Distinguishing between them is the challenge given unto us by the Lord. Now then, there is bread by the door—fresh from the oven. Break it together with us, and come back to us soon. Here—and nowhere else—shall you find your solace. Come and listen to the others testifying, and then let us meet again to discuss their examples. I see your doubt, but you must take this first step out of trust."

When Ceton takes his first bite of the rye cake—still warm—he realizes he is not eating out of politeness but because he is hungry, and that he can barely afford anything else.

30

Ceton heads home late in the stifling night, the words of the Dissenters still gnawing away at him. Drunkards have sought shelter in doorways and on doorsteps, even drunker for having learned that it is better to exchange their last coins for spirits than to wake with their pockets picked by deft fingers. The most hardened have turned their pockets inside out to save the pickpockets the trouble, knowing that the more ill-disposed of the street's pack usually make their displeasure known after fruitless efforts through kicks or blows. The cobbles in the alley that lead to the courtyard where he rents his chamber are invisible in the dark, but he can hear his soles breaking the crust of filth left by the day, shoveled in the direction of the gutters, thicker than customary, a crust of summer snow. His soles slide in the mire and terrify swarms of flies into flight. In the courtyard, a sow advanced in years snores in her sty, which has been subtly adorned with all manner of tinkling scrap to betray the presence of nocturnal thieves. Before stepping from the shadows, he halts, warned by some uncanny sense of another's presence. The moon is obscured, but as he waits the starlight reveals a small figure, and when the recognition becomes mutual it addresses him with a girl's voice lowered to a whisper.

"Sir?"

He's seen her before—one of the many children who run about the quarter. Her parents neglect her, but she has become old enough to disregard the younger brothers and sisters she has been tasked with overseeing, knowing that the punishments promised are rarely remembered if she only returns at those times when drunkenness has taken its toll. She surely intends to make him a milestone in her inescapable path towards the maidens' rooms on Bagge's Row for which fate has so clearly cast her.

"I've been waiting for you for many hours, sir."

Before he has time to answer, she places a finger to her lips to silence him. "And I am not the only one."

She waves him closer and gestures to him how best to peer round the corner of the building, up towards his chamber's only window. It takes time before the night shows him what she wants him to see. On the other side of the pane burns a faint glow, imperceptible to anyone not seeking its presence: someone is waiting inside.

"They came at twilight. Had they been visiting a willing host, they would have lit a flame by now. Instead, they wait in silence and they have closed the door so that no one will know of their presence."

Ceton retreats into the shelter of the alley.

"Do you know who they are? Have you seen them?"

"I know the watchman Cardell by name. His companion is thin and pinched—even from a distance one could tell he wasn't like the others. They had someone else with them—from the Chamber of Police, to judge from the badge around his neck."

"To what do I owe this benevolence?"

"You have been renting for a long time, sir, and you're one of us. What would the City-between-the-Bridges be if we neighbors didn't watch each other's backs? But one good deed merits another. Perhaps you have a few coins leftover in your purse, sir?"

With a grunt, Ceton selects blindly from those few coins he still has, certain that he can at least keep what he owes in rent, given that he can no longer return to his room. He hands her a shilling, but as he turns to leave he feels her small hand on his jacket sleeve.

"Sir? Surely I've earned more than that."

She has raised her voice slightly, and the moment he hushes her he realizes he is being robbed by someone armed with the advantage. He passes her another shilling to keep company with the first, but she backs away, leaving his hand hanging untouched between them.

"They're standing by up there—I've seen them—they're ready to surprise you as soon as they hear your footsteps in the stairwell, sir. If I were to scream, they would be here in a flash. It could happen so easily. I'm just a child out after bedtime, and the night is filled with dangers."

"The moon is covered, it's dark as pitch, and if I turn a corner their efforts would be in vain—just like yours."

She shrugs.

"Perhaps they'll be lucky when guessing your escape route. The odds are even. You might have noticed, sir, that someone seems to have knocked over the dung barrel here in the courtyard, and heels can easily slip in the filth, especially those of one in a hurry."

He can sense her smug smile, as well as the circumstances of the accident.

"What price would be reasonable?"

"Your whole purse, sir, and anything else of value that you have."

"So let us take a few steps back, sufficiently close for our friends to hear you cry out but sufficiently far for me to get away should you conceive of doubling your profit by alerting my guests in the hope of a reward."

The girl nods at the reasonability of the suggestion, but she knows the ways of her world. She stops on the spot where she can still walk away safely, beyond his reach should he dare lunge for her. With the first steps of his escape prepared, he passes her the purse with the final coins he owns.

"You may not be so successful if we meet again."

She shrugs at him while stowing her prize beneath her skirts, and her voice is indifferent.

"Last year I had nine friends in this block the same age as me. Three of them saw in the new year underground, a fourth succumbed to the chills in the spring, one is on the streets, another is in the orphanage. I'll seize my chance when life offers it and leave the morrow to those who can afford it."

31

Lars Svala has a good voice for preaching—an emotionally charged baritone of the kind that can carry to all ears and be heard without difficulty. The assembled people listen with a reverence bordering on euphoria, and many who seem incapable of containing their emotions rock from foot to foot in time to an inaudible pulse. Ceton allows his gaze to roam over the crowd that today counts perhaps fifty and he is surprised: all four estates mix here without distinction. Here are apprentice journeymen and their masters, easily recognized by their coarse fists, bent backs, and faces tanned full of wrinkles from squinting at their task in failing light. They stand shoulder to shoulder with fishermen, destitute ragamuffins, young priests in black cassocks. At irregular intervals, the light catches the brass buttons on the well-brushed coat and golden watch chain dangling down the waistcoat of a member of the upper ranks. Despite their difference in rank, they all wear the same facial expression. Ceton is put in mind of a shoal of netted fish, each yearning to escape through the same narrow aperture, but try as they might, these people are unable to stop themselves heeding the voice now addressing them. The people once again begin to sway on their feet to the melody of the words.

"Even when we come into the world we are filled with sin, the off-spring of a family that have offended our Father and justly been banished from His garden. But the Lord showed us mercy and in our time of need sent us His only born son as salvation through His sacrifice. High on Calvary, Jesus was hung on the cross, still unredeemed for His actions, until a soldier was sent forth to find out whether there was any life remaining. Longinus was his name, and he seized his lance and thrust it deep into Jesus's side. Thus the red hole in our Savior's breast was opened, through which His heart was finally revealed to the people. Our path to His bound-less love has been cleared; the gates of heaven are not adorned with pearls and gems but by the edges of His wound, that lacerated flesh, and all the people fell to their knees before the light emanating from it, and the holy blood that so profusely flowed."

Svala's passion, and the warmth radiating across the bodies packed into the hall, have made sweat break out on his brow. He pauses in his sermon, stepping to one side and pointing to the simple chalice waiting on the altar cloth.

"We drink the same blood now in commemoration of Him, and we eat His flesh. Receive it with devotion, and when the body is put to your lips, close your eyes and know that you might just as well be drinking directly from the tip of Longinus's lance, like leeches on the holy body, gathered to suckle for the sake of salvation."

Before communion, the believers testify. Two youths stand beside the altar—so alike they could be siblings. Both have some growing left to do in their bodies, neither yet twenty. One of them is taller and probably older; he takes a step forward, with some hesitation, after glancing at his companion, whose chin is resting on his chest, a fringe of hair obscuring his eyes and the tears that have already begun to stream down his cheeks, his face contorted into a grimace. The elder boy takes a trembling breath and begins to speak.

"My name is Albrecht, and my cousin is called Wilhelm. We come from the south—born as subjects to Frederick Augustus the Just."

He speaks fluently, with only occasional idiosyncrasies of vocabulary to betray his mother tongue.

"We are apprentices both; our trade is smithwork. Wilhelm is still not old enough to do much more than manage the bellows, while I have begun shaping blanks with tongs and hammer."

He stumbles on his words and hesitates, unsure how to continue.

"We . . . our home has long been the scene of neighbors' wars, and when adversity became too much in our village we were sent north to Rostock as they knew that there was a land across the water where Louisa Ulrika had been made queen, and where others from our parts might be welcome perhaps. Our family has always feared God, and we were given the best upbringing under the priest. No blame for what has happened can descend on them."

He loses his train of thought for a moment, and searches for the right words.

"We were sent away together and made to promise that we would care for each other, each never far from the other's side. But soon we agreed that there were three of us on the journey—and that the third of our number was the Devil. He cast his net over us, and we, we . . ."

In the silence, all that is audible are the younger man's sobs and the sound of the congregation: many breaths, weight shifting on creaking planks, coughs.

"Feelings grew between us that should not exist between anyone other than man and woman. The temptation of the flesh became worse and worse with each step we took, increasingly difficult to resist. Terrible is our suffering, for we both know that our souls are damned the very moment that temptation overcomes us. We are strangers here, and did not know where to turn for help in our distress until Wilhelm remembered the village of Herrnhut near our own, where the late count once gave sanctuary to all in his parish. Our joy was great when we found that his people were also in Stockholm."

His speech becomes increasingly incoherent until his voice cracks and sobbing forces him to stop. Only after a few deep breaths does he manage to collect himself sufficiently to bring his tale to a conclusion, his eyes now cast down, his shoulders shaking.

"Our master that we serve in Stockholm has in his kindness shown us the same room where we have been given one single bunk to share. We dare not do so, afeared as we are of being led into sin, and while Wilhelm takes the bed I have made my own bed on the floor. Yet we rarely sleep. Every night we pray together to Jesus Christ to deliver us and alleviate our anguish, and for the bloody bridegroom Himself to come and wrap His arms around us, and to make use of all the love that the Evil One wants to employ to lead us into the ways of sin. We . . . we ask for your prayers to overcome the blight that besets us."

....

After communion, Lars Svala offers his tobacco pouch to Ceton to stuff his borrowed clay pipe. They each light up from the last tallow candle in the hall before Svala blows it out and they sit down on a bench in the small garden. The last of the faithful have passed through the gate, strengthened by the body and blood of Christ. The sound of washerwomen in Cat's Bay striking their boards can be heard in time with the cries of the fish sellers, and from the Royal Garden come occasional laughter and cries from the flâneurs who have sought out the shelter of the shrubbery to escape the blazing sun. The day is warm, as ever in this long summer. Svala breaks the silence.

"What have you to say about this evening's testimony?"

Ceton allows the cool smoke to waft across his tongue, inhales deeply, and lets it escape through the broken corner of his mouth—on the side facing away from his host.

"To love and have love requited—not in every lifetime is such a favor granted. Fate has given them the time and opportunity to satisfy their desires without disturbing anyone else. They are in the bloom of their lives, both ornaments of their kind. The only thing I am inclined to call a sin is that they are forsaking the companionship that has so clearly been placed within reach. And speaking of sin, were it such a thing, it was not one that the late King Gustav considered himself above, not to mention Baron Reuterholm. There is only one thing I can think of that the two agreed upon, and that was the joy of the company of beautiful boys. The Greek love germinates here, there, and everywhere. Of those who harbor it, we can say neither better nor worse than of anyone else."

"What then of eternity? What of the damnation of souls?"

"Why would any God have created a being in His image and filled it to the brim with urges that displease Him? Given the power, why breed anything less than perfect?"

"Our faith teaches us to resist temptation in order to make our own choice between good and evil."

"Are we a game then? A bored creator's amusement? Where one single entity is omnipotent, there is no space for the free will of others. He knew what the outcome would be, and He could have righted every wrong with the turn of a hand, instead of behaving like a child lashing a dying animal with a stick from sheer curiosity. If their faith lasts sixty years, each one of those lads will be alone as an old man, hand on a crutch where his beloved might have been. Through the tears of regret, they will look back at a wasted life, the only comfort being that little of the suffering remains."

"My friend, what do you believe awaits us on the other side?"

Ceton bends forward to rub a stain from his thigh.

"Nothing. What else? The thought holds no horror for me. Look at the natural world around us, which allows nothing to go to waste. Nor are we lost. Today we are people, tomorrow we become worms, the day after flies. Is that not permanence? But no consciousness remains, no soul, no gifts in the life to come to be gained through supposed virtue, no penalty for imagined crimes."

Lars Svala laughs quietly. The sun is still high in the blue sky above the spire of Jakob Church.

"Your words strengthen me in my faith. Who but God can have put you in my path? Never has there been a soul in greater need than yours. Break bread with us before you go."

Ceton greedily eats what is offered. Svala turns away to let him sate his hunger in peace before he asks his question.

"My friend, did you sleep outside last night?"

Ceton inspects the clothes he is wearing and at once sees the same thing as Svala. His coat and trousers are stained, marked by the filth of the streets. An attempt to brush the worst from the breeches has had the opposite result, and he notices that his hands have evaded the washbasin for far too long. He shrugs—the only response of a fallen gentleman to a question that stings too much to merit an honest answer. Lars Svala allows his gaze to survey the garden beyond and betrays no pity when he makes his offer.

"There is water by the kitchen. Soap too. We have a bed here for anyone who needs it, in a room that may be humble, but where all the essentials are within reach. Ask the maid and she will show you the way, and I shall ask her to lay out clothes that you may borrow while she washes the ones you are currently wearing."

32

He has been banished from Gallows Hill. It has become his habit to trudge down towards the Stream, wait a while by the water, and squint towards the North Bridge, where wood has been used to make temporary vaults above the bridge abutments that have been neglected since they rose from their pilings. Below him, the torrent from the swollen lake thunders along, hungry waves leaping up towards him, their white foam clawing its way up the stone walls of the channel. Ceton follows the water along onto Church Islet where the slaughterhouses are located by the shore beside jetties sunk deep into the ground. He climbs some distance up the hill leading to the church and finds himself a spot where the gap between the houses affords him a view of the slaughterhouse yard. Above him, the clock strikes and announces the beginning of yet another grim day of toil. The craftsmen whose appearance has quickly become as familiar to him as their names are unknown shuffle out into the yard one by one, tying their aprons on and stretching their stiff arms and backs. Then they lead in the first ox of the day, which reluctantly allows itself to be tethered to the pole, lowing in the pen. The cloth bound across its eyes isn't enough to soothe its anxiety since it possesses other senses that warn it of impending misfortune. The butchers exchange glances and begin the routine they all know without a single word. A gangly lad raises his blade and places the calming palm of his hand on the ox's head while balancing the sharp point in the crease of his thumb and forefinger. He nods at the animal's executioner, who spits into his fists, wields his club, and with practiced skill drives the iron into the ox's forehead with a crash like that of firewood cracking in the heat. The ox tips onto its side in shock and lies there like an epileptic, all four legs moving, and Ceton wonders what kind of thoughts are spinning around in these final moments. Perhaps none at all.

Given that it is the first of the morning, the butchers stand awhile to contemplate the convulsions in a concession to the seriousness of death before it becomes yet another working day. They nod at each other in recognition of a job well done. The lad grins proudly at his master, his face splattered. He did his duty, not letting go of his grip too soon so that the blow missed, and not too late so that the club struck his forearms.

The blood pulses red across the cobbles of the yard in a growing puddle, and Ceton follows the brief moments of mortal struggle while holding his breath, to no avail. Before evening comes to dull the edge of the butcher's blade, there remain some dozen animals—perhaps a score if he is fortunate. That isn't many to feed a city, but prices have shot up as the crops have fared badly. He finds a better vantage point as the next ox is led in.

Afterwards, he directs his feet towards the Moravian Brethren, past the Nonpareil. Within, they are rehearsing: loud voices carry into the street, and when they pause, the hoists and windlasses of the theatrical machinery rattle. Someone shakes a sheet of metal to mimic the sound of thunder.

33

Bolin receives him differently upon his return visit, the manner quickly agreed upon through an exchange of messages: Ceton is still directed to the back entrance, but this time he is led into a different room. Ceton feels hope germinating—the kind that fills the breast of a gambler when the odds are raised and the stakes grow higher. Sconces line the corridor walls, his passage causing the flames to flicker, their rear mirrors scattering rays of light here and there, and for a few moments his senses are fooled: it feels as if the floor and walls are swaying around him, the pattern of the wallpaper and the dado rail suddenly undulating like waves. Yet again, he has gained admission to the world that was once his, every surface the gaze lights upon refined, and the very air itself filled with what were once ordinary smells, evoking memories: potpourri in bowls placed to spread their fragrance, lavender from the linen cabinets, wine decanted prior to a meal, meat being roasted and vegetables simmering in the pot, spices from distant lands. Assurance grows within him, for if his hastily written proposal hadn't aroused interest he would never have come this far. There is too much luxury here to sully it with his blood, and given Bolin's inclinations towards pragmatism things would have been done more simply. They would have left him to his fate, and had they preferred to silence him they would have used the kind of gag that consists of a henchman lurking in an alley with a nondescript piece of steel in his fist and robbery as pretext.

He is even more bolstered by the fact that his appearance is somewhat improved ahead of this meeting. Just as Lars Svala promised, his clothes have been rinsed and rubbed, and while many of the stains put up resistance beyond the powers of soap, the fabric itself has regained an overall state of cleanliness. Dressed like this, he finds it easier to rise to his full height. There was a worn-out comb in his chamber and his beard and hair are now free from knots. Then two mirrored doors open, and he is shown in to meet the fate that his erstwhile brothers have chosen for him.

There are more of them now, a handful in conversation by the window, Anselm Bolin with one hand resting on the stiffened edge of his tailcoat, and the other on the top of his cane. He staggers half a lap around the carved ivory as his joints lament.

"Ah, Tycho."

The other three nod at him, flushed and perspiring in their elegant suits. Accustomed as he is to reading the nuances of etiquette, he finds the greeting to be measured but lacking in hostility. That is how a pariah bringing hope is received—a runner returning from convalescence on whom money can once again be bet, albeit with reservations. He knows their faces of old. Two were guests at Three Roses's wedding and crowded in around the bridal bed. Bolin and the others exchange meaningful looks before the former staggers across to a table by the wall and ostentatiously pushes a small silver basket of confectionery towards Ceton.

"Bonbon?"

Ceton knows the variety: sweet liqueur under a cocoa shell. His mouth is watering, but he chastens temptation through force of will. Bolin shrugs.

"Well. You already know Tosse, Sneckenfelt, and Stjärnborg. They collectively represent the brothers' attitudes at large: one spoke in favor of your case at a plenary of the brothers, and with a warmth that was met with sympathy. One did the opposite. One is irresolute. I have declined to offer my own views and am confining myself to acting as mouthpiece."

Clumsily, but with practiced habit, Bolin places his weight on the arm of a chair and allows himself to sink down, leaning his cane against the wall.

"I have brought your case before the brothers following receipt of your dispatch. I shall be honest, Tycho: rarely have I seen our order embroiled in such controversy. The two sides appeared well balanced against each other, and neither was more accommodating than the other. I shall spare you the worst of your detractors' views regarding your character. It took some time before a more or less edifying conversation occurred."

He clears his throat and shifts positions on the chair before continuing.

"Let us leave old antipathy behind us and settle for observing that you have a history that has not gone unnoticed, and that has claimed some victims in terms of fraternal love. Instead, let us focus on your most recent escapade: Three Roses's wedding. Those who were at the event were able to recall fond memories, and described you as a considerate host. Also stated in your favor was the fact that this gesture of reconciliation towards our order came about when you were still in a strong position and your will could thus be regarded as heartfelt. That you have now been compelled—indeed forced—to come to us is, however, difficult to question, and there were those who plainly asked what kind of man has so few friends that he must turn to his enemies for support . . ."

Stjärnborg induces a cough and glances at Bolin reproachfully.

"Well, that is as well as may be. The event at Three Roses's was scrutinized closely, and I shan't conceal the fact that a number of critical voices were raised. Several of the brothers felt the entire affair was rather vulgar and a renunciation of the sort of finesse upon which our order prides itself. A gullible young man in a stupor, a peasant girl hopelessly outnumbered. A further circumstance is the gain you made on the affair in retrospect: the boy was reportedly admitted to Dane's Bay in a feeble-minded state while you carved gold out of the guardianship. There were some injured voices who asserted that you exploited the Furies for your own ends, thus inviting the brothers' displeasure upon yourself. Others praised your cunning, and regarded the maneuver as an example of your genius. In the end, however, a compromise was reached."

Bolin extends an arm towards his companions.

"Together with the gentlemen here, I am a member of your party committee, here to vote for or against the proposal that you present in its entirety. If the aforementioned proposal is deemed satisfactory, we have been granted access to a purse from which the required resources may be obtained. It is a fair size—after all, pleasures of this kind are our order's very raison d'être."

Ceton's thoughts turn to the congregation's loaned bed, with its hard base, the bedbugs, the dry bread where each mouthful has to be washed down with water to pass his throat. Anselm Bolin holds out his arms, exchanging glances with his other guests.

"Well then. Gentlemen, please take your seats. Tycho, perhaps you prefer to stand?"

....

Afterwards, the other guests leave him with Bolin, one by one. The last to go is Gillis Tosse, who grabs his arm in the corridor and leans in close, his teeth blackened and his piggish eyes red, the lingering slenderness of his youth losing the battle against the pounds being hung around his waist by voluptuousness. A whisper in his ear.

"You and I have never seen eye to eye, and it is thus with the utmost satisfaction that I wish to tell you the following. I gave you my vote for one reason: if the brothers' appetite is not sated by what you put on the table, then you shall in turn become the main course—the kind one need lend just enough rope to hang himself. And what you proposed may sound impressive, but it will never succeed. If you believe otherwise then you are a fool. It will be a pleasure to witness your fall, and from the best vantage point."

Ceton responds with a smile—his first in a long time—and feels the brittle crust of his cheek cracking at the corner of his mouth and the taste of iron on his tongue. That old, familiar sensation. Once again, he and his enemies are equals. No, not equals: he is restored far, far above them.

....

Once they are alone, Bolin passes him a handkerchief and Ceton holds the silk against his bleeding cheek while Bolin kneads his stiff leg, extended across a velvet-upholstered ottoman, his fingers going as close to the ache as he dares with a grimace of discomfort.

"There are some final details to be negotiated between ourselves, Tycho, and there are now plenty of spare seats. Won't you sit down?"

Ceton does as invited.

"The matter you raised with me on your last visit, Tycho: your hunting dogs. I have taken the liberty of securing an informant in the Chamber of

Police—someone with knowledge of both men. He was not cheap—we all know that the Academy has only been abolished temporarily, and is sure to be resurrected once the young king is of age. Old Schröderheim is at death's door and will hardly see the end of the summer. I was forced to promise the old man's vacant seat to secure my source, but now the man is ours."

"And?"

"On your heels you have Emil Winge, younger brother to the once renowned Cecil, latterly deceased. This Winge has taken his brother's place at Indebetou House. By virtue of the successes he has achieved through his work, he cannot be cleared out of the way with ease—certainly not without questions being asked of the kind our order has always sought to avoid with the utmost caution. *Esse non videri*, as you well know."

Bolin loosens his cravat without awaiting a response.

"It is another matter with the other one. This Cardell. A fellow who has long lived hand-to-mouth and rarely far from danger. If you found his corpse with its throat cut, no one would be particularly surprised. Nevertheless, I would prefer there to be an explanation available for the curious, and in that respect I have engaged a representative. A soldier in days of yore, just like Cardell. Indeed, a loose acquaintance. He is now making the rounds of the inns where similar fellows drown their sorrows, slandering Cardell with no great discretion in the hope of finding someone who harbors the same grudge. When such a man makes himself known, we shall induce the said individual to take the blame for any counterfire."

34

And so busy days return to Tycho Ceton, long missed but more demanding than he remembers. There is much to be put in order, and no room for mistakes. Only now does he see what marks the suffering of the winter has left upon him. Maintaining his thoughts fatigues him and leaves him with an aching pain across the temples, and when the evenings grow late and he seeks his bed, he falls unconditionally into the arms of Morpheus, as dead to the world as any drunk under a bench. But his dreams bring him a foretaste of triumph. Fragments of what is to come are played out, each detail beyond censure, and when he wakes it is with a bittersweet feeling as the memory of the images of sleep melt away to be replaced by stark reality. Nevertheless, there is one dividend: Lars Svala's ragged sheets and worn bunk are easier to endure now. Previously, he was nought but a simple supplicant, grateful for a roof over his head, at the mercy of others' discretion. Now? Poverty is merely his disguise of choice. The bites of the lice stop itching with the realization that they are self-inflicted, that a door that was closed is once again open, and that what awaits on the other side is no longer frightening but tempting.

In his room, Ceton pulls out the small parcel he has been carrying inside his coat. The paper is of an unfamiliar make, coarse and gray—the kind that testifies to a long journey. The seller did not make himself easy to find. Ceton went himself to the sloop whose odd shape leaked almost beyond the limits of seaworthiness, and which was shrouded in a stench of cinnamon that stuck in his nostrils but was still unable to conceal the acrid rot of the timber. Belowdecks awaited a seaman grown old before his time, his face so sooty that only the wrinkles channeling the sweat away remained clean, running at random angles through the black. As on so many occasions before, Ceton is reminded that greed unites all men with a language of its own. Coins strive to be in new hands, goods too, and despite the fact that neither of them can utter a word that is understood by the other, meaning is found. Grunts, gestures, and grimaces invoke the spirit of business. He inspected the goods carefully, haggling as best he could while his counterparty wrung his hands and feigned disappointment as he waved goodbye to the wake extending behind him through waters to the other side of the world. Eventually, a deal was done, and both were quite pleased with the compromise reached.

Now, by the light of the tallow candle, Ceton is able to indulge himself in examining his purchase anew, and a gnawing suspicion is confirmed. Something is wrong. The color is not right. He carefully tips the package on end and shakes it until three of the small beetles land in the palm of his hand and lie there, stiff and weightless. To be safe, he counts those remaining in the fold of paper—another nine, a dozen in total. He holds his hand closer to the light. The ones he has seen before have been more golden in color, and these glitter green in a shade he has never before seen—one that seems unreal to him, as though they are miniature guests from a world more frivolous than his own. He knows that he must ensure their effect. There is a knock on the door and he carefully returns the three beetles to their kin.

Lars Svala enters uninvited, clears his throat awkwardly, and remains standing while Ceton carefully conceals the packet in the pocket of his waistcoat.

"After the service, I saw you in conversation with the boys from the south. You left together for the Royal Garden and it was a long time before you came back."

His answer is slow in coming and the sun is dazzling through the window, the room hot as a bakehouse, the joists creaking in the dry air, and when Tycho Ceton turns halfway around on the stool towards the man in his doorway, Lars Svala forgets his question for a moment. In that instant, it crosses his mind that his old guest is gone and a new one has moved in. Ceton rubs his bare chin and angles the cracked box mirror for a better view.

"My beard was itching. I'm glad to be rid of it, finally."

The rag he used as a towel is lying on the table stained red, soiled each time the blade of the knife caught the edges of wounds. Reminded of the shave, he grimaces to stretch his naked cheeks, the left corner of his mouth longer than its neighbor. With a final glance in the mirror, he turns around and gives Svala his full attention.

"Please forgive my vanity. Yes, I have had many a conversation with Albrecht and Wilhelm. The Royal Garden is cool in the evening, and we meet each evening to talk. They are obliging lads, and I am flattered by their confidence."

"What do you want with them?"

"Am I not part of the communion, just as the others are? I've been alone for so long. It's no wonder that I enjoy company."

"Theirs in particular and no one else's? Is there any specific reason?"

"What makes you ask?"

Lars Svala sits down on the edge of the bed and his fingers pull the collar of his shirt away from his sweaty neck. He frowns in annoyance.

"I'm worried about them. Anyone who has ever harbored feelings of tenderness for another can see the anguish they are suffering. They only have each other, but they still want more, and the lures of lust are troubling during our younger years. Our Lord must see something special in these two to line their path with such tribulation."

He stands up again, restless, and paces back and forth across the floor as far as the space allows.

"And I know your view on the matter. I am afraid that even one single poorly chosen word may nudge them into depravity."

"Is your God's voice so weak that mine is easier to hear?"

Lars Svala sees Ceton in the counterlight, the rays slanting across him leaving a dark swath across his face. He cannot say for certain whether Ceton is sneering or whether it is just the play of the shadows across the gaping scar on his cheek. He lets the question go unanswered, and Ceton continues.

"You should know that I am grateful for all that I have received here. It has been to me like an ascetic's period of fasting. You have expanded my world; I could not help but wonder if I had got hold of the wrong end of the stick. I have tried to unravel the nature of existence through the eyes of others, and it has been in vain. Now I wonder if there aren't better ways to do so."

Ceton leans forward on his stool, slowly.

"How small-minded He is in His omnipotence. Your God. How He frets over our pitiful sins. Let me ask you a question, given your priestly leanings: Do you think there could be any blasphemy strong enough to rouse Him from His lofty distaste? One that might shake Him from His fluffy chaise longue in the sky and make Him show Himself among us mortals?"

"What can there be that He has not already seen? He works out of sight. His ways are inscrutable."

Ceton opens his hand, and what he is holding in it sends a reflection of the sun into Svala's face. Squinting, he sees that it is a ducat, gold and shimmering in the way that only gold can be.

"You were once a gambling man. If you were still, would you care to take a wager with me on their souls?"

For a moment, Svala feels the stab of dizziness in his belly.

"Would you take the side of the Evil One?"

"There is just you and me here."

Lars Svala shudders in the heat.

"The time has come for you to leave us, my friend. Nothing would have pleased me more than to give you the gift of faith, but if you are spreading unrest in the flock I have been tasked with guarding then you leave me with no choice but to show you out of the pasture."

The memories come unwanted, from the ecstasy of drunken evenings, filled with games of faro and ombre, the very rush of life never so irrepressible as when the dice tumbled and cards were turned, profit and ruin present in one and the same breath.

"And I never gamble any longer, least of all with things that don't belong to me."

"Not all battles are ours to choose. Sometimes we must play; otherwise the loss is inevitable."

Ceton tosses the coin into the air and catches it deftly.

"We have grown close to each other, I would venture. The boys and I. They are both simple creatures, but lovable in their simplicity. Youth and beauty have bestowed upon them a value, albeit a corruptible one, and no less consuming given that in the manner of the young they are so unaware of it. Do you know why the bet is one you can never win? Do you know why they would follow me rather than you if faced with the choice?"

Lars Svala knows, but he casts his eyes down in shame while Ceton twists the knife in the wound.

"They are welcome in your group solely through mercy. You want to recast them into God-fearing little lambs—into something they are not. Deep down, you hate them. They may be confused, but deep down they know their nature. During prayers, their skin stings as judgmental stares pour from the eyes of others. The promise of sin rests upon them like a cloud of anxiety, and is of such a distinctive nature that the likes of you cannot reconcile yourselves with it. I alone see them for what they are, and wish them to be nothing else. I alone do not judge them."

"Yet more cause for you to move on. Your time as a guest is at an end."

Ceton cocks his head to one side.

"I have a favor to ask you. The last one."

Lars Svala wrinkles his nose in a baffled grimace, as if these words were the ones he least expected to hear.

"Well?"

"During my time in the Caribbean, I had the misfortune to contract a particular illness—chills of a most severe kind. I recovered but soon came to realize that it was a kind I can never fully be rid of. It lies fallow between its fits and starts, always ready to flare up and leave me lying wherever my knees give way. The power of its onslaughts varies from time to time, and it is never easy to predict."

"And now it is brewing?"

Ceton nods with feigned earnestness.

"It is coming now, and tonight promises to be difficult. Will you allow me this final evening here in a room that I have grown accustomed to and where I may rest undisturbed? The fever has already set in and my muscles are sore. As soon as my legs will carry me again, I promise to be on my way."

Svala hesitates, torn between his own instinct and the promises that bind his world together.

"I . . ."

Ceton struggles not to betray with his face the win that he knows in advance is his, grateful for his disfigured cheek.

"A certain man went down from Jerusalem to Jericho, and fell among thieves, which stripped him of his raiment, and wounded him, and departed, leaving him half-dead."

Svala smiles reluctantly and finishes the verse.

"And by chance there came down a certain priest that way: and when he saw him, he passed by on the other side. There is nothing wrong with your biblical knowledge, despite your heathen ways. No, this priest shall not pass you by."

Once more alone in his room, Ceton closes the door, shakes loose three of the small green beetles, and crumbles them between his thumb and forefinger into a mug filled with water before throwing his head back and draining it.

35

First nothing. Then gradually an unfamiliar noise, ghostly waves striking against the shore of reality, intensifying until the room is shaking and his vision is cloudy. Ceton hears an unfamiliar sound and realizes that it is him gnashing his teeth. He sweats in ever-heavier flushes, every part of his body suddenly in revolt at the emerald-green vermin ravaging its fluids. Worse and worse: the shadows of the room take on menacing forms; angles that were once straight lean towards him and then away. He casts himself on and off the bunk, the rough blanket first wrapped around him then discarded. He hears himself laughing, crying, and howling until his vision darkens and leaves him alone in an empty space.

Out of the darkness a voice, a lamentation. As a matter of course, the dream asserts its reality: around him is Saxnäs, and he is no bigger than a boy with scars—still unhealed—from the pox, woken from fever to a world where his father no longer exists. Amid the cottages of the dying is a silence reserved for him alone. The words of God have fallen silent along with his father's voice, and not even prayer brings him peace any longer. He walks between the walls of the houses on the same errand for which he recently accompanied his father, carrying water in a bottle, a rag to bathe feverish brows, Bible and hymn book discarded in the gutter.

He follows a path, a furrow carved in damp snow. Each time he stumbles, heavy flakes tumble down and fill the crack between the leather of his shoe and his woollen stocking, stinging for a few moments before melting and cooling. He knows where he is going. Once he arrives he kicks the timber walls of the cottage to knock the crusts of snow off his soles, then steps inside and peers about the murky kitchen, looking for a wooden stick to thrust into the glow visible beneath the ash. Then there is light, a flame flaring up in the darkness, and it is he who grasps its source. A simple candlestick, a brass pipe to hold the stump above a saucer to catch dripping wax. A loop to provide his finger with a grip.

He follows the sound of the coughing—wet, dejected jolts between sobbing inhalations. The smell bites his nostrils. A lowly abode. Karl Johan is at death's door, his face swollen with blisters. His body shudders when he senses company in the chamber, and Tycho moves away from the feeble hand that gropes towards him. Karl Johan was a big man with a voice of authority—one that carried far enough to rebuke an errant farmhand on the far side of the field. The weight has dropped away from him until all that is left is an assortment of bones in an overcapacious leather sack. Of the voice, all that remains are shallow sighs.

"Ulrika? My Ulrika, is that you?"

Tycho has stopped replying to the dying. Interaction is beyond them. Johan's wife has been lying cold in her grave for the past week, while he is so far gone that oblivion and hope have set aside all reason. Tycho sits on his stool next to the box-bed for a long time, observing each breath, occasionally searching for a pulse at the wrist. He has kept vigil at enough bedsides to sense the arrival of death, and when Karl Johan begins to wheeze he slips off his stool, plucking up the courage to open a swollen eyelid. The pupil tries vainly to shrink away from the harsh light, and he has to use both hands to force the eye to remain wide open. The man resists, spurring Tycho to use a firmer grip, firmer than necessary given that the distaste for touch he has felt since his recovery colors his judgment. He applies his weight to the dying man and holds his breath, waiting as his fingertips become damp with tears. Then the death rattle right into his face—a final, impure exhalation from what was recently human, and it is over, and he is none the wiser than he was before. The eye glides to rest on stiffening muscles, and the face bears no testimony. There lingers no fear of purgatory nor sign of bliss at a glimpse of the pearly gates. Just emptiness. The past. These meager departures from life in miserable struggles give him nothing, worthy only of the base existences they conclude. He has to get out, away, must seek his answers far away in the world. Outside darkness has fallen. The piece of sky that the window has framed is filled by scores of stars. He feels their weight on his shoulders, beautiful and indifferent. Tycho lingers on his knees alongside the bed. The prayers he learned as a boy itch at his tongue through the power of habit—they want to get out. He is only able to mumble them halfheartedly. Then all of a sudden there is light in the room, and from the glow he gets answers.

"My son, have trust, I am here with you."

The darkness gives way, a shimmering hand caresses his shoulder, and he turns and sees his father clad in light, his head crowned by a halo, his face gentle in triumphant piety and free from pus-filled boils. At first he feels the triumph of a conviction confirmed. Then comes the death-blow of horror—an icicle tip speared into his heart, a blow to the head hard enough to blind. He opens his mouth to stutter his question.

36

A cold, damp cloth against his brow: Lars Svala holds it in place while Ceton turns his head on the pillow and he only removes it when they make eye contact and he discerns a glimmer of sense within. Morning light streams through the window, rays at sharp angles penetrating a cloud of dust lethargically circulating above the floor.

All Ceton's limbs are in order, responding as they ought. Only his belly throbs with pain, like a wicked fist clenched with all its force, refusing to give in. He can feel each heartbeat as if it were a hammer to an anvil. He pushes back the ragged blanket to better cool off, and Svala tactfully averts his gaze. Ceton tests his voice, cracked and husky to begin with.

"How long?"

"All night long."

Ceton sees how tired he is after his long vigil. Svala's eyes are exhausted, dark rings under them.

"You must forgive my intrusion. Your cries became voluble. I feared you might do yourself some harm."

Svala passes him a mug of water and tops it up from a jug after Ceton drains it.

"Is it over? Do you feel better? Your brow is no longer so hot."

His muscles aching, Ceton sits up and swings his legs down to the floor. His entire body is sore, but nothing has been destroyed, nothing is broken.

"Yes. It has rarely been worse. Everything is a haze."

Svala rises and rubs his face.

"Will you excuse me? If I am to get any sleep before the day hurries on without me, it must be now."

Ceton nods in reply.

"Yes, of course. And thank you."

"There is fresh water from the well in the basin. I fetched it not an hour ago when you seemed out of danger."

He pauses with a hand on the knob of the door.

"I . . ."

Then, with a shrug, the preacher changes his mind, before opening the door and closing it behind him.

Ceton waits until he hears the wooden stairs stop their creaking lament, and footsteps on the gravel beneath the window, before he staggers, bent double, to the chipped basin, rolling down his breeches and standing on his toes to relieve his tender member, locked in a discolored spasm and stiff as a cudgel. Afterwards, the worst is over, some of the blood recedes and the swelling goes down, and he can but laugh at it all—at the unfamiliar beetles with their peculiar shade of green. Not because they were the wrong kind or too old—on the contrary, they were fresh, full of the special power because they were not given the opportunity to languish in an apothecary's urn. He took too much. Far too much. He has more than enough for the purpose he has in mind—one ought to do it, one and a half to be sure. *Come*, he thinks to himself, opening his hands at his sides as if about to distribute the sacramental wafer. *Come, all is ready.*

37

He has acquired writing materials, ink and paper, and fills sheet after sheet with lists of all that must be done, constantly vigilant to maintain the correct order. He has been lent a boy by Bolin to run those errands that must be done in daylight—visits to the pharmacists who have previously aided the company with remedies that few request and that are usually denied—but Ceton himself shuns the light, only crossing his threshold when the long shadows take shape with dusk. He goes to the Opera's workshops, where the tailors hunch cross-legged over his patterns. Nothing is left to chance, and there are many alterations to be made in the process. The wrong fabric, too broad a girth. Sometimes he meets Bolin there. The old man has thawed considerably and struggles to stay away, unable to conceal his germinating enthusiasm for what in his view is beginning to attain its proper quality. Back home in the City-between-the-Bridges, his butterflies wait, neglected, a thick swarm with wings spread in simulated flight, each one soaring on its own needle.

They walk together past the bridgeworks. The Stream is drowsy and lethargic in the evening heat, the sky so light that only Sirius and Capella are able to put up any fight at all against the evening blush. Bolin limps alongside him under the tower of the Nonpareil, where they stop to shelter for a while and contemplate the sparse assortment of masts out by the Ship's Bridge and at the yards by the Salt Sea. Few. Fewer than last year and the year before. So it has been ever since the wound in the king's back sucked the final breath out of His Majesty: last year's nightmarish output is this year's idle dream. The trading houses are on their knees. Those who have keys to the coffers embezzle with an inexorable logic: they may as well drain the dead of all blood before it turns rancid. Bolin clasps his hands together on the shaft of his cane behind his back.

"How are your preparations progressing?"

Out across the water, bats chase about, their roving flight and rapid movements impossible to mistake.

"All in accordance with expectation. Everything is in order."

Restlessly, Bolin drags his bad leg into a more comfortable position, scratching his thigh under the gaiter that has been buttoned all the way from the knee down over his shoe. He seems unsure how to say what needs to be said.

"You know just as well as I do how difficult it is to keep things undercover in a group as tight-knit as ours."

"What you mean, Bolin, is that you can't keep a secret."

Despite the darkness, Ceton thinks he can see the man changing color as the blood rises to his cheeks. He can picture it: Bolin infected with enthusiasm for Ceton's proposal, its details bubbling away in his throat until the wine saps his judgment and out it all flows. *For your ears only, don't pass it on.* Bolin has staked his reputation, and regardless of whether Ceton departs in triumph or failure, Bolin will have to shoulder his fair share. How quickly their positions have shifted! The drunkenness of power washes over Ceton, unfamiliar after such long abstinence, and in the dizziness of the moment he almost feels gratitude towards the old man. He smiles a smile that cannot be mistaken and sees Bolin shudder with displeasure.

"It is all one to me."

Bolin squints at random among the ships.

"I must admit that I could have said less. Nevertheless. Expectations have grown high—the brothers talk of little else. I am merely eager to ensure that everything proceeds as agreed."

"There is no cause for concern. There is but one final thing for me to seek assurances about, and then we can set the date and time."

"The location? What are your thoughts?"

Ceton turns his back to the water until Bolin follows his gaze and interprets its meaning.

"The Arsenal Theater at the Nonpareil? Are you out of your mind?"

Ceton shakes his head.

"Nothing else will do. We don't want to disappoint anyone—least of all now that you yourself have helped to make expectations what they are. I have no doubt that the appropriate contacts can be mustered among the brothers. Would you be so good as to make inquiries on my behalf, Bolin?"

Bolin extends his arms in a gesture that is part irritation, part resignation. He clears his throat and spits self-consciously, swaying restlessly back and forth before he is able to conclude the matter at hand.

"I wonder if it is not perhaps time for you to seek out new quarters, Tycho. I have arranged a suite at mine. All comforts are at your disposal. There is a dividing door, but I have placed a bookcase before it so that you may feel undisturbed. What do you say? There is a cabinet awaiting, filled with garments I believe you may appreciate."

Ceton's eyes narrow in response to this generosity.

"A timely offer, and truth be told, a tempting one. To the extent that one wonders what thorn such a rose may conceal."

Bolin fixes his gaze to the ground to hide his blush.

"My ambush did not go as planned. The result was a mishap of precedence. I must concede that I gravely underestimated the intended victim. Now the situation has been made worse by the fact that Cardell is alerted to the danger, and I cannot in good conscience abuse the resources of the Kindly Ones on such perilous ground. Not without a stronger mandate. I can only apologize."

Bolin is quick to continue.

"At any rate, I have some newspapers that may be of assistance to you. My source informed me that Cardell has since last autumn spent all his waking hours in pursuit of a girl—an escaped workhouse inmate—and with as guilty a countenance as if he himself sold her soul to the said hole."

Ceton nods in understanding.

"I can probably guess whose mother she is, and wherein the guilt lies."

"Cardell has had no luck thus far. But Johan Erik Edman's henchmen in the Chamber of Police are also searching for a girl—also an escaped workhouse inmate—for an entirely different reason. A watchman who attended the premiere of *The Reconciled Father* to prevent the whores from jerking off the rabble in the dark corners of the parterre glimpsed her in the theater alongside a lad who appeared to be leading her, or was perhaps her pimp. My informant tells me that both cases pertain to the same girl: her name is Anna Stina Knapp. Before the war made a cripple of him, our observant watchman ran errands for the Martin brothers in the hope that they would recognize his artistic gifts, and today he always carries paper and charcoal wherever he goes. He had time to draw a likeness of the couple. Copies have now been posted to every customs booth, police barracks, and jail."

"Will you ask your contact for a copy of the sketch?"

"It is done. And chin up, Tycho. If our plans succeed and the brothers take mercy upon you, then neither of these gentlemen is likely to grow too much older."

38

"Good God, it's hot."

Magnus Ullholm snatches the wig from his head and mops his brow with the lamb's skin. Edman is sitting at his desk in just his shirt, his jacket hanging over the back of the chair and his waistcoat folded on top. He fans himself with a bundle of papers.

"Yet we have shade here for at least half the day. Every room on the south side is deserted. Anyone who wanders in there at noon is baked to stone like a troll."

Edman raises a glass, and its contents clink as he cradles it.

"At least we have deep cellars packed with chips of ice."

He drinks with sensual pleasure, gulp by gulp, until it is all gone, then sets the glass down, behaving as if nothing has happened for several moments before inviting his guest to help himself from the jug. Ullholm refreshes himself in silence while Edman watches.

"So no girl despite weeks of reconnaissance. The Gustavian conspiracy proceeds undisturbed."

Ullholm gasps for air for a moment after draining his glass, doing his best to stifle his obvious satisfaction with a downcast expression.

"Our efforts continue."

Edman grimaces in distaste.

"Yet more inquiries?"

"We have plenty of informants about the maiden's rooms. Or, more precisely, the constables and my own men are under orders to ask dutifully routine questions when fucking on credit. We have been searching for the Knapp girl by those means for a long time—I took it for granted that she had returned to her whorish ways again. But all in all, it seems she has not. The divisional superintendents have inspected their households for tenants matching the description, but that has turned up nothing either. A few other useful things have come up, though. Have rumors of the ball already reached you?"

"Which one? People seem to do nothing but dance, despite the heat. How they manage is beyond my wit."

Ullholm leans in closer, eager at the good fortune of being the first to share some juicy gossip.

"It is still a few weeks distant. And in this case it is in your own neighborhood. They are to host a whores' ball in the north wing of the Castle. By Prince Fredrik's consent in the rooms the queen has abandoned for the season."

Edman brushes an unruly lock of hair back from his receding hairline, leans forward, and laces his fingers together to rest his chin upon them. After some reflection, he purses his lips.

"The court will be scandalized; tongues will wag until the end of the year. The feeble-minded will allow themselves to be diverted, the wives of state will chatter like hens, the prince will be sent to Tullgarn Palace in disgrace. Reuterholm will shout and scream and make a din; no one else who matters is likely to care significantly. We can operate in peace. Good! Let the whores grease the axle of state for a change."

His face settles in an expression of satisfaction before he finds his thread anew.

"What does this affair have to do with the girl?"

"I have a passing fancy."

Ullholm's artificial pause serves only to annoy, and Edman's tone is enough to sweep the satisfied smile off his lips.

"Out with it then."

"A general inquisition among the indigent. We block the bridges and sweep the City-between-the-Bridges clean, one quarter at a time. Watchmen, constables, and my own men will work together. I've spoken to Lode, and he to Reuterholm. It will pose no obstacle to make it appear as good statecraft. Stray folk have no friends. They are a burden on us all."

Edman chews a thumbnail while considering the proposal.

"When?"

"I envisage the day after the ball. A Friday. From early dawn all through the day—for as long as we need. The monstrous regiment will be out of the way, still in the same beds to which their duties have led them. Likewise those dignitaries who attended the ball, nursing severe headaches. Only the rabble will remain. We will blockade every bridge, move quarter by quarter from Castle Hill heading south and flush out every stairwell, attic, passage, and unguarded space to be found. The district superintendents will shake every landlord from their bed to count their tenants. Those of good morals will naturally be excepted. Each and every person unable to account for themselves will be forced to head towards the Southern Isle. That is where we shall close the net. Then we shall separate the wheat from the chaff, and any loose and idle soul shall be sent to the rasp and the spinning wheel. If the Knapp girl is to be found in the City-between-the-Bridges, we shall find her there too—mingling with her equals."

Edman nods his assent, counting down the days in his head.

"Use the remaining time well. Waste no spare moment. Set those of your men who are literate to the task of petitioning the newspapers about beggars and vagrants, and make sure that every single letter is printed. Drive public opinion. Guard the bridges. Keep me informed."

39

Baron Reuterholm's Ordinance of Abundance from the summer of last year all began with coffee. The prohibition was met with the same obedience that applied to every similar decree: nonchalance from the rich, disregard by the thirsty, exploitation by the resourceful. Among the foreign diplomatic corps, consigned to the frozen north for their sins, this affront was more than honor could endure: not only had statecraft forced them to engage in a humiliating courtship of the regency's capricious peacocks, but now they were not even permitted to alleviate their suffering with this black gold. Reuterholm, an upstart whose sole mandate lay in his access to the Duke's bored ear, was ignored, and in the diplomatic clubs the silver coffee service was used just as diligently as ever. Quick to take offense, the regime also took notice of this contempt for Swedish law, and the entire ambassadorial staff was summoned before the governor under the pretense of discussing new political developments. Instead, the dignitaries were scolded for their coffee-drinking ways, but the regime had little awareness of the gift they were issuing to their guests from afar in the form of a pretext for indignantly bidding farewell to this crumbling kingdom, this formerly great power now staggering about like a drunk on the brink of the abyss. The kingdom stood alone, cut off from the Continent, the same Sweden that was already living on handouts from abroad and relying on the benevolence of foreign powers for old times' sake. From across the Baltic, the rattle of Russian grindstones could be discerned—a whisper of imminent retribution for the injustices of the previous decade. The Russian fleet consigned to the bottom of Svensksund had been resurrected, bigger, better, and ready to cast anchor. The only defense Sweden had to offer was its courage. What choice was there? Reuterholm entered into negotiations with revolutionary France, the gangrene of Europe, and now, incomprehensibly, it has happened: Sweden has recognized the newborn republic in exchange for the replenishment of its almost empty state coffers, every coin given harvested from ditches where guillotined corpses are stacked twelve feet deep. Sweden, alone in Europe, has been harried into the arms of the universal enemy in the name of stupidity.

But the brothers prefer to speak of other matters, since Reuterholm is a numbskull, the kingdom is going to hell, and every man would be well advised to save his own skin. The heat of August broils Stockholm with undiminished strength and renders the city excruciating—the plume of winged insects laying siege to the City-between-the-Bridges can be seen with the naked eye from far beyond the city limits. Yet there are more brothers than usual here, now that September is nigh. Ordinarily, they shun the city and seek out the cool elsewhere, making for distant summer delights inland, but rumor and expectation have brought them together prematurely. They collect in different kinds of swarms: as guests in each other's drawing rooms, where they drink coffee shamelessly, given that any crime punishable by a fine is openly regarded as permissible to all who can pay their way; in secluded corners of ballrooms, where special handshakes allow them to identify each other; in closed groups that gather in some *petite maison* where they summon procuresses to display what new wares the failed harvest has chased in from the countryside: fresh boys and girls who, although thin in flesh, have so far been spared the blemishes and bruises of city life, those that have some life left in them, and who yet harbor the vain hope that the price at which they sell themselves will buy them something better and render such nights the exception. Those, in other words, for whom the profession has not become routine, who are still capable of exhibiting feelings of desire or fear, or both, or in quick succession. Wares of that kind perish quickly; they decay, their market value plunges, and before you know it, the lump of lead that their dreams have clung to has dragged them down to a point of no return.

But the brothers enjoy them while they can, and for those who can pay, the opportunities seem endless. Pleasures of that sort also demand variation. One grows tired of the same kind of different things. One may think one has found a new source of amusement, but then the morrow comes, and that which once shone so brightly seems at once lackluster and monotonous. Curiosity circulates: What is that disfigured devil up to? What is Tycho Ceton doing? Surely the man is out of his mind, irrespective of how one measures such things? But then again, all those strange whims and quarrels of his may be a confected distraction. Stupid he is not. Bolin's men leak like sieves, selling all that they know for as cheaply as it takes for someone to crack open a barrel and allow them to drink themselves to a stupor. Ceton has bought Spanish fly. The news comes as a disappointment. Who, after all, has not had recourse to such things? Admittedly a member will stand upright if the dose is correct, but it will itch and sting too, and is not the very action itself testament to something awry? The odds on Ceton's future shorten.

There seems to be one thing upon which all are agreed: regardless of its outcome, there can be no losers here. If the spectacle fulfils its promise, then everyone will be happy; if not, then there is always Ceton's fall to delight them. Comments are made at his expense, only half in jest. As Gillis Tosse says, in a stage-whisper:

"If he does not supply satisfaction, I have always wondered how many sailors' cocks would fit in that cut cheek, and if it is too tight, then we can always widen the other corner of the mouth too."

Everyone laughs, but the oppressive heat contains an impatience, a frustration with waiting. The weather must shift soon. The summer cannot last forever; somewhere a thunderstorm is brewing, awaiting discharge. The storm draws near. Nothing can be more certain. And, deliciously, here comes the news that a date has now been set, the invitations circulated by old Bolin himself, so eager that he appears to walk more easily on that gout-ridden foot of his that has bothered him for as long as anyone can remember. A venue has been found—and not just any venue, mind you. The audacity! Rehearsals are being conducted in the utmost secrecy.

40

Bolin has contacts; by having a drunken patron vouch for the organizers' dealings, the Nonpareil is theirs—the new Royal Theater. Negotiations of this kind have always been food and drink to Anselm Bolin, and with well-practiced steps he steers the conversation with the theater's manager until it comes to seem that the idea of nightly rehearsals and a midnight premiere are the man's own suggestions. Now they may come and go as they wish, undisturbed and unseen. The price is easily negotiated down—not that the brothers are poor, but merely as a matter of principle. There are many details to finalize, for the brothers are accustomed to the best and will accept nothing else. The whole place must be spick and span ahead of the premiere; the lighting must be perfect. The performance will be a private one, and no uninvited guests will be allowed to linger. They will take care of the cleaning afterwards themselves, and offer assurances that the facilities will be left in the same condition in which they were received. The manager chuckles at the secrecy. Like all those who oversee desirable venues in Stockholm, he has been courted by his fair share of the city's many orders, each more eccentric than the last, and he winks knowingly at Bolin. Surely they must be planning to stage some kind of erotic comedy—one where the actresses' nipples can be seen through their chiffon costumes, an entertainment designed to please those whose lewd desire has for so long outlived performance? Bolin cannot bring himself to wink back, preferring to pretend that he is flummoxed to have been so easily seen through. The agreed sum changes hands.

Ceton has paced the length and breadth of the stage, examined the backdrops, and selected one for each act. Bolin's man and another borrowed aide—a deaf mute from birth—have been shown those parts of

Johan Schef's newly built theatrical machinery that are needed for the curtain and scenes, a Gordian tangle of ropes, blocks, pulleys, and clattering wooden levers, wheels, and winches that spread out below, above, and behind the stage. Those who, barely two years earlier, witnessed the premiere of *The Jealous Neapolitan*, sprung from the late king's own pen, still speak of their incredulity at the extraordinary spectacle they had witnessed—an Italian valley inside the building, replete with Gothic castle in the background, dowsed in rain and shaken by thunder—before seeing the set move, revealing it to be nothing but a stylish illusion. For the first act, Ceton has found a rural backdrop on which a road winds away into the upstage depths towards a distant walled town beneath a sky that depending on the lighting can show storms or merely harmless white clouds. He has left the stage itself almost empty—here there is nothing but a carpet of sorts to mark out the road as it extends towards the auditorium. If you stand on top of it the distortion falls flat, but he has examined the effect from different angles around the auditorium and found it believable enough, especially in low lighting. For the second act, there is a dark olive grove full of crouching, knotted trees. But it is the mirrors that are giving him the greatest concerns: he is aware that everything must be as visible as possible. The loan of the large mirrors was not easy to secure, nor was it a straightforward undertaking to align them correctly for all the audience to benefit. Each one costs a fortune and must be handled accordingly.

It is with a feeling of elation that Ceton walks up the center aisle between the standing areas separated into their sections. The auditorium rises high above him, the balconies climbing towards the ceiling in three galleries, each decorated with ornate garlands running along hanging arches with rows of stylized lyres, white and golden on pale blue grounds. Everything looks brand-new. The colors and gold leaf shine resplendently. Not even the most assiduous could find a speck of dirt—the soot from tallow flames has not had time to soil the ceiling. This place is full of fragrances: the hemp of the rope and the fresh timber, recently sawn and carved, the pigment of the paint and the potpourri of the dressing rooms. As the building ages, all these will perish in the same sour stable scent—the stench of dirty bodies crammed in as closely together as possible without them actually demanding refunds on their tickets. But there is a long way to go, and Ceton does not intend to make a return visit. He goes through it all in his head one last time from beginning to end, his own tasks as well as those of others. His helpers are waiting, yawning, backstage, eager to go home, and he releases them after testing their understanding with questions until every answer is to his satisfaction. He stretches as soon as they have left him, rolling his head from shoulder to shoulder to alleviate the tension of expectation, and then he steps onto the stage to rehearse the final part alone. He bows to the audience, honored, a step diagonally backwards with one foot, one arm in front of his waist, the other to the side. Over and over. He can already hear their jubilation. He bows so deeply that not even the front row can see his sneer.

41

The night comes and gathers the brothers. Masked men around the midnight hour are no unfamiliar sight around the theaters and palaces of the city—masquerades are once again in fashion following the brief mourning period in the echo of the shots at the Opera. One can once again deck oneself out in armlets and dominoes without being accused of being a Jacobin, and the city has resumed its best-loved occupation— because only under the protection of a mask can one mix unconstrainedly, equals in the knowledge that the hand one has caressed during the minuet may belong to anybody, just as yours too may. Such arrangements spur acts that would otherwise be impossible. Night disguises clumsiness as assertion, chastity dares yield to lechery, and even the most timid ventures a love sonnet. With only one's eyes visible through the holes cut in silken hoods or paper masks, one's intentions can still be made clear. Complete anonymity is difficult, however. The city is small, and the slightest mannerism can quickly betray one. But one does what one can. The countess and her companion exchange gowns. The count borrows a corporal's uniform, the son of a merchant a harlequin costume. Immediately they permit themselves an adventure that is partly another's. A kiss, an embrace behind the tapestry, a friend for the night. All agree on one truth: those who are beautiful may be poor, but those who are ugly must be rich. One makes one's choices, approaching whichever one covets most hotly.

The brothers are of a different sort. Most know each other, but the masks are customary. Never the same mask twice, so the rule goes. They are available to borrow for those who wish to, but many come in new ones, custom-made. Witches, billy goats, knight's helmets, plague doctors. Some are alone, but many arrive in small groups, fresh from the event still going on in the north wing of the Castle, where they have drunk a lot, endured the worst of the heat, discussed the evening's expectations and tried to guess its theme. It is not done to dress up too soon—most make their way into the Royal Garden, where the hedges have shapelessly sprawled in anticipation of the shears that have themselves been trimmed by the governor's office, and when they return they are enfolded in new guises. From a distance, voices and tones can be heard from the Conservatory, where a ball has drawn to a close, with boisterous parties lingering in the warm evening, not wanting to hurry away. A lone violinist has been persuaded to continue playing an accompaniment, and whoever caresses the strings must have been bribed with spirits, because it is well known that the happier and drunker fiddlers are, the more minor their key becomes. The garden has grown wild and is full of shadows where the streetwalkers prowl, aware that many a fellow has not been granted the favors he sought and is prepared to pay for rapid gratification. The brothers' presence draws them towards the Stream. The streetwalkers are chased off by masked men uttering exhilarated and predatory cries, in the certainty that the night bears more refined bliss in its bosom. The palace is offset at an angle to the garden behind it, and the twilight grants a space where one can pass water against the facade in privacy while a stone carving of Mars gazes down from its plinth above the gate, flanked by blind windows.

The evening is beautiful and the Nonpareil is as pristine as ever, its spires, turrets, and chimneys reaching towards the stars, the iron tiles of its angled roof forming a staircase to heaven itself. Many a voice has been raised at the palace's inappropriate transformation into a theater, since every stone in its facade seems dedicated to bloodlust: a frieze lines up cannons, mortars, standards, encampments, and flanks of cavalrymen brandishing sabres. There are lion's head ornaments and decapitated Turks' heads, Roman warriors with plumed helms. Those dreaming their way back to the glories of battle bemoan the fate of the Nonpareil, deriding her new status as the repository of wooden swords, cardboard shields, and silken armor. But to the amusement of the brothers, such decoration is once again apposite.

The firmament darkens, lending the palace the allure of the unknown, a fairy-tale air. From the tower of Jakob the bells chime midnight. Bolin himself stands by the stone steps, clad in a stag's crown and furs. No one is able to cross the threshold without grasping his outstretched hand with the proper grip and whispering a name in his ear, but some have over-refreshed themselves to the limit of indiscretion, and he commits them to memory for reprimand. He exchanges meaningful looks with those he knows so well that no mask can disguise. He hides it well, but his stomach is turning over with expectation and in anticipation of the dangerous path into which he voluntarily stepped. He wonders how he has managed to put himself in such a position, but is unable to summon any remorse. It has been a long time since he last staked anything—so long that he has forgotten the thrill that only risk can offer.

....

"Are you ready?"

Ceton sits in the borrowed chamber two storeys up in the southeast tower—one of those that are otherwise reserved for actors when preparing or resting between acts—with Albrecht on a chair in front of him. Ceton passes him a glass and pours wine into it from a bottle—not too much, but enough to banish any stage fright. The boy cannot conceal the trembling of his hand, and Ceton adjusts his voice accordingly, making it soft and suave by way of encouragement.

"You have nothing to worry about. I've told you many times before. This congregation is different to those you have seen before. Svala's flock are simple by their nature. Meager souls who cannot help but judge others. Even if they disguise their silence as piety, they would prefer to give you their curses than their prayers. Tonight, the listeners are noble and well-meaning. They want to hear your story. Spare them no details. Your voice will carry better than you think, for our guests are here to listen, and the auditorium has been built to enhance voices from the stage. Do not be afraid, for you are among friends."

Albrecht attempts a nervous smile and drinks the wine. Ceton inspects his attire for the tenth time. Prior to the first act, it is the same as that which he normally wears, with worn breeches and a linen shirt sooty and pocked by flying embers from the hearth. Ceton has no pocket watch, but if midnight has not yet passed then it must be soon.

"It's time. Come, let us go. I shall accompany you to the stage and I will be right behind the curtain the whole time."

....

The backstage area is deserted. Bolin's henchmen have taken up their positions in the wings, but their route to the stage is clear: down two sets of stairs and then under. Below the auditorium lies a triple maze of corridors with a shortcut for actors to bypass the intricate waltz of the ropes that operate the scenery. There is something ghostly about these abandoned spaces, these places that exist only to make the fantasies of the spectacle possible. The suspended counterweights of the flies drum against the partitions, stirred by the drafts generated within such a vast building. For all that the stage and auditorium appear exquisite, everywhere you look down here there are glimpses of the violence perpetrated on the building. Floors have been pried up and walls demolished, makeshift staircases rendered permanent when the coffers ran short. Corridors that once led somewhere are now dead ends filled with clutter. Some doors have been nailed shut, others lifted clear of their hinges. The new has preyed upon the old, and here—beneath the surface—the result is repulsive. Ceton illuminates their way with his lamp, constantly alert to the fact that Albrecht is following in his footsteps. Before long, they hear the hubbub—hundreds of voices showing them the way. Bolin's voice strains to be heard.

"Gentlemen! Pray be silent for a tragedy in three acts!"

....

From behind the curtain, Ceton signals to Bolin's man for them to begin—who in turn pats his deaf and mute companion on the shoulder until comprehension is passed on. Reluctantly, Ceton squeezes Albrecht's upper arm in the hope that the gesture will inculcate courage.

"Out you go. Don't be afraid. Wait until they have seen you and fallen silent. Then talk. If you lose your thread, look to me and I'll give you a few words to get you going again."

Taking hesitant steps, Albrecht crosses the line that the shadow of the curtain has drawn diagonally across the boards of the stage, moving slowly and haltingly, like a frightened animal. The light falls upon him, and Ceton hears a change in the hubbub in the auditorium as the attentive alert their neighbors that the drama is ready to begin. Then hissing shushes those accustomed to speaking until they are done. Eventually, there is silence of the kind that can only be afforded by a room full of people. Ceton cannot resist peering out from behind the curtain, and there he sees them—for the first time in a long time: the brothers, all gathered in their majesty. Ranged by rank and temperament across the three rows of the parterre. Cats, lions, fool's caps. Ceton has prepared Albrecht well. The boy knows what to expect. Ceton has promised that it is worth it—the congregation has its own peculiarities just like the Moravians in the Royal Garden have theirs, and where is the harm in it, so long as everything is done in honor of the Almighty? The difference is that this congregation will attend upon his words attentively and with sympathy, and if anyone can help it will be them.

....

The lad is everything Ceton has hoped for. His feelings are as heartfelt as if he exhibited them naked, incapable of hiding anything. His voice trembles but carries, the tears come but do not disrupt—rather, they heighten the emotion. He reminds them of love of the kind they have forgotten— for those who have ever been granted it. The innocence and sincerity of youth, its hopes and promises. He tells of his forefathers' faith, of the incarnation of the bloody bridegroom, of the Moravians' belief in the mystery of wounds. They follow his every step from Prussia to Stockholm, his companionship. He shows a sample of his work that he has brought with him—already hammered into the correct shape. Regret and pain. Wilhelm. Ceton hears the silence change tone to rapt attention—no one dares even cough. Barely a breath is audible. He assumes that the masks in the auditorium have taken on new roles as they also conceal tears. The boy's humble words find an echo in even the most worldly. Many hearts, long since scarred, bleed again—and a bewildering twinge of pain flourishes in a limb supposedly amputated and forgotten. They are reminded of love of a sort that is no longer permitted to germinate in the soil of cynical excess: heartfelt, pure. So ends his tale; he bows his head as the words peter out, and for a moment you could hear a pin drop between the balconies. Then the applause erupts, augmented by supportive cries and whistles. Confused by the response, Albrecht looks quizzically at Ceton while wiping his cheeks on his sleeves, and Ceton mimics a bow until the boy understands and repeats it. He draws Albrecht offstage with a gesture, and leads him back to the dressing room to prepare the second act of the evening. He hears Bolin's voice rise above the noise.

"Champagne awaits you in the foyer, gentlemen! The interval shall last an hour."

42

Ceton leads Albrecht back the way they came. The boy's relief is palpable—a faint intoxication following a trial that has gone better than expected. Once back in the dressing room, he drinks willingly that which he is offered without question—the same champagne as the brothers, albeit adulterated. Ceton flatters, fantasizes, is attentive to the effects, estimates the timing for the dose to be just right.

The brothers stand out in the hall and far up the wide staircase, sousing themselves and freeing tongues that have been obliged to rest. What they have been given is not what they expected, and the mood is passionate. They don't know what to think—many seem reluctant to say anything at all. Reddened eyes in swollen flesh indicate more sentimentality than anyone previously suspected. Others are disquieted and feel their time has been wasted, but they also know that a second act awaits them and do not want to deliver a verdict before the performance is over—perhaps he is playing with them, that man who one can never be sure is smiling or not, and better to stay quiet than say things one must subsequently take back. Over drinks all can agree. In anticipation of the second act, there is a preponderant benevolence—boredom is, after all, their chief scourge. All they have wanted has been available to them since childhood, but that freedom is itself a cause for concern, because what is to be done when the final wish has been granted? What can fill life, once all curiosity has been satisfied? At Madame Sachs's at the Red Sheds one could be entertained by the unexpected, but that establishment is long gone, the imperial house's walls that formerly echoed with lustful moans now furnished with bookshelves full of apocryphal works and ringing with the hymns of Dissenters. The brothers dwell upon what they have heard, playing guessing games as to the sequel. The more they guess, the more the nervousness spreads, for in all traces of expectation there lingers the shadow of disappointment.

Bolin's man has dressed the scene for the second act. The mirrors, the flats, all the rest. From the dressing room, Ceton counts the bells recalling the audience for the continuation of the performance. One, then two, then the third. He plies Albrecht with a few more sips, the lad now beyond any capacity for resistance, like a sleepwalker, but still vigorous, still capable. They make for the stage again, Ceton's whispered words of encouragement coming in a never-ending stream. The lad has to be led by the hand.

Absolute silence has descended upon the auditorium. The lamps are extinguished; only in the center of the stage is there a pool of light. Albrecht is so compliant and dazed that Ceton is able to prop him against a wall before he goes onto the stage. In his fists he already has the tools made to his specifications, for this night only. One is a hammer, the other an awl of sorts, forged in a single piece. The handle tapers into a pointed cone, its length and gauge carefully modulated. He is sweating and has to wipe both hands on the thighs of his breeches before seeking a fresh grip. His heart is pounding—he knows this is the critical moment for him, always so disgusted by proximity to others. The bedroom adjacent to the Tin Tower flickers through his mind's eye, and he pinches his arm to conjure the picture in full. A deep breath, then the stage is his. Ten paces to its center, no more. Everything has been prepared according to his instructions. He finds the spot he seeks, counting the ribs on the right-hand side from the bottom up. The black dot of a solitary birthmark appears to mark the spot. Then he places the point of the awl against the skin, feels the body tense in response to its cold touch, takes aim with the hammer and strikes. The scream is muffled. It takes more force than he had expected—the flesh putting up resistance—and he loses count of his blows before the awl penetrates deep enough and the stalwart bars of the rib cage have given way sufficiently. Disgusted, he watches the red torrent bubble and suck as the lung below finds a new airway. Then it is done. He hurries again to Albrecht's side, shoos his obedient body onto the stage, and unfastens his change of costume—the linen shift that is all that covers him, laced at the back. Heavy arms allow themselves to be easily slipped free. He is led out naked, his path identified by his manhood hardened by the Spanish fly.

Wilhelm is lying outstretched before him in the center of the stage, fettered to a cross wedged at the right height above trestles clad in foliage—silk palm leaves borrowed from the props department. He is resting in the circumference of mirrors with nothing but a narrow loincloth shielding his modesty, slathered with oil that makes his tender skin shimmer as he trembles. Slender limbs can barely move the ropes that bind them. Beautiful, so beautiful. His hair has been brushed back, and a thorn of crowns on his pale temples has drawn small drops of red; his hands and feet are already marked. The face of the Savior has been painted carefully onto the cloth wrapped around his head, his mouth stuffed with rags underneath. Ceton leads Albrecht the final steps, looking into the rolling eyes where confusion and desire dance on the ruins of sense, and he leans in to his ear.

"The bloody bridegroom awaits. See, his side wound opens just for you. There is your salvation."

The pliancy of the wound offers no resistance. Ceton takes a few steps back as it begins, the sound of the act the only noise in the auditorium. As if bewitched, he holds his breath and dares not blink because it will come at any moment—the moment he has been waiting for, that which has so long been refused to him. He listens for the insurrection of creation itself—divine wrath capable of shaking the firmaments, making the ground tremble and cracking the earth into webs of chasms. Wilhelm lets out a stifled cough like a bark from a dog in a cellar, gasping for air under his mask. At his side, the sweat pours off Albrecht, every muscle tensed with effort. Ceton forces his eyelids to remain open even though his eyes are filling with tears from the sight of what is occurring onstage. The hair on his arms stands on end; the shivering grips him by the neck. Below the actors, the puddle stops expanding. Then the final sigh—a protracted wheezing as the lungs' bellows give up. The blood no longer flows, the heart has stopped. Albrecht continues for a while as if nothing has happened, but the flesh cools about him and even in his intoxication he realizes that something is wrong—something has been lost beyond salvation. And for the first time, Ceton dares to shift his gaze and sees his own face in the mirror, contorted into a stiff mask of unsparing fear as the ovations begin behind him, never to end. Somewhere he hears Bolin's cry.

"Break! A break before the final act! An hour!"

The hammer remains in Ceton's hand. He raises it towards his own image.

PART THREE

Inquisition
SPRING AND SUMMER 1795

O noble Reuterholm, my lord! Your glory now I sing,
My muse, redoubled with each year, will mount to loftier wing.
Your valiant deeds my waken'd song shall ever more inspire!
To History's grand canvas now my lines must seek t'aspire.
> —Carl Gustaf af Leopold, 1795

43

There are unknown paths that welcome only the few, and Elias draws a map of them in his mind, helped by the testimony of his own eyes and the awareness of his own ability. A barrel stands by a wall in the alley, tall enough to provide support for a foot to reach a stone ledge revealed by falling plaster, a step allows small fingers to grasp a window frame, a cellar window bar is rusty enough to allow itself to be bowed and let through any who are thin enough. Elias is nothing if not slim, almost twelve years old but with childhood prolonged by hunger, lagging behind and meager across the belly and breast. His smallness is an asset he exploits while it lasts. He can still feign innocence and timidity, gaining admission where no one notices, playing dumb by way of excuse. Few are as good at the art as he. For three years it paid his rent in the orphanage, where he was entrusted only with the simplest of tasks in return for soup and shelter; so impossible was it to bargain him away for fosterage in the country that they eventually stopped taking him on the trips. Elias Blockhead. Boredom was his only enemy, the slow hours in bed when no one could be bothered to ask after him, without any entertainment other than the changing light beyond the window. In retrospect, he misses those idle hours. But he was robbed by age, like everyone else. Arrangements were put in place for him to be moved to the rasp house—an altogether different place where the doors were locked at night, indolence was countered with a slap, and lads who were unable to protect themselves became substitutes for absent wives. He will never forget Matron Ebba's dropped jaw when she left the gate ajar and he seized his opportunity; he closed the mouth he had purposely left hanging open around his swollen tongue and wiped the drool from his chin, leaning close enough to whisper into her ear. She gave such a start that she dropped her bucket.

"To hell with you, you old witch, and thanks for the soup."

And so out through the gate, free as a bird in the crown of a tree, out of reach, fleeing the scene to seek his fortune in the City-between-the-Bridges. He allowed himself a laugh of mockery and joy in response to her belated retort. But even for the quick-witted, life outside the walls is hard.

The route he is following does not test his skills. He knows it of old. A stake supports his one foot, allowing him to reach the top of the wall. He pulls himself up to check that no one is standing in the windows or in the courtyard within, before swinging up his legs and then crawling along its crest until he reaches the gable of the building. The metal gutter might easily give way under a heavier grip, but not his—he heaves himself up and crawls carefully to avoid slipping. The corner building has a copper-clad roof unlike its tiled neighbors. He leaves his mismatched shoes in the gully and wiggles barefoot across the cloudy surface, which is rugged and firm against his bare skin. Up to the window, without a sound. It is open, secured in place by a stay, and the room inside is empty. They have made it as beautiful as they can: the scent of potpourri emanates from a jardinière, and the vases are filled with braided reeds in anticipation of fresh spring flowers. He gets into position and waits.

....

At last, the door is brusquely knocked open, and in hurries a stout woman wrapped in colored tulle, her face and chest covered in white makeup, cinnabar on her lips and cheeks. She brings with her a cloud of nauseating scent: sweat beneath rosewater. He knows her as Little Platen, and her mere presence makes hatred burn like bile in his throat. She even calls herself von Plat nowadays, impudently comfortable in borrowed plumes, claiming to be an heiress, leaving it unsaid whether it be as a cousin, sister, or daughter. Among the street people there are few who believe her, and others who can recall her baptismal name, but then it is the credulity of the customers that is important. Elias sinks farther down as she inspects the room ahead of the assignation, slapping the pillows a few times to ensure they stand to attention on the chaise longue, nudging the hand of the table pendulum clock a few circuits with her index finger to make the time right so as not to betray the clockwork that has stood still for years.

Elias holds his breath in expectation, and he is lucky: the next guest to enter the room is the one he has been waiting for, and she claims his attention to the limits of foolhardiness. She is so beautiful, so beautiful. How old? He has barely learned to distinguish the years from each other among the older folk, but she can barely be thirty. Time has been kind to her: her body is still girlish, the occasional wrinkle on her face solely pleasing in effect. She wears her hair tied up with a blue silk ribbon, and a dress in rose-red muslin in honor of the day. Within these walls, the Ordinance of Abundance has been set aside. Little Platen knows how to grease the right palms, so much so that they dare to entertain worthy guests with the coffee service. Sugar, sugar box, Sugar Klara. That is how she is referred to by those who are familiar with her renown. But Miss Klara is her name. She is followed by Little Platen's maid, who has a sack over her head to spare the world the sight of the ravages of the French disease, her back stooped, arms covered in black barnacles and curved before their time into the wrinkled claws of an old woman. She carries with her a feather duster, broom, and bucket, and hurries to sweep the places identified by Little Platen, whisking spiders' webs out of the ceiling corners, before hurrying away again with the filth.

Little Platen takes Klara by the shoulders and straightens her up for inspection. With a moistened thumb, she flattens an eyebrow and mutters to herself, but everything seems largely satisfactory. To Elias's ears, her voice is like the croak of a magpie.

"Well. I suppose that will have to do. I'll fetch him now. Stand by until I ring the bell."

"What sort of man is he?"

Klara's voice is that of a nightingale by comparison.

"Debutant, or close enough, I dare say. No sophistication in taste. But he may be able to cultivate some with your assistance. Play your cards right and you will have an admirer in your pocket who will last a long time."

Elias cannot see Klara's expression, but when Platen continues he realizes she must have made clear her displeasure.

"Come, Klara. Look at Charlotta Slottsberg. Look at Sophie Hagman. They started on the street and had nothing more in their favor than you do. And see how it went. Princes and dukes fell in love, and hey presto! they are mistresses in court, married off to some compliant count for appearances' sake. Of course, Slottsberg was stupid and let success go to her head—she believed herself to be superior and became reviled for it. But little Sophie knew to be polite and demure, and soon there was no fine salon in which she was not welcome. Summers at Drottningholm Palace, Christmas festivities at the Castle. But now she has been dismissed and Prince Fredrik sleeps alone once again. It is high time that a new talent moves into Little China."

"How shall I ever get there if all you give me are burghers' sons who want to be rid of their virginity?"

Little Platen's voice is cold now. Cold and harsh.

"Those who wish to go somewhere must first refine their art."

Klara laughs mockingly.

"Lying on your back and closing your eyes for five minutes, pretending to groan loudly occasionally by way of encouragement? What more have I to learn that I have not learned in the years I have been yours?"

"Stupid girl. That is not the art. When a man wishes to empty himself, anyone will do. It is the game around it that demands skill. To give and hold back. Ensuring that he chooses you and no one else, over and over; that he lies awake at night and pines, as if his cock were carved from wood. That was an art they knew—Slottsberg and Hagman—and one of which you still have much to learn."

Klara is left at a loss, and Platen opens the doors through which they came.

"Enough. Your next subject is waiting downstairs."

She leaves the room, and Klara takes the side door to the adjacent chamber. Elias carefully shifts his weight on his toes and elbows until he has shuffled over to the next window, and there she is, sitting before the mirror on the dressing table. Scattered across the tabletop is everything associated with her trade: boxes of trinkets, small knives for powder, a spatula for makeup alongside various brushes, earpicks, and a tongue scraper. Her face is red and swollen at first, and she wipes a tear from the corner of her eye, breathing deeply to master herself. Then she takes a pair of tweezers and pulls a straggling hair from her eyebrow. For a long time she sits there looking at her own reflection, eyeing her face from different angles, testing smiles and pouting her lips. Worry creases her forehead when she runs her fingers over the skin around her eyes and neck. Elias holds his breath so as not to disturb this tender moment. On so few occasions has he been given the opportunity to see her up close, undisturbed, just the two of them together. But there is already a racket coming from the far room, and Klara is awakened from her daydream, hurrying to scrape some powder from the box and dab her face. He can hear Little Platen courting her guest, and he moves carefully back to survey the spectacle.

"Mr. Balthazar, is it? Is that a name we may add to the books?"

"By all means."

The man who answers is barely more than an adolescent. He hovers on the spot, rolling his hat between his hands.

"I'm sure you understand that I'm not in the habit of seeking out establishments such as this. The banns have been read for me in church and soon I shall be a bridegroom, and friends who cherish marriage have advised me to acquire some experience in the arts of Freyja."

"You don't want to disappoint your bride."

"Quite. Quite."

"You are a sensible man, and your friends have given you good advice. Won't you sit down? Now, let me tell you. Your wife will be most gratified by a man as caring as you, and not just in bed."

She lays a familiar hand on his arm.

"As soon as I ring the bell, the girl will come in: Miss Klara. If you like what you see, just give me a brief nod and I shall leave you alone. Have you any questions, sir?"

He shakes his head, swallowing hard to summon words. "None."

"Well then."

Little Platen shakes a bell and a gentle tinkling is heard. Klara enters, and as always Elias is fascinated by her transformation and how easily she settles into new mannerisms. She smiles at the guest—a shy smile, but shy as if it were taking all her strength to master her curiosity. Elias spots that the guest is pleased, albeit dumbfounded; only after a long pause does he remember what he must do—he gives his approval to Little Platen and they are left alone. He is like putty in her hands, like a bullock allowing itself to be led by the horns, without knowing whether it is to slaughter or pasture. Elias has seen her do this before with reluctant fascination. Her speech is both simple and ambiguous as she weaves an unaffected incantation over what must occur, making it seem spontaneous and to their mutual delight. She is good. Soon she will have pried his trousers down to his knees and settled him flat on the sofa, having bamboozled him with enough nonsense for him to forget his dread and show his manhood. She lies down in front of him with her back against his chest, taking his member in her hand as he lets out a trembling sigh. While the guest's eyes remain closed, Klara sneaks out a small vial of oil, pouring it into the palm of her hand and then allowing the stiff and oiled organ to slip back and forth between her thighs. The guest is too captivated to notice the difference, groaning ever louder in his pursuit of *la petite mort*. Elias has seen enough. Under cover of the noise, he creeps away to the edge of the roof and puts his hands to his ears. By the time he removes one, it is already over. He waits.

....

The guest leaves first. Then they emerge on the steps below him—Klara and the maid—just as they always do afterwards. Klara has changed out of the borrowed dress into her usual simple cotton skirt, and has left the blue silk ribbon and knotted her French hood underneath her chin. They sit down on the step, each with a broken clay pipe, the maid rolling the sacking far enough up her face to be able to smoke unhindered, turning away from Klara to spare her the sight and affording more of it to Elias. He shudders, and swallows to keep down what little food he has had. It is as if her face has rotted before its time. Elias knows that the disease is an occupational hazard for those who are unlucky. They call it the devil's kiss, and while he knows it to be nothing more than one blight among many, the words paint terrible pictures: Satan himself, his hooves bringing him close enough to lean over and embrace one of the beauties, venom and slime dripping from his yearning lips, and then the kiss, long and lecherous, a wide-open gape and a split tongue diving deep into the throat. Wherever its touch is felt, the flesh is laid bare in rancid wounds that linger and expand until the rot goes deep enough to corrode the very bone, the nose sinking away, the face devastated. He must hurry—hurry before his mother suffers the same fate. He fixes his eyes upon Klara—her beauty even more striking in such company. Klara's sigh draws a question from the maid.

"Well, how was he?"

The words slur slightly, adulterated by her deformity.

"If that wasn't his first time, then it can't have been far from it."

"Easy money, then."

Klara takes a deep drag, holds her breath, and tilts her head back so far that Elias fears discovery before he spots that her eyes are shut.

"And yet I'm tired."

She exhales the smoke into the darkening sky.

"Elsa, tell me truthfully. Am I still beautiful?"

"My dear Klara, you are as radiant as the sun. None is your equal. Platen knows that too. That's why she's tough on you."

The cracked lips fumble through the compliments, and Klara sighs. Her voice betrays bitterness.

"Tell me of a sun that does not set."

She scrapes the pipe clean with a stick, brushing flakes of tobacco from her lap.

"To hell with her and her beautiful words. Had I a better way then I would take it. Well, Elsa, farewell for today."

She takes the gate through the wall, and as soon as Elsa has also left the courtyard to return to her duties, Elias hurries down. He catches up with Klara quickly because he knows she is on her way home and he knows where that is. He follows her from a safe distance all the way to the door of the house where she lives, still with her mother and father, even though her younger sisters have been married off and flown the nest. When she gets home, it is the same story as ever—Elias knows as much because he has heard it many times before. Where have you been? Why so late? Does your reputation mean nothing to you? It isn't just yourself that you bring shame to! But once she has shared the coins she has earned, they lay down their weapons for the time being, and she is able to buy a grim peace at the price of a few shillings.

44

Only with the morning does Elias return. Spring is wet and cold, the departing winter sulky and perverse, refusing to leave without a struggle. He knows a baker whose boys are weary and absent-minded in the morning, and who happily cool off from the warmth of the oven by leaving the window wide open. He carries the loaf he has taken inside his jacket, still warm like a living thing. He has water in a jug from the square, which is where it tastes best—sweet and cold. He takes care not to be seen. The city is cramped and full, every district swarming with people. Yet he still prefers the City-between-the-Bridges over what lies beyond the city limits. Tenements and rooms so full that everyone is nameless. Those who know the art of moving among people unnoticed, who use only those routes that offer other distractions, might well have been wandering in the kingdom of the blind.

In the Cerberus quarter, he has found a neglected hole of a cellar, long since dedicated to the storage of rubbish left behind by generations of tenants, which landlords would prefer to stow away rather than go to the trouble of auctioning off; there is always the risk that doing so might bring legal action on the owners' return. He has tipped a table over on the stairs leading up to the door, and he has piled up junk from the whole alley to conceal the window crevice. A small crack remains, too narrow for an adult, and each time he hurries inside he ensures that no one is looking towards his bolt-hole and clutches his crotch as if he were seeking privacy. He slips lightly down, met by the staircase of stacked objects he has built.

For a moment he is worried, and then his eyes grow used to the dark and he sees her. She sits in the dark as usual—the girl—almost motionless except for the breathing that makes her sway slowly back and forth. Elias calms down, feeling his heartbeats returning to normal, steps closer, and kneels before her.

"Can I look at you?"

He pours water onto a rag and begins to wash her face as gently as he can. When he is satisfied, he removes the shirt that is only hanging around her shoulders and bathes her arms, neck, and torso.

"Now let's make your hair fine."

It is not always that he has soap, and not always that he can wash her completely clean. Now he fills a chipped bowl with water, uses his hands to whip up the soapsuds, and then begins to carefully rub—scalp first and then all the way to the tips of the hair. As ever, he is ashamed by the gleam of the blond color. It has been sullied by the dirt, and he is reminded of how long has passed since the last time. When the final bubble bursts under his careful fingers, he leans her forward and pours water out of the jug to rinse it clean.

The comb is one of his most prized possessions. It is speckled brown, carved out of one piece. Held against the sun, it is almost translucent in places. He has heard it called tortoiseshell, but he has never been able to imagine the animal that might bear something like it. For the sake of the comb, he took an exceptional risk—a brazen theft worth one or two years of penal servitude with a chain around his leg. But the joy each time he uses it is one he rarely otherwise feels. It glides through her thick hair with a long whisper, and seems to share its luster with her flaxen blond locks. He counts each stroke.

"I went to see Mother today, at Little Platen's. I wish you could have seen her. She's the most beautiful of them all, the most beautiful in the city. No wonder Platen watches over her like a hawk."

Tears of indignation appear in his eyes, and Elias blinks to rid himself of them. Here he is the man of the house, and blubbering like a child will not do. He must be brave, must use his thumb and forefinger to grasp the paltry flesh of his left arm and pinch it until the pain drives away the thought. He spits over his shoulder as if Platen's name were an invocation of evil forces.

"I have seen the men that Platen has in her pay. Big, rough creatures.

Everyone does as she says out of fear. Mother has to work off her debt. What other choice has she?"

He lets the teeth of the comb tug at the hair, holding one hand underneath to guide the locks. Soon she will be deloused.

"Mother doesn't understand how debts of the street work. They're never paid. More is added with each passing week than can be chipped away. She will never be free without help."

A solitary tear makes it out of his eye, despite his best efforts. He chokes a sob against his arm, and realizes he has lost count of how many brushes he has done. He starts again. He is still not good at counting—he struggles to keep track of the tens—but he stops when he thinks he has reached one hundred. The uniformity of the strokes is a comfort to him.

"Let's have breakfast."

It isn't easy to ply her with food. He has to break off pieces of bread the right size, soak them in water, and gently caress her lips until her mouth falls open as if for old times' sake, and if he isn't careful he'll finish the whole loaf while she is still grinding through her first mouthful. He remembers with shame all the occasions that has happened, and now he splits the loaf first, taking only from his own half. When she is done, he fetches a chamber pot—cracked but serviceable—and puts it under her before waiting. Afterwards, he cleans her. It is no great endeavor. He still remembers the first time, the blood trickling down her legs, when he thought she was going to die but could not understand why. They laughed in his face when he rushed to the pharmacy with a made-up story about a young sister under his care. Thus he learned that a woman bleeds every month from the time she comes of age, and he was sent away with linen strips to still the worst of it and to be changed frequently. Since he has started eavesdropping on the girls outside the Lizard, he has learned more about the power of the month over the female body, how the arrival of the bleeding must be counted carefully and marked in the calendar, because only on specific days can a man's seed take root in the womb, and on these days certain services must be avoided. In the evenings, he tells the girl all that he has heard. Now he no longer has to wash her. The bleeding has stopped altogether. Once again when he asked why, he was mocked. Is she fat or thin, they asked in reply. Thin, he said.

"Then it's famine."

He picked a flower on his way here—one that has obligingly broken ground where two stones left an open patch. He puts it in her hair, its yellow color deprived of its shine in the gray light of the cellar, and for a while he allows himself to just sit there and look at her. She looks better now that he has made her beautiful. She needs more flesh—she is much too thin—but her skin does not lack luster, and her hair falls well. The same cannot be said for her head. She does not speak, sinking even further into her silence. She moves more in sleep than wakefulness, tossing anxiously back and forth, and only when she is asleep most deeply do the murmured words come. Elias listens as best he can, every word a key to unknown locks.

The first time he saw her, she had two children. One girl, one boy. She came with them to the orphanage. She saw him for who he was—like no other did. She gave them her own bread, blueberries too. The children are gone now. Sometimes he wonders if they would still be alive if he had not spoken so openly of the hardships of the orphanage and scared her off. But no. They do not weigh upon his conscience. Everything he said was true. They would be just as dead, only their suffering prolonged.

She must have kept vigil by the embers for a long time until a wind came and wrenched the ash away with it across the bay towards the city and she followed it. Only on the fourth day after the fire did he dare venture across Klara Bridge. Like all other spoils on offer, the ashes were raked through according to rank: first the adult street scavengers, then the older children, and last those such as himself, all in the vain hope that chance or cunning would bestow upon them something the others had missed. And lo! Barely had he made it to the other side before he spotted her sitting on the stony shore, alone and still, sooty and barefoot, as if dead to the world. He took her hand and she followed him, gently, as if in a dream.

45

He has held what he has been carrying before him while running bent double through the drizzle, but once down on the cellar floor Elias's grip shifts until the bundle is concealed behind his back.

"Look what I have for you."

She pays no heed, still lying on the floor curled up as if she were a child, though at least she isn't sucking her thumb, but Elias is used to this, and in his head he answers on her behalf, easily imagining the replies that hover between desire and suspicion. With a triumphant smile, he produces his gift from the sack he is carrying. It is a dress. Even he must admit that the darkness of the cellar somewhat diminishes its shine.

"Just wait till you see the colors. White and blue, as blue as can be without angering the constables. It was hanging high up on a clothesline above the small yard in Pomona. It wasn't easy to get hold of, you know. One wrong step and I would have broken my neck."

He crawls next to her, brushing the hair out of her face with a tender finger and leaning forward to whisper in her ear.

"Tonight we're going to the theater. Mother is going to dance! Finally you'll get to see her."

The girl's body is heavy, but she is nevertheless oddly pliable. If one pushes, pokes, and pinches her a little, she does as one wishes, even though there's nothing much upstairs and every movement is sluggish as if underwater. He gets her onto her feet and holds her by the shoulders until he is certain that her legs will carry her. Then he pulls the dress over her head, adjusting the straps over the shoulders, and then takes a step back and gives her a reproachful look.

"I know. It isn't a good fit. Not yet. Have some patience. There's more in the sack."

Elias pulls out a depleted pincushion, and with great patience begins to fold the cloth around her body, pinning it into a better fit. Only once does he slip and draw blood, but that does not rouse her in the slightest. It takes him a long time, because the art is new to him, even if he has seen Platen do the same for both Klara and others. The dress, which could originally have fitted two of her, has now been taken in. It has been no easy work to ply her with enough food to allow her to regain some flesh on her meager bones, but he is glad to see that it has borne fruit: the once sunken chest has filled out somewhat, and waist and hips can now be distinguished. He has no hoop skirt to hold out the cloth, but he knows the fashions are in flux anyway and that the fine noblewomen prefer to wrap themselves in simple materials with straight lines rather than large ball gowns with fabric over a farthingale, and he settles for pinning the hem and letting the rest hang as best it can. In the end, he is satisfied; he does a circuit of her, taking a few steps away to contemplate her from a distance. He nods his own approval.

"It's best we're off. It won't start for a while, but we have a way to go and you're not so quick on your feet."

To get her out, he has to go up the steps and laboriously roll aside the table that bars the door. After the racket of doing so, he listens for a long time, welcoming the silence that greets him, attentive to whether anyone in the building has been disturbed or their curiosity has been awakened. He slides back the bolt, holds on to reduce the burden on the hinges, and then he takes her by the hand and begins to lead her out. The rain has stopped, the afternoon light seeping through dissipating clouds. Disappointed, Elias realizes that his skills as a tailor only come into their own in poorer light, but it is too late and anyway there isn't long left until evening comes to his rescue. He finds himself a puddle of water that is still clear, dips his hands into it, and washes his face and hair. Passively, the girl waits to be led wherever the road may go.

The grinding routine of the orphanage has granted Elias a patience that few are given. He knows that crowded scenes that easily weary the impatient can provide enormous diversion to those capable of paying attention to detail. Their slow progress troubles him not at all. He leads her with one arm around the waist, the other clasping her hand, carefully ensuring her plumage avoids obstacles and uncleanliness. She shambles forward, barely lifting her feet, and each protruding edge or loose stone would be enough to fell her to the ground where the dress would be stained and torn to rags. By the time they reach the bridge across the Stream, the dress already looks better again—forgiven by the dusk. Occasionally he shares a few words of encouragement with her, and finds that even if she doesn't seem to hear him, it gives him further courage because now he can see the four towers, he can see people already gathering along the quay and in the Royal Garden, ready for the evening's performance.

Once they join the masses, the movement of the flow of people carries them up the stairs to a man in grubby livery.

"Ticket?"

Elias shakes his head, confused, because he doesn't have one—all he has are the coins he has heard admission costs. The guard shakes his head as if stifling a scolding, peers over his shoulder, takes the coins, and pockets them before jerking his neck to show them in without condescending to address them. When his gaze takes in the girl's face, his features freeze into sudden doubt.

"Oi, brat, how much has your sister had to drink?"

He makes to grab them, but those behind them push impatiently forward and they are already beyond reach.

"If she throws up in the auditorium then I'll wring both your necks!"

Elias need only follow the others onto the parterre. He gapes, unprepared for what awaits him, because above him the room opens up—it is so big that it accommodates its own sky, in which angels hang, gazing down upon the mortals. Along the walls are people, already seated, and their lorgnettes flash in the light of the sconces. Before long the penny drops, and he laughs because never before has it been made so clear to him: crammed in down here are the commoners, who must settle for standing on their own two feet, while above, the rich have upholstered chairs. Up by the stage there is a screened-off box hung with draperies between pilasters clad in gold leaf. At the front there sits a man in his prime, straight-backed in evening dress, with a white wig and a blue-and-white cross on his chest. Elias tugs at the nearest arm and points.

"Who is that? Who is the man sitting there?"

The man turns around in surprise and looks initially inconvenienced, but melts at the prospect of gossip and leans down to be better heard.

"It's Prince Fredrik Adolf himself. Look how glum he is. You can see his lower lip hanging from here."

"Why?"

"Duke Karl has gone to Skåne and taken our little king to be with him. The last time the Duke left, little brother Fredrik got to take his seat and wield the gavel in the council of state, but Fredrik neglected his duties in favor of hunting and other distractions. Now all trust is forfeit. It can hardly be a surprise to him, but he is surly nonetheless. Everyone wants something for nothing, even if few are crowned with success."

They have to stand and wait on the floor for a long time before the curtain finally rises and the performance begins. The same man who enlightened him before whispers from the corner of his mouth.

"That's Hjortsberg, the leading man, the one with the brush and palette. The finest actor to be found in the high north."

The drama begins. Elias's nerves make it difficult for him to follow the plot, and the people up onstage speak quickly and affectedly. Something about a daughter who has married for love, and now her father is angry and she is sad despite her fortune. Like everyone else, he laughs at the dapper Captain Strutz, who behaves comically, lisping in French and stumbling over his saber, a jester of unrequited tenderness. In the break between acts a dance troupe provides entertainment, and finally he sees her, Miss Klara, in a yellow dress. He points her out to the girl—so loudly that others angrily hush him.

"There's Mother. The blond one to the left. Isn't she beautiful?"

With his heart in his mouth, he follows the performance, terrified that she will break a heel or slip on the boards and be mocked by the audience. But it passes without a hitch and when the row of identically dressed girls curtsy to the applause, Klara raises her skirt higher than the others, showing a slender leg naked halfway up to the knee and turning her head towards the box. The applause rises and the entire group leave the stage to whistles and claps. Elias has seen what he came for, and would happily leave straight after the end of the third act were it not for the crowd and the prompter's appeal.

"Don't go yet! The author's going to speak and receive ovations."

A young man is led onstage, barely more than a lad, his neck exposed and his cravat hanging loose. He speaks too quietly to make himself heard, and at first they shout at him to speak up, but when they see him blush and hear him slurring and stammering, they realize that he is most definitely intoxicated. Enthusiastic calls follow, inciting him to make a fool of himself until the management sends forth their men to lead him away and save him from himself. Only now does Elias notice that the man beside them has pulled apart the seams in the side of the girl's dress to make himself a slit and he is fumbling between her legs with his hand. Elias strikes his arm away with an angry shout and the man smiles at him derisively.

"Shame on you, boy. Have I not done you a good turn? May I not frolic a little by way of recompense—surely it does no harm? Perhaps I am taking something she has not enough of for all who want it? And besides, who are you to take that tone? For I most certainly hear no objections from her."

46

Once outside, Elias's good mood has been replaced with dejection. The thrill he felt in his belly from the vision of Klara has given way to an anxious ache. When he looks at the girl now, it is apparent to him that his efforts have been in vain. She is like a doll clumsily dressed up by an uncomprehending child. Her skin is gray and sallow, her hair lank. The dress he was so proud of is ugly and ragged, hanging like a limp sail, even worse now that his inadequate fastening has been pulled apart. He erred from the very first moment. The occasion made him a thief, and he should have known better. What was he thinking, pinching a garment from the poor quarter of Pomona? The fabric is worn and the colors faded, the vapor of others' bodies lingering despite laundering. A dress like this must be able to count more years than their combined ages—a multiple hand-me-down not even fine enough to accompany its owner to their last resting place. He shakes his head. This will not do. Not at all. He tugs her by the arm, harder than necessary, until her legs obediently move.

Someone is following them. Elias doesn't know how he knows, because initially there are many going the same way, but he makes a habit of glancing over his shoulder. One never knows what dangers lurk behind your back awaiting their moment, and he sees a shape—lean and lopsided. While others hasten to reach their homes before the evening grows later, it is as if an invisible rope is tugging the stalker along behind them on the same course and at the same pace. Perhaps its limp is feigned as a way of walking as slowly as he and the girl, or perhaps it is in fact a pursuit—albeit one the stranger is ill-equipped for. Elias does what he can to hurry along, ducking round a street corner into an alley where he knows he will find an opening into a courtyard with other escape routes. He chooses one of them on the spur of the moment, rounds another corner, and shoves the girl ahead of him, underneath an abandoned carriage. His tries hard to breathe deeply and quietly, and puts a hand across the girl's mouth to subdue her too. Soon he hears the footsteps he has been waiting for, and their irregular step confirms the limp to be genuine. They stagger back and forth as their owner seeks out new lines of sight, peering round corners in the hope of catching a glimpse of the backs of the prey. He can hear from the voice that it is a man when the profanities begin—gross oaths improvised with the sensitivity of a virtuoso. He takes out his anger on a broken funnel, with a kick that sees it rattle away across the cobbles. Through the spokes of the carriage wheel, Elias sees him leaving. Blue jacket, dented hat, dirty white swordbelt with a whip instead of a blade. A watchman—typical of his kind, an emaciated and discarded soldier whose toes have been blown away or cut off, or his legs broken and so badly healed that they must constantly languish in splints. Elias looks quizzically at the girl's indifferent face.

"Sometimes I wish you could talk."

He takes her by the hand and leads her away to safety.

47

Elias has fallen asleep. It has become easier with the passing of the weeks, now that the summer is half-done and the heat has mastered the city. There has hardly been time to feel gratitude that one need no longer freeze before the heat becomes a torment, but it is still preferable. He rejoices in dozing off, feeling all his troubles fade away into blessed indifference as his eyelids slide together and his existence is put on hold. Now he wakes with a start, and as soon as he moves he feels unexpected pain, because all around him the roof sheeting is so hot that his skin aches; the heat can only be endured where his own sleeping body has been in shade. His lips have cracked and his thirst is great, and for a few moments he is confused before he realizes where he is, and why and how he has been awoken. He is lying beneath the window, and from the room there come voices. Her hoarse croaking—the jailer, the witch:

"Copenhagen is on fire. Have you heard?"

"Surely everyone has by now, and I can't believe you sent for me to help you mourn the Danes."

Platen chuckles artificially at Klara's witticism.

"No, my sweet, you haven't made any great secret of the fact that my establishment is too small for you of late, and that your gifts have not been displayed as they should be. And I, for my own part, have sought your diligent patience and promised that better times are coming."

"I . . ."

"Well, let us set aside these long-standing grudges. If you listen carefully then you will soon hear good fortune knocking on our door."

Elias peeks over the edge of the window. Klara and Little Platen are alone in the room, the latter inviting Klara to sit down on the sofa with a sweeping gesture.

"You are most definitely too young to remember, and even I had barely been deflowered. It was one summer—sixty-eight, or perhaps sixty-nine. They threw a ball at the Castle, in the rooms belonging to the Military College. Hasenkampff was host—a lewd fellow whose proposal to Baroness Wrangel had been accepted, but despite his married status he remained a monarch among libertines, and likewise in high standing at court given the amusement as his impudence. He wanted to host a carnival to surpass all others, and at Stockholm Castle itself. Well, Miss Torstensson, foremost among the city's procuresses, was tasked with inspecting the monstrous regiment for action. She gathered them all together—the most beautiful, the best, the most notorious. Asunander was there, the Dress, Lambkin, At-tendée, Spaas. Such a gathering of society ladies has never been seen, before or since. The ballroom was not large, but in the adjacent corridor there were a dozen offices for officials that had been equipped in honor of the evening with bunks and mattresses. There they relieved each other with increasing frequency as the evening progressed. It became wilder and wilder. After midnight, I saw Kjellström dancing a minuet in just her bodice, passed from embrace to embrace. She was only some twenty or so years of age, beautiful as the day. A few hours later, the lovers lay in heaps under gut-tering candle stumps, everyone sharing what they had and no one able to say who had taken and who had given. There was naturally a great scan-dal afterwards—the papers wrote of nothing else for weeks. Poems were composed in homage to the heroics of that night, and in mockery of those who fell short—a tribute to love or in defense of morality. The only person punished was the attendant, who was given his marching orders."

Little Platen has slowly approached the window, absent-minded in her recollections—she is so close that Elias doesn't dare breathe because a single glance down would reveal where he lies. But then she spins around on her heel, throwing out her arms for dramatic effect.

"It was almost thirty years ago. Now they're going to do it again. The Military College may have moved out and the dowager queen may have moved in, but she is at Ulriksdal for the summer. The north wing is to be made ours for a night."

At first, Klara is silent for a moment, a meekness that testifies to doubts. "Is the memory of the Castle's overseers no longer than that?"

"Ah, but only now do we get to the best bit! Prince Fredrik Adolf has given it his blessing. He is already out of favor at the Castle, and now he wants to thumb his nose at all of them, right in front of little Reuterholm and his pretty courtiers. It's his own idea, and they say the prince himself shall attend the event—incognito, of course, but you'll make quick work of penetrating his disguise once you have the opportunity to see him up close. Here is your chance, my restless little sweet. The one you have so feverishly pined after. Give him a night he will never forget—one that he will want to experience again—and happiness shall be yours for all time, for eternity."

"When?"

"The last week of August, on the Thursday. Go down to Elsa and talk of clothes."

He hears the door creak under its own weight and Little Platen crossing the floor alone. While she is in the room he dare not move. Fatigue washes over him again, insidiously stifling the elation he feels at what he has heard, and soon he can no longer keep his eyes open. When he wakes up, the moment is so similar to the last that at first he thinks he must be dreaming, but then he sees that the shadows have grown longer and that the afternoon has already turned to evening. There is yet another conversation taking place in the room, and when he peers inside he sees Platen talking to a girl he has never seen before, brazen in appearance despite her youth. The words however are familiar.

". . . and happiness shall be yours for all time, for eternity."

48

E lias pushes the heavy pendulum of the handle back and forth, and soon water emerges from the mouth of the lion—at first in a feeble pulse, but soon in a steady cascade. The summer has grown agonizing in its heat. After a moment of hesitation, he sticks his whole head underneath the jet of water and feels his entire being rejoicing through stinging skin. When he can no longer keep it there, he takes a step back and shakes himself before cupping his hands to catch the water, which he drinks in deep gulps. Behind him, an old woman swears halfheartedly at the splashing. Others join the chorus—there are many who think this street urchin has a nerve to queue among folk who need the water for more sensible things. But for a brief moment, the heat of the sun feels like a caress on his wet skin, and he leans back with his nose towards the sky.

When he first spots it, he thinks he must be seeing things, because the moment he looks back down at the earth the round sun continues to hover in his sights. It is a piece of paper pasted to the stone of the well, and when he steps closer he is able to confirm his first impression. It is her—the girl—drawn with a few simple lines, but still unmistakeably her. High cheekbones and a small brow, empty eyes set in beautiful features. And next to her a boy, shorter, with a blunt nose and matted hair. He snatches the paper and runs towards the stairs by the Stock Exchange. In the shade of the arcade, he examines his reflection in a window, moving his face back and forth to make the image swerve beneath the bubbles in the glass as he compares himself with the drawing. Surely it is him. Someone has drawn them covertly. Beneath, there is something written. Elias cannot read it—he has never understood how ornate ink can be transformed into language for common folk to understand. While others were forced onto cramped benches to learn the catechisms of Luther, Gråberg, and Svebilius by heart, they stuck a twig broom in his hand and left him in the yard, and when the others came streaming out with the backs of their hands striped by the cane, he laughed to himself happily. Now he feels regret, as he does more frequently since taking life into his own hands. The secrets of scripture are closed to him, and panic squeezes his chest as he screws up his eyes over and over before opening them and looking down at the sheet of paper as if he could surprise the meaning of the words out of it before his ignorance washes over them. To no avail. Instead, Elias rubs his thumb against his illustrated face until the features are blurred. He runs over to the first man he spots, an apprentice painter carrying a bucket of lime and brushes, his other arm threaded through a ladder, and stands in his way.

"Please can you read this?"

At first the man thinks he is making fun of him and he looks around for a group of friends on the lookout to laugh at him. Then he sees Elias's seriousness, his red face and his breath panting with agitation, and he bends down to look.

"First it says 'Boy.' Then . . ."

His lips move without emitting any sound until his patience runs short and he blushes at his meager attempt.

"Why don't you fuck off, you little brat, if you know what's good for you."

He turns his body, making the end of the ladder swivel dangerously and Elias only just manages to avoid its blow. He takes his leave at a dash.

"You'd best lime your face so the shame doesn't show so much, you son of a bitch."

He runs down towards Ironmonger's Square, and by the time he reaches the corner where anonymous lampoons and pasquinades are usually posted, he spots another notice just like the first. There is yet another down by the pump. He rips both of them down and stuffs them into his trousers. There is one more on one of the pilasters of the German Well. Down on the long street he eventually stops an older man whose vanity can be flattered into reading. The man makes a great to-do of the enterprise, tucking the frame of his spectacles over his ears with ceremony and peering reproachfully at Elias over the top of them as he clears his throat.

"Boy, if you are seeking a buyer for your wares, seek me out at your convenience."

Then the name of a street and the number of a door.

49

What Elias must do forces him into unfamiliar territory, driving him to take risks of the kind he otherwise avoids. His years in the city have taught him the craft of thievery. It is simple: be nondescript, strike when attention is elsewhere, be quick, don't be greedy, keep guilt off your face. Now he notices new difficulties—ones that he cannot overcome by himself. The goods he seeks are only available in places where he ought not to be. As soon as he shows his dirty face and worn-out rags, conversations fall silent and people stare at him crossly, waiting for him to state his errand. The apprentice pharmacists at the Raven chase him back over the threshold the very moment he crosses it. Instead, he assumes a position outside and he waits. He tries to peer inside to see what is being bought, but to little avail. Backs obscure and the light dazzles. Often maids go inside and shop in groups of two or more. There is no option but to rely on chance. When someone walks alone he follows her, and where the crowd is at its thickest he steps on her heel, pushes her back, and makes her trip, and as others hurry to help her, the cloth bundle she bore is nowhere to be found. He has rounded the corner into an alley, then another, and another as he roots through the items for what he seeks. He must repeat the process several times, watching over the Crown, the Angel, and the Swan too. The tins and boxes are covered in labels he cannot read, and he must open each and every one to examine their contents. Pills and powders are chucked into the gutter.

Nevertheless, the dress is hardest—and most important. It has to be perfect this time, not like last time. The ignominy of the theater is fresh in his memory, but he comforts himself with the fact that he would prefer to have blundered in the past than to be condemned to do so in future. On the streets, all is gray and dull; clothes are only to hide nudity, devoid of all playfulness and ostentation. There are no drapers in the city who dare openly advertise better goods either, and on the clotheslines crisscrossing the narrow skies of the alleys hang only items of little value. Elias now knows that he started at the wrong end last time, and once the solution occurs to him it seems obvious. Why pinch a dress at random rather than seeing it on the right model? He strolls about the square and the Ship's Bridge from dawn until late into the evening, when the revelers at the Stock Exchange have danced themselves to exhaustion. The illuminations of the windows spill their lights onto the steps, and from his hideout by the well he is able to catch a glimpse of wives and daughters in their finery, just before their escorts drape shawls and coats over their shoulders to protect them from the evening breeze and to flatter their own chivalry. Many parties are then swept away by carriage, but for some a servant awaits to light the way with a lantern on a holder. Finding the right one is a long-winded task, but Elias knows that patience is the poor man's asset and he accepts the task with equanimity, trying to find the best vantage point from which to broaden his view.

He sees her for the first time one morning, led by her governess: the dress is pale blue and invites the dawn light to play in its folds, hemmed in lace. A shawl covers her shoulders. The girl is slim at the waist and hips, her hair blond; she could be a younger sister. He hurries closer, but in the crowd she is lost and when he picks an alley at random he finds he has chosen the wrong one. He runs back to the square and tries another, but the opportunity has slipped through his fingers. With a sob in his throat, he pounds his knees with his fists while bent double catching his breath.

He has to wait a week before he finds her in the same place, and this time he is ready. This time the dress is pink, albeit pale so as not to challenge the Ordinance of Abundance. She carries a parasol to shield her white skin from the sun, and when he creeps closer he hears her humming to herself while her governess assumes a stern expression and urges her to hurry. The closer he gets, the more certain he is. She is the right one.

They disappear into a courtyard, and before long Elias hears hesitant notes climbing a scale before descending again. He follows and ventures to a low-set window. The girl is sitting at a harpsichord, her cheeks slightly blushing. The governess has absorbed herself in a book while the music tutor—a young man in a neat waistcoat—has found the best spot from which to feast his eyes on the girl's décolletage under the pretext of observing her fingering. When the lesson draws to a close, Elias follows them home. He is careful, but soon notices that he appears to be invisible, and the closer he gets to them the better he understands why: their two worlds merely overlap in the moment—they use the same streets but for journeys so disparate that he might just as well be a phantom to them.

It takes time for him to learn her habits. Rarely is she alone, always in tow behind the governess. Often they spend their days at home on higher floors of which Elias is denied sight. He acquaints himself with the house as best as he can, staying late into the evening to learn the sequence in which the rooms are extinguished, following the flickering through the windows as it pilots the household to bed. He soon knows where she sleeps. He knows not what the fine folk do with all their rooms, but guesses that the dressing room must be beside it. Music lessons are on Tuesdays, and on Thursdays she meets a dance tutor, but the daylight discourages him from making an attempt. Rather, he chooses the eve of a holiday when she accompanies her parents to a ball and the governess appears to be alone in the house. Elias's courage grows with each evening he spends by the walls of the house. As always, time seems to rush through the summer months as if it prefers the dark and cold, the nights becoming ever blacker, and he knows now that the window illuminated from within becomes like a mirror if the background is dark enough. He has tested his theory outside the inns, tapping on the window and sticking out his tongue at the lecherous men inside, but he has received nothing but puzzled expressions in response and no scoldings. When the governess is alone on the bottom floor, he can follow her from room to room, close enough to mist the glass. He sees her swiping tasty morsels from the larder, and examining herself before the mirror, wrapped in her mistress's stole, before lying down on the chaise longue and slipping a hand under her nightshirt, breathing heavily.

With time, Elias has come to know the girl's entire wardrobe. He knows what he most wants: something similar to what Klara usually wears, something light and airy, easily tied at the waist with a silk ribbon and made from a cloth so fine that its caress practically shows the body beneath. A garment where provocation and modesty are accommodated on equal terms. Preferably the blue one. The one he saw her in the first time.

50

E lias believes he has found the best way in. An adjacent, lower building leans against her house. From the neighboring roof, he ought
to be able to reach a window if fortune is on his side. The alley outside
is narrow—even in the event that someone were to pass, the facades
hardly encourage sky-gazing. He awaits the evening, sees the party leave,
squints in at the governess who is pinching plum brandy and yawning
with increasing frequency.

The stairwell next door is of a far inferior kind, and he uses it to gain
access to the roof through a hatch. He has blackened himself to resemble
a chimney sweep, and now he leaves black handprints on everything he
touches. Tiles here, treacherous ones that creak under his weight, each
one ready to crack and send its shards down into the alley like a shower
of hail. He carefully climbs up the slope towards the point where the roof
ridge meets the next building. Once up there, he follows it to the corner.
Nauseous and frightened, he stares down—frozen to the spot for a while
in this dreadful place where the difference between safety and doom is
a single step. The abyss whispers its invitation to him, and he closes his
eyes and embraces the warm stone until its voice falls silent. He must edge
round the corner, find a grip on the dormer window, and get a foot onto
the sill. He feels plaster crumbling under his hand, which is in turn stained
yellow by vitriol. Yet he finds a better grip the next time he tries, his slippery sweat absorbed by stone chips. His grip holds. Now his foot. He
hesitates, but crouched halfway round the corner he realizes that the way
back is now just as risky as the one ahead, and he makes his choice. For
a second he sways on the edge, digging in his heels and fingers to wedge
himself firmly, and an urgent craving suddenly drops into his lap. Beyond

all rhyme and reason, he can tell that he needs to piss; he must empty himself at any cost, and without being able to change his grip he holds a leg out over the void and lets it run. When he is done, the blessed relief that descends trumps the discomfort. Once satisfied, he notices that he has managed to keep his foothold dry. He uses an elbow to press against the windowpane. Panic resurfaces when he finds its resistance greater than expected, and each new attempt also pushes his own body towards disaster. Eventually it cracks with a resigned crunch, and he carefully picks away the shards until his hand can reach inside to lift the latch. Inside the room, his legs shake until they will no longer carry him. He crouches and wraps his arms around his chest, closing his eyes and humming a song to himself—a melody that he likes, but only those of its words that bring comfort, not fear, over and over.

"A boy stood by a flowing stream, between rich sheaves of rye, and gazing on the water's gleam, his own fair form did spy."

Life has taught him that feelings are just as much a part of the body as the mind, and that time itself is the best comfort. After a while, he feels better. He pays attention to the ongoing silence within, and when he is sure, he leaves the shelf-lined box room by carefully nudging the door ajar, creeping across the corridor, and trying to find his bearings.

His long hours spent outside serve him well. He can count the doors, and gets the right one on the first attempt. It is the daughter's dressing room—right beside the bedroom where the night-light goes out first. Although the dim light turns all colors to gray, he finds what he is looking for almost immediately. The blue dress is hanging alongside the others, and he carefully lifts it out. He doesn't want to risk staining it with his dirty hands, so he nudges wardrobes and chests ajar, searching for something appropriate to wrap his booty in.

....

He pulls out a drawer at random and finds it full of clothes of a kind he hasn't seen before. He holds one of the garments up in the dark, and wonders to begin with whether they are discarded children's clothes. It takes a while for him to realize that it must be a skirt worn underneath the others—closest to the body. The feeling that consumes him is strange and unfamiliar, but also tickles him, and he buries his face in the fabric, saturated with the scent of lavender. Elias glances out through the window and listens carefully before opening the connecting door. Her bedroom is silent and dark, the sheets on the bed neatly stretched out between its four posts. He touches the material, soft as a breeze, and hesitates, but knows that he has been given an opportunity that will surely never come again. Taking care so as not to make the bed creak, he crawls up on it, finds his spot, and feels the yield below. The softness of the bed takes his breath away—the bed is like a forgiving embrace, as far from the wooden bunks of the orphanage as a high-floating cloud. He pulls the quilt aside and has to put a hand to his mouth to prevent himself from laughing out loud at the feeling of it in his hand. It hardly seems to be of this world, neither solid nor liquid, light but warm, the cloth shimmering with delicate flowers but so pliable that their texture is barely tangible. He carefully crawls underneath it, feeling its weight over his body, feeling the tension ease in a sobbing sigh.

Above him there is an undulating cloth ceiling where waxed and folded paper stars hang suspended from threads. Leaning against the pillow beside him is a knitted doll, her hair in braids, coquettish in her small dress and with a beautifully embroidered face that smiles at his touch as if he were a welcome guest in her world of thoughtfulness and opulence. He reaches for her, hugs her in his arms, and places his cheek against the crown of her head.

....

He is awoken by noise from the corridor, steps coming closer. He barely makes it out of the bed before the door opens, staggering on numb legs that threaten to give way. The blood rushes to his head and his eyes darken, and he only just manages to catch her at the doorway, draw her into the dark, and grip her so as to prevent her from crying out her surprise.

51

Only after midnight does Elias venture out from his hiding place down on the Ship's Bridge in a corner behind a barrel, shrouded in the musty vapor of rainwater. He gently tries the ankle he twisted in his flight down the steep stairs, opening and closing fists that ache where he pounded fruitlessly against the inside of the door before he managed to muster the sense to try the bolt. The house empty, the governess's snoring still audible. Then out, away. Someone must have brought the girl home early and dropped her off at the gate. His hands are stiff as if cramped, as if every tendon has locked into a firm grip—only by bending and prying does he manage to straighten the fingers, the pain running up into his forearms.

There are blood spatters on the blue dress, an ugly stain that he has been staring at for hours, bent double over the bundled-up fabric he has been hugging in his arms. Now he sees yet more on his own sleeve. He hobbles down to the wharf where he can most easily reach the water and kneels by the bottom of the steps to scrub the cloth clean. A sudden sob takes him by surprise as the washing awakens memories. The blood was his own that time, because they beat him often in his early days at the orphanage. He knew back then that they would never stop if he gave them the obedience they demanded, and instead he transformed his face into one that was blank and expressionless, his body limp and sluggish, and he let them hit him until they grew tired. The tears and trembling only came when he was alone and no one could see him. Thus he taught them that the cane was of almost no avail with little Elias, who was too stupid to feel pain like the others, and soon he was only whipped for the sake of it, when someone lost their temper and needed a pliable body upon which to direct their rage, someone without the wit to question what he was being punished for and who wouldn't tell afterwards. How he loathed them in secret, their faces absurd amid the grimaces of their rage, like infants who had soiled their swaddling clothes. Never had he seen himself in their place. If only he hadn't fallen asleep. If only she had wanted to stay quiet. But beneath his silencing hands the scream quivered, and none of the words he chose for comfort would make it stop.

The seawater is black and oily on his fingers. Time and again he dips a fold of the dress into it and rubs the cloth against himself. The light is poor, no colors can be distinguished, and his tears dazzle him—but he can see enough to tell that the stain won't come out, ever. He shivers in the heat of the high summer's eve.

52

"Damn this confounded summer. It's a wonder the wells haven't run dry. But soon it will be over."

Johan Erik Edman gives Ullholm a look as the chief of police stands in the doorway, clutching his wig and hat, mopping sweat from his brow using the sleeve of his jacket. Edman grunts in response, and Ullholm seeks out a chair to sit on.

"How goes the hunt?"

Edman shakes his head and loosens his cravat.

"Reuterholm is desperate. With each passing day, he becomes harder to deal with. I think it is at its worst now: he remains omnipotent, although he realizes his days are numbered. This year will be his last. If he is to succeed in burning King Gustav's legacy and salting its soil, it is now that it must occur. I take it you have seen the pamphlets?"

"I've only heard about them, not read them."

"If nothing else, the fellow is a genius when it comes to undermining his own ambitions, and I believe I know why: it cannot be easy to comprehend how normal folk think if you have only ever seen them from the castle window. Well, the first is a printed letter from the Swedish ambassador in Naples, who refutes the allegations that he arranged the assassination of Armfelt, with a zeal that verges on fire and brimstone. *Entre nous*, there are few who are capable of being so upset about anything other than the truth. The second is a set of letters written by Armfelt to the conspirators who have already faced the courts, published to further insinuate their guilt. The public seem to agree that the first letter was authored with less dignity than becomes a representative of the kingdom, and that the others are a petty attempt to sprinkle salt on the wounds of those who have already taken their punishment. The only result is that those who have hitherto doubted that the Baron is a small-minded bastard with a long memory have found it increasingly difficult to assert their case."

He holds out his hands in resignation, falling silent and then finding a new subject.

"What shall you do next, Magnus? Once Reuterholm has gone home to Finland and the king takes the throne?"

"I'm quite contented where I am. When Reuterholm and Armfelt are both forgotten, I shall sleep late into the morning and see to my health. And do you know something, Johan Erik? I have considered the matter carefully: it takes a lot for a chief of police to be held accountable for something. What's more, the role is far too visible. The day they tire of me they will have to grant me an honorable discharge as evidence of their satisfaction with my zeal. Anything else would be proof of their own stupidity. What about you?"

Edman grimaces.

"You have it easy. Everyone knows who the chief of police is, but a keeper of the records can easily be dismissed without any harm to the Crown, even if its powers are for the moment limited. If I am to succeed old Lode as chancellor of justice, I must prove my competence in office without acquiring enemies. I must be zealous and rise above politics, gain the respect of all, but cause no offense. There are no comfortable laps upon which to be dandled—that much I must admit. Which brings us to today's topic: if we can just find Anna Stina Knapp and the letter from Rudenschöld, then neither of us need worry about the future. It will resolve itself. Is everything ready for the big day?"

Ullholm smiles in response, quite certain.

"It must be said that it hasn't been easy patching together the necessary strands, but yes, everything is ready. The constables will begin at the Mint and sweep the city clean. They have practiced the maneuver and will continue to do so until the last moment. The vagrants will be driven towards the Southern Isle. That will be the end of them. Including the Knapp girl. It will be one hell of a scene, Johan Erik. One the city shan't forget in a hurry."

53

Elias wakes early to memories of an anxious night during which he tossed and turned in the vain hope of finding a position that would cradle him to peace. It seems to him that his nights have all been the same of late: memories of that soft bed soon replaced by nightmares. An awakening, and then it all begins again in a hopeless maelstrom before the dawn light brings its comfort. He splashes water from the jug onto his face, and he is at once clearheaded, the meandering thoughts that have peopled his slumber with blurry caricatures now clean and straightforward: day is here. Tonight it is due to happen. Exhilaration and fear are mixed in equal measure. He stretches his arms above his head over his filthy blanket. Somewhere inside the drift of rubbish there is the sound of a rattling escape: a rat frightened by the sound of him. He rubs his eyes clear and turns over, and there she is, lying with her eyes half-open, staring into nothingness. Each morning is the same: for a moment cold shivers run down his spine before her small chest betrays a breath and lets him know that she is still alive. Sometimes he wonders if she ever sleeps, because he has never managed to catch her with the peace of sleep written on her face. She stands still at her crossroads between sleep and wakefulness, her eyelids half-closed, her face slack, only her brow and temples occasionally disturbed by an anxiety that creeps beneath the skin. Elias mixes a fistful of oats with water in a bowl, stirs it with his fingers, and sets it aside to soak before he begins feeding her a little at a time. Each pinch of food necessitates a reminder to swallow. He brushes her hair back to reach her better.

"We've got a lot to do today. You must be patient—do you hear me?— and try to help me as best you can, even if it will be difficult."

....

He fetches water from the well. It is early and the few people who have already risen from bed are still drowsy, yawning constantly. It is already hot—the day promises to be sweltering, the culmination of the week just gone. Back in the cellar, he crumbles a shard of rose-scented soap into flakes, dissolving them in water, pulling the shirt over her head and scooping the liquid over her hair in an attempt to create a cleansing lather. He washes her from head to toe—all over. Afterwards, he moves her onto the floor, where a slanting beam of light filters through the glass and he can see better. Nervously, he spreads out the summer's stolen goods before him, small tins of every kind, and opens them one at a time to expose their secrets. Anxiously, he chooses one at random—some white and claggy stuff—and begins rubbing her skin with it. He has tried to see what Klara does in front of her mirror, and he knows that the red goes on the lips and cheeks, the black around the eyes. On several occasions, he has to wash it off and start again. Since time is passing, he listens for the chime of the bells, feeling grateful for his advance planning.

Finally, the dress. He has almost forgotten what it looks like, hidden away ever since he brought it here, but now he separates its creases and measures it against her shoulders. Eagerly he pulls it over her head, ties its ribbons, and finds all his hopes have been surpassed. It is a perfect match for her blue eyes, and while its owner was younger, the width is right. Attired for festivities, the meager body is no longer a symbol of poverty, but instead of moderation, humility, innocence.

"Let me look at you."

He leads her in a circle with both her hands in his, and what he sees makes his eyes fill with tears of emotion.

"How beautiful you are."

He bows to her and extends his foot in courteous invitation, and then begins to move her gently round and round, luring the vacant body into a sluggish dance.

....

When the hour has struck and the light has departed from the alley, he wraps his blanket around her—the one that serves him as his bed—and lets the hem hang over her eyes. Once outside, he chooses Priest's Street rather than be visible on Long Street, which is full of people even at this late hour, and each time they encounter an empty alley he takes it, preferring an undisturbed circuitous route over a direct one. Outside the inns people gather in clusters, their shirtsleeves rolled up and their buttons undone to better cool their bodies. People curse the warm beer from those innkeepers who lack better storage. They continue to be fleeced for anything that is meat—those who are poor and thoroughly sick of crusts must gnaw on salted pork like a becalmed sailor. Elias steers her around them as best as he can, muttering words of encouragement and praying silently that no loose cobble will trip them now that the goal is within sight.

Finding the right place is not hard. Up by the Castle, the outer courtyard is deserted, except by a doorway in the far corner where lamplight spills onto the cobblestones. Outside stands a man in uniform of a kind that Elias has never seen before. The man inspects them while twirling his mustache, and a wry smile crosses his lips.

"Well, well, well, aren't you a strange one? So, what have you got under the cloth?"

Elias lets the blanket fall away and the guard's eyes widen before he is able to speak again.

"Is that supposed to be for entertainment?"

Elias nods eagerly.

"Yes. Yes, for entertainment."

"And it's been agreed?"

He prefers to nod silently rather than betray a lie with his voice. For a moment, the man ponders while his fingers twist the hairs on his lip into a point. Then he shrugs and jerks his head.

"Well. Dash it all. Who am I to judge the tastes and preferences of others? At least she's young. Well then, in you go."

Inside the door, there is a stairwell big enough to house a whole block, with room enough for two people to bed down on each step. From above come echoes of laughter and loud speech. Sconces with double wax candles light their way until they reach a double door, each of its halves open, and attached to the wall by velvet ties. It is like a cave in a kingdom of purest light, and Elias hesitates in trepidation. Never has he seen the night illuminated like this. Of course, just like others he has lingered outside the illu-minated facades of the Conservatory and the Stock Exchange, and gaped as he has tried to sate his gaze on the tamed flames dancing behind the windows, but that beauty was always bittersweet. The glow that beamed out was just what was superfluous, and the many arms of the candelabra marked a kind of boundary—one that he and his peers never dared to cross, condemned to turn their backs on it and wander into the cold and darkness; only the most fortunate might squint in the light of a glowing hearth or meager spill. Now he is welcomed at the door, yet simultaneously struck by the immensity of stepping over its threshold. Then he hears the musicians warming up, and beyond the doorway sees a formally attired gentleman chasing a woman in wide skirts, so that his coattails flutter. She lets out a coquettish squeal as she laughingly flees, and the spell is broken. Elias turns to scrutinize the girl, caressing her hair smooth.

"This is when it counts. Do you hear?"

Then he takes her by the arm and they step into the light.

54

He is dazzled, but only when the tears overpower him does he close his eyes. Together they seek shelter along the wall where a bouquet of flowers on a table shield them both from view for the time being. The room is suffocating him with its pomp. It is as big as the theater, with a ceiling that rises high above their heads. The vaulted frescos of the sky are entwined with golden foliage. Cherubs play tag among the clouds. The walls around them are no less ornate than the ceiling: golden panels, wallpaper so beautifully patterned that he has to touch it to convince himself that it is a mere woven illusion. Strangers stare down at the room from their distant worlds in paintings larger than life size, and each as lifelike as himself. The women graciously smile from hoods of gossamer lace festooned with roses, their pet marmots peeping out from the ornate boxes they clutch; the men are stern and commanding, posed in front of battlefields and fleets, their chests a mass of gold insignia, medals, and ribbons. The windows are set in deep niches. Far below are the stables of the Islet of the Holy Ghost and the bridges to the Northern Isle.

....

The small group of musicians has begun to play, at first with unobtrusive strokes intended to fill the pauses in conversation, but before long a group of gentlemen drain their glasses and each leads a lady to the center of the dance floor. The dancing begins, and the music becomes louder and quicker. Everywhere there are people roving about. Many are wearing masks, either those held up on a stick or that are simple bands, with holes cut out for eyes and tied at the backs of their heads. Some wear bigger masks designed to resemble animals or fanciful creatures, and they frighten him. Elias spends a long time looking before he catches sight of the face he is looking for—grateful at least that she has shown herself unmasked. He takes the girl by the hand, moving closer, until he finds a moment when she is standing alone. Little Platen gives him a look of consternation when he stands in front of her—the sort of look she would have directed at a muddy puddle that had flowed into the place she wanted to place her heel. She has already half turned away before he stops her.

"Wait."

She is surprised enough to be addressed that she stops midstep.

"It's about Klara."

"I beg your pardon?"

She peers at them both through a lorgnette.

"You don't need her any longer. You can let her go. I want to take her away from here."

There is a pause while Platen tries to interpret the testimony of her own ears. Elias takes a step to one side and pulls the girl with him so that she is standing right in front of her.

"I have another one to offer in exchange. She's younger and more beautiful. She can serve you for longer."

Platen's jaw is working in vain to force sounds from her lips as her head turns between them, one to the other. Then she laughs.

"That? A famished gutter cat? Who would want one of those? And what are those rags she's wearing? And why is she made up as a harlequin?"

She lifts the girl's cheek with a sharp finger, turning the face back and forth to try to catch the vacant stare—in vain.

"And what's wrong with her?"

Elias's lip trembles, bereft at the criticism of his toils. Little Platen turns to the woman beside her.

"Klara! If you be in my thrall then say so. Have I ever forced you into anything? Are you not free to come and go from my chambers at your own discretion?"

Klara is beautiful in her dress, so fine that its white color is made pink by her skin. She is wearing her hair up, held in place by ornate pins. For the first time she pays heed to Platen's supplicants, and gives them an indifferent glance after surveying the dance floor and the gathered groups with the eyes of a hawk.

"What? No, of course not. What kind of question is that?"

Little Platen raises an eyebrow at Elias, but she is obliged to purse her lips at his doubtful expression.

"Simply to be rid of you quicker. Well, Klara, would you be good enough to explain to this brat the nature of our dealings?"

Klara laughs as if it were a game she does not understand but is still expected to participate in. She leans towards Elias, her voice adopting the tone of a teacher explaining the simplest of things to a child.

"I want to meet gentlemen who will give me gifts in return for my tenderness. Pining men come to Platen; she introduces us and lends us a room—in return for a share of what is given."

Platen's posture is suddenly as straight as a plumb line. Her wrinkled neck stretches out and a finger flies out to point while she pulls Klara in by her waist to allow her to look along her arm. There is a handsome man in a wig and smart uniform, on whose chest grandiose stars and medals jostle for attention. His mask covers his face from the tip of his nose to the middle of his forehead.

"There. Isn't that him? Fredrik Adolf? And is he not unattended? Now, Klara. The iron is hot. Strike for all you are worth."

Klara hurries away, moving so quickly that the wine spills from her glass and leaves a trail of drips on the wooden floor. Little Platen turns back to Elias.

"I don't want to make a scene for which others may wish to blame me. But if you trouble me—or Klara—again then I promise that I shall shout for a guard and have you driven out of the door. You and your famished street whore."

With those words, she turns on her heel and makes to follow Klara's damp footsteps.

55

Elias pulls the girl back to his nook. There are so many seeking attention that they remain undisturbed. The candles burn low, the hours of late summer twilight linger for a long time before night is permitted to fall. The musicians grow ever drunker and more careless, and the notes become discordant while the tempo becomes irregular—but no one notices a thing, everyone lost in the maelstrom of their urges. The group in strange masks depart shortly prior to midnight, but those remaining do not lament those places made vacant in unfamiliar arms. The dance continues until a couple take a fancy to each other: the gentleman takes his lady by the waist and leads her out into the corridor in the hope of finding a room with a free bed. A rapidly diminishing number are to be found, and once drunkenness has blunted all inhibitions, necessity nullifies all laws. At first they copulate behind curtains and tapestries, but soon they do so openly, soon with pride, competing to bare themselves with the least shame: in the bay windows, within a circle of onlookers in the center of the floor with their own garments as their bed. Flickering flames play with masks and shapes—it is hard to see where one body ends and another begins; all are cast together into something that Elias can no longer interpret as fully human. He takes the girl by the hand and leads her back downstairs, afraid that sooner or later someone will be without a partner and will take her from him.

He sits her down against the castle facade, crouching down alongside her and letting time dry his tears. They wait. They are not alone. Down by the facade of the outer courtyard, servants await their masters. Some have gone to sleep as best they can, curled around their unlit lanterns to avoid being robbed in their slumbers. Others take turns with their lit candles while they play cards. The flames flicker in the wind blowing off the sea—the kind of wind that presages a storm. Elias glimpses the maid Elsa among those sleeping, with her head in her sack and her body twitching on the strings of her dreams.

The darkness gives way, the stars disappearing one by one in the blush of morning as it heralds the newly lit bonfire that will soon rise from the shiny mirror of the bay. The streaks of dawn are red in that way that makes seamen batten down their hatches. Far away across the sea thunder rumbles. The debauchees forsake the party, some alone, others in pairs, yet others in groups, and Elias is back on his feet, shifting from foot to foot to scan each face before it is lost into the alleys, staggering on uncertain feet. Then he sees Little Platen and without a thought he is on his feet, blocking her path again. She walks alone, her gaze cloudy and with the careful small steps used by the practiced drunk on Stockholm's capricious cobblestones. She is surrounded by a miasma of sour wine.

"Where is she?"

She is more intoxicated than he thought. Her expression is one of incomprehension before she recalls with effort where she has seen him before and what his business is. She opens her mouth as if to dismiss him, but then stops herself and starts again.

"How long have you been waiting?"

"All night long."

She claps her hands together with a croaking laugh.

"I think she pulled it off."

Little Platen looks around for a better audience, but there isn't one, and with triumph written on her face she turns back to Elias.

"Prince Fredrik. I saw them go. He took her to his own quarters. Other ladies of the evening have to settle for straw mattresses and floorboards, but not Sugar Klara. She got a four-poster and down bolster, silk sheets, and sable blanket."

Elsa is by their side now, making herself known to her mistress before running over to a manservant who has just begun to pilot his master homeward, in order to light her wick from his lantern. Upon her return, they all stand still for a moment of peculiar silence until a sound makes them turn towards the Castle.

Klara walks slowly, limping towards them in a dress whose ties have been torn apart by an impatient lover, and that can now only be kept together by holding her arm across her body. Her second hand is cupped to her sex, where blood has penetrated through the cloth and run down her bare legs. When she reaches the light from Elsa's lantern, they see his grip still visible on blue skin. Her lip is split and her face red, her cheeks moist with tears and snot.

"It wasn't him. It was someone else in the prince's entourage. But he let me believe what I wanted to. And I let him hurt me in front of his friends, who gathered in a circle. No matter what he did, I pretended I liked it as best as I could . . . Until he let the mask drop and they all laughed—laughed heartily at the stupid little whore and her fruitless greed. They've ruined me. I've been torn asunder. It has no effect on them. What will I do?"

Elias's heart beats faster than ever. He sees his chance, better than he could have hoped for, and again he drags the girl forward with an encircling arm, having pulled her up from her position against the wall. He holds her by the shoulders in front of Little Platen.

"What about now? Do you want to swap now?"

Little Platen blinks in surprise, shaking her head, dumbfounded.

"Why?"

Elias wipes his eyes with a dirty sleeve.

"She's my mother. She left me in the orphanage because she was given no other choice."

Klara reels on the spot, Platen reluctantly supporting her, careful to protect the hem of her own dress from stains.

"Klara? Is what the boy says true?"

She shakes her head.

"No. I've never had a baby."

Elias's voice rises to a pitiful wail.

"You may not have given your own name, but the matron saw you when you brought me in swaddling clothes and she has seen you since then! She didn't know that I was listening, but I heard her say that my mother is among the Lizard girls, with Little Platen."

Little Platen lets out a whinnying laugh.

"Now the pieces are falling into place. Didn't you have a bun in the oven, Elsa? And isn't the boy old enough? You told me you were going to get an abortion—wasn't that why I gave you an advance? And then you took him to the orphanage instead."

In the silence a sob emerges from Elsa's sack, and while she stumbles she manages to intercept the fall of the lantern enough for it to remain upright on the cobbles. The cloth that conceals her face is not enough— she covers it with her hands too to muffle the tears and sobbing. At first Elias stands there as if paralyzed, before releasing the girl and going to his mother. She tries to defend herself when he moves her hands, but it does not take much force for his will to prevail, rather the tenderness of his touch. She snuffles as he lifts the edge of the sack and reveals the face that is no longer there. The devil's kiss has taken her nose, climbed up a corroded cleft between her eyes, and consumed her forehead between festoons of bulging blisters. Holes in her cheeks devour her tears as torn lips slur his name.

"Elias. My Elias."

His trembling fingers let go of the cloth that has covered her. As she raises her hand to touch him he recoils, betraying his horror with a gasp. He wraps his arms around his head and crouches, curving his back to tuck his head between his knees, forming an orb of nothing but hard surfaces. The gravity of the moment seems to infect even Platen, who takes Elsa by the arm gently but commandingly. Her voice is muffled, devoid of the merriment of intoxication.

"Come on, Elsa, let's go. You too, Klara."

They help to lead away the maid, and among the sound of footsteps Elias hears sobs muffled in the distance. When he dares to open his eyes again, all is as it was. They have left the lantern behind. It captures his gaze until the wick sparkles and dies with a sputter. The cold is taking its toll, and he rises on stiff legs and fumbles for the girl's hand with his, grasping it and turning to lead her away into the city.

"Come on, let's go."

He is oblivious to the drizzle that has begun to fall, and far away there is a quiet rumble. Below them in the stables by the bridge across the North Stream, men have begun to gather in small groups, clapping their arms against their sides as they wait to be called into formation, passing bottles around, helping to adjust each other's uniforms to save time and effort later on.

56

There is no order whatsoever in front of the stables on the Islet of the Holy Ghost. Captain Lennartsson of the Castle Guard moves between the small groups of men clustering together. Most are his own *corps de garde*, but there are also plenty of watchmen, and while he has on occasion encountered former comrades in arms among their ranks, he is disgusted to see them gathered now in such numbers: if they weren't rotten before, then the rot has taken them now. An assortment of lecherous cripples set up to do the dirty work no one else is willing to. His own men are slightly more impressive, though that isn't saying very much. His practiced gaze darts over uniforms and equipment, although it is a habit he has tried to break ever since leaving army service, because there are so many flawed details it is better to try to see the bigger picture, albeit with blurred vision: the white cuffs of the waist-length jackets are dirty, frayed, and unbuttoned, used sporadically as handkerchiefs and gloves. All the swordbelts and gaiters have seen better days, while the hats sport buckled brims and threadbare plumes. Jackets, breeches—everything is stained. Lennartsson knows just as well as anyone that uniforms are often worn in the inns of the city, in violation of regulations, preferably after closing time, in order to drink for free. God help him if he ordered an inspection of polished weapons, because more than half the rapiers are surely rusted into their scabbards. But at least they are unlikely to be called for today, and better that than some fool being overeager and causing a bloodbath. Well, such is his dirty linen, and there's no point washing it in public now.

Everyone is sleepy, and the yawns run from one to another like messengers. Some of them stink, staring phlegmatically into space now that drunkenness is turning into a hangover—those who, with the perverse logic of the soldier, have regarded the early muster hour as a pretext not to go to bed at all. It can hardly be called morning, but the sun is already casting sharp shadows, driving away more and more of the dark with every passing minute. To crown it all, the summer weather finally seems to be at an end, and while Lennartsson—like everyone else—has wished the heat gone more times than he remembers, the storm could have held off for another day. Far across the sea thunder has been rumbling for the past hour. Perhaps they might dare to hope that it will pour out all its rage on the waves and archipelago, but they are hardly likely to escape the rain. The sky to the west is an angry red, and with the creeping light come strong gusts of wind. There has been a weathervane over by the corner of the guards' barracks for as long as anyone can remember, occasionally replaced, and viewed with equanimity by commanders who know when to choose their battles. The soldiers have attributed prophetic powers to it, and he has been infected in turn—rarely does he begin the day without glancing in its direction. Last night, the wooden finger of its oracular judgment was pointing down, towards the cracked ground that must soon be submerged. Isn't that drizzle he can now already feel?

As he walks among the men, he exchanges meaningful glances with the noncommissioned officers he finds among them. A nod is enough to set it all in motion, his unspoken order climbing down the ranks to the half-dozen corporals who clap their hands loudly to interrupt the tittle-tattle and line their men up in rows. The inspection is not made any longer than necessary—the names of any absentees are taken, reports are filed, and Lennartsson tells them to stand at ease.

"You know what you have to do. We have been practicing dry runs for two weeks—now this is for real. One file on each corner, two men left in post, the rest to go through the quarter one door at a time in the order they come. Every nook and cranny—leave no stone unturned. Regroup and repeat at the next street corner, keeping an eye on the nearest file to your left and right prior to advancing. And so on. Anyone who is found to be loose and idle is to be dealt with—none of you have been in the guard for so little time that you have not learned to distinguish plain folk from riffraff. Err on the side of arrest—if there is a brat unable to account for herself then those who defend her will have to resolve the misunderstanding at the Southern Isle. Those you apprehend are to be sent back into custody; those who run for it you are to drive forward without breaking the line. Take advantage of the early hour, because surprise is on our side, and as the day goes on the rabble will go to ground with ever increasing guile. Let us be quick so that we have cleaned up by evening. Good luck, and I will see you at the lock gates."

Ostentatiously, he turns to the undisciplined mass of watchmen who have been gazing at the formation of the guard in bewilderment.

"And you are all to help where you can. Use what skill you have. Do not stand in the way—if you do, you'll risk spending the night in the rasp house, because by the time we reach the lock gates you are liable to be so drunk and your uniforms so filthy that it will be difficult to distinguish you from the lowlife."

The constables know when they are being joked with, and laugh as if by command, ridiculing the watchmen. Before discipline crumbles entirely, Lennartsson breaks off and speaks up more powerfully.

"Let's rake this confounded dunghill clean once and for all. Should your patience begin to run short as the day grows long, then by all means take it out on the vermin whose fault it is that you must toil, but keep it within reason. I do not want to requisition any carts for removal. If these bastards can't move under their own steam, then I shall bloody well make sure that the man responsible drags the stretcher himself. Hold the line. Proceed!"

57

The city watch descend upon the city in a row, an arc spanning from the Knights' Isle Bridge in the west to the empty plinth beneath the castle where the late King Gustav promised to return one day in a mantle of bronze. They move in a blue line past the Castle and the palaces by Castle Hill and Ship's Bridge, and into the muddle of houses and doors in the quarters of Phaeton, Pygmalion, Cepheus, and Cassiopeia, and get even sweatier in the smaller quarters between the new streets. It is not long before they encounter their first quarry. A mother and daughter are woken in the doorway where they have bedded down in a corner, and the scene turns dramatic when the mother—far too slow to have any hope of escape—urges her child to run, but her hesitation ends in the arms of a soldier. Both are sent back, their fate left to others to decide. Perhaps they will be parted, the mother sent to the workhouse and the child up to the Northern Isle; perhaps they have a home outside of the parish to which they will be sent on a cart. In a hayloft, a whole heap of street urchins are surprised—the boys clinging tightly to each other to keep the heat in. They put up better resistance, and of seven all but two escape. It is no easy task catching nimble, barefoot runners when clad in gaitered boots. They must hope for better luck in their hunt when the noose is tightened and the lock gates are within their sights. Yet the defeat is enough to alter the atmosphere. The hunt is on the move, bloodlust aroused when the cockiest of the escapees stops in the middle of the alley to pull down his breeches and show his buttocks to his pursuers. They clear Phaeton, they clear Pygmalion. People who have been sleeping in stairwells lie for all they are worth: one has lost their key in the gutter, one is the landlady's cousin from the country, one is a despised husband who has quarrelled with his wife, who is now prepared to lie about the very marriage itself to be rid of the man she recently pledged allegiance to in sickness and in health, to hell with it. Their work is not difficult. It is all too easy to see who sleeps outside and who has their own stove. Few are such hardened liars that they can make themselves credible when their collar is in another's fist. Where there is any doubt, they pass judgment quickly and harshly, and always to the defendant's detriment, the truth entrusted to the men behind the column, just to be rid of the torrent of words that fly in their faces like chaff.

The drizzle continues to fall, so lightly that the heat of bodies in motion dries clothes from within before the damp spreads. Now the news is out and all sense of ambush is gone. The beggar brats and vagrants are warned by their peers, who can be seen leaving their hiding places long before the watch approach, running along the alleys in the hope of reaching safety beyond the lock gates, among the poor quarters clinging to the mountainside, where the law does not reach. The wind is worse—it has increased in strength so much that it whistles between the buildings, playing the quarters like an organ, and any who catch occasional glimpses of the sea between the houses are horrified by the blue and black clouds rising from water to sky.

With the arrival of morning, the whole city is on the move and aware of what is happening. In front of the line, the daily grind begins—the best way to avoid removal and demonstrate that one is not loose and idle. Some of the more resourceful officers make matters even more efficient by going on ahead to warn people that they are to be counted imminently, and most are sharp enough to gather the household together and stay out of the way as the buildings are searched from attic to cellar. The atmosphere behind the line is different. The odd person who has managed to induce an acquaintance to vouch for them is recognized by the watchmen in respect of previous misdemeanors and unable to account for themselves upon further prompting; they are grabbed by the arms and sent away. For others there is no longer any risk of being mistaken for quarry. All that remains is entertainment. Few have any feelings for the rabble—day in, day out, they are lazy and idle, their life lived at the expense of others. The worst ones steal like magpies or entice honest men to forget their vows, while others merely stoop to peck at the crumbs that have fallen from the tables laid by honorable folk. It is high time that they get what they have for so long deserved! The spectators go from house to house, up through the recently searched stairwells, before crowding around windows to get the best view of the quarter that is next due for inquisition.

Behind the blue line an impromptu baggage train has arisen. Some innkeepers have loaded up a borrowed cart with beer kegs, cracking open one after another and offering the watch the chance to refresh themselves in return for a few pennies. Familiar faces are allowed to drink on credit when their purse gapes empty, every debt carefully added to the accounts. The idea quickly runs rampant and is imitated—soon every innkeeper is asserting his right to the cobblestones outside his door, carts loaded with drink are denied passage, and quarrels lead to fisticuffs, while the watch help themselves from neglected barrels, leaving taps running and beer spraying straight into the gutter to test how soon thirst will trump discipline. The corporals bellow at the provost marshals to keep their men reasonably sober with the aid of the cane, but wherever the ground slopes away it is clear for all to see. Chaos awaits. The closer they come to the lock gates, the more escapees are crowded into every available hiding place—many are even on the rooftops. One of the watchmen treads on a cracked roof tile and falls through the roof into a pigsty; he is carried out by his comrades roaring with laughter, his thigh broken and his uniform covered in piglet shit. The officers are quick to rein in the spread of rumors in order to goad the men into action: listen up—the rabble are taking up arms. They're fighting back. One of ours is at death's door, the victim of a base and shabby trick. Retaliation is called for—the honor of the corps has been questioned.

Sabers are impractical—they sway about at the men's sides and get in the way when they are running. One man is assigned to stand guard over the abandoned weapons while they arm themselves instead with the best weapons to hand. Stones are kicked loose. A barrel is flung to the ground, its hoops removed and the staves made into cudgels for two dozen men. Everything that can be used as a drum or cymbal is torn down, and they begin to clatter as if in a rhythm determined by bloodlust itself. Those who have nothing else stamp their feet and pound their fists. The pulse unites into one troop what might otherwise have fallen apart, and the watchmen find the line again, advancing through the alleys, flogging women, children, and drunkards who lack the wit or strength to move out of the way in time. The wails of the flogged fill the voids between the thunder of the rooftop kettledrum that is the city itself.

The thunder remains at a distance for now, its cracks remote and the flash of the lightning glimpsed across the archipelago, but the rain intensifies and the wind brings down the drops at a steep angle. It is a warm rain, one that is incapable of cooling in the insanity that is spreading quarter by quarter. It obscures the vision and deafens the ears, and allows deeds that others might have stopped to continue unabated. The blood that spatters into the gutters is washed away just as quickly as it came. Wet uniform jackets are rolled up and stowed in windows; the men with the barrel staves are soon in shirts that have been dyed pink in a blend of blood and rain.

58

Circumstances conspire to keep Elias ignorant of what is going on—he who is usually, in the manner of the street urchin, so responsive to the shifts of the city, who through some nameless sense discerns every change in temperament as if the alleys were veins and its heartbeats were felt under his own bare feet. Now he is sleeping, dead to the world after a long night's vigil, as if his body seeks to comfort his disappointment in the only way at its disposal. The feet that slap against wet stones outside the cellar window are his first warning, and he is startled out of his curled-up sleep as if anticipating a blow. Having assured himself the girl is still asleep, or as close as she can get, he climbs up and wriggles out of the window as quickly as he can. He is soaked to the skin in the space of a moment, squinting with his hand cupped against his forehead to see better. Others hurry past him, often blindly, and he has to take care to avoid being knocked down. In the alleys farther up the hill towards the square the din is terrible—a persistent rumble with a chorus of screams and shouts. A boy younger than himself comes running, and Elias steps into his path and grabs him by the scruff of his shirt.

"What's going on?"

The boy is bleeding from a nick somewhere on his scalp, and struggles as best he can to continue his flight.

"Just answer and I'll let go."

"The constables are coming. I didn't know there were that many. They're moving in a line and searching every quarter. If you're loose and idle they'll nab you. I've heard that the ones they arrest are being dragged to the steps of the Stock Exchange and beheaded on the spot."

Elias can't help but glance at the ground where the water flowing down the square is splashing across both their feet. It is distinctly brown thanks to the mud that has dried to dust over the past hot weeks.

"What fairy tales are these?"

The boy grabs hold of his own shirt and yanks it free from Elias's fist.

"Why don't you go and ask them yourself—or just stay put. They'll soon be here."

Around him, the doors are closed and locked, the householders protecting their properties in anticipation of an inspection by the watch. Farthest down, most have chosen to bolt the shutters across their windows. Their curious faces can be glimpsed in rows behind dusty panes of glass higher up the facades. Elias continues up the street until he sees with his own eyes the men approaching in a slow march of blue and white that disperses all in its path. He turns and runs back whence he came.

....

The girl's body is sluggish and intransigent. He pushes her up the steps, encountering an old woman inside the doorway who glances at them sharply with a wry smile.

"Well, well, well. Here are our sponger tenants from the cellar . . . Time for you to kiss your easy days goodbye."

She unlocks the door and opens it for them into an alley wet enough to run a mill wheel.

"You'd better hurry up if you want to save your skins. Don't say I never did anything for you."

Elias pulls the girl behind him; she is immediately just as soaked as he, and he leads her towards the Southern Isle as quickly as he can. Behind them beats a thunderous pulse, like the steps of a colossus in remorseless chase. When they reach the final building and the alley opens out, he sees the trap awaiting them. Both drawbridges are up, the blue one and the red one, and there are watchmen and guards all over the place, ready to intercept those fleeing the city. It is raining too hard for him to see the island across the water, but he can easily imagine what is going on: clusters of watchmen ready to fasten shackles around the defenseless and lead them to the Island of Scar for their betterment and education. The ragamuffins are flooding in from both the Ship's Bridge and the new streets with suffi-cient haste to demonstrate to him that there is no escape route to be found there either. The ships that are usually a leap away from the quay have withdrawn to the outlying buoys or lie at anchor to prevent those flee-ing from seeking hiding places on board, and with commerce temporarily interrupted the crew are huddled in oilskins along the rails to follow the spectacle.

Everywhere there are wails and screams, people tumbling over each other. Those who are able fend off the inevitable as far ahead of them-selves as they can, joining a cluster in front of the millhouse, midway between their pursuers and the men waiting by the lock gates. Their combined mass sways restlessly in the rain, unable to stand still and equally powerless to find a way out. The street urchins still have power in their legs and refuse to believe that their young limbs, which have hitherto saved them from most things, will soon run out of luck. As if it were some new game, they race to and fro between the shrinking boundaries of liberty.

Elias tugs the girl in beside a house wall where they are almost pro-tected from the rain as long as the capricious wind shows them mercy. He senses an injustice whose acquaintance he has made previously: never are thoughts more sluggish than when danger draws near and they are most needed. For a moment, he can do nothing but stare in one direc-tion and then the other, blinking as if drowsy to keep the water out of his eyes, while the din of the alleys grows ever closer. The wind whips around them, his nose stings, and at once he knows what he must do. He takes her by the waist and shoves her into a run.

They stagger across the square and down towards the water. Over on Knights' Isle, he catches sight of blue jackets on the approach, and he re-mains bent double to avoid attracting any more of their attention than is necessary. Soon they are obscured by the row of public privies. The stench intensifies. A dark shape looms before them. His hands rest on the wooden fence barring their way.

It is the Flies' Meet. He has never been so close before—he has only ever seen the place from a distance, and that distance has never been shorter than necessary. Only the waste-women venture here, nightsoil collectors working in pairs, with their splashing barrels hoisted on poles over sore shoulders. It is a legendary place, the subject of jokes and pranks, as well as darker tales in which the unfortunate are buried there by miscreants, the appropriate punishment meted out by the court of the street to those deserving of it. The roundworm makes its home in the entrails of everyone, and sometimes they are expelled, and rumor has it they can survive here outside the guts, growing stronger, as long as snakes, big enough to strangle young rats if they are careless enough. The depth of the mound is disputed, as is its age. A deity, an idol of shit, stacked five fathoms high and three times that in breadth. Many a time he has heard the Flies' Meet compared with the still-unveiled equestrian statue of old King Gustav Adolf outside the Opera, which is so top-heavy, people say, no one can understand how it could stay upright without the scaffolding propping it up. They sneer at that big, black monstrosity and then point to the south and say, *there*, over there, should you ever want to see one, is a truly irrefutable monument to the efforts of mankind.

The closer they get, the louder the buzzing grows, becoming a rumble to rival the rain's. They're everywhere, small black bodies that crawl over every surface in indolent intoxication, taking off heavily to tumble drunkenly through the air to their next blowout. A tall wooden fence binds the dungheap, reinforced by upright posts to ensure that the bulging planks do not burst and submerge the Grain Harbor. A simple staircase has been built to make it easier to tip barrels over the woodwork, and they take one step at a time until all that remains is to straddle the obstacle and then jump across to the other side. The sludge has already reached the top, and is overflowing where the uneven boards are at their lowest. He helps her up first, then sits alongside her, testing the depth with his foot and feeling the languid quagmire sucking against his calf with no hint of a bottom. A deep breath in quiet gratitude for the rain he so recently cursed, and then they jump.

The slurry comes up to their chests down here, in the ditch formed where the rain has planed the sides of the heap. The shock is considerable, even though he prepared for it as best he could. The unfamiliar mass is heavier and denser than water; he can feel it squeezing his breast and making it hard to breathe, while far below him his feet are being dragged into a tighter grip. The stench is like a slap to the face, a poisonous unseen creature, pungent and stinging and with endless variations of foulness. Floating in the quagmire are seeds, fishbones, fruit pits. Everything is brought here—everything that the people of the city have to give—and that dizzying thought is a step towards madness. He strains air through his lips even though he doesn't want to open them any more than he must, and for a while strange shapes begin to dance across his field of vision and dizziness swims through his head. His mouth is filled with flies; he has them on his nose, his eyelids, every inch of his skin. He vomits, once then twice, drooling bile and adding his spittle to the filth. Once voided, he screws his eyes so tightly shut that his face convulses, pinching his arm with white knuckles until the pain cleanses his mind.

Only now he is able to think about the girl. He turns around and there she is, unaffected, albeit with her arms around her torso, suddenly freezing. He takes her hand and begins to trudge along the inside of the fence, dragging her along. They are still not safe—they are fully visible to anyone who looks inside. He chooses the part of the incline that seems least steep, and begins to climb. Over and over, he slides down into the sludge to be mocked by the furrows he has plowed with his scrabbling fingers on his way up, testimony to how little progress he made and how much remains to go. In the end, he tries the fence in the hope of finding a tool, and the wood is brittle enough to allow a sharp shard to be broken off it. Then he digs out—step by step—a staircase towards the sputtering sky, holes deep enough to give support to hands and feet. Once the way ahead is free, he shakes the girl's shoulders. She gives no answer. The effort and hopelessness make him cry, and he hears his voice crack.

"Now you have to help me. You have to climb. Otherwise they'll catch us both and take me to the rasp and you to the workhouse."

The final utterance seems to be a password of some kind, because now she begins to move. She slowly allows herself to be helped up. He follows behind, helping each foot to find the right position, and eventually they reach the top of the mound—the flat summit has sunk in the middle into a hollow, a rancid puddle deep enough to cover a prostrate body. Elias helps her into position and lies down close beside her to share what body heat they have. He shakes as the water and wind chill him, but finally everything goes numb: he floats weightless atop this mountain of excrement, leaving his body to be violated, no longer feeling the live blanket of winged insects even when they are crawling across his lips or drinking from the corners of his eyes, and at last he is still, hidden by the torrential rain and the densely gathering twilight.

59

Dreaming and wakefulness are hard to tell apart. His mind is like a flame in a draft. The evening light dissipates and morning comes, and between them falls a timeless abyss. The light shifts from one direction to another. It remains cloudy, but the rain has stopped and the wind has died down. The morning paints their shelter in its true colors, even more repulsive in plain sight. Elias hears murmuring voices and, shortly after, the splash of a barrel being emptied over the fence. The vessel rattles as it is carried down and away, and the waste-women's clogs clatter out of earshot. He's warm, even though he shouldn't be. That scares him. He puts his hand to his brow—it's hot as sheet metal warmed by the sun.

He carefully rolls onto his belly and lifts his head to look around. The blue jackets have gone from the lock gates, and the drawbridges have been put back down to provide free access. The seamen have begun their day, eager to recoup what the preceding day cost them. Fishing boats are coming in from the archipelago, keen to unload what their nets have gathered. His body remains stiff and unwilling. He holds his hands in front of him, pale under the sludge, the flesh wrinkly and spongy like that of one who has drowned. He shakes the girl to life and does what he can to ensure a safe climb, to no avail. His mind is sluggish and his movements clumsy, and his limbs refuse to do as they are told. They slide down, him first and her following. Hand over hand, he pulls himself along the fence until he can heave himself over the edge where the steps are and pull her along behind him.

Once on solid ground, he finds he is no longer able to walk upright. His feet provide no stability, his toes are blue, and only once he has rubbed his legs for a long time can he feel the blood flowing painfully. Having done his own, he turns to hers and only now does the quality of the shivers change and show him how cold he is. He needs her support just as much as she needs his, and together they stagger towards the channel and into the water until it reaches high enough for them to crouch up to their shoulders. He casts water over her hair, helping her out of the soiled party dress, wriggles his own shirt over his head, and shakes the garments underwater to rinse them clean. He wrings them as dry as he can, and hangs them on a broken oar. Elias wraps his arms around his calves, perches his chin on his knees, and together they wait to dry, naked, gnarled with goose pimples each time the wind gusts along the shoreline.

....

Their clothes are still damp when they make their way in among the houses, her hand in his. Elias can feel how the essence of the city has shifted from one day to the next. His kind have been weeded out. The quarters have been drained of the loose and idle—their nooks and street corners are gaping empty. Their lives have been driven out of the dead-end alleys and arches where they previously sought shade and shelter. There are no echoes or quarrels and games; the refuges of the day before have been reduced to a rubbish tip or thoroughfare. Left behind, of course, are the industrious, dashing back and forth under the burden of duty, just as unperturbed as they are undisturbed. Down by the Ship's Bridge, the well-heeled stroll along and he imagines that they are showing off their watch chains more openly than ever now, given how many deft fingers have been put to the rasp instead. The city belongs to others now, and Elias keeps his body close to the facades and his eyes to the street, afraid his cover may be blown. But no one pays him any attention, and the few watchmen he sees yawn indifferently, tired and satiated with action.

Everywhere he can hear the change in the weather under discussion. A salute to mark the burial of the summer is how they refer to the thunder that has now died down. Two men share a bag of tobacco on a step where an old woman is sitting with a carding comb alongside a basket of wool.

"Well, autumn is on the way now. Then winter, and with a poor harvest at that. Save yourselves, all who can."

"Would that the summer had been cooler, but we are bound to forgive the heat as time passes."

The woman squints up at the clouds and rubs her sore joints with a resolute grimace.

"There's more water up there, and it's coming soon. So say my knees."

The night has left a chill in Elias that will not pass. The wind has sharpened teeth, but it isn't cold. Yet he is freezing and sweating in turns. He is shaking and he draws the girl closer to cadge her warmth, only to have to fan himself with his shirt because the skin across his ribs is glowing and blushing in angry splodges. He can tell they both still stink. It will take more than a wash in the dirty waters of the Grain Harbor after a night in the bosom of the Flies' Meet. Nevertheless, he is in better condition than she. Her dress is hanging off her in rags, the hem half-gone, dragging along behind her like a tail. What color it once was can no longer be accurately discerned. Her hair hangs in knots he has not been able to untangle, and her skin is pale and swollen all over.

60

The door he seeks, the number of which he so carefully committed to memory, is down towards the sea. He knocks, first unobtrusively and then harder, and the servant who opens the door a crack asks him what his business is, with a voice distorted by the fingers he has quickly moved to pinch his nose. A febrile sweat breaks out across Elias's brow, and he sways giddily on unsteady feet. A cough has come in its wake, a tickle ensconced in his throat that obstinately remains there no matter how he claws at it with muffled barks.

"I have something I want to sell."

The servant nods curtly, turns on his heel without a word, and leaves them to wait.

"There must be a doctor—someone who can make her beautiful again. More beautiful than Klara. But that has its price. Mercury, hemlock, clean bandages, a bed in a room smoked with fir twigs. I'm sure they'll give me thirty daler. Perhaps double. If it's worth pasting our faces to every well in the city then you must be worth thirty to him."

The sound of footsteps is once again audible in the hallway. Elias has to support himself against the plastered wall of the house.

"It's warm in there. There's food to eat. I don't know what they want you for, but how could it be worse than it is with me?"

He sways on the spot. A reverie draws its veil across his eyes. He smiles.

"The doctor's knife will cut away all the bad, so that it may grow back new and more beautiful. She will be so beautiful. Perhaps beautiful enough for Prince Fredrik himself. Perhaps we'll live happily ever after."

When the door opens again, it is a strange face he is presented with. He can't tell whether or not it is smiling. Elias proffers the notice, soaked into a smudgy clump, the drawing barely perceptible: blurry figures, two small phantoms consigned to haunt a haze of diluted ink.

PART FOUR

Rest by This Stream
AUTUMN AND WINTER 1795

Death's soft bosom
gives sweet relief
when the heart is sick.
Fortune's tricks,
the adverse odds
of malicious gods,
love's burning grief
all hounded us here.
They pause at the tomb
and leave us there.
　　　　　　—Carl Lindegren, 1795

61

Cardell dances with Petter Pettersson beneath the moon on the shore of the Island of Scar. He blinks the sweat out of his eyes, forcing recalcitrant legs into attack and retreat, all in pursuit of the best position. He is beset with cramps, but the fact that he is still capable of movement is a surprise. All around them, shadowy figures are revealed by the glow of their pipes, but he cannot allow his attention to be diverted because here comes the cane out of the darkness, and a lash like a musket shot next to his head leaves his ears ringing. Pettersson is wielding it with his left hand, and now the right comes whistling in and cuts into Cardell's back as he bends forward to avoid being hit, lunging forward with his wooden fist towards the soft belly but missing. Another time, they exchange glancing blows, Cardell feeling braided leather tear at his neck, a fist bouncing off the shoulder he raised to protect his cheek, the stump of his arm burning when he thrusts forward his left arm and strikes flesh, a groan confirming its impact.

The battle finds its pace. They come together, exchange blows, back away to weigh up what has been given and received. Cardell gnashes his teeth at the injustice. On another day he would have acquitted himself better—any other day at all. His limbs will not obey him as they should: he is slow, and his blows do not land where his aim is directed. He cannot fathom why he is still staggering about, why Pettersson hasn't ended it all, and he guesses that it is no more than the cat toying with the rat.

His mind is clouded, and all that remains is a single thing: his entire being has been reduced to a body fighting for survival at the cost of another's life. There is a certain freedom too. He recognizes it of old. Pure battle, flesh against flesh on terms as equal as they can be, the kind that cannot be resolved by gunpowder-packed iron and the whims of chance, warfare for the frightened and wary. No such doubt can be brought to a place such as this—all that was recently difficult is forgotten in the face of what is now plain and obvious. Farewell to why. Now there is only space for how. He no longer knows whether his grimace is the work of the convulsions, or whether it originates from the ecstasy of battle—the furious predator's tribute to his created destiny.

Cardell fights dirty, he fights practically. Each movement is adapted for its ends at the smallest possible cost. In the military, he saw others try to give combat a shape, surrounding it with ceremony: slight young men with foils and rigid postures, one hand on their hip and their feet performing a prim minuet. Such things disgusted him—a perverse game played by cadets who believe that death in war only afflicts others and is ideally sweet and glorious. Those who have never seen grown men whimper and call their mother's name as they vainly try to wind their spilled entrails back into their belly.

Salt stings in the wounds, small pains hiding the greater one. But there is also a sound that does not belong here, and he has been hearing it for a long time now. Someone is crying with sobs of despair. A lamenting howl. Is it himself? No. It takes a while for him to realize that it is Petter Pettersson. Tears clouding his vision, Cardell moves towards the other body, taking the long, slouching step that puts the blow within his reach. All force emanates from the hip, his body spins around, and the moonlight dazzles him as he sticks his left arm into a blast furnace. He feels another saltiness, different in essence from his own sweat, spatter across his face and lips, leaving behind the taste of iron.

The big body is felled and his own knees turn to stone. He creeps closer, not daring to believe in his own victory—wise from old mistakes. He crawls until he is lying straight across Pettersson, listening for the hiss of the lungs, seeking out the big veins in the neck with his good hand. For a moment there is a rattle and wheeze in the chest, a phantom simply seeking out its old haunts. His fingers touch upon something weak, but Cardell cannot tell whether the heart that beats is his alone or both of theirs. Then it is gone—whatever it was—and beneath him the blood falls silent and thickens in the vessels. His own will falters, the last of his power draining away, and they lie there in an embrace as intimate as a pair of lovers after their dance. The heat is gone, the duel is over, and in those places where the spirit of battle is now withdrawing its mercy, pain hurries into its place in all its glory. Wounds he did not feel when they were inflicted upon him flare up all over, uniting in a single, boiling ache.

Now he feels hands on his body. Feebly, he flails at these new, unseen enemies tugging at him, and then he remembers something else. He knows that there is something missing, that his mission is not yet complete, and he fumbles in the jacket beneath him. His fingers are numb, but he can make out the rustle of paper through heartbeats that give solitary shape to a thunderous silence. He closes his fist around what he has found, scrunching it into a ball small enough to be concealed in his hand. Then he is lifted up, they set him on his two feet, others step in to support the weight he can no longer carry himself. They lead him away.

62

A police constable comes loping after him along the street as soon as Emil shows his face up at Castle Hill, and hurries to his side.

"Hold on, Little Ghost! I was just on my way to see you. They've found another, not far from the first. The body has been left at Jakob Church this time."

A small party has already gathered in the cemetery. The tower watchman himself, a shamefaced expression directed at the ground, stands alongside the parson in his black cassock. Not far away, accustomed to shunning company, there are two gravediggers whom Winge recognizes from the Johannes burial ground, both resting beside the stretcher they have set down in the grass. They all look frozen in the damp air, most of all the man who found the body and raised the alarm.

Winge pulls his Beurling from his waistcoat pocket and checks the time. It is a little after seven. He compares it to the tower clock and finds that his own is twenty minutes fast. He adjusts the hands and turns the small key on the chain until the spring is wound. The priest rubs his shoulders and stamps his feet on the spot in ill-concealed impatience until Winge is done and turns to him. The answers come before he need ask.

"Mark here found him, and the sinner must have been asleep at his post because he didn't see anyone come or go. Isn't that right, Mark? One moment there is peace and quiet in the churchyard, the next second a body that has fallen from the sky? God help us. You bring shame upon your profession. With tower watchmen such as you, it's a miracle the city hasn't been turned into a field of ash to make Copenhagen seem a blessed paradise. Believe me when I say that this indolence will not go unnoticed in your pay."

A vestment has been laid across the deceased. Winge folds the white linen to one side. The tower watchman turns away with a groan, closely followed by the priest. The gravediggers crane their necks curiously, with the air of connoisseurs. Yet another lad, albeit a little older than the one he took his leave of the day before yesterday. He is lying on his back, his arms clasped across his chest, as peaceful as if he were lying here in intoxication or fatigue, or asleep during evening prayers. The pallor and mortal wound betray the illusion. There is a tear in the shirt, red at the edges, and when Winge carefully separates the stiff crusts of cloth, he sees the same shape etched into flesh in the side where the soft belly stops and the ribs begin. Lying next to the body is a piece of metal, a little longer than his arm and black, flat-hammered, and pointed at one end.

"Was it one of you who laid him out?"

The tower watchman shakes his head.

"No, my lord. I found him just that way. I only left him to ring my little bell to raise the alarm. I took the alb from the vestry and laid it over him, that's all."

The priest glances at him sternly.

"And it will scarcely ever be clean again."

Winge raises his voice so that it will carry to the gravediggers.

"Help me to turn him onto his side."

The men's rough fists are surprisingly gentle in grip. He hears them muttering as they roll the corpse over, and he guesses that the words are somewhere in the hinterland between prayer and incantation. Every craft that concerns itself with life and death has its own mores and superstitions. He crouches, and he finds the twin of the wound to the left of the vertebrae of the spine. No blood stains the ground. Cecil's whisper is in his ear.

"The one that you call Jesus from the Royal Garden . . . is he still in the morgue at Johannes?"

The older of the two gravediggers nods.

"Yes. The pit was supposed to have been dug already, but that was Joakim's job and he has lumbago. Thankfully the heat is gone, but regardless of who handles the shovel he needs to go into the ground before day's end."

The younger one shifts his weight nervously in response to Winge's silence.

"Jesus, that is. Not Joakim."

Winge points to the dead man.

"Can you stretcher him up to Johannes? Don't let anyone wash him as yet. I want to carry out my examination first. Lay them beside each other. I shall follow you at my own pace."

The stretcher, tensed between stooping backs, hurries off in advance along the edge of the Royal Garden and on along thoroughfares never tamed by cobbles. The gutter trickles past on his right-hand side in its shallow descent from the Bog down to Cat's Bay, upon whose shore the fishing boats empty their bilges. The earth that has for so long lain dry and cracked has drunk itself unthirsty, and each time he treads outside the paths where the footsteps of others have compacted the mud, he sinks deep enough to stain his stockings. The summer is over—the one that seemed to have settled upon the city for all time and eternity. The air is heavy; low clouds above him brood upon more rain and the east wind promises a prompt chill.

....

They are both lying in the morgue, each stretcher supported on a pair of simple trestles. Jesus, kept aboveground for much too long by infirmity, is ever more deeply painted in the colors of death. Beneath the torso are a flush of stains ranging from pale yellow to deepest red. Blackening veins meander like vines. Acid fumes emanate from the hole in the chest. The other lies alongside, and Emil begins with the clothes: they are simple and worn, those of a poor man, but not a vagabond. The white sections left unsullied by the past day testify to a shirt that has seen the laundry tub and scrubbing board on a weekly basis. The trousers have been repaired, new seams overlapping the old where the joins between fabrics have worn and the sections have come apart. When he is satisfied, he has to go and ask for a sharp knife because the body is stiff and reluctant to shift from its position. He cuts the shirt at the sides, and the trousers along the leg, until the clothes no longer hold together and can be lifted away in parts. Once they are pulled free, he presses the bundle to his face and inhales through his nostrils, and yes—there is a scent that does not belong, not rain or earth or the iron of blood. Smoke. Both shirt and trousers reek of it.

Cecil says the fists—palpate the fists. He gently forces apart the clasped hands and strokes the fingers and palms. The calluses are rough to the touch, accustomed to the grip of tools.

He takes a step back to contemplate the two of them at the same time. The right-hand one is younger than the one on the left, albeit not by much. They could well have been companions. One is blond and one is dark; the older has coarser limbs, his body clad in muscles, halfway to manhood. Winge takes a step to one side to give his full attention to the most recently discovered body. He places a finger on the chest and presses, and the mark does not whiten. Death came to both on the same day.

Cecil says the blood above the crotch and groin is not from the stab wound. Emil seeks another wound by way of explanation without finding one. He stands there for a long time in silence, nodding to himself in time with the drone of the flies, and his gaze flickers from the diaphragm of the one on the left to the chest of the one on the right. He moves closer to compare even more closely, places a hand to his brow, and turns away.

Emil leaves the morgue for a while, crumbling tobacco into his pipe until it is brimming, spilling yet more with trembling fingers, before seeking out the nearest smoking chimney to ask its owner for a light. He holds the pipe close to the fire until it is lit, then he returns inside. He allows his fingers to comb the curly hair until he finds what he seeks, several of the same thing. The small shards of mirror catch the light when he holds them up to the rays from the window, breaking the white light into a variety of colors. Cecil says he fell on his sword. Cecil says that here lies a Judas beside our Jesus.

63

Tycho Ceton paces back and forth across the floor of the drawing room, dragging his heels so much that Bolin's gaze is drawn anxiously to the expensive carpet.

"You have to be patient."

"But why?"

Bolin shifts his foot to a better position with a grimace.

"The performance was a success and no mistake, Tycho. After the first act they didn't know what to think. The second act took them by storm. Who has seen anything the like of it? A memory for life. I had my doubts about the third act until the last, but it all went off without a hitch. And the finale when the blacksmith lad rose from his self-spilled puddle as if from the dead and staggered down to the parterre and out, with the spear straight through his body . . . I don't know if you saw, but there were those among the brothers who thought we had been trifling with them and that the whole thing was just a farce with beetroot juice and crushed tomatoes. They were close to his body—close enough to touch him and be spattered by the still-pumping heart. The blade must have stanched the blood in that position, and struck just the right spot given the circumstances, but nevertheless . . . What an achievement! What desire, what *esprit*! Passion in the biblical sense to follow on from the earthly. Surely no one has ever earned their ovations more than that boy."

Ceton nods in irritation.

"So what's the problem if everyone is satisfied?"

Bolin rubs his hands together as if to squeeze more sensation out of wrinkled palms.

"Your own character was found to be . . . peculiar. You smashed the mirrors at the close of the second act without anyone understanding why. It didn't seem to be part of the whole, but rather something spontaneous, and everything seemed to come off despite your presence rather than because of it. There is speculation as to your reasons. You gave grist to the mill of your enemies, and they are not going to forfeit their opportunity to defame you—they claim you to be unsound of mind. The more cunning have used the success of the performance as its own argument: that the genius who has staged such an event cannot be trusted, and lines have been crossed as far as our order is concerned. More wine?"

Ceton holds out his glass and Bolin pours from the silver decanter, using the pause to change subject.

"But surely not everything is in a minor key? You have the Knapp girl safely contained in your chamber—the one that the persistent watchman has been searching for. I have no doubt she is of use to you now? It's not only the Lord Our Father who extends His helping hand most willingly to those who help themselves. It wouldn't hurt your case with the brothers if I could inform them that you were at least free of your pursuers, your problems solved by your own head."

"In the state she is in, she is of little use to me."

"Perhaps you should ensure it improves."

Bolin shakes an expression of disappointment off his face and seeks out a better disposition.

"Well, we can do nothing but wait and see. The brothers are to meet again soon, and never have so many voices been raised in your defense. Until then, you are quite comfortable here, are you not?"

Bolin raises his own refilled glass in a toast.

"Have trust, Tycho. The deciding voice may very well be my own, if my count is not mistaken."

64

His bunk. Home. A spasm arches his back, forcing Cardell's head backwards along with his heels, convulsing his body until his bones creak in competition with the wooden frame and base. Only for a while— then it releases and he falls back, panting, to where sleep awaits. He twists and turns his big body like a roast on a spit, but as ever there is only one position where he can find any peace: curled up like a child with the stump of his arm hugged to his chest and the rest of his body wrapped around it. In the depths of torpor, the chills of his fever dreams run amok. Memories of his ruin, frozen in old tableaux. The dead flock around Cardell—so close that he barely dares draw breath.

He is on the waves at Svensksund, on the deck of the *Ingeborg*—she who is condemned to become a wreck. Her fate is inescapable: she alone has been chosen from the line of battle. A weak point in her hull tempts the Russian cannon, the seas already high, the shot fired at random across a battle zone where no hit ought to be possible. The crash, the fire, the stores of gunpowder that threaten to explode. The impact rocks the gun mountings on deck. Men are hurled back and forth, broken and ragged, daubing the planks red. Their anguish forsakes the bass notes of manhood and cracks into shrill howls stripped of all dignity; vocal cords thrum to no avail, defenseless against the burning and the din of the wind. Now they are drowning in the insatiable sea, and he is alone on the deck, shackled by the anchor chain. Now his grip on Johan Hjelm's collar is slipping, and yet another friend is lost, the buttons of the uniform and the wide-open whites of the eyes visible a foot below the oily mirror that is the surface of the water, then gone, but etched in his field of vision as if by white-hot needles. Now he is being rescued, delirious with chills after hours exposed to the elements, but strong hands are not enough to break him loose. Now they are comparing knives, passing the sharpest from hand to hand to whoever has drawn the short straw. At first he feels nothing, his arm long since numb. Then everything. It never gets better.

Now his boot loses its grip on the slippery bottom of Larder Lake, and beneath him the depths open, a swollen corpse his lifebuoy. An embrace, a promise drunkenly murmured.

Now Cecil Winge is smiling at him in the glow of the smoking tallow candles of Cellar Hamburg; he turns and opens the door, not onto Postmaster's Hill but into a black abyss. Now he is standing by Winge's grave—one of just a few. Dust to dust.

Now he is running cowering through the flames in the corridors of Horn Hill. The Red Hare roars with hunger and delirium. The children scream their prayers for mercy that does not come. Now he is carrying her children in his arms. Now they are falling from his grasp. Now Erik Three Roses is dying by his hand, part crushed, part drowned.

....

The weight of the ghosts presses him from all sides—the burnt and the drowned united in their envy at all that has been taken from them and still remains his. Where is the justice? He is suffocating, suffocating, is woken when the bunk beneath him falls away and he hits the floor, and the pain in his stump flares like phosphorus to newly opened eyes. The gate of hell was once opened to him, but only his arm made it through before it was closed again. Its flesh is being roasted ahead of time, tender enough to melt on the tongue when they come to celebrate his own arrival. Every morning he tells himself: never has it hurt as much as it did tonight. Each time the pain wakes him, he strikes the stump against the boards to gain a more worldly pain, a more comprehensible one, and when someone who must have recently moved in hammers the wall in defense of their sleep he roars profanities back at them.

....

Night. A tallow candle cradles its flame; a face, rain against the window. Emil Winge hunched over a manuscript held inside gilded leather. He recognizes the portfolio. Three Roses's testimony from Tycho Ceton's chamber. Cardell's breathing must have betrayed his condition, because Emil comes, bathes his brow, strains water for him to drink through gritted teeth, pressing his fingers against his wrist. He has nothing to offer by way of resistance.

"Didn't I tell you to clean your wound?"

He cannot answer. His jaw is locked so tightly his teeth are creaking.

"It's lockjaw. Tetanus. I've had doctors come here with their mercury—first one and then another—but they can do nothing. Your body is a battlefield beyond aid. You will defeat the blight yourself, or you won't. I will be here when I can, until we know."

Capitulation. A return to torpor.

....

He wakes yet again, and Winge is still reading. Something else now. A crumpled letter. His senses are too slippery to allow for any grip. He falls again into the abyss.

....

When he next wakes he finds the cramps have eased enough for him to open his mouth. He can move, albeit not much, and he turns in the bed and lifts his back, which has been chafing against the sheets. The very act of changing position is a mercy, and must suffice. Winge comes in the evening, offering him water. Light and darkness do somersaults through the room as the days merge into one. They speak when he can, as briefly as possible. Only later, when he is strong enough to sit upright, does Winge produce a long object wrapped in coarse cloth. He produces the hidden object from beneath Cardell's bed, holding it with both hands. An iron rod shaped into a flat point and marked by the blows of a hammer.

"Jean Michael, do you know what this is?"

He proffers his hand, and after hesitating Winge places the object on the palm of his hand. It is heavier than Cardell expected—until he realizes that it is he who has been weakened. It is a hand's breadth shorter than two cubits. He weighs it in his hand, feeling for the point where the blade weighs evenly.

"Yes. I've seen my fair share."

"Well?"

"It is a sword blank. After it was fully forged and hardened, it would be rubbed shiny and sent to the engraver to be carved with the king's monogram. Then to the brassfounder for a brass hilt. Eventually it would be issued to a fresh-faced cavalry officer to hang from his belt, where it would be of little use other than for his self-esteem. He might have an opportunity to wave it in the direction of danger, but all bloodletting in close combat is left to the men and their angled bayonets."

Winge nods to himself, satisfied with the answer.

"The Military College ought to have lists of those engaged for the forging work."

"Tell me what you are thinking."

"The second body that was found, our Judas, was a blacksmith's apprentice. His clothes reeked with smoke from the hearth, his right arm was stronger than his left, his right hand was hard and calloused. His arms are pale where gloves have shielded them from the sun, his shoulders red with white stripes where the apron has sat. I believe he fell on his own craftsmanship."

"By his own hand?"

"Such is my thesis. But someone moved him afterwards—someone who wished him well."

"What about me? Give me something to do."

"The gentlemen who knocked on your door last summer hardly did so in the hope of plundering your fortune from you. Something else is behind it. When you're well enough, do you think you could find out more?"

"The Furies? Has Ceton won their favor?"

"That's what I believe, but let us not paint with our imagination before reality condescends to sit to us."

"You seem to believe a great deal that you are keeping secret."

"First, one more question, if I may. What if there had been a mirror in the anatomical theater on the evening we were there, and Ceton had caught a glimpse of himself in the condition you describe. Do you think he would have appreciated what he saw?"

"Hardly."

Winge nods to himself, chewing on a cuticle.

"Well, my thought is that Jesus and Judas are both the work of Ceton, cast in their roles both for the sake of the Furies and for his own sake— a spectacle of sorts. He seeks their mercy. That is what logic says. It is not only his best chance to be rid of us, but also to return to the existence that he desires. It was on his behalf that an ambush was sprung against your life. You're hardly living incognito—someone gave up your door number."

"What about you, then? I kept vigil in your stairwell with the same thought in mind. No one came."

"I'm close to the Chamber of Police for the time being. My own demise might lead to awkward questions being asked. Speaking of which, here is your pay from the Chamber. I asked them to add what you receive from the Stockholm Watch and demand compensation from them."

Winge makes to place the cloth purse on the table, but stops himself and instead picks up the paper lying on it: name after name in bloodspattered lines.

"But it's not just me who prefers to keep quiet rather than speak too soon. What is this?"

Cardell makes to sit up straighter, but has to give in with a groan.

"The girl. Anna Stina. Last year she was sent into the workhouse through a secret passage to seek out Rudenschöld, who was there for several nights awaiting transfer. She was supposed to extract a letter listing all Gustavians recruited to Armfelt's cause and who were ready to bear arms against Reuterholm and the regency. The conspirators don't know each other's names, and thus the revolution lies fallow. The workhouse custodian, Pettersson, took it off her as a pledge, indifferent as to its value. It has languished with him ever since, while all parties have searched in vain for the girl."

Emil Winge turns pale, and returns the paper to the table carefully as if it were a snake with poison dripping from its fangs.

"My God."

Cardell grunts his agreement.

"Jean Michael, what are your politics?"

"Well versed enough not to prefer the despots of yesterday over today's without careful consideration."

"So you intend to do nothing?"

"That letter is worth her life and that of many others, to boot. But she remains missing. It stays where it is."

"Keep it safe whatever you do."

65

Emil Winge's steps take him ever farther south across the Southern Isle to places he has only heard about but never seen with his own eyes. After the lock gates, he passes the church that houses his brother's ashes, rising among hills crowned by windmills hissing in the wind. At least the climb returns some warmth to him. On the other side of the hill, poverty awaits. The stones of a solitary poorhouse rise above wooden shacks of a kind that the danger of fire have seen prohibited elsewhere. Every now and then the manufactories make themselves known through scent and sound before he sees them. Leaf tobacco and brimming vats of paint sting his nostrils, set to the theme of the foremen's instructions and abuse, with misery and excuses by way of counterpoint. Old residences have been claimed, their once-stately interiors torn apart to make way for spinning wheels and carpenter's benches. The wind casts its force at him, stopping him midstep as if he has struck an unseen barrier. His stomach is turning and he has to put a hand across his nose and take deep breaths to control himself, bent double as if ducking beneath a stench that puts the Flies' Meet to shame. And between two houses he sees it, like a clearing in the settlement—a wide tarn whose greasy surface breaks up the light into stripes of unfamiliar colors as it laps against its swampy shores. Against all common sense, he staggers closer, because he has heard the name and the tale and he wants to see if they have done justice. This is the Larder. Its waters are barely more than a bubbling pulp, muddied to black by all that it has been entrusted with that others wish to forget, surrounded by square paddocks for nightsoil carriers to ease their burden, a few tufts of grass divulging that they have so far been left undisturbed. An ox head is swimming a few cubits out, sluggishly contemplating him for a while with an eye over which the flies crawl unperturbed before something shifts in the deeps and upends the carcass in a leisurely dive. Over his shoulder there is a brooding presence that reminds him that this is the *fons et origo* of the Cardell he knows—the beginning of everything. He turns and hurries away, preferring to take a detour rather than test its shores any further.

Before long he has to ask for directions, and gets nothing but an obliging wave in response: on, on. The nose that he has now been able to unpinch comes to his rescue. He scents charcoal, turns into the wind that has helped him, and follows his nose. The forge is behind a wall, open and free, to frustrate the fire that might one day creep out of the hearth and demand retribution. His hand on the gate is enough for the smith to leave his bellows and come to meet him.

"If you seek service then I must say you look rather slender. But I'm not picky."

The words are said half in jest. The blacksmith pours water onto his face from a barrel, wiping the soot from his brow on his shirtsleeve, brushing his fists against his apron and showing Winge to a block upon which to sit. This is not the first visit of this kind that Winge has made—had it not been for the names struck out on his list of men engaged by the Military College, he would have lost count long ago. They talk awhile. The smith harps on the same garrulous string that they all do.

"Time is out of joint. To hell with Svensksund. Not that I wish a Russian for king, but if the battle had only ended somewhat equally we would have had many a year of war yet. I remember eighty-eight and eighty-nine. The hammers were clattering away day and night. We had to equip every soldier with a rapier and bayonet, billhook and cutlass. Us children of the household went down to the weighing scales on the orders of the Crown, and each man with a license for forging work could demand any price he liked for his work with no further ado. When the guild held a ball, we were the equals of the knights, in new clothes and silver buckles on our shoes and silver buttons on our breeches. Now I stand here among dust and ashes in leather and rags, with two daughters for whom I have no dowry to give, and if they are ever to be married they must use their sex to bait their traps and threaten to shame the reluctant fathers."

He spits into the earth.

"The war carried us forward. What else spurs mankind to brilliance, other than the knowledge that an enemy prowls the borders, ready to thrust a sword into your back, shackle your son to the yoke, and make harlots of both your wife and daughter?"

Winge lets the smith talk, lighting his pipe from a stick ignited in the hearth.

"Look at the City-between-the-Bridges as it has become. So stuffed to the brim with loose folk without wit or work that they were compelled to weed them out by inquisition. They're already streaming back in, more of them and more brazen. A good war would have licked them into shape. The best would have come home again, and we would have been shot of the worst. Every cohort must be weeded out if they are to germinate. Those who survive come home to the spoils of war, and to be blunt, our fields are better at feeding the few than the many. Only blood will do when we have to grease the axle of society. All know it, but few speak the truth. Now famine is here, the grim sister of peace."

He sighs remorsefully.

"They say the late king himself started the war as a Machiavellian scheme to blame the Russians. Well, so what? He knew his subjects well. Not many raise their voices to toast Gustav's honor any longer, but we still remember the song, we smiths, and we sing it with longing."

Winge unwraps the sword blank from its cloth and passes it to the smith, who receives it with the air of a connoisseur.

"A good example of what I'm talking about. Not more than one hundred years ago, a weapon such as this wouldn't have been good for much. You had to stop in battle to allow both sides to knock their blades straight and sharpen new edges. Today we tease the coal under the crucible with the bellows and achieve a heat that would make the devil himself sweat, and then we harden the steel. Once this is done, you can slay a regiment before its edge needs to be put to the whetstone."

The blacksmith brings the steel to his eye to examine its length, and then glances nervously at Winge.

"Does this stem from my own hearth?"

"Such is my question to you."

The smith lays the blank on the side of his fist, seeking its center of gravity.

"Is this about my apprentice? The hammer marks bear Albrecht's character. Are you from the Consistory? Has the boy gone too far in his superstitions?"

"I'm from the Chamber of Police."

"Worse still."

"Tell me about him."

The blacksmith extends his arms.

"The boy had talent. All that he lacked was the time to learn. You should know that the profession is not an easy one to acquire. Power in the arm, accuracy and judgment, zeal and a good head—otherwise the ingots are forfeit. When I became an apprentice, I did the initiation—just like all the others. The older boys pissed in a bowl, held me over it, and shaved my head, and my God it stung, no less in my spirits than my scalp. Albrecht is on the way to the same baptism, I should say, if only people would have some understanding for his foreign descent. Albrecht came from the south—he and his cousin—with a letter of recommendation. We're family, so it seems, at least by a few winding branches. I took him on as an apprentice and Wilhelm as coal boy to handle the bellows until his arms became strong enough to help at the anvil."

"And their faith?"

"Both Moravians. Naturally I noticed that they shunned mass and said their own prayers in a foreign language. But they were industrious and gentle lads nonetheless, and they made it easy for me to turn a deaf ear. Good apprentices don't grow on trees—especially not those who barely ask for more than a plate on the table and a roof over their heads in return for their efforts."

"Albrecht is the bigger of the two, blond-haired, with smith's fists, and Wilhelm is dark and slim, and they are so alike they might be brothers?"

He nods.

"On Friday morning they were late to rise, like they have never been before. I searched for them in their room. No one had slept there; and there has been no news since then. I have had to fire the hearth alone, master and boy all in one. Do you have them in your custody? What have they done?"

Winge sits silently absorbed in his own thoughts for a while.

"Find new lads. These ones will not return."

The blacksmith opens his mouth to ask more, but their eyes meet and he closes it again. Both rise, Winge to leave and the smith to blow warmth back into the glow again. He takes a deep sigh as he closes his fist around the handle of the bellows.

"Perhaps this is the punishment for my sin of letting Dissenters hammer the Lord's gifts."

"What is?"

The blacksmith gives him a look as if he has understood nothing. "Peace, of course."

When he is on the far side of the gate, he hears the blacksmith humming in time with the puffing of the bellows.

"I sing to my king, to Gustav the Great, whose implacable fate is to balance the scales till Sweden prevails in all matters of state."

66

The rain streams down over the rooftops, leaking droplets that cool Cardell's chamber. Day and night merge, the fits of cramp reducing in strength and time with each passing day. Cardell is nothing if not a practiced convalescent. He knows how best to pass the time in a sickbed. He sleeps as much as he can, his exhausted body grateful for the rest, and when wakefulness forces itself upon him he is able to reduce even that to a kind of torpor in which he stares vacantly into space with infinite patience and forces every thought to move slowly enough to fill the time. Before an open window he slumbers dreamlessly, snoring like a clubbed ox, and night by night the chills are driven from his body. As soon as he is able to, he staggers out, lying in wait in the stairwell until he can grab the middle son of the family downstairs by the scruff of the neck, promising untold riches to the delighted and eager lad in exchange for the errand of carrying up a few meals from the nearest inn. He devours what is brought as if he has never seen food before and without a thought for the slate on which his debts are tallied, just as grateful for sour herring as he is for salted pork, and he showers the boy with praise the day he stumbles through the door bent double under a half cask of beer.

Left to his own devices, Cardell dwells upon something that bothers him, refusing to leave him alone. His whole life seems to consist of interludes between battles. He has encountered superior odds and more evenly matched resistance, and he has always been able to give as good as he has got, or more. Over and over, he replays his brawl with Petter Pettersson, blow by blow and step by step, and each time he comes to the same conclusion. His opponent was bigger, faster, hit harder, and was just as hardened as himself. Yet he alone remains alive. It is as if he is hag-ridden by a guilty conscience of a kind he cannot explain, the sense of having colluded with some unknown injustice. And outside it is already autumn.

Feeling himself stronger, he begins to move a little more. First across the floor of the room, no more than ten steps back and forth, conquering one crack in the floorboards at a time. He tries his strength first on the chair, then the table, then the bunk. He walks up and down the stairs until his heart is pounding and his throat burns. Then out, once again within the walls of Sodom in the City-between-the-Bridges, once around the quarter before returning. Stronger with each passing day. Eventually, he makes it all the way to Ironmonger's Square, where he waits until the girls come with their baskets, and he spreads the word that he is looking for Lotta Erika, erstwhile stepdaughter of Frans Gry in Mary Magdalene.

With the seed sown, he takes a broomstick for a crutch and limps down to the harbor to find a cart. A man who has just unloaded his takes him north without payment after Cardell proves himself to be both obliging and broke, on boards marked by the white dust of their recently delivered sacks of flour. At the customs gate, he thanks him for the lift, and talks a while to the men, who shrug and wave him through. He is out of shape, the sweat forming under his shirt and jacket from the effort of wading through withering grass and having to balance on uneven tufts. Once he has forced his way through the bushes at the edge of the forest, he reaches easier ground and soon finds paths he remembers, passing a meadow where twigs have been bound into crosses to mark hidden hollows, along the stream that springs from its source up the hill, and in under the trees where stones have been laid out in a circle around charred twigs. There is no one here, but he goes down on one knee to touch the ashes. The warmth of the fire still lingers on in the ground.

"You're here?"

He doesn't hear her coming. When he turns his head she is standing close by: Lisa Forlorn, just as he remembers her. Everything she has endured seems to have bought her the mercy of time itself. The same worn garments, the same face. The port-wine stain almost hides it, but he catches a wrinkle of concern when she scrutinizes him.

"You aren't taking proper care of yourself."

"Lord knows it must be bad when one gets pity from tramps. Spare your feelings of tenderness. I have been sick, but my strength is returning by the day. Soon I will be better than I was before."

He falls silent, self-conscious, and then he answers the question she hasn't asked.

"I haven't found her yet."

Lisa Forlorn comes closer, sitting down on a fallen branch.

"Autumn is upon us. I've waited as long as I can. Winter is coming, wandering south from its summer hide, closer by the day. The fox and the hare are digging their burrows deeper. Soon it will be the wolf's time. The fire that dies down will be ever harder to light among damp splinters. If I am to keep ahead of it I must go south."

He nods.

"That's as I thought. I'm glad I found you while there was time. I haven't given up. I want you to know that."

They sit together for a while longer before he leaves her, and Lisa Forlorn hears his groans and profanities long after he has laboriously stumbled his way across the scrub and roots. Up by the burrow, her pack has been ready for many days. Everything is prepared and she need only weave some branches to conceal the entrance to the burrow before slinging the pack on her back. First she takes the path up towards Owl's Bay, where she knows there is still alumroot and fivespot growing, picks herself an armful, and then returns the way she came to the meadow on the forest hill. She finds the right place, clearing the ground of twigs and grass. All summer she has slept here, curled up on top of the patch where just a foot or so of soil separates her from the child she has never seen, but the nights have grown too cold, the rain cutting mercilessly into her skin and the wind harrying the open spot as if in revenge for the lull that has endured beneath the crowns of the Great Shade. If she lingers, the wreath she is leaving on the grave will be one made from her own bones. She hums slowly as she braids another in farewell, the blue flowers glowing between the deep red leaves, hoping that it will be blanket enough to warm the earth until the year turns.

67

Ceton scratches his scar, once again overgrown with itchy stubble, inspecting for the thousandth time the rooms put at his disposal by Anselm Bolin while the Kindly Ones deliberate. He regrets ever asking Bolin for assistance with his pursuers, because now they all know that the Chamber of Police is unraveling his past, and meticulousness is a virtue they hold in high esteem. The fool and the cripple carry weight—reason enough to keep him at a distance and refuse him everything he was promised. Each and every one seems entrenched in his own view. The bile of bitterness stings his throat day and night, but he cannot really claim to be surprised. He is himself the best man for the job, and others' help is never really to be counted upon. Thank goodness for the drawing from the Stockholm Watch and his own resourcefulness. The boy came. The girl is his, albeit in a state so poor that her value is decidedly low. Now he awaits expertise, pacing back and forth, glancing with each turn at the pocket watch he has allowed himself to indulge in as a replacement for the one that got stepped on. It is close enough to the appointed hour that one of Bolin's servants shows in his guest without censure. Ceton scrutinizes him with a practiced eye. The man is young, his clothes worn, but his gaze is servile and the bow is the right one.

"Welcome. Perhaps we have met before? My protégé Erik Three Roses was under the care of Dane's Bay until as recently as last year. I am Tycho Ceton."

The doctor has a commonplace face that Ceton is unable to recall. Nor does his guest seem to have any memories of past encounters, fleeting as they might have been, but he frowns out of courtesy.

"I saw Three Roses on occasion as I worked alongside Professor

Hagström to observe and learn. A hopeless case in the end, as far as I understand, and one that has left quite an aggravating reputation in its wake as far as management of the asylum goes."

Abashed, he stares down and fiddles with a worn cuff link.

"Forgive me, it was not my intention to express myself so bluntly. I have been among my peers for far too long. We who have sworn the Hippocratic oath have a harsh jargon, and it may be that it is our way of drawing a veil over all-too-tender emotions. I swear the words house nothing but concern."

"Concern unites us. What would we be without love of our neighbor? Barely has poor Erik been wrenched from my care than I once again find myself made guardian of one whom life has trodden upon."

"That is why you have sent for me? For a consultation?"

"Assuredly."

Some coins change hands and Ceton opens the door to the adjacent room. Sitting on his bed is the girl, in just her nightshirt. A maid holds her upright with her hands at her shoulders, and stows away a gruel spoon and jug when Ceton signals to her to withdraw. The doctor settles the sides of the spectacles that he does not need but has assumed in honor of his mentor over his ears, rolls up his sleeves, and raises an eyebrow at Ceton.

"May I?"

"Of course—if you would be so good as to clothe your thoughts in words as soon as they arise."

He considers her for a while with a critical gaze.

"Well, it is a girl of between fifteen and twenty years of age. The age is hard to determine in a face so devoid of expression."

He grasps the thighs and calves, moving each leg back and forth, repeating the movements with each arm, and feeling the torso and back.

"She appears to be in good shape despite her privation, retaining the flexibility of youth in her movement, unsullied by visible vices. The belly has the stretch marks of recent pregnancy."

He moves a hand back and forth in front of her face without eliciting any reaction, first slowly and then with mock violence, both from side to side and towards the face. He turns her head first towards the window, then towards the wall.

"The eyes are unseeing and the gaze does not attach; the pupils do not dilate or contract."

Fingers seek out a pulse to capture the beating of the heart, counting them for a while in time with the passage of the pocket watch. He raises an arm and lets it fall. Then he sits in his own thoughts for a while until his hand shoots out without warning and pinches the flesh on her side.

"The heart is strong and beats evenly at a pace befitting her age. Sudden stimuli leave her unmoved."

He removes his glasses, polishes the lenses with the corner of his cravat, and carefully stows them in the pocket of his waistcoat before turning back to Ceton.

"May I ask whether anything in particular has prompted this state of affairs?"

"Let us say revolutionary events of a violent nature."

"How long ago?"

"Winter of last year."

The doctor nods as if the response was expected.

"Then it is as I thought. The mind—or the soul if you prefer—has strayed from its domicile. In circumstances such as this, we try to create enough stimulus in the body for the mind to be lured back. In years gone by, we grafted scabies onto the sick, but today we have more modern methods to turn to: a swing bed where the convalescents are thrown about in a wide circle to instill a terror so strong that the madness gives way and their true self is returned to its rightful place. It is an impressive sight to see in action—a triumph of mechanics. I myself have counted more than one hundred and twenty revolutions per minute—with such force that all the blood is forced to the head and falls as tears."

"And from the shackles of this swing bed the recently mad are led out healthy of mind and body?"

The doctor is momentarily tongue-tied.

"The mechanism is fairly new. Unsurprisingly, further time is required to refine the method, and not even the best remedies offer a certain outcome since each affliction follows its own course. What is irrefutable is that it has worked wonders where laxatives have performed badly. If you wish, I can make inquiries about a suitable time?"

Ceton rubs his coarse chin.

"I think I shall spare my charge your swing bed for the time being. But I declare that you have given me much to think about, and those coins I have spent I consider well used."

He accompanies the doctor to the door.

"There is one more thing, Doctor. Just as you now know where I conduct myself, so I have gone to the trouble of determining where you live. If you wish to forget my address then I shall have no cause to remember yours."

68

Getting directions is not difficult—any police constable is capable of setting him on the right course. They know the Moravians well. Their preacher, Svala, has proselytized in the City-between-the-Bridges late in the evening for many years, ranting beneath a flame in the square with a handful of faithfuls as guard of honor until the constables routinely arrive to move them on. The home of the congregation is no secret, even if few outsiders have cause to go there. Its land extends from the shadow beneath the alley that flanks the Royal Garden as far as the shores of Cat's Bay beside Packer's Square. They have been here since the century was young, tolerated at the time due to their small numbers, and now due to their big ones. The revival has spread widely without regard for the boundaries that inhibit all worldly things: from low to high, young to old, all the way up to the state rooms at court where not only the dowager queen but also little King Gustav Adolf have lent time and ears to the false doctrine. The Church is biding its time. The clergy curse heresy from their pulpits, threatening purgatory.

Emil Winge's path passes by Jakob Church, past a silent Nonpareil with its blind windows, currently inactive and barred as the theater is quarrelling over the autumn program and all rehearsals have been postponed while awaiting harmony. Behind the walls lies the Royal Garden, now empty and defoliated, the leaves of the trees gathered in wet drifts in the corners where they have been blown by the wind. Winge turns his collar farther up his neck, raises his shoulders, and bows his head to protect himself from its fumbling chill.

Facing the Royal Garden is the manor house, two storeys of brick. An equally large building with paler plaster is visible just behind, alongside small wooden buildings, all of them raised on timber frames higher than a man can reach. Irresolute about where he should be going, Winge climbs the steps to the main door and gives the clapper a few hasty knocks. A maid opens with an air of disgruntlement and speaks in a whisper as if to compensate for the racket.

"The widow is taking a nap."

Winge gives her the name Blom mentioned, and she leads him through the building's interior, now past its prime, and out the other side. Squeezed between the houses are apple trees, the branches laden with fruit, baskets and ladders testifying to the ongoing harvest. She makes towards the other larger building but stops with a small exclamation en route, and gestures in among the trees where a man is stretching to pick the branches clean.

"Lars! The gentleman is asking for Lars."

He wears only a shirt despite the chill, and yet mops sweat from his brow and bows his head to acknowledge Winge. At first the man strikes Winge as an unlikely churchman, rough as a carpenter, with a long salt-and-pepper beard, but he soon changes his mind. There is a gentleness in his face, and he can understand how God's words emanating from a source such as this must assume a natural credibility.

"I am Lars Svala, at your service."

"Emil Winge. I have come on behalf of the Chamber of Police."

Svala hesitates for a moment before nodding curtly. Under the apple trees, they have laid out a raked path with a crossroads in the center that branches off in all directions. They begin to walk around together, Svala clearly set on letting Emil lead the dance.

"I don't know much about your faith."

"Probably more than you think. We all worship the same God. The difference is that we reserve the right to worship Him on our own terms and to distance ourselves from the position of the Church. We abstain from middlemen in salvation."

"No wonder the Church is doing what they can to be rid of you."

Winge discerns a blush around Svala's brow, and hears his breathing grow heavier.

"What priest wouldn't sing such verses when his own livelihood is at stake? Is it right that the bishop gorges himself in his palace using money with which the congregation has been encouraged to buy plots in paradise, though God Himself would not tax a penny more than a grain of sand?"

He falls silent, at once abashed.

"Forgive me. As you can tell, the subject is close to my heart. Here is a bench—let us sit."

"You venerate the same sacrament and commandments?"

"Of course."

"Would you say that a man who is versed in the words of God demands a higher standard of virtue than one who is ignorant?"

Svala nods thoughtfully.

"A sin committed without intent may be easier to forgive, for the Lord as for those made in His likeness."

"The punishment for the conscious misdemeanor is worse?"

"That is reasonable."

"And if that man of learning be you, and the sin is to perpetuate an untruth?"

A melancholy smile crosses Svala's face.

"Then I am embroiled in my own faith. Well, if your questions lead me to a confession then I am glad that at least it has not been entrusted to a fool."

"There is something else I wish to say first. I know the city watch repel you back across the bridges when you proselytize in the evenings, but I come on different business. I harbor no grudge towards your congregation, and I cannot pass judgment on a faith that I cannot possibly value in comparison with another—I mean no ill towards anyone who does not have misdeeds upon their conscience. You don't know me, but I still ask that you trust my word."

Lars Svala considers him for a moment before sighing.

"I have spoken to representatives of the powers that be in the past, but you seem quite different to me. I am the shepherd of my flock, unworthy as I am, and not unaccustomed to reading others. I do not see any malice in you. I shall do as you say."

Winge gestures towards the grove of trees.

"You've left your coat and hat below the ladder. Yet I see mourning crape among the folds."

"A lamb has been taken by the wolf."

"Did the lamb answer to the name of Albrecht?"

Lars Svala's surprise is plain upon his face.

"How can you know?"

"Was it you who moved him to Jakob Church, or another from your flock?"

Svala places his large hands on his knees, as if he is ready to be clapped in irons.

"It was I and I alone."

"Will you tell me in your own words, from the beginning?"

"I was awake at night—I know not why—listening to the wind as it grew with each passing hour. It was as if I were awaiting ruin. There was a noise down in the courtyard, and once I had lit a lantern I found Albrecht there, felled with steel through his body. I asked who had hurt him so badly, and he placed his hand to his own breast. There was nothing that I could do for him other than to give a benediction and hold his hands in his final moments. Dawn was near. I carried him to my room to watch over him. You must understand that it was no easy decision that I made—my responsibility is to my entire flock, and there are many who wish us ill. An incident of this kind might harm us more than we can recover from. I waited all day and when the night came again I carried him to the church-yard, laying him out for the priest to find at morning light. Better to be in the church's consecrated earth than eternal damnation."

"Did he acquire his injury in your courtyard? Was there blood?"

"No."

"Do you know where he had come from?"

"His left shoe was filled with blood and left a trail. I did not follow it any farther than to the gate. By then the rain had already begun and the traces were diminishing with each passing minute."

"But which direction?"

Svala points towards the Stream and Winge nods.

"He can't have walked far if what you say is true. Are you missing any lambs other than this one?"

Svala's expression shifts into open supplication.

"Wilhelm. His cousin. Do not tell me that the boy has a part in this too."

Winge feels gratitude that he is not a man of Svala's kind, bound to the truth under threat of the purification of purgatory. Emil is free to give Lars Svala the gift of his silence. He changes subject.

"Do you worship the image of the Lord? Would you show me your place of prayer?"

Svala remains still for a few moments before bowing his head in reluctant gratitude at the insight he has been spared, rising and leading Winge towards the preaching hall. Inside, benches stand in rows, simple planks on trestles, arranged in semicircles to reduce the distance to the altar. At the front there is a crucifix where the Savior hangs on His nails, crowned with thorns. Winge approaches it to see better in the dim light, and finds on the wooden figure every detail that he has already seen in the flesh.

"Tell me about the wounds."

"There are five. One in each place where nails have been driven through the hands and feet, and finally the tear where the Roman legionary Longinus directed his lance."

Winge allows his fingers to caress the right-hand side of the rib cage where the woodcarver has laboriously and deftly whittled a gaping wound, narrower at each end, and with edges parted like the leaves of a newly broken bud, like red lips. Svala's voice becomes dreamlike in his explanation.

"The bloody thoracic wound. It is the subject of special veneration because beneath it the sacred heart is bared, ready to receive each sinner in the embrace of salvation."

Winge stands there for a long time absorbed in his own thoughts before he turns around.

"Tycho Ceton. Is the name familiar? A scar by the mouth makes him easy to distinguish from others."

Svala stands there pale and silent, unable to disguise his quaking body.

"So this is his work? All of it?"

"Have your paths crossed?"

"He came to us in the evening when we were spreading the Lord's word in the City-between-the-Bridges. His distressed soul seemed to shine to me like a bonfire, and for the sake of his salvation I gave him a bed for the summer."

"He lived here, under your own roof?"

"Soon enough I began to sense whom I had invited across our threshold. But who but a sinner is worth the trouble of saving? Thus I interpreted my calling. I still had hope and God by my side—hope that has now been lost. How to subjugate that devil which knows to take advantage of all that is good, that only allows himself to be destroyed by one who is willing to sin just as badly as he?"

Winge nods at the question, leaving it open. He makes certain of the practicalities: when Ceton came, when he left, what he saw, what he said. Once every detail appears to have been clarified to his satisfaction, he makes to leave but then stops himself.

"Do you know that he is the son of a man of God?"

Svala turns away with a brief nod.

"That much I guessed."

He hesitates a moment before continuing.

"I wanted to drive him out but he asked me for one final favor: he said that in his time in the south he had succumbed to a fever that would not leave him in peace; he felt that a fit was imminent and he asked to stay until the chills had abated."

Svala hesitates, shifting his weight from foot to foot and undoing a button on the shirt under which he has begun to sweat.

"I couldn't resist making my way to his door. I listened to his anguish, and when I heard his cries I went into the chamber in the hope of being of more assistance, if only to prevent him from doing harm to himself. He was barely in his senses, tossing to and fro in bed, and suddenly I was tempted and reflected that this opportunity would never return."

"What did you do?"

" 'My son,' I said, 'have trust, for I am here with you—both the Lord and I.' And this is a double sin I accomplish here, for I took advantage of his weakness, and now I break the sacred confidence between each man and his priest."

"And Ceton? What did he say?"

"He looked at me in a way that made clear to me that the fever had replaced my face with that of another. In his daze, he took my words literally. First it was a triumph and relief to him, so it seemed to me, as if something he had long hoped for had just come to pass. Then his expression was replaced with one of horror and he shook, the anxiety radiating from him. He grabbed my arm. I still bear the marks from his nails. 'Father, has he seen what pains I have gone to in order to find him? What it has cost? Can he see that my heart is pure?' I realized he thought himself dead and resurrected. 'My son,' I said, 'the Lord is love—he forgives his children all.' And with that his face was smoothed into one of blessed relief, and I knew that I had done him a kind deed. He fell back into a torpor, and when he next woke it was as if nothing had happened and what memories he had were but a dream. He left us, just as he promised."

Lars Svala cranes his neck, turning towards the crucifix.

"So lies another sacrament broken under my heel. I am glad that it happened before the eyes of Our Lord, so that He may Himself determine whether I have done right or wrong. I submit myself to His mercy, now as ever. I hope that my violation of the oath is not in vain. For Albrecht. For Wilhelm."

They walk outside. On their way through the orchard, Svala turns again to Winge.

"What are your beliefs, Emil Winge?"

"I have heard it said that God is the form we have given to what reason cannot explain."

A resigned smile crosses Svala's face, as if the words are all too familiar. They stop at the gate.

"For my own part, I have heard it said that had God not existed, then it would have been necessary to invent Him."

Emil returns his smile.

"Who is ensnaring whom?"

69

Tongues are wagging. Cardell has only had to wait a single night before there is a scratching at the door and a neighbor tells him that a girl is asking after him in the street.

She curtsies, made shy by the time that has passed since they last spoke.

"Mickel, they say you have been on your deathbed."

"A mere scratch. I'm lazy and dull by nature—I like a good rest. How are you, Lotta?"

Her face cracks into a smile.

"It's just me and Mother now. She grieved a little, but freedom suits her, and the old man left us what little he had. I don't have to mention his name when introducing myself, which is good. This winter, I will stow my basket and start milking over Danto way in a warm barn with good walls."

"That pleases me."

For a moment they stand in silence, Cardell grateful to share in her happiness, if only for a minute.

"Lotta, the last time we met you gave me words of warning about your late stepfather, may he rest in peace. Do you know more? Were there companions of his you had not seen before during his final days?"

"There was a man I didn't recognize. I heard them through the wall, drinking together into the night, talking as if they were old friends. If only I could remember his name. I don't think I ever heard it clearly even then. It was short and foreign."

"Did you hear what they were talking about?"

"The war, I think. Memories."

"Did Gry drink in the same places as before, or did he seek out new springs?"

"He went to the Last Farthing now and then. He usually couldn't be bothered to trudge over there before."

Cardell gives her his thanks. He knows he ought to wait for more of his strength to return, but his time in the chamber has become too much for him. The walk beyond the customs gate was exhausting, but seems to have done him good nonetheless, because if he tries hard enough he can walk without a limp. Up in his room, he fastens the wooden fist into place, the grip of the straps unfamiliar on the stump that has been free for a long time now. He grimaces when he tries its weight in different positions. To hell with it. Surely he looks strong and dangerous, even if appearances can be deceptive.

....

Johan Kreutz has drunk too much of late—that much he is reminded of each morning when he is forced to spend an hour in the privy suffering the anguishes of hell before his sour stomach allows itself to be persuaded to release its wretched burden. He rejoices that the spirits are at least being chalked up, because nothing tastes as good as a debt left for the morrow, and were he one day to break his neck down by the town wharf, then it would all be free—a comfort as good as any. The lip cracked by Cardell's wooden fist—may it burn in hell—has reminded him of how weak his proud flesh has become with age. Time and again, the wound has broken open and he has been forced to pull away the scab to get at it to rub it clean, and now he has a wound so ugly that he must behold his lost beauty each time he examines his reflection in the mirror or a puddle. The coins Bolin promised him for Cardell's departure from this life have slipped through his fingers, and in their place are the bloodstains left by Frans Gry, slain for no good reason. Occasionally, when he is drunk, his emotions well up and he is capable of passing a tear over the deceased, but each time he sobers up it feels better, because a man like Gry is just as well off dead as alive.

Kreutz has stayed away from the Last Farthing for a few weeks to allow any traces he may have left to go cold, but no one seems bothered and against all reason he thus feels all the more aggrieved by existence. Does his path through this world pass others by completely? Damn it to hell. It is late. Blurry bodies sway on the benches, and he has surely tested that fool of an innkeeper's patience enough. It is time to go home. He raises the beer tankard to his mouth and leans back, and when he lowers it again it slips from his hand and falls into the straw on the floor. His groggy body follows it under the table just as soon as it can, where it cowers for a while, but to no avail. When he opens his eyes, Cardell is standing over him with his face cleft into a broad grin.

"Well, if it isn't Warrant Officer Kreutz. I haven't seen you since *The Fatherland*. Or did we cross paths on the *Lovisa* too? The pain in my arm may have clouded my memories."

Kreutz weighs up the option of denying his own name, but recognizes the battle as lost. Instead, he assumes a pensive air and pretends not to remember Cardell.

"Carlander?"

Cardell lets out a magnanimous laugh.

"Cardell. Mickel Cardell. I was one gun deck down from you at Hogland. Then I transferred to the *Ingeborg*. And you went to the *Torborg*?"

"The *Styrbjörn*."

"Practically shipmates."

To Kreutz's horror, Cardell straddles the bench and sits down next to him, gripping Kreutz by the shoulder with his good right arm and squeezing it as if they were lifelong blood brothers. And Cardell waves for refills—of both beer and spirit—just as Kreutz is feeling for the first time since last summer that he's had more than his distress called for. He politely demurs, but Cardell appears to be in magnificent form and wants to reminisce about the war.

"Drink up, my brother! On me. Damn it to hell—cheers!"

Kreutz plays along as best he can, while fear grinds away like a millstone in his belly and a cold sweat pours down his stiff back. He is accustomed to treating every coincidence with suspicion, and the odds against a man whose arm he blindly tore at just weeks ago just happening to sit down to drink alongside him to compare tales from the Battle of Viborg seem particularly high. At the same time, he is feverishly sifting through memories of the man he knew fleetingly during the war against the one he is now speaking with. He was never the most artful of men, was Cardell. A born sergeant, and nothing more. Able and dutiful within his own narrow limits, lacking in imagination and intelligence. Nor does Kreutz remember any of the cunning in him that ran rampant among the enlisted men. There were many of them who gathered each evening between huts and in encampments to roll dice and turn over worn cards—games where sleight of hand and downright lies were the hallmarks of success. He never saw Cardell in those circles. A fool, in short. At the mercy of distress and poverty. Surely a fellow couldn't change that much in just a few years? The thought gives him comfort, and Kreutz finally shrugs his shoulders as the strong drink makes it all much of a muchness: What can he do other than play along and hope for the best? Soon they are laughing, comparing scars, swaying on the bench as if the Gulf of Finland were rising up from under the leaky floorboards of the Last Farthing.

"That's quite the thick lip you've picked up."

"Some pauper left a rake lying out in the dark. And by the way, you're a fine one to talk."

....

Eventually, they are thrown out into the cold night by the innkeeper. They linger in the courtyard awhile before Kreutz embarks upon the speech he has spent the past hour preparing—a mixture of thanks and false promises to meet again soon. But Cardell puts an arm around his neck.

"No, no, don't let's put it off. I have both beer and spirits at home—and black bread for a late supper. The night is young, and you still haven't told me how the *Estates of the Realm* was lost."

It does not go unnoticed by Kreutz that the direction Cardell wishes to lead him in is not in the direction of the Southern Isle and his room at Cutter's Alley, but up the hill towards the muddle of buildings and the spire of Katarina.

"Is it far? My old limbs are stiff. The years are taking their toll."

"Not far at all, and if you nod off then you're most welcome to stay the night. I've rented rooms in Katarina for many years now. You can sleep well there at night without being disturbed by the racket in the City-between-the-Bridges."

Kreutz can't help but meet his gaze for a brief moment, before quickly turning his head so as not to reveal his own emotions. The lie has come to light now, and he is no more than the rat being toyed with by the cat. His only hope is that there is still some doubt and that he'll manage to dodge the claws by feigning innocence; he prays that Cardell doesn't know that he knows. He stretches and lets out a good-natured laugh.

"Well then, brother, lead the way. I'll be damned if I turn down another drink."

As they walk, Kreutz talks about the navy's defeat at the Battle of Reval, where two ships of the line were lost, repeating word for word what he heard from a comrade who claimed to be one of those who set the *Estates of the Realm* alight rather than see her surrendered to the Russians. Where his memory fails him, he exaggerates freely; meanwhile Cardell leads him through the gate into Katarina churchyard. But it is not the shortcut to their unknown destination that he surmised. Cardell stops him and shushes him. At their feet, the gravediggers have left a pit open and the shovels are stuck in the heap of earth beside it. For a while, they both stand there in silence. Cardell's voice is free from all slurring when he speaks.

"Why, Johan, you're sweating like a whore in church."

"What's this, Mickel? Why have we stopped? What about the soft tack and ration?"

"Here's the bed I promised you. And the men have left a shovel so that I may tuck you in properly. You should be snug in there for the night. And beyond."

"What kind of joke is this?"

Cardell is holding something between his thumb and forefinger. It glimmers like amber in the moonlight.

"Here's a front tooth I found in my stairwell just the other week, just as yellow as your other ones. Shall we see if it fits the gap in your upper jaw?"

Kreutz's lips slam shut like a church door around his exculpatory grimace.

"Give over, Johan. Your hand hasn't been more than two inches from that knife since we took our first steps out of the inn. If you're going to draw the blade then it's high time you did it. Have you had enough sense to clean the blade this time? Last time you gave me lockjaw. I'm still suffering the aftereffects. Possibly enough to give you an honest chance."

Kreutz looks down at his own body's betrayal. His right fist is clutching the hilt of the knife so tightly his knuckles are white. With a trembling hand he draws the blade from the sheath, stained with rust and rot, meets Cardell's dark gaze, and feels the terror draining his willingness to fight, before dropping the knife out of reach, his hands up in surrender.

"Well then, Johan. You shall have one more choice before the night is over. Either you climb into that hole and lie down at the bottom, whereupon I fill it up and you shuffle off this mortal coil with your dignity intact. Or you give me the name of your employer and show me his door this very night."

Kreutz hears an unfamiliar sound as he stands there, seemingly frozen stiff. Intoxication shakes him as if he were standing dizzily at the edge of the abyss. He hears a whispering sound like the wind in the trees of the churchyard, although the air is quite still and cold as death itself. For a second it crosses his mind that it is a whisper from the occupants of the graves, welcoming him into the ground to warm their frozen bones. He feels heat spreading down his legs, and while he knows that all he is doing is pissing in his breeches, it is a good feeling, a comforting warmth that recalls him to life and all its pain and pleasure, more of the former and less of the latter with each passing year, but never at a price greater than he is willing to pay; it lets him know that the choice he has been given is no choice at all.

70

Autumn offers them a morning of frosted silver as Tycho Ceton leads the girl down towards the Ship's Bridge where a barouche waits to carry them both along the quay, past the Castle and across the bridges. He keeps her wrapped in a woollen coat, careful to ensure she does not freeze even though she gives no signs of doing so.

Their journey takes them across the square where the Opera and Sofia Albertina's palace mirror one another, turning by the tower of Klara Church to avoid the hill, and trundling on along the paved thoroughfare of Queen Street between elegant brick houses. Ceton sits alongside the girl, one arm around her to protect the loose-limbed body from the jolting of the wheels.

"It's time we talked seriously, you and I. Your name is Anna Stina Knapp. Last year your twins were given sanctuary at the Horn Hill orphanage. Horn Hill was my creation, and their admission was realized following an agreement that I struck with one Jean Michael Cardell. I seem to recall that your children's names were Maja and Karl. Both of them burned, together with many others, when Horn Hill was turned to ash last autumn."

Ceton waits. The girl betrays no reaction to his words, her gaze listless, moving only with her swaying head.

"What you don't know is that Cardell is to blame for the fire."

Ceton catches a glimpse of the Observatory on its hill, and knows their destination is close.

"It all went as follows. Part of my philanthropy consisted of acting as guardian to a young nobleman who had become unable to pay his debts—a certain Erik Three Roses. Erik suffered from an affliction of the mind that, time and again, maddened him into a rage that left him with no abiding memories of what he had done. His young bride fell victim to this shortcoming on their wedding night. My affection for Erik did not allow me to surrender him to the administration of justice. My thought instead was that if only Erik could recover, the true perpetrator of the killing would also be avenged. But despite paying a pretty penny for the finest treatment Dane's Bay hospital had to offer, his condition deteriorated and there was no choice but to move him to the asylum—for his own safety as well as others'. There, his delusions were encouraged. Cardell and his accomplice, one Emil Winge, had been tasked by Erik's mother-in-law with clearing her son-in-law's name. Cardell settled on directing his suspicions at me. Why? It took me a long time to understand it all."

When the carriage stops on the street, he guides her out, helping her to find her footing before leading her through the gate in the fence that surrounds the Common Orphanage.

"Cardell crossed paths with me during his inquiries. I gladly showed him round Horn Hill—justifiably proud of all that I had achieved. Shortly thereafter, he sought me out again—this time with the intent of inducing me to accept two children into my care. Twins; Maja and Karl were their names. Lacking both resources and faith in my benevolence, he immediately resorted to threats: if I accommodated him, then I would remain unmolested; otherwise he would do all in his power to concoct evidence to my detriment. I took the twins, regardless of inducements: such care was the very purpose of the building."

With his arm under hers, he leads her forward. The surface beneath their feet changes from the muddy mire of the street to the swept paving of the courtyard.

"Shortly after that, the building was in flames. Horn Hill burned to the ground. Few children were able to save themselves—around a hundred burned inside, including your own. The arsonist was Erik Three Roses, recently escaped from the lunatic asylum, who has been placed under decidedly closer guard since then. The reason? Cardell had said too much in front of Three Roses: he loudly aired his suspicions that I—of all people—had orchestrated his own tragedy for my own dark ends. Erik, in despair, was prone to grasp at any straw that promised to restore his innocence to him."

In the center of the courtyard sloping towards the water there is a well. A woman is waiting there, her arms full.

"It is a terrible world that we call home, Anna Stina. Scratch the surface of any good deed with your fingernail and you shall find it has only been thinly plated over other substances. You must have seen it before and know it just as well as I."

He comes to a halt out of earshot of the woman, holding Anna Stina by the shoulders and trying to catch her gaze.

"It was no mistake that Cardell bore false testimony against me before Erik. He did so with malice aforethought. Surely he too, just like Erik, hoped that I would fall prey to the flames in my guest room at Horn Hill, my ashes strewn to conceal his lies for all eternity. But fate wanted me elsewhere that night, and I was not the intended victim in the first place. It was the lives of your children that he coveted. He wanted Maja and Karl out of this world."

He lowers his voice yet further, his broken mouth close enough to her ear to warm it when he exhales.

"We see it in nature all the time—the disciples of Linnaeus testify to it. Bears and lions devour those cubs that bear the scent of another's paternity without mercy. Surely you must know that he craves you? Surely he must have tried to steal a kiss some time? He is too old for you, and knows it himself, but if anyone can turn the head of a man it is Cupid, his arrows unleashed while blindfolded. He saw himself by your side in some chamber somewhere, sufficient to his watchman's pay—it was all the same to him, so long as it was big enough for a bed for the two of you. But in the future he desired, there was no room for the children you had conceived with another—no brats to disturb his lust with their cries and whines. Maja and Karl were in his way. When he came to me with his proposal, he drank deeply of my wine—better than he was accustomed to, I dare say—and it quickly went to his head. Drunk, he let the cat out of the bag regarding his hopes: that you would allow yourself to be persuaded to surrender your babes for good when you saw what care Horn Hill offered. But alas, he soon became aware of the power of a mother's love, and realized that all you wanted was to free your twins as soon as you had the means. At that very moment, their fate was sealed."

He leads her to the well. The courtyard lies empty. From an unseen hall comes a chorus of spinning wheels, each one creaking, whirring, and thumping at its own pace in one vast combined din.

"Matron! I see that you have brought all that I asked for. Now leave us alone in the courtyard for a while and I shall call you when we are done."

The woman hesitates before handing over her burden into Ceton's arms, but he clicks his tongue reproachfully.

"Come, come, I happen to be in charge of an orphanage."

They are two infants, neither of them a year old, each in swaddling clothes. One is asleep; the other looks astonished at the unfamiliar embrace. Ceton holds them both in front of Anna Stina.

"Anna Stina, I am sorry about what must now happen, but time leaves me no other option. These two nameless children are of the kind left at the orphanage every week by girls who have happened upon misfortune. We are free to give them names for the moment according to our own discretion. Let us name the boy Karl. The girl shall be Maja."

He carefully puts the two of them down in the bucket standing next to the well—it is more than big enough to accommodate them. Now the girl also wakes up, and with the inscrutable gaze of an infant she takes in her surroundings with equanimity. Ceton hushes them, and still humming he lifts the bucket over the edge of the well. At the same time he puts a hand to the rope holding it over the depths through a hoist. Hand over hand, he follows the rope a few steps from the well to the place where Anna Stina is standing. He shifts his grip to stand behind her back, as if embracing her, and gently moves her slack hands onto the rope, helping to braid her fingers around the coarse hemp.

"Are you ready, Anna Stina? Soon I will let go and the grip will be yours alone. Come back to the world."

They stand together in silence for a moment, their breathing following the same rhythm. The boy lets out a gurgling squeak in complaint at the hard wood and the warmth he has been deprived of; the little girl has closed her eyes again, sedated by the swaying cradle of the bucket. Then Ceton lets go.

71

Winge opens wide a pair of doors on sprung hinges, and when they slam behind him the lantern issued to him by the attendant is no longer sufficient. He was warned—although the day is not far gone, there are no windows to admit the light, and the room is too big to give the lantern's glow anything to fall upon. Blindly, he staggers across the parterre, through the empty standing space defined by the barriers marking the difference in ticket price. His eyes slowly adjust. The gold leaf flashes in the dark from swags and garlands higher up. Shadows the size of houses surround him, the shadow cast by the arms of the chandelier a spider crawling across the painted ceiling. He is struck by the unreality of the place—a vast space separated from the material world, not unlike a church but consecrated to a deity of another kind, erected to accommodate illusions and affected mannerisms. Outside, the city is all too close, but the thick walls stifle all sound and the silence reigns absolute.

Standing in front of the apron stage, the dark space looms above him like a black sconce, and he must edge to the side before he finds a stepladder to grant him access. Up here, the emptiness is even more palpable. Looking outwards, the boundaries of the stage are delineated by the two halves of the curtain, tied back in tassels of twisted gold, and between them nothing but the void of an empty auditorium. He shudders. A particular kind of horror lingers in abandoned places that usually teem with life. He checks his gaze and concentrates on the task at hand, lowering the light towards the spot that seems to him the most promising: the very center of the stage. Yes, right there. A stain, blurred and faded into almost nothing but a memory, but still discernible to any who look—big and dark, spreading across the boards. He gets down on his knees to scratch a dark flake from the timber. He moistens his palm with his lips and lays his find there, rubbing it with his thumb to tempt it back into its original form. The glow of the lantern is yellow, leaving colors hard to make out, but he is in no doubt that the daylight awaiting him outside will show the red of a drop of blood. He holds up the lantern and looks around again, and between the boards there glitters an answer. The colors of the rainbow ensnared between splinters and knotholes. Shards of a mirror, wedged where no brush has been able to reach.

72

Like a snake in flight, the rope rushes through Anna Stina's hands, leaving a searing burn on her palm and fingers. Just for a moment. Then it stops and sticks fast, the weight of the bucket tugging at arms and shoulders and forcing her forward in staggering footsteps until she has to lean back in a movement that would once have been natural but now seems unfamiliar. Muscles that have lain fallow for months are tried, and the effort takes her breath away. Almost immediately, she begins to shake, feeling the inexorable heaviness of the other end of the rope pulling downward. Strength drains from her numb fingers; her knees shake and her heels crunch as they seek a grip in the gravel.

"Well, Anna Stina, didn't I know it? Welcome to the world of the living."

Ceton's voice is low, and what is worse, far too distant. He has backed off and is standing too many steps away to rush to her aid should her grip loosen. She searches for the words, forming her tongue and lips around those alien things.

"Help me."

"Happily. But not until you prove to me that you are here to stay and won't escape back to your shadow world as soon as there is an open road to do so. You have to want it, Anna Stina; otherwise nothing is worthwhile. Pull the bucket out of the well and you can have my help."

The lament of the children rises from the hole with a strange resonance from the echo of brick-lined walls. Anna Stina hears herself reply in the same language, trembling sobs torn from her breast. She tries to make her body obey, but in vain. Once upon a time she would have hauled the bucket out hand over hand, easy as anything, even if it had been full to the brim with water, but now her fists are locked around the rope, afraid to slip. Time is against her: her strength is already draining away by the second. A trickling drizzle has begun to fall on them. She seeks a solution, and although panic makes her sluggish, it comes to her. She moves on foot, first one and then the other, over and over, turning her body around. The rope follows, winding its way around her waist, and with each slow pirouette she takes, the weight becomes steadier and the searing pain in her fingers milder. One step at a time, she moves closer to the round, brick-built shape of the well. The bucket meets here there, and then Ceton is beside her, lifting it to the safety of the edge and down to the ground. Relief takes the last of her strength and her legs give way. She feels the rain pricking her skin, feels her borrowed clothes hanging sodden and heavy, and in its wake come the grief and pain. She slaps her face with her hands without being able to stop the tears. Ceton stands unmoved next to her in the rain, now with the children in his arms, protected under the coat that hangs from his shoulders.

"The little ones are cold and hungry, and it is high time they get under cover where there is gruel and a cot. Do you want to take them in to the matron?"

She nods, and once she has got to her feet he helps her to move first the girl and then the boy. Anna Stina remembers—she remembers how the burden of a child is unlike any other, how they find their place, how warm small bodies shape themselves against hers, how light they are for all their weight. She looks at their swollen faces and in the difference between them the memory of her own children returns, bittersweet, small things she had thought were lost forever: laughter lines, a snub nose, a wrinkle where the brow frowns. These are not Maja and Karl—they are strangers with borrowed names. She walks with difficulty, one step at a time. Ceton does not hurry her, remaining silent and staying one step ahead, opening the door with a cautionary gesture towards the high threshold.

73

Emil Winge has barely crossed Cardell's threshold before the watchman waves at him to turn around.

"Let's go downstairs for a bite to eat. My stomach is rumbling like a king's salute."

Winge conceals his surprise badly.

"I didn't think you were supposed to be on your feet for weeks yet."

Cardell grimaces as he stretches his back and neck.

"Don't count on me in a fight, but I've always had good strong flesh. It's not always easy to say whether that's a boon or a punishment."

They file down the stairs and into the alley. Cardell pauses for a moment, sniffing in both directions before nodding up the hill.

"They've just killed a hen up the way, I think. I can smell the pot simmering."

The room is like so many of the city's other inns: a nook with room for five—twice that if intoxication permits. It is still early, and the only person present is the gangly innkeeper himself, hunched over his stove, his mouth opening to notify his guests that he hasn't yet opened before he recognizes Cardell.

"Oh, it's you. Well, take a seat. The stew won't be ready for a while yet, but if you'd like bread I can give you yesterday's loaf cheap."

Cardell taps the hard bread against the edge of the table and it echoes like wood on wood.

"Yesterday's, you say . . . Did you add stone flour to the dough? Do you expect me to grind away at this without anything to dip it in and pay you for my trouble? Rats have lost their teeth on less."

The innkeeper shrugs sullenly.

"Pay me whatever it's worth."

Cardell rolls a shilling across the tabletop.

"This is for the stew. Two bowls. And beer and water. The bread is on the house."

The man catches the coin in his fist with infallible reflexes, bows with a grimace, and retreats to his stove, where he slowly and with infinite patience peels turnips from a basket, pinching the blade of the knife against his thumb in a spiral along the perimeter of the tubers. Cardell helps himself to a tankard from the cask, drinking until it burns his throat and setting it down with a clatter.

"Anselm Bolin."

"Who?"

"That's the name of the chap who paid to have me stabbed by hired heavies in my own chamber. He made the mistake of seeking out the services of Johan Kreutz, an old scoundrel I remember from the war. They wanted to make the murder look like an old grudge between shipmates. I caught up with Kreutz yesterday and it didn't take much to make him sing like a blackbird and then lead me to Bolin's door."

"Where?"

"Glaucus, with a door onto Fork Alley."

Winge hesitates for a moment before responding.

"I don't wish to detract from your discovery, but was that altogether wise, Jean Michael? In your state?"

Cardell gives him a cold look.

"That I have been sick does not make me a child for all time and eternity. I'm a grown man, capable of making my own decisions by my own judgment."

Emil is first to look away.

"I, for my part, have been to visit the Dissenters in the Royal Garden. It was they whom Ceton sought out after we rumbled his lair. I know the names of the dead. Albrecht and Wilhelm had the misfortune to cross paths with Ceton and reveal their weaknesses. They were cast as the leads in Ceton's attempt to regain favor with the Furies."

"And Bolin?"

"Ceton's patron among the ranks of the Kindly Ones, I should guess.

If we're lucky, he is still harboring Ceton behind the door you have found."

"So?"

"I must go to Blom and inquire about the Chamber of Police's resources. Access to the domains of the Ship's Bridge nobility is not granted freely—there would be a scandal. Everyone and their dog is liable to have their cellars stacked to the rafters with untaxed goods, and if police constables were to intrude unannounced then every merchant would raise a common cause until they had Ullholm's head on a platter as a gift of atonement. The Stock Exchange trumps lineage more and more with each passing year, and not even Reuterholm will dare turn a blind eye to their influence. First we must substantiate Ceton's presence. Then we take him. One way or another."

Cardell nods briefly, craning his neck to try to form an understanding of just how long their host means to take with the stew. He drains his tankard.

"May I ask you something, Emil?"

"By all means."

"Just what was there unspoken between you and your brother?"

"We chose different paths. Our father had peculiar ideas about how to raise a child. Cecil found a way to play Father's game on his own terms, and it served him well until the blight took him. I chose to be a contrarian, and for that I suffered much hurt for little reward. Now I find myself in a position where I must think like Cecil, and each time I do so it is his voice that I hear. My inferences, my logic, my reasoning: it is as if he whispers the words into my ear."

Cardell pushes the tankard away and looks thoughtfully at Emil for a while.

"It's more than that, isn't it? Once before, you saw him in the street—dead as he was. Do you still see him?"

"You know of my illness of old. It has improved, but I am not recovered."

"How often?"

"What does it matter? I know just as well as you that the threshold of the grave can only be crossed in one direction. It is no ghost that haunts me—merely a chimera, and one that serves to make the memory of him yet more bitter. When this is over and I no longer need the expertise that I ascribe to him, he will leave me in peace."

"You have struck a deal with your own delusion?"

Emil looks away rather than responding, and Cardell leans back on his bench, two movements that break the confidence between them like a string stretched to breaking point.

"Well, I am not your child nor do I wish you were mine. It is just that I was raised next to a forest that superstition filled with eldritch things, and it seems to me that my entire literary education comprised old wives' tales where those who make pacts with things understood by no man meet with an adverse fate. More I cannot add. But there is something else too."

"Well?"

Cardell fixes his gaze on Winge, watching to see whether his expression will match his words.

"Petter Pettersson."

Winge shrugs.

"The custodian of the workhouse?"

Cardell drums his fingers on the tabletop for a while as the innkeeper carries two deep dishes over to them.

"Forget that I said anything."

74

In the room by the Ship's Bridge there is chocolate steaming in a pot set to keep warm in the niche of the tiled stove. Anna Stina glances at it, unaccustomed to impressions being accompanied by thoughts. She allows herself to be shown to an armchair drawn close to the radiating heat, and with Tycho Ceton opposite. She warms her sore fingers against her body, raising the drink to her mouth occasionally. It burns, and the bite of the cocoa is strong enough to bring tears to her eyes.

"Let us speak on the basis of mutual trust, Anna Stina. Firstly, a question to satisfy my curiosity. Were you in there the whole time? Do you remember the year that has gone by?"

She nods in confirmation.

"I was there, although remotely. There was just nothing I saw that I was concerned about—nothing seemed worth the effort."

"Were you on the King's Isle when Horn Hill burned down?"

Language comes slowly, allowing itself to be reluctantly recaptured, full of stutters and hesitation.

"I was on the Scar when the bells began to chime. The fire lit up the sky. It was as if I already knew—as if they were ringing for Maja and Karl. I ran. I didn't arrive until the place was in ashes."

"And then?"

"I sat there for a long time. Men came to put it out. No one took any notice. Some older children had survived, albeit badly burnt and with broken bones after leaping from roofs or windows. At last, I walked away and back towards the city until I began thinking about why. Each step was slower than the last. The more I thought, the fewer answers I found. Eventually, I left the path and walked until water barred my way, then I sat down and stayed there. The hopelessness became a crippling embrace. Some fishermen's children came to ask what the matter was, but they left me alone when I didn't answer. I remember wondering how long I needed to sit there before hunger would take me. Or the cold. And I found I didn't care about that either."

"The lad who found you, the one who brought you to my door?"

"Yes. He wouldn't let me be. We had met once before at the Common Orphanage when I came to leave Maja and Karl. I didn't know what he wanted, but it didn't matter to me anyway. I no longer had any will to say no. He gave me bread to eat, wetting it in water and forcing it between my lips. When it was easier to swallow than not to, I did. Otherwise I didn't."

"So do you hold a grudge against those of us who have helped?"

"How could I do otherwise? All I wanted was to be left alone long enough for death to bring its mercy to me and let me kiss the blade of its scythe before the blow struck. He comes uninvited to many. Was it so much to ask that I should go early?"

"You've heard my truth. He who is to blame for the death of your children remains at liberty. Don't you care about that either, now that you know? Is there no wrath to accompany the hopelessness?"

She sits quietly for a moment, her gaze seeking the flames crackling in the open stove.

"That's what this is about, isn't it? You want me to kill Cardell. I, who can get closer to him than others. Not for my sake, but for your own ends."

"Let us rather say that our ends run in parallel. I built a house for the protection of one hundred children. He burned it down—a black stain in the grass of the King's Isle is all there is to mark their grave. I was their only defense, and I came off badly when they needed me most. The watchman would gladly pin the blame on me still, because he must. Without painting me as a maniac, how else could he pretend to be innocent?"

He bows his head, raising it again with a question.

"Was I right in my guess? Has he made overtures before?"

She remembers a fire in the woods, a bloody fragment, her heart in her throat, an advance denied.

"He once tried to kiss me."

"You didn't want to?"

"No."

Ceton sighs, shaking his head.

"They say that murdered children can never lie peacefully at rest until their deaths have been avenged. They wander frozen between the worlds, lighting small candles to illuminate the scene of the crime in the hope of justice. Two are yours—the other ninety-eight belong to me. So isn't this what we both want? To balance the scales that have for far too long weighed against us? If so, I will help you. For my own part, Cardell is out of reach. I retain no power—I live by the benevolence of others. But to you he will open his door. You, he will let into his life."

He pauses, gesturing at the door.

"If you don't want to, then I can't force you, and you are free to go when you please. If there is anything else I can do for you, then you need only ask, although I cannot promise much."

She closes her eyes and searches within for an answer. Out of darkness it rises.

"Yes. That's what I want too."

"I shall give you a knife that is sharp. I shall show you where he lives. When you are strong enough."

75

Out to sea, the clouds are stacked high, still against a pale gray background. Winge passes the main square and pushes through the alleys behind Grill's House and into the maelstrom that is Cepheus, with one eye on the cathedral clock tower telling him that he is on time for his meeting with Isak Blom. Nevertheless, he walks briskly, eager to get answers to his inquiry about the house in the Glaucus quarter. He sees the waiting figure from a distance. Only when he gets closer does he see that it is someone other than the man he has been expecting. The man is leaning heavily on a cane; he is finely dressed without extravagance, his cheeks marked by smallpox. He raises his hat in greeting and reveals a bare head with a few stubborn strands of hair across it.

"My name is Bolin. Anselm Bolin."

"Emil Winge."

Bolin gestures towards a planed board across two trestles serving as a bench against a wall in a spot where the autumn sun is spilling across the rooftops.

"Why don't we sit? My gout plagues me, and never so much as when it wants to tell us what we already know: winter will soon be upon us."

"By all means."

Bolin sits down heavily, positioning his sore leg with his hands and sighing gratefully at the relief.

"It has come to my attention that you have sought the mandate of the Chamber of Police to place my home under surveillance. This would be an unfortunate development—one that I seek to forestall through this informal conversation between us."

"Your vigilance is well served by good contacts."

"I have always taken pains to be my friends' friend. I would be most ungrateful were I to share their names here. Now, my sources also tell me that you have become an esteemed figure in the Chamber since you first appeared in the autumn of last year, your sole recommendation being the memory of your esteemed late brother. I am told that you have a future there—one that it would be a pity to forsake, both for your own sake and for that of all those malefactors who will go free if the task is left to less able men."

Winge can guess what is coming, and lets it happen without interruption.

"Live and let live has always been my doctrine, and I am most reluctant to speak with such bluntness as I do now, but I see no better way forward. If you maintain your interest in me and that enterprise that I have been tasked with representing, then you give me no choice but to use my influence to deprive you of the support of the Chamber of Police. I would far rather that we met here at this crossroads, like strangers heading in opposite directions who speak awhile during our brief rest before professing our mutual respect for one another and moving on to our respective destinations, into the wide world where the odds are high that we shall ever encounter each other again."

"You're threatening me?"

"No, not yet. I harbor hopes that I shall not be obliged to do so."

Winge nods, thoughtfully taking out his clay pipe and beginning to pack it full. He excuses himself for a moment, poking his head through a window from which the waft of baking emanates, before returning with his pipe lit.

"Perhaps you would like to tell me a little about yourself, Mr. Bolin? If not to make our conversation more convivial, then to allow me to lay firmer ground upon which to stand in my decision?"

"I am but a humble official in the autumn of my years. Once I was a young man with aspirations. I attached myself to the company of the Kindly Ones through a love of adventure, and I rose through the ranks without trace. I have been secretary for a number of years for no other reason than that I am mediocre enough in my image to make the choice easy for all parties. I take minutes when the inner circle meets, and later when voting. I do what I can to sow concord among the brothers, albeit at times with some little trouble, because it is a stubborn fraternity to which stronger wills than mine are gladly drawn."

"And Tycho Ceton?"

"It would be a mistake to judge us all by the example of Tycho. Had it been up to me alone, he would never have been admitted. He may be shrewd enough to dupe the foolish, but the fact that he found two brothers gullible enough to sponsor him fills me with despair. But what is done is done. He is ours—akin to a delinquent child that no one has taught to distinguish between a chamber pot and a jardinière—and we can do nothing other than take that responsibility that now accrues to us."

"The Furies have not always shown him their kindliness."

"That name has had its day. We change it intermittently."

"What will it be instead?"

"I dare say we will vote on it in due course. I gather that the Bacchants is leading the field."

Bolin lowers his voice, leaning in closer.

"Regardless of the name, what has been said is true. Tycho fell out of favor. But he was given the chance to restore trust, with mixed results. The world would be simpler if Tycho were free to become your quarry, but enough of the brothers see a value in him, and then there is, of course, the principle of it all. Hence my sitting here now."

"The Moravian boys' performance at the Nonpareil fell on fertile ground."

Bolin smiles and raises his eyebrows, miming a demure ovation.

"Gracious, that's quick work, Emil Winge. I note that your abilities have not been exaggerated. The respect you garner makes me no less eager that we reach an understanding. Well, it must be said that the spectacle was controversial. It was not to everyone's taste. Too subtle for some, much too vulgar for others. But nonetheless, many saw advantages to tipping the scales in Tycho's favor—for the time being. These are bad times, Winge, for both the kingdom and its subjects, and there is enormous boredom. In the era of the Ordinance of Abundance, diversions have become a rare commodity. I venture that even Tycho's detractors cannot help wondering what he will think of next. Well, the time available to me is drawing to a close. Where do we stand?"

"If you haven't threatened me yet, then it's high time."

Bolin sighs, rises heavily, and takes a few one-legged hops before his bad leg finds the right position.

"Winge, you're still a young man. You're quite an acceptable conversationalist, especially since it seems to be an increasing rarity to meet anyone who can handle ambiguity with finesse, let alone from your generation—depleted though the war has left your ranks. But let me be clear: You surely understand that I am here humbling myself at least in part to prevent you from laying down your life prematurely? I do not wish to share any part in that guilt—you may reasonably live a long life of prosperity. Yet you have set your course on an unnavigable path. It does not lead to a victory that can be won. Take good advice and you will be left alone—both you and your one-handed henchman. Otherwise, you will not."

"You underestimate Jean Michael. That mistake has been the last made by many."

"I would have been better served by that warning last summer. But I swear that I am not in the habit of making the same mistake twice."

"Goodbye then, Mr. Bolin. I shall soon come to Castle Hill with a bid to reveal your hand."

76

Cardell opens his eyes and through the slit of the window he sees the aftermath of the first frost of the season. The roofs are white in the still morning air, glistening in the light cast by sunrise. He is warm-blooded by nature, warming up when he pulls on his jacket and coat, stockings and boots, and makes his way downstairs. Outside, the air is cool and fresh. He senses a shift in the temperament of all those who have begun their working day in this splendor. It is, by definition, bad news. The winter is making itself felt, cruel and merciless, its path annually lined with drunks frozen solid, suffocated by frost in the gutter where they fell asleep or the doorway in which they sought shelter. The cold will sting the skin and crawl right into the marrow until even the thought of ever being warm again seems vain. The very light itself will wane day by day, the working days shortening accordingly, the poor purblind in the glow of the hearth and hunched over the flame of a taper. But it is also beautiful—this white death—and for a few hours the City-between-the-Bridges glitters as if she had dressed for a feast in robes of the whitest silk and a diamond tiara. Cardell climbs the hill below the cathedral tower and emerges beyond the castle facade, arriving at the door to Indebetou House, which is ajar to admit the morning's stream of personnel. In the hall there is a basket of dry bread—the previous day's oven harvest deposited by some baker serving an informal sentence. With well-practiced impudence, Cardell helps himself to a crust, breaking it apart and stuffing it into his mouth. An officiously uniformed constable looks at him quizzically and Cardell uses his password.

"Sorry?"

He chews and swallows, making a better attempt.

"Isak Blom."

"Not here yet. The secretary usually puts in an appearance eventually. If you can find his office then you're welcome to take a seat and wait by the door."

Cardell takes a step closer and lowers his voice.

"Is there coffee? And don't you start quoting the Ordinance of Abundance at me. Your work is hard and demanding, and I cannot quite fathom how you're able to find the strength to run the errands of justice day in day out without greasing the wheels. Given everything that you confiscate, there must be a copper pot simmering away somewhere."

The constable gives the matter a moment's thought before jerking his head towards a storey up.

"Follow your nose. Let them know Josefsson sent you and you'll get what you need—with a nip too."

Cardell puts a grateful hand on the man's shoulder.

"This world may be a shameless dunghill, but it is my heartfelt hope that a just reward awaits you in the next."

....

Strengthened, and with his mood considerably improved, Cardell waits outside Blom's room, his wooden fist slung over his shoulder and his right hand wrapped around the stump for warmth. He paces back and forth while he waits. The stones of the building bear the chill of the night, and the meager wood supplied to feed the tiled stoves is of little use. He catches Blom's eye as soon as the rotund secretary turns the corner, and Blom stops on the spot, surprise and worry written across his face. Cardell raises his only palm in a gesture of peace.

"See here, Blom—for once I haven't come to cause you a nuisance."

Inside his office, Blom sits down and rubs his brow.

"Blom, I come to you in supplication."

The secretary stops Cardell with a gesture.

"No, Cardell. Let me speak first. There's nothing I can do. For me, the matter is already far beyond reach."

"Blom . . ."

"I understand your disappointment, but Ullholm himself has passed his decree and for as long as he remains in post it will be uncontestable. He is likely to remain for a long time, given that he seems to possess every quality most prized by the gentlemen at the Castle."

"What are you talking about?"

Blom hesitates, wrinkling his nose in confusion.

"And you? What are you talking about?"

"I came to ask you for help—undeserving as I may be. It concerns Petter Pettersson, until recently the custodian at the workhouse on the Island of Scar. One of two, if I am not much mistaken."

Blom removes his spectacles and rubs the confusion from his eyes with a sigh.

"I know of Pettersson. He was rapped across the knuckles the other year for having overenthusiastically taken the life of a weary workhouse inmate with his whip, and I dare say it says much about the desirability of the post that he was reinstated without any further measures. So?"

"Pettersson met his demise at the end of the summer after coming second place in a fight with some daring assailant who shall, as far as I am concerned, remain nameless."

Cardell leans forward over the desk while Blom leans back in his chair, keen to maintain a distance between them.

"Pettersson was an ox of a man. He did not do himself justice. I want to know whether there were any unusual circumstances on the evening when he was killed."

"You're in the watch yourself—albeit only by name. Surely there are people you can ask directly?"

"I fear you overestimate my popularity, Mr. Blom. In the ranks of the watchmen, I am generally regarded as a truant, a conceited bastard who thinks himself too good for the shitty drudgery he'd prefer to leave to others. I'm not well positioned to find fault with their misconceptions."

Blom ponders in silence, and Cardell leans back in his chair to give the secretary more air.

"The gods know I'm already deeply indebted to you, and I've given you little cause for benevolence. Let that knowledge testify to the importance of this matter. I beg of you most humbly, dear Isak, pretty please, with honey and molasses on top . . ."

"Let it go. Think of it as your severance payment."

"Sorry?"

"Emil. I gather you haven't heard, and I apologize for being the bearer of bad news. He has fallen out of favor. His powers have been rescinded. As of yesterday, he is persona non grata in the Chamber—what authority he once had on sufferance has been reduced to nothing. I dare say the same applies to you."

77

A knock on Winge's door yields no response, but when Cardell tries the handle it glides open on squealing hinges, revealing joyless stone walls and darkness. Winge is sitting on his bed, staring at what fills the table beneath the window in such numbers that the very floorboards are bowed. Bottles. Cardell crosses the floor and picks one up, removing the stopper to smell the contents. A quick glance around him reveals that the one he is holding is the first to have been opened, and that no empty glasses are spread across the floor.

"These are fine wares, Emil, and plenty of them too. The very best."

Winge nods absently, still without looking at his guest. Cardell pulls out one of the two chairs in the room so that he may sit down between Winge and his treasure. He can hear how his voice is laced with anger, even though he does what he can to master himself.

"So you find yourself in difficult straits, and this is the best solution within reach? I must say I still remember how it ended last time. I had to wipe the vomit from your bare skin, and hold you as still as I could because you were shaking violently enough to hurt yourself. I'll say again what I said then, in case you've forgotten: if you take that path again then there is no turning back."

Their eyes meet for the first time, and Emil shakes his head.

"You misunderstand, Jean Michael. The bottles aren't mine. As far as I'm concerned, they're not even bottles in the first place."

"Then what are they?"

"They're a message. I found them here—just as they stand now."

"Who from?"

"Anselm Bolin. The implication could not be clearer. He is telling me that he knows where I am to be found, that he can gain access whenever he wishes, and that he knows my weaknesses better than I ever imagined he did. I have no doubt that it is a mercy of sorts, albeit a cruel one. He warned me when we spoke, and his warning took effect when I tested him. And yet I am magnanimously being offered a way to dodge destruction: all I must do is drink with the same lust I once did, and his problems will be forgotten. Mine too."

"How long have you been sitting here?"

"I don't know. What time is it now? Since I returned from the Chamber of Police. That must have been yesterday."

"You're not considering drinking it?"

Emil swallows and brushes a hand over the corners of his mouth.

"The thought had crossed my mind."

"Dismiss it from your mind. Surely there are other options."

Winge stares at him with a hollow gaze from bloodshot eyes.

"What would that be, Jean Michael? Tell me. I believed I had the mandate of the Chamber of Police, but alas! None of the work I have done counts in our favor. We have no resources left at our disposal, no one who can help us. The mere act of doing something is no longer a just battle in the name of the law. It is merely arbitrary violence. We've been reduced to bandits. Disturbers of the peace."

Cardell is on his feet, thrust into motion by a frustration too great to quell. He paces back and forth across the floorboards, gesticulating with his good arm as if to summon words that keep sticking in his throat. In the end, he comes to a stop and hisses what he has been wanting to say.

"It isn't my lot to think. Each to his own. Have I ever asked you to flog sailors to force information out of them, you with your seven-stone-weakling frame and matchwood limbs? I have played my part. Now play yours."

Winge shakes his head.

"I can't. I've turned it all inside out. I cannot find a solution."

"Then you haven't finished thinking."

Cardell tears his hair, feeling the pain each time his nails catch the scars on his burnt skin. He turns, groping for the bolt of the door. The misery in Emil's farewell serves only to irritate him.

"Jean Michael? Won't you take the bottles away from here?"

"Why, Emil? The whole city is flooded in spirits. There is temptation for you in every doorway. If you don't want to drink, don't do it. The choice is yours—now as it always was."

Cardell is already halfway out, but hesitates for a moment with one foot across the threshold before he turns one last time.

"If you don't have the wits to find your own solution, ask your brother."

78

Anna Stina Knapp considers the chamber that is now hers. Big, filled with all that she may need. It is at the end of a corridor, and all other activity that occurs in the house she hears at a distance—footsteps on floorboards above, remote sounds from kitchens and washrooms, deep muffled voices in the distance, too muddled to be interpreted. The door is not locked. It has been made clear to her that she is neither a captive here nor bound by any debt, free to open it at any time of her choosing, turn left into the corridor, cross the kitchen, and climb the stairs into the courtyard before heading into the City-between-the-Bridges. Her host hides nothing from her, answers any question she asks, makes his intentions clear, and helps her to understand them fully. Tycho Ceton has decided that the truth is his ally, and that the only requirement for everything to happen is her own willing complicity. And why should she leave? Here she has everything—not in excess, but still in an abundance beyond all imagination in comparison with past years. They serve her three meals a day, and each morning a pail of hot water is carried in alongside fresh linen towels for washing and drying, and a shaving of soap on a dish. Her body has only slowly grown accustomed to solid food in such quantities. At first it protested, repelling all that it was given, forcing her onto her knees over the chamber pot, her belly cramping. Nevertheless, she persevered, forcing it into submission. Her body is regaining its shape. Her protruding ribs are concealed beneath new flesh, the slack skin of her legs and arms has filled out, her cheeks are finding their past roundness. The dressing table has a mirror, and she often sits in front of it. With each passing day, she looks less and less like a famished street girl—a stranger with a vacant gaze—and more and more like herself. Each passing day rejuvenates her.

It is as if time has reversed its flow. In the evenings they eat together, returning to one and the same conversation. He asks about the life that was hers, and she tells him, surprised how life is infused into all those she lost along the way. Mother Maja, Lisa Forlorn, her sister in suffering at the workhouse on Scar, Johanna.

At night, she dreams of her children—Maja and Karl. Their burnt skin has cooled to a charred crust. Now they are cold. They each carry a candle, but the flames seem to give no warmth. The thirst and hunger become worse with each passing day. Their limbs are as thin as twigs. Dreadfully weak, they stagger to and fro on faltering legs in the ash that still marks where Horn Hill burned to the ground. Around them, the world is empty and dark, the living only discernible as shadows in the distance, imperceptible, ghosts in the world of the ghosts. Wordlessly, Maja and Karl scream with hoarse voices that are barely audible over the cold wind whipping between the soot and the scorched tufts of grass. She knows what they're saying. *Mother, where are you? Mother, why have you left us here?* Anna Stina awakens in a cold sweat, entwined in damp sheets, with a despair that has nowhere to seek solace except in anger. Only in its thundering proximity can her grief be drowned out. She is frightened by her thoughts, but must listen to them, nonetheless. Cardell. Tilting his neck for her kiss. Her children's death a hidden glint in a lewd gaze.

Ceton comes to her in the afternoons, always sensitive to her wishes. He seems to know inherently what is best suited to her temperament in the moment: to listen, to speak, to sit in companionable silence. Beyond the window it is gray. It is the winter that leeches color from everything. Heavy drops patter against the windows in angry bursts as the wind off the sea flays the city. Occasionally the rain is mixed with damp snowflakes, making melting snail's trails down the panes. In one corner of the room is a tiled stove. They set an armful of wood alight in the morning and another in the evening—enough for the patterned roundel to spread its warmth all day long.

One morning she feels a tenderness across her bosom, sore joints, pressure at her forehead. So long has passed that she wonders whether it really is the monthly bleeding that has returned, or merely a chill of the kind that creeps up on people when the warm months of the year begin to fail. The following day she begins to bleed, silently and scantly, for the first time in months. She has to ask for bandages, quickly procured without question. A few days later it is over, and she counts a few more, over and over again to be certain, and when Ceton comes to her in the afternoon she gives him the news she knows he wants to hear most of all.

"I'm ready to go. Let me see your knife."

79

The City-between-the-Bridges has its own voice in the hubbub of the crowd, and the months that Emil Winge has spent here have taught him to interpret its meaning. He has heard the promises of spring resounding through the first warm nights of the year, the subdued speech of Sunday mass, the elated anticipation on execution day. This morning it is indignation, anger, surprise, and malice—in shouts and raised voices, and brisk feet on cobbles on the way to notify those who have avoided the news in the sanctity of their homes. The night has brought him no peace. He has lain awake, hearing the city waking like an anthill disturbed by a twig thrust in by a boy. Even before he has had time to pull the waist of his breeches over his shirt, he knows that something has happened— something important—and he hurries out and downstairs into the chill that so many have chosen to defy. The first bookstall he sees bears witness to the fact that the printers have shared his vigil. The city's newspapers are already in their second editions, hastily printed sheets filled with careless, rushed mistakes. He has money enough to buy one and then another, skimming a third over the shoulder of a red and bloated gentleman who regards him with timid eyes. There are many being shoved about in the crowd, and among the crush of bodies there is one he knows well, one who whispers in his ear with a chilly gust of grave dust.

Cecil says this is your chance. Cecil says this changes everything.

80

Something is brewing; Castle Hill is full of people. Cardell hears voices from the many small groups that have gathered. Some appear outraged; others have lowered their voices to whispers. Guards have been posted at the door of Indebetou House—a few sturdy police constables with a practiced air of boredom, ignoring those of an inquiring disposition. Cardell has little opportunity to penetrate the assembled ranks, and deems he has but a slim chance of gaining access solely by using his gift of the gab—the men by the door are of the kind that have made careers out of neither listening nor understanding. Doubtful, he waits. He sees a few being let through—far too few—and he goes around the building. Before long, he finds the back door—it, too, guarded, but considerably less mobbed. He sends in word to Blom with a hurrying sergeant, and the secretary soon peers out of the crack in the door, his hat already on his head and his coat over his arm.

"You came at the right time, Cardell. I'm escaping the field. Lead the way to freedom."

....

One of the inns serving hot chocolate in the hope of making a few pennies at the expense of the shuttered coffee shops allows them to crowd around a rickety gateleg table. Cardell asserts his entitlement with sharp elbows and a menacing look until they secure a corner to themselves.

"What's going on?"

Blom looks at Cardell, flabbergasted.

"You don't know? You must be the last one in the city. Don't you read the papers? Don't you have any friends?"

Cardell reaches for one of the sheets and squints at the paragraphs.

"The last time I read the paper, poets were bickering about meter. I generally consider people to be a bloody rabble, and it seems the feeling is usually mutual."

Blom leans in closer and lowers his voice as if sharing a secret.

"Last night the Duke himself was ambushed. A pack of assassins had concealed themselves outside Drottningholm Palace in the bushes in the gardens, their weapons loaded. The shot was audible from inside."

"Has Duke Karl been shot?"

Blom shakes his head.

"No, no. The conspirators were mistaken. The Duke is amorous by nature and on occasion he takes shortcuts through the park en route to his nocturnal liaisons, but this time he was lucky. They opened fire on a corporal in his bodyguard whose build and posture was sufficiently similar to the Duke's to be mistaken at a distance under cover of darkness. They missed him too, but he had quite a hole in his jacket to show where the bullet went when he ran to the palace to raise the alarm. They've been searching for the marksman and his two cronies all night long without success—the hunt remains under way."

"Who fired?"

"No doubt the Gustavians. Armfelt's instigators may have gone to ground, but they are still there. They want to see the young prince take on his father's fallen mantle, and with the Duke out of the way the regency would collapse like a house of cards in a gale."

"Oh. So nothing has really happened. The situation is unchanged. Much ado about nothing."

"And that's true too. But the political consequences, Cardell, will be far-reaching. Such aggression is precisely what Reuterholm needs to step up his persecution of anyone that he disagrees with. He won't be slow to depict the shooting as revenge for the permanent closure of the *Extra Post*—an act by those ready to spill blood in order to spread whatever rot they want without censure. Up at the Castle and in Indebetou House, everyone is running around like headless chickens in hopes of their zeal and loyalty being observed, despite the fact that the conspirators remain anonymous and there is little of value to be done. Hence my retreat."

Cardell clears his throat and searches for the right words, but as so often is forced to settle for the first, best ones that come to mind.

"As it happens, I was seeking you out on another matter, Mr. Secretary."

Blom is startled, and then perks up.

"Of course. Forgive me. The mystery of the battle-shy custodian."

"Well?"

"I've made my inquiries. His colleague Hybinette, who shared Pettersson's office, had his fair share to say on the matter, and all for the price of a few tankards of beer. I can confirm your suspicions. There were most particular circumstances at play that evening."

Blom pauses for dramatic effect, and Cardell tries to please the secretary by forcing his aching facial features into something resembling breathless anticipation.

"Petter Pettersson was removed from office that very morning. Inspector Krook himself notified him, and there was no possibility of appeal. The man was dispatched that very day—even after so many years' service."

"Well I'll be damned."

"Hybinette, who was not too late to put his own house in order, made certain to inform himself of the course of events. Krook received an official visit early that morning from someone who was able to document his authority and who claimed to be investigating various alleged acts of misconduct at the workhouse, now that many benefactors' gazes had been directed there in these difficult times when other establishments for the improvement of citizens' character have ceased to be. It related to recurring, arbitrary punishments of workhouse inmates for little reason other than the fact that Pettersson seemed to derive pleasure from it. Krook was persuaded to accompany him to the workhouse to see this unsatisfactory state of affairs, and it just so happened that Pettersson had set about painting the well red with blood, and all that with a prick that was troubling the seams of his breeches far down his thigh. Inquiries among the men established that the girl—new to the workhouse and unfamiliar with its customs—had committed the sole misdemeanor of asking whether she could have an extra crust for breakfast. Next, Krook inspected the cottage hospital and there he found a sound explanation for the establishment's terrible output. The rest you can work out for yourself. Petter Pettersson was never seen again sober, and—to borrow Hybinette's apt words—he appeared to have nothing to live for. Then the duel came to pass, and whoever it was killed him almost certainly did him the favor he most wished for."

Cardell kneads his eyelids with the fingers of his right hand. In the darkness, there are sundry will-o'-the-wisps flickering.

"And Krook's visitor?"

....

When Cardell knocks on Winge's door, there is no reply, and this time it remains closed. He peers through the keyhole, moving his head back and forth to get the best view of the room. The bottles are still neatly lined up on the table, their stoppers untouched and the glass dusty. Otherwise it is empty.

Emil is instead waiting for him in his own chamber at Cutter's Alley where the broken door affords free access to all who feel so inclined. His lap is covered in the white sheets of the day's newspapers.

"I've done as you wished. I've found a solution."

81

Like a fortune teller with her cards, Emil lays the sheets of newspaper on the table in front of Cardell. Each has selected the printer's largest typeface for their headlines. The news is easily summarized, while the remainder is filled with speculation written in haste in the night just gone. Most of the papers have run extra editions—a new one for each piece of fresh information discovered, each supposedly from a well-informed source who has been able to provide comment. Cardell gestures querulously at this game of patience.

"I assume that this failed assassination attempt on the Duke is on your mind?"

Emil Winge nods.

"Yes. I've scoured every bookstall for newspapers. There is much that is unclear about what has happened. I sense that all is not as it seems to be."

"What do you mean?"

"The oldest ruse in war is to appear the injured party and thus be able to attack with cavalry mounted on the high horses of justice. Perhaps this spectacle was staged. The Gustavians that Reuterholm hates so much seem to be biding their time. In this way, the Baron can demonstrate that they continue to pose a danger. The fired-upon guard is the only witness. The point is that it doesn't make any difference. The Chamber of Police is Reuterholm's puppet. Any conclusions drawn will be those that best serve the regime. Not that it matters to us."

"Precisely my own thought. The bigwigs can shoot each other as much as they like as far as I'm concerned. Still, I expect you came with a purpose other than enticing me to become a subscriber."

"I shall get to that. For the time being, all you need know is that I've found a solution to our problems. Two things are lacking to make it possible."

"Well?"

"The girl, Anna Stina Knapp, the one you have sought for so long. We need her."

"And the other?"

Winge turns away, seeking the light streaming in, squinting towards it.

"I need to disprove the categorical imperative."

"What?"

"Jean Michael, I have qualms. I don't know if this solution that I have found can be justified."

"Are you pulling my leg?"

Winge shakes his head, his mouth clamped shut into a defiant line.

"Is all that we have done to fall flat due to your tender conscience? Did we not swear a promise—you and I—for the victory that may be won, for which no price would be too high?"

"I said qualms. The word implies that I need some time to think. There's something I have to do—something I've long postponed."

Cardell trudges back and forth across the floor before eventually coming to a halt, leaning against his good arm with his face to the wall. He masters his heavy breathing, making an effort to regain the calm he has almost lost. With a sigh he turns back to Emil, and is surprised by the gentleness in his own voice.

"Well, Emil. Do what you must and let me know what happens next."

Winge gathers the newspapers from the table, folding them into a bundle and tucking them into his coat pocket on his way out. He stops in the doorway.

"You're taking it with greater equanimity than I dared hope for."

"I don't suppose what you come up with makes much difference. I've been fruitlessly seeking her for a year. There's nothing to make me believe my luck will suddenly change now."

82

The linden trees that once lined the parks of the great houses have shed their leaves on the Meadowland. The wind is capricious; Cat's Bay is swollen and sluggish after the simmering dog days, and its fumes can only be detected occasionally, and faintly at that. Emil Winge passes the tower of Hedvig Eleonora and the parish poorhouse. Here the wooden huts jostle together quarter by quarter, ill-equipped for the coming winter. Children play awkwardly between the walls, their lips blue and knees red, each trying to keep moving to continue out the cold. Farther away, the buildings become sparser, separated by fields with tilled soil or cattle huddled flank to flank. The patterns of the streets become harder to follow, and he doesn't know their names. He has to ask using the only name he knows, choosing to question the elderly in the hope of longer memories. Thus he is conducted through the crossroads with gestures of shifting certainty.

....

The cottage he seeks is remote, behind a wall and sheltered behind a groaning apple tree. A ladder is raised to its crown, and balancing at the top there is a man who has undone his coat to cool off. He supports himself on the branches to reach the red fruits, and one by one he drops them down to a woman who laughs as she catches them in her apron and then puts them in her basket. The man says something that Winge does not hear, and the woman laughs again. She is beautiful. No longer young, but the years have been kind to her, and what signs of age there are she wears like an adornment: lines where her cheeks have been creased by smiling, a network of nascent wrinkles around her eyes. The man appears to be a few years younger, handsome in his loose-fitting attire and slim in body, with a well-groomed mustache and healthy complexion. Emil stands for a moment watching them from the gateway in the wall until the woman catches sight of him and drops the apple she has just caught. From up in the crown there comes a surprised exclamation from the man as the next fruit hits the ground and rolls away into the grass. The ladder creaks unhappily as the man climbs down, while the woman stumbles closer, pale as snow.

"Cecil?"

Emil shakes his head.

"Emil. His brother."

The gate is separating them when the man approaches, stepping between them, his cheeks flushed with the knowledge that something is wrong and that the uninvited guest is to blame. His voice is harsh, with the tone of one accustomed to giving orders and seeing them obeyed.

"What is your business here?"

His wife puts a hand on his arm.

"Johan, would you do me a favor and leave us alone for a while?"

His expression is exchanged for one of surprise, and he looks from one to the other, clearly in two minds.

"Emil is my brother-in-law."

The man opens his mouth to say something, but closes it again. He takes the hand she has placed on his arm, raises it to his lips, and kisses it. Then he steps aside to open the gate and let himself out, and Emil in, with a reserved nod and an eloquent eye, his parting words just as much for Emil's sake as hers.

"I'm very close by if you need me, Emma. You just have to call."

He buttons up his jacket, pointedly beginning to walk slowly along the wall while taking a bite from the last apple he picked.

Emil and Emma stand there awhile without either being able to bring themselves to say the first word. The cry of a child from inside the house comes to their rescue.

"He's starting to wake up. Come inside with me."

The red-painted, half-timbered cottage is sturdy, each log carefully bound with flax. There are only two rooms, one with a stove and the other with a bed. The baby is in his cradle, and when Emma sees that he has woken and is staring at her with big blue eyes, she picks him up in her arms and sits down on a chair. She offers another, similar chair to Emil.

"Erik will be two in December. We are trying to wean him, but when Johan isn't here I often secretly spoil him."

The boy has spotted the stranger, and while Emma wraps her shawl around her to veil her bosom, he looks at Emil in astonishment as he in turn seeks out familiar features in the chubby face.

"Is he . . ."

"Cecil's? I can feel your gaze. It's something I have often wondered. But I have never found an answer by those means. Johan and I have chosen to let him belong to the father who is at hand."

She moves the child into position under the shawl. Embarrassed, Emil turns away from the smacking sounds—an intruder in a place he does not belong, the shawl making little difference. At first she takes no notice, but soon he feels a similar look turned his way.

"You're so like him."

"So many people say."

"Then you might understand the wounds that your visit opens. Why have you come?"

Emil fidgets, at once uncertain of the words he has so carefully prepared on his way.

"Did he ever speak about me?"

"Yes, Emil. He spoke of you often."

"In that case, you know how often I was a nuisance to him. Even now he is gone I cannot stop. I have come for my own reasons."

"So why?"

"We had different ways of looking at things, Cecil and I. Now it's too late to reconcile. The closest I can come to that is trying to understand the choices he made in the evening of his life, and seeing where they led."

He gropes for the right words, in vain, and for a long time she lets him sit there unaided.

"You speak of me and Johan."

He nods, his cheeks red, without daring to look her in the eye.

"I gather that you know of the circumstances already. There aren't many who can boast of that knowledge."

"Cecil confided in a friend who in turn told it to me. I have not passed it on."

She stretches her back, as if defiant in her honesty.

"Then you know that Cecil himself chose me a lover. He must have searched for a long time before he found Johan, and he spent a lot of time in his company to assure himself that he was the right man. I often think about what it must have felt like. Well, everything turned out as he intended, until a little stroke felled a great oak, and Cecil stumbled into the pit he'd so carefully dug for us. He left me and Johan alone with the guilt, but no one to blame but ourselves."

She shifts the babe to her other breast.

"Like everything that Cecil turned his hand to, he did it well. The shame ought to have torn us asunder. After his friend died, Johan wanted nothing more than to seek service in a foreign army where the enemy's volleys would determine his fate. My anguish was no less. It took me time to reconcile myself with Cecil's intentions, and to make Johan understand that we would best honor his memory by loving each other and forgiving our infidelity."

"Are you happy together?"

She nods.

"Yes. How else can we justify Cecil's sacrifice? We both mourned his death. Last year we married. The baby had already been born, but the priest understood the situation and did us a good deed by entering him into the register under Johan's name. The war is over, and with that all opportunities for promotion. We shall have to make do with his meager corporal's pay for a long time, but when poverty troubles me it is a comfort that my husband is whole and unscathed. Truth be told, we have enough. Not in abundance, but still. The house is small, but is big enough for three, and if more come, then we'll make room. We have bread and milk, sometimes meat at the weekend, and apples from the tree. In the summer the sun shines, in the winter we have wood, when the wood runs out we have each other. Cecil gave us all this. Whatever bitterness I still feel, I will heal with gratitude."

Emil remains still on the chair for a while, as if committing every word to memory. The baby is full, burping with satisfaction and babbling in the cradle as Emma buttons up her shirt.

"What was it you came to hear, Emil?"

"Yes. Well, it was that. Thank you very much."

She follows him to the door, and just as he is about to step outside she takes him by the arm. Surprised, he turns and feels her hand on his cheek. For a moment they stand there before she closes her eyes and leans forward to kiss the lips he knows are not his.

"Thank you for coming."

....

Out of sight, he is compelled to seek the support of a fence, trying to marshal thoughts cavorting in chaos. He staggers off like a drunk, taking no notice when he happens upon the corporal on his way. The words he has listened to buzz in his head, casting implications all round him; the ground is unsteady. Some children take him for a drunk and fall into a parade around his winding path, laughing and shouting until the distance and his disinterest drive them elsewhere. Emil pays them no heed. He doesn't know where he is going, lost without caring, impervious to the increasing chill of the afternoon. Heaven and earth are swaying, there are flashes before his eyes, tears and laughter come, one replacing the other from the storm within him.

83

Cardell trudges his dreary round with routine his guiding star. What else is there to do? It has now been a long time since the City-between-the-Bridges ran out of new roads to offer him, and every face he encounters he seems to have met before and dismissed. The beggars have flocked back to the city since the inquisition of the summer, because the final hope of the year is at death's door. Already the frost slays by night. Soon the daytime chill will be too severe to permit anyone to sit unsheltered in the city. Distress will come to all, and there will be no help for it. Darkness is coming ever faster: there are just a few mean hours of gray light between late morning and early evening. Above him, the clouds seem to rest upon the columns of the chimneys. The world itself has a low ceiling.

He is slow in stride, his muscles still sluggish and stiff, painful when stretched, and in the shady arches and dark nooks it is only his old clothing and obvious destitution that protect him from the thieves. His steps take him around the City-between-the-Bridges from lake to sea, from saltwater quay to freshwater harbor, from royal castle to common privy. He has nothing for his pains. Emil's chamber is empty and locked. His own is equally desolate. He gets a piece of bread on the way up; beer is drunk from a borrowed jug and necked quickly to relieve his hunger. Up in the room it is cold, and there is nothing for him to do other than adjust the rags that some more resourceful tenant left to block the cracks in the window, wrapping his coat more tightly around himself and waiting for his own body heat to warm the chamber. He sits upright on his bunk, listening to the church bells counting down the hours and quarters until the day's end, when the tower watchman takes over with his hoarse shouts. He dozes intermittently, woken by cramps in his neck and back before falling asleep again. From the hinterlands of slumber, he conjures the inner city and continues to wander its cobbles. But only in his dreams is Anna Stina waiting, and then he finds her, with equal parts triumph and trepidation.

....

He is woken by a creaking hinge, and blinks into the dark. He is not alone. Doubting the testimony of his own eyes, he rubs his face but the distorted image remains. There she is, absolutely still on the threshold, as if its damaged border is the boundary of the dream itself. Panic squeezes his chest, smothering every possible word. All he can do is sit still and continue to look, afraid that any reckless move will set this nightmare into flight. Nor does she move. A shiny surface catches a beam from the window, and he sees the dagger in her hand. He finds his voice, albeit one so hoarse it barely carries.

"I've been searching for you for a long time, Anna. Many lost days and nights. Where have you been?"

"Away."

He moves forward to the edge of the bunk to see her better. She seems whole and clean, pale but healthy, and he rejoices for her, come what may, remaining silent and giving her the time she needs to begin.

"My children are dead. They say the fault is yours."

An abyss opens beneath him, and he feels the dizziness in his belly as he falls and falls.

"They do not lie."

He rises from his place and goes to her. She raises her weapon.

"If you have come to collect what I owe you, then I shall not deny you that, Anna. The guilt weighs heavily. All that I have is yours in payment. I only wish it were more—enough to buy you something of value."

He laboriously crouches, kneeling before her. Then he raises his good hand and places it on the back of her hand where it is wrapped around the hilt of the knife. He brings it closer until the point reaches his throat, in the hollow above his ribs where the skin seems to stretch across a void.

"Here. Strike here to be sure, and it will be quick. You won't need much force. I've seen it before. But there will be a lot of blood, Anna, so be sure to step aside if you don't want it all over you."

Only through an effort of will is he able to let go of her hand. Warm in the dark. Just as hard as it is to close his eyes. He does it anyway—not for his sake but for hers—and he thinks that this is more than he has asked for. The past is making itself known. He doesn't know whether he says the words aloud or only thinks them.

"This has always been about us. You and I—with a sharp blade between us. Third time is the charm."

Hell comes to him from the depths, a glow from far down, eager to complete the enlistment initiated by the fire at Horn Hill. He hears a sound far away—the clatter of its gates flung wide open in anticipation of his arrival. But when he opens his eyes he sees the knife has fallen to the floor, and Anna Stina is on the chair. He puts a hand to his throat—the wound there is so small that wiping away a single drop makes it nothing. Without knowing why, he feels resentment. He was ready, but is now refused, living and unforgiven. He feels once again the sting of the debt that must be paid, but has been left to accrue yet more interest.

"Wasn't this why you came?"

"I came to confirm what I never should have doubted."

"What?"

"That there is a difference between doing good for one's own ends and doing evil with the best of intentions. You didn't kill my children on purpose."

"No. Out of stupidity. Stray words uttered in anger before ears I thought deaf. I placed in the hands of Erik Three Roses the weapon he needed for vengeance."

The shame of hearing his offense clad in words makes him fall silent. A vain hope parts his lips again, but the fear behind the question is yet greater.

"Are you going to forgive me now that you have let me live?"

"I didn't say that."

"So what now?"

She strokes the burnt skin on his crown, her touch as gentle as a moth's wing. He can feel her shuddering through her fingertips, and it is echoed in his own flesh.

"I don't know for certain where death takes us. Maja and Karl had so little time. In my dreams, I see a shadow world where souls denied life wander about. Perhaps there is such a place. Maybe that was where they were born from. They were given a human home in my womb, albeit for just a few short months. Now they are back where they came from. Perhaps they are waiting to be called back. In the night, I hear them calling for their mother with what language they have. I want them back with me. If not both, then at least one."

Far away, the hour of two o'clock is cried out, and as so often in the winter the sky seems ashamed of the gaze of those awake and dares only show itself at night. Now the clouds part for the stars.

"You know my past, Mickel. Men have never done me anything but harm. You have destroyed me, and I will never look upon you with joy or derive pleasure from what you have to give. But now I need a child. And I only have you."

Speechless, Cardell shakes his head.

"Look me in the eye and tell me this isn't what you have long wanted."

"Not like this, Anna. Never like this."

"Elias told me everything—everything he learned from eavesdropping at the windows of ladies of the night. The streetwalkers count the days carefully and know to miss those evenings where the risk is greatest that their duties will bear fruit. I've done the very opposite. For me, that time has arrived. Now. You mentioned your debt. I am here to redeem it."

She is wearing a shirt that she unbuttons with difficulty, her nakedness revealed sparingly by the light of the stars.

"Will it be easier for you if I pretend to like it?"

They both pretend.

84

Winge knocks on Cardell's broken chamber door in the early morning; the sun has not yet risen and its rays are only sufficient to etch the horizon. He hears the struggle from the other side and Cardell's steps as he shuffles across the floor. A crack shows half his burnt face and swollen eye. He does not open it any more than that.

"Go down and wait for me in the street, Emil. I'll be down as soon as I've finished powdering my wig."

Cutter's Alley is in shadow, and the only lamp in the quarter that is lit during the night has used its final drops of oil and reeks of dying wick. The cold has clad the cobbles in rimy fur, while the white points of the hoarfrost climb the windows of the alley. Winge stamps his feet on the spot to keep warm until the door slams and Cardell comes down the stairs and out into the gutter. Neither of them proposes any direction, but their feet turn towards the light and the Ship's Bridge, where masts and rigging soon filter the morning sun above them.

"What's the matter, Jean Michael?"

"I don't want to talk about it."

Cardell remains silent for a while, pointing his wooden fist towards a coil of rope with space for them both to sit on.

"What of you, Emil? How has your night been? I was passing your chamber yesterday evening and there was no one to be found. Whatever happened seems to have done you good, but where have you been?"

"I cannot say with certainty. I believe I have been walking around the city. Where exactly is neither here nor there. I needed time to think."

"All night? In this cold?"

"Yes."

"And was it worth the trouble?"

"Yes, Jean Michael. Everything is clear now."

"What is?"

"That I've been a fool my whole life—a clown fencing against shadows. I went to see my sister-in-law yesterday. There my brother had left substantiation for hypotheses I have rejected for as long as I can recall. At the same time, I know I am right, Jean Michael. So how do opposing principles intertwine, when one man's right must mean another's wrong?"

Cardell shrugs, his brow wrinkled. Emil closes his eyes and seeks out the sun with his face, its glowing disc engaged in leisurely escape from the cloud cover.

"We limp our way through the disorder of existence with whatever means we have at our disposal. Around us we erect symbols and ascribe value to them to bring order to the confusion, all at our own discretion. We fatten them unto greatness, before willingly submitting to them. We seem like a race born to slavery, all of us. The lies we hum to ourselves by way of comfort become the bellows for the hearth where we forge our own shackles."

"What lies?"

"All that we afford to faith in our foolishness. If they are not lies, then at least the truth of one is no greater than that of any other. Right and wrong are in the eye of the beholder."

"And you, now? Are you going to believe in nothing? What will move us forward?"

Emil shakes his head.

"No, not at all. I am free to believe what I please. But I now choose myself, unaffected by the force of habit. All my defiance against my father and Cecil—what has it been for, except to confirm the value of their delusion, my opposition equal to their zeal? Reason was our golden calf. The truth is that every person stands alone and free to make his own choices the very moment he rejects the oppression of the learned. It is as easy as lifting a veil, but it is nevertheless a yoke gone from my shoulders. I have vainly sought to mediate my doubts between two conflicting doctrines. Never again. My choices need not be consistent in the eyes of others. I answer to no one. Only now do I understand. I am free, Jean Michael. Finally free. Free in mind and soul."

"And Cecil?"

"Gone. Like a shadow before the light. Banished and forgiven. He shall not bother me anymore. May he rest in peace, safe in his grave. I wish he had been granted a longer life, but we are all counters in the game of chance."

Cardell sighs, turning towards the sun the part of his face not ravaged by the fire.

"I shan't pretend to understand what you are talking about, Emil, but it is sufficient for one of us to do so. I interpret it to mean that your qualms have been set aside. So what is the lie of the land, and what shall we do next?"

"Erik Three Roses and his Linnea, the poor Schildt cousin, the Colling widow, the Moravian lads Albrecht and Wilhelm whose lives we were incapable of saving, ready as we were—I cannot leave their fates unresolved, condemning them to oblivion. Their innocence must see the light of day. Tycho Ceton must face justice—his story must be told to all who can hear, his guilt presented as evidence."

"His brothers will surely do what they can to protect him."

"Indeed. And therein lies our second task. The Furies must be brought to nothing. In this regard my qualms remain, for the only weapon that we have to hand is blunt and will strike blows against all with the same, indiscriminate force. We ourselves must commit perjury, and those crimes we ensnare them for will not be those for which they ought to answer. The path of justice is crooked. Bearing that in mind, do you wish to proceed?"

Cardell scratches a louse bite behind his ear and spits a jet of tobacco strongly enough to change the course of a swimming duck.

"Damn them all to hell. Whatever path they take has little impact upon me, as long as they stay on it."

"That leaves only the girl. The list must come from her own hand, to guarantee its provenance."

Cardell pretends to track a gull with his gaze until it swoops away.

"I know where she is to be found."

85

Illuminated windows spill their trembling light onto the steps of the Stock Exchange.

Gillis Tosse has loosened his cravat and unbuttoned his waistcoat and shirt, the flushed skin of his chest bared to the wind now besieging the square. The cold does not bother him—it may be the scourge of poorer men, but to him it offers nothing but cool refreshment. Inside, the dance continues without him, heels hammering out a tempo on the floorboards, and between the clattering the music meanders. He is familiar with the melody without knowing its name, and he whistles along for a while before giving up the attempt to remain in tune. He is drunk, but there is room for more, and he brings the goblet of wine to his lips and tilts his head back to reach the final drops. The world shifts as his neck flexes. The square's desolate destitution falls away; he sees an opening between the clouds where the stars crowd through—beautiful and distant—and he greets them like brothers in silent triumph. Each one shines for him alone. The giddy weight of his head is tipping him over and he has to step backwards to keep his balance, but his heel soon encounters a higher step and he falls. Behind him, the rise of the steps is there to take his weight and—unharmed—he finds himself a seat. His wig slips off, and he erupts into a whinnying laugh. Here come the plebeians to the rescue, in the hope of a tip. He is helped to his feet, but the grip feels strange, and when he fumbles about he feels the hand that has helped him—it is hard and motionless. He blinks and looks from one to the other, suddenly pale. Two faces he vaguely remembers. Incredulous, Tosse shakes his head.

"This has happened once before."

The big one's good hand grabs him by the arm and leads him down the steps without leaving any room for choice, while Tosse squints at the small one.

"Are they messing with me? Bloody hell, what have they put in the wine?"

They come to a halt behind the building, with Niklas church tower looming above them. Tosse rocks on unsteady feet back and forth between the facade and the wooden fist. The watchman's voice is a raspy bass, as if tuned with threats and abuse in mind.

"Yes, we've met before, and on this very spot. Two years since. Thank goodness you are a predictable crowd, you bon vivants. You never miss a ball at the Stock Exchange."

Tosse points a finger of accusation at Emil.

"What business have you here? After all, you're dead. Didn't I celebrate with champagne? Damn it, what a faux pas. Bloody bad manners."

"Allow me to introduce Emil Winge."

Tosse nods slowly, his eyes narrowing, buttoning his shirt back up now that the heat of the dance has left his spirit-numbed skin.

"Younger brother. Very much alike. Of course. I remember from my Uppsala days. The perpetual student. Well, what is the meaning of this?"

The small one's voice is also not unlike that of his brother, albeit less hoarse.

"We have come with an offer you will find hard to resist."

"Permit me to air my doubts."

"We want to help you live longer."

Gillis Tosse feels the intoxication begin to give way to weightier things, and with its departure he feels his commanding presence resting securely on its foundations. What anxiety he recently harbored seems ridiculous.

"You're threatening me! Me? On a Saturday night while there is a ball going on? I am not without protection. I can have you flogged like hogs at the snap of a finger."

Annoyed, Tosse notes that his fingers have failed him, depriving him of the full effect of his retort. He makes to leave, but the wooden fist shoves him and he rebounds so quickly that the back of his head strikes the plaster.

"Shut your mouth and listen, if you know what's good for you."

Emil Winge lowers his voice and steps closer.

"You remember the pillorying of Magdalena Rudenschöld in the autumn of last year. She was in the workhouse for a while before they moved her to better quarters. From there she was able to smuggle out a letter—a list of all those ready to fall into rank behind Armfelt and bear arms in the revolution, hitherto divided and unknown even to each other. The letter was then lost. Until now. We have it in our possession."

"What does that have to do with me? I don't give a damn about politics. I wouldn't hesitate to piss on Gustav's chapel if I needed to, and if some of the drops fell onto Reuterholm's coattails then I wouldn't be all that bothered either."

"Surely you're shrewd enough to realize what would happen to everyone whose names appear in the letter if it were to fall into the hands of the regime—especially at present, when the Duke himself has been fired upon in the palace gardens."

"I wouldn't envy them their fates. Rudenschöld got off lightly, solely for having breasts and a pussy. The Baron would have the men whipped, each and every one of them, and would then have them transported to Hammarby to meet their end as a warning to others—and few would kick up a fuss. Anckarström would be watching from his station in hell and consider his final hours easier by comparison."

"It would be a simple matter to add your name to the list. There is plenty of room at the bottom of the paper."

The blood drains from Tosse's face. He gropes for words with which to reply but seems unable to squeeze even a syllable past his lips, seeking support from the wall and hearing the crack of his own limbs being broken on the rack and the hissing of glowing tongs. He searches for an escape route without finding one—not to the left, not to the right—and in the end he opts to allow his knees to give way, vomiting on the very spot on which he stands. Winge and Cardell wait until his sobbing has stopped and the spittle has subsided. Tosse's voice is one of resigned misery as he fumbles for support to stand up again.

"How may I be of service?"

Winge crouches rather than waiting for Tosse's vain attempts to regain his balance to succeed.

"The Furies—of which you are a member—have an inner circle, don't they? The brothers who choose which motions are put to a vote?"

"It seems we're going to call ourselves the Bacchants now."

"It makes no difference. Answer the question."

"Yes. Yes, that's right. The coterie. But which of the brothers have been entrusted with that task is not known to all."

"Find the names for us."

"How?"

Cardell growls.

"If it were easy we would do it ourselves rather than wading through your vomit. Solve the problem."

Winge is more conciliatory in his address.

"Anselm Bolin. If anyone has a register of members it will be him, surely? Pay him a visit. Find the register. Give us the names. Cardell here will accompany you and wait outside."

Neither of them is able to interpret a word of Tosse's noises. Cardell rolls his head from side to side to iron out a crick in his neck.

"I heard they cut Anckarström's dick off and rubbed it in his face before he laid his neck on the block."

Tosse's belly is empty, but the yellow bile runs fluently enough in the gutter.

86

Gillis Tosse hesitates for a moment, his fist raised before Bolin's door on Fork Alley. He doesn't have to turn his head to remind himself that he is being watched. Cardell is waiting by the corner up the hill, unseen in the shadows beneath an extinguished streetlamp. Sobriety has begun to make itself known, and in its footsteps comes the cold. Tosse is so cold he is shaking, and he slaps his chest, belly, and shoulders to warm the skin. Then he steels himself and allows his knuckles to descend. There is light in a third-floor window, and before long he hears the lamentation of the stairs within, at a slow pace befitting the master of the house and his gouty leg. When the door is opened a crack, it is Bolin himself who sticks his nose out and gives him a look of equal parts surprise and irritation.

"Tosse? What is the meaning of this? It is gone midnight."

"We must speak, Anselm. Please be so good as to admit me."

Bolin purses his lips at the overfamiliar mode of address, leaning in closer and sniffing the air.

"Are you drunk?"

Tosse sighs dejectedly.

"Not as merrily as I was before."

For a while he stands there in silence, stamping his feet on the spot, until Bolin shrugs and takes a clumsy step to one side.

"Well, you'd best come in. Age has banished sleep, in any case."

Bolin makes his way slowly up the stairs, supporting himself on a crutch and the balustrade, and Gillis Tosse follows behind him. They ascend towards the light. A sole flame burns in the candelabra in Bolin's private drawing room. Halfway there they encounter Bolin's servant, still drowsy, his shirt hanging over his rump, clearly woken by the knocking and quick to have risen for duty. He hurries to light the wax candle's neighbors on the many polished arms.

"Gillis, would you like some coffee?"

"If we share the jug, most certainly."

Bolin waves his manservant away and lowers himself carefully into a battered armchair whose cushion already bears a deep impression of him. He painstakingly stuffs his pipe, and Tosse passes him a light. The servant soon returns with a steaming copper pot on a tray, alongside porcelain cups so fine that Tosse thinks he can see the glow of candlelight clear through them, along with a plate of wheat biscuits half-dipped into solidified cocoa. Around them the cabinets throng with butterflies, each one threaded onto a silver pin. Several of the doors are open, and attached to a loose cushion there are a number of brittle pairs of wings waiting to be assigned their rightful places. Bolin pours coffee into the cups while Tosse takes in his surroundings.

"Where are the butterflies going?"

Bolin shrugs and sips his coffee.

"It's a funny thing, Tosse. So often I think I've found the perfect way to file them, but barely am I satisfied before my opinion shifts and it occurs to me that my *Papilionidae* belong next to my *Nymphalidae* due to their wing ribs, and I spend a whole night moving them. Then I rise in the light of morning and the colors assail my eyes, and I move them all back again."

Bolin takes a deep drag from his pipe, slowly allowing the smoke to rise from his mouth as he tilts his head back and half-closes his eyes.

"This is going to be about Tycho Ceton, isn't it?"

"Is he still with you?"

"He remains my guest, but he has his own suite and I take care to bolt the door separating his rooms from mine at night. There is no need to worry about him."

"But this name-change business smarts more than I am prepared to endure."

"Am I to interpret it that you are traditionally inclined in your tastes when it comes to the Greek tragedies?"

"What?"

"Oh. Nothing more than raillery."

Bolin rubs his tired eyes, and Tosse refills his host's empty cup while seizing the opportunity to look around the room. His heart skips a beat at the sight of the beautiful gilded leather folder on Bolin's desk—the one he last saw under Bolin's arm when he was receiving the brothers on the steps of the Nonpareil, ticking off each name whispered into his ear. Bolin's voice is flat as he continues.

"I don't understand why you attach such importance to such a banal thing. It has been the society's custom to change its appellation at regular intervals, as and when the opportunity arises and inspiration strikes. That happened in the form of Ceton's masquerade. It makes our footsteps harder to follow over time—to the benefit of us all. We do not want for men of letters in our ranks, and someone noted the similarities to the fate of King Pentheus at the hands of Dionysus's followers. Hence the name. The connection to Ceton is peripheral, and the idea is not his."

"Nonetheless."

"What is it about him that riles you so?"

"He isn't one of us."

"You don't understand him. That frightens you. I don't blame you, for that is nature's way. What we do not understand we cannot predict, and therefore cannot trust."

"What about you, then? You understand him?"

"I would say so—but then I also know enough about his origins to speculate upon his motives. Most of us seek pleasure in life, but for Tycho it is death that is of interest. Most of what he says in order to win our favor is borrowed, somewhat naively, from his French books, by authors for whom reality is only ever a distant host. Well, it's a long story. You may have a point, but there are many intersections between our interests. *Quod erat demonstrandum.*"

Bolin drains his cup for the second time and grimaces at the grounds. He leans forward on his chair, his face ill-suited to conveying confidences.

"Think of Tycho Ceton as an exotic animal—a patterned snake or a monkey in an amusing hat. A pleasant distraction—albeit bought at the price of some labor—and one that can't be introduced into fine rooms without a chaperone. Perhaps the creature grows bigger than intended until the trouble outweighs the pleasure, or it becomes impudent enough to bite the hand that feeds it, and that is the day when it must be returned to the wild. It offers satisfaction for as long as it lasts, and no longer. But dangerous it is not."

Tosse fidgets on his chair before crossing his legs. The coffee is awakening his waterworks. With a suppressed groan, he reaches over to refill Bolin's cup a third time, cursing the bladder that Bolin's gout has no doubt allowed him to exercise to the limits of elasticity. He raises the pot high to ensure a resonant jet of liquid, and almost loses his grip completely when his prayers are suddenly answered.

"Do excuse me a moment, Tosse. Nature calls."

While Bolin slowly rises and limps towards the concealed nook containing his chamber pot, Tosse makes a great show of examining the rows of winged insects, but as soon as the footsteps have creaked far enough across the floor, he is on his feet and behind the desk. His hands trembling, he opens the leaves of the folio until he finds what he seeks. He tears out the page and tucks it into his waistcoat.

87

Cardell wonders whether he is imagining things when he senses something in the air—a sensation he cannot put his finger on, one that is at once alien and familiar. He tells himself that he is getting worked up for nothing—that waiting in the shadows feeds delusions. All around him, the city has fallen silent. The debauchees seek the support of each other's shoulders as they cross the thresholds of inns and wend their way home. A bluecoat makes his rounds with brisk footsteps, eager not to waste a moment more than necessary beyond the confines of the guardroom. Lights still burn in a handful of windows, the buckled glass occasionally haunted by swaying phantoms on their way to and from the privy. Such are the poor inns, which after midnight transform from drinking den to dormitory, in which the frozen homeless huddle together seeking each other's warmth. Sleeping bodies in tight rows generate a heat that seems to grow greater than the sum of its parts in a charity normally alien to nature. The windows are streaked with condensation.

Down the hill, Cardell hears the door open and voices raised in farewell, and, shortly after, Gillis Tosse's footsteps echoing in the empty alley. He waits awhile at his corner before impatience drives him out of cover to walk towards the waiting man. Tosse gropes inside his waistcoat and holds the crumpled paper away from himself as if it burns his fingers, his sentences staccato amid the hiccups that have overcome him.

"Here. Take it. Now leave me be. Do I have your word?"

Cardell nods.

"Yes."

Tosse shakes his body, muttering to himself.

"Fuck me, what a night. I wonder if the ball is still going. I wonder if I've got time to drink enough to wake up oblivious."

Left alone, Cardell begins to walk back up the hill towards Cutter's Alley, but then he stops. The night is late: those few lamps they have bothered to light have drunk their oil, but there is one still burning at the corner of East Street, and the light draws him towards it as if he were a moth. He has to use his single hand to smooth the folds of the paper against the breast of his jacket. It takes a while before his eyes are equal to their task. The lamp is no more than a suspended metal bucket sparsely punched with holes to spare the flame from the wind, and in order to illuminate the carefully written letters with the swarming points of light, he has to move the sheet back and forth while chilly gusts frustrate his efforts. He has never been a quick reader, and it takes him even longer to reconcile himself to the ornate penmanship. He reads the names one by one, lowers the paper, then reads again. Over and over he makes to leave, only to seek out a better shaft of light by which to read. In the end, he lowers the paper and stands there with his head bowed. As if dizzy, he is obliged to seek out the support of the wall, where his wooden fist slips on the frosty plaster. Rather than dance on the spot to remain upright, he leans heavily against the wall and lets the strength leave his knees, sinking down to a crouch, where he sits with his good arm around his head. He sits like that for a long time, slowly rocking back and forth. The hour is called out from the German Tower. Then there is a chilly caress against his cheek, and he opens his eyes, at once aware of the source of the feeling he has been ruminating upon all night: snow-filled clouds. Now they are scattering their load over the City-between-the-Bridges.

....

Around him all is white, shrouded in soft flakes falling heavily into the alleys with a rustling whisper. It is as if the city is wrapped in a shroud of redemption, and Cardell fumbles to find a grip and get to his feet. Then he brushes the snow off his body and tarnishes the white carpet with his boots, a row of dark stains marring its purity all the way back down the hill. He follows the path that Gillis Tosse previously took, tracking it back to the same door.

88

Emil Winge goes from shop to shop, his scarf wrapped around his face to avoid identifying himself any more than he must. Others are doing the same thing, because the cold is biting into skin and teasing noses until they stream. No one will particularly remember him. He searches among reams of paper for the right one, and the hours are all that help him distinguish one sheet from another, until they are as distinct to him as animals of different species in a world that was previously hidden to him, despite his years of reading. The color is the first thing he notices. What he previously saw as nothing more than white has come to accommodate an endless range of diversity, from shades of brown and yellow to gray and ivory. On one occasion, he is tempted into a recognition of what he is searching for, until he realizes he must have been mistaken: it is from the light glare of the snow outside that he recognizes the hue.

Color is not the only thing to be considered. The densities differ, from thin tissue to sheets so thick they leave jagged creases when folded. The surface pattern is a third consideration: easy to disregard from a distance, but when held close to the eye and angled to the light it becomes a landscape to be differentiated from others. Masses of different materials stiffen into papers of various kinds: cotton, wool, flax, hemp, sometimes with petals added for scent or for an improvised effect. Emil has risked taking a torn corner with him, to help his chances, careful not to smudge it any further with his bare fingers. His task is made even more difficult by its history. The sheet was once part of a batch, but how closely does it resemble its fellows now? It has been aged by its privations. Time after time he despairs, and with each passing hour he realizes that the best he can hope to achieve is a compromise among too many factors to adequately consider. He makes his choice, the best he can do. After that: ink.

Down by the lock gates, the boys test the night-old ice with chapped legs. Insensitive to the cold in their enthusiasm, they compete to see who can get closest to the open channel dryshod. The salty water bleeds into their footprints. A large quantity of snow has fallen and its clearance has been neglected. People are directed to tamped-down paths through what were until recently streets wide enough for all. Now people must push and shove, wielding profanities and elbows. Emil knows the city well enough to follow its preeminent rule: biggest first. Aware of his size, he waits his turn, hopping from foot to foot to keep warm.

Cardell has directed him to new quarters—with Widow Gry and her daughter Lotta on the Southern Isle, far from the bait in Bolin's net. He doesn't have room to sleep stretched out in the corner they have set aside for him, but it is enough and he has been able to set up a plank of wood by the window by way of a desk. Now he is hurrying to make the most of what daylight still remains. The widow seems to accommodate him quite contentedly. She is a nurturing sort, and he guesses that his miserable person has become the welcome object of her maternal emotions, now that her only living daughter is merely awaiting the onset of spring before moving into her own abode. She saves him what few scraps their diet permits, pressing him at the table to help himself to porridge and soup. By way of payment, he has helped the girl to improve her reading—she is a good student and he a better teacher than he thought. Within him, the voice that was Cecil's rests in silence. Doubts and anxiety likewise. Within him, a room has been sealed off, a door to a library full of reason and logic closed. He does not miss it—he does not need it any longer. He gratefully bids farewell to cunning and calculation, to intrigue and strategy. Every necessary thought has been carried through to its conclusion. All that remains is execution.

He must give himself the time to thaw his frozen hands before he can begin. The art is harder than he remembers from the winters spent in his student quarters. For a long time, his fingers remain white and numb, even though he shakes them and then warms them in his armpits at intervals. When he is satisfied, he carefully applies the knife to the quill, testing its nib over and over until it draws lines of the same width as on the list that he lays before him with caution, as if any hasty movement might consign it to dust. He has bought himself enough cheap paper to practice, and two sheets of the right kind to give himself more than one chance. Then he begins to write, at first slowly and carefully, in order to learn each and every peculiarity of Magdalena Rudenschöld's penmanship—acquired long ago under the careful instruction of a private tutor—and later sumptuously, in order to better dress treachery in ink, and in glaring contrast to the handwriting that characterized Bolin's records. Over and over, Emil copies the names—the actual ones first, then those from Bolin's list—with increasing speed and fluency. The names he must record appear to have been hastily scrawled, which hardly surprises him, given Tosse's condition and urgency. At the stroke of two, dusk sets in, and he lights a tallow candle to pilot him through the darkness. Diligence dulls his senses. He dedicates several more hours to his task before testing the first one of the real sheets and nodding appreciatively at the result. Almost there. All the pieces required to make the whole are falling into place. By morning, the forgery will be complete, the letter exactly as if Rudenschöld herself had clasped the quill. Then the tallow gasps and gives up its final breath in a reeking plume of smoke, and Emil Winge extinguishes its glow with a moistened thumb; he curls up, still dressed, and falls asleep, exhausted and full of confidence, to the sound of the widow's snores from the other side of the wall.

....

He spends the next morning refining every last detail to perfection, wearing the edges of the paper and aging it with creases and grime before wrapping every garment he has tightly around his body and braving the cold for his meeting with Cardell. The coffeehouse doors remain shuttered, and they have agreed to meet at the cathedral. In the pews they pray through chattering teeth, many here less out of the fear of God than to find shelter from the cold winds. The vergers take it in turns to scrutinize the assembled masses and give a dressing-down to those who have taken up postures comfortable enough to catch a few winks, or who are discovered with bottles in hand or intoxicated. The choir is rehearsing by the chancel, the boys' cheerfulness contrasting with the conductor's short-tempered hangover. Occasionally a phrase or chord rises above the murmured prayers and scuffling feet, and the harmony of the clear voices resonates around the space. Winge and Cardell take cover behind the fluted pillars, following a way through the nave to find an undisturbed corner by the plinth where St. George on his steed rises above the defeated dragon. Emil hands over his work, which he has been carrying inside his waistcoat with the palm of his hand on top of it all the way from the Southern Isle, worried about pickpockets and stray winds.

"Give it to the girl. She knows where to go, doesn't she? After that, our fate rests in her hands. You have told her what she must tell the guard to secure an audience with Edman?"

"You don't have to worry."

"Is she capable? Can she account for her movements if she is examined on the spot?"

"You know what she has gone through in this life. What are Edman's questions in comparison, however shrewd they are?"

"Edman is nothing if not resourceful. If all goes as we hope, his actions are unlikely to be subject to any delay. I give them an hour or less. We must wait at Bolin's until the soldiers arrive, and as soon as they have dragged Bolin away we must reach Ceton before he smells a rat. Then he will be ours. I have the evidence ready, as well as dispatches to the newspapers and notices to fix to street corners should the Chamber of Police prove intractable. But I don't think that will be necessary. Magnus Ullholm is crafty enough to spot a good story when he sees it. If he turns a deaf ear to it, then it will nevertheless grow legs. Robbed of other options, he will doubtless choose to profit by the affair as best he can, and take full credit for Ceton being brought to justice and conveyed to Gallows Hill."

Emil bites his thumbnail and nods to himself, as if lining up each factor all over again and evaluating his conclusions. Then he raises his gaze to the saint above them, clad in gilded armor, sword drawn to inflict a mortal wound on the likeness of evil.

"There shall we stand, Jean Michael. Tomorrow."

89

ardell wakes up in the night. He feels her warmth under his hand, and he remembers another similar feeling. When the piece was loaded and aimed on its mounting, and he was waiting for the right moment between wave crest and trough to fire, he used to shoo away the gun crew, taking care to ensure that none of his men lingered and risked crushed feet from the wrath of the recoil. He alone remained waiting for a while at his post, his palm on the hot metal of the barrel, spellbound and terrified by the preposterousness of its explosive force—its jurisdiction over life and death, made inescapable by its smoldering fuse. The memory brings goose pimples up on him. Sleep escapes him for a long time, casting its thin membrane over the moment, only for him to burst into wakefulness again.

The room is so dark that at first he cannot say whether his eyes are open or not, but Cardell knows to collect himself, and he waits. He hears her unseen movements, feels the blanket shift and with the passage of the moment light is borne to him out of the dark. A solitary, soft streak, a silver string floating in the abyss: her shoulders, arm, and waist. For a while, she remains like that, and Cardell is equally still, all the will he is not wasting on praying for respite from the passing of time required to carve her form into his memory, capturing its beauty like a bubble in solid glass.

She is sitting on the edge of the bunk, moving quietly so as not to disturb him, brushing the floor for her shirt with gentle fingers. He wishes it lost, but she soon finds it and stretches her back to pull it over her head, and then her weight is lifted from the bed. She crouches for her skirt and stands up dressed. Three steps away she finds her coat where it was discarded, her feet much too light to sound upon the floorboards. Then he feels her fingers stroking his burnt cheek.

"Mickel?"

He opens his eyes to look into hers.

"You burned yourself when you tried to save them, didn't you? You ran into the fire."

"To no avail."

He turns his face away in shame. Her hand turns it back again, cool and smooth, impossible to resist, even though it is no stronger than a seedling, and she leans in closer to kiss the stinging skin.

"Mickel, what could be more beautiful to me?"

She remains for a while longer until morning light finds them both on the bunk and chases away the dream they dreamed. Once again she rises, gathering her clothes.

"This is the last night."

"I know that."

"Goodbye."

What can he say? Which words could be enough?

"Goodbye, Anna—take care."

Then she is gone, and he lies there rigid as a dead man as dawn slowly paints his room with its palette of black and white.

90

They wait together in the alley, concealed behind a wooden cart tipped onto its end. The snowfall has stopped and visibility is clear. Eyes watering, they can see straight to Anselm Bolin's door. The wind plays whimsically between the buildings, going in one direction and then the other, occasionally dusting them with flakes scuffed from the edge of roofs. They move closer and closer to each other until they are huddled up shoulder to shoulder to conserve what warmth remains. Winge is shifting from one foot to the other, and Cardell, mute and still, leaves him to his dance. For a third time, Winge gives up his vain attempts to lure a spark into taking hold in the tobacco stuffed into his pipe.

"You asked me before what I am going to do when this is all over, Jean Michael. I think I know now."

"Oh?"

"I met my sister-in-law and was given a glimpse of the life Cecil should have had. I've never approached such matters before—out of ignorance. Perhaps such things are within my reach too, for what it is worth. Perhaps a human being can be made even from one such as I, perhaps one who is worthy of another's love. After today, all obstacles shall be gone and I will have no other excuses left than cowardice."

"Anyone calling you a coward will have to answer to me afterwards."

Emil takes a rapid step back to better conceal himself.

"Men on the hill. Here they come."

There are four of them, each in the blue jacket and plumed hat of the guard, speckled with snow. They are keeping pace with their leader as best as they can, although the ground causes them difficulty. Each right glove grips a saber. They come to a halt by Bolin's door, and one of their number climbs the steps to hammer upon it. An unseen hand opens it from within, and one by one the men climb up and kick the snow off their gaiters against the facade. Emil pulls his watch from his pocket to check the time, nodding contentedly.

"Just as planned. So far, so good."

While they wait, the snow begins to fall again, and soon it is whirling wildly enough to force them to squint between aching fingers to maintain their view. Winge counts a quarter of an hour, and then the small troop emerges from the door again, more of them now, one of them being led out with a firm grip on each arm. This time it is Cardell's turn to be restless. Of the two leading the way, one is limping with the support of his cane, barely visible under wolf furs. Emil's voice conveys his dismay.

"Bolin is at the front. Someone else is under arrest."

Cardell puts a hand on Emil's shoulder.

"Emil, this was the only way."

"What?"

"You made me swear to it. You did."

"Jean Michael, what's going on?"

"The victory that remains to be won."

"Why?"

"Tosse gave me a page torn from the register of the Furies' inner circle and I read it. Your plan was the best one, Emil, but it would have been of little use with those names. A hare cannot go to the wolves with the half-eaten carcass of his friend and then denounce the law of the jungle. All you would have got for your trouble was a knife in the gut and a free pass to the bottom of Cat's Bay, your boots filled with rocks, and the right to sway there at five fathoms until only your bare bones marked the spot. The dice were always loaded to our detriment. We just didn't know how badly."

"Edman himself? Lode? Reuterholm? The Duke Regent? Modée?"

Cardell lets out a reluctant sigh, shaking his head.

"Names of that kind. Best you don't know."

Emil's eyes widen despite the heavy snow, his gaze vacant while his mind rushes between conclusions.

"So you cut a deal with Bolin. You gave me a different list. What I took to be Tosse's careless transcript was your own."

He cannot conceal his confusion.

"But Jean Michael, if we are so powerless, what did you have to bargain with?"

"I selected two names I didn't recognize from Tosse's misappropriated list and said they were also included in Rudenschöld's letter. I told a barefaced lie to Bolin and silently prayed that if his brethren were worth anything to him he would accommodate me."

"And when he comes to realize he has been deceived?"

Cardell is clutching the letter Emil prepared in his hand.

"He won't. Now they're there among names I selected from the newspapers or plucked from thin air. His, I have struck out."

"What do you receive in exchange?"

"A life for a life. Yours, Emil, first and foremost. You forced my hand."

"How?"

"Was it not you who first saved me? I spoke with Blom and asked him to make inquiries on my behalf. I know why Petter Pettersson is swimming in the deeps of Knights' Bay, pale and rancid. It would have been me, had it not been for you. You went to Krook and took him to the workhouse to see with his own eyes the stone in his shoe. Pettersson's departure was by your hand. We weren't to be friends, Emil. Wasn't that what you said? If you wanted to see a different ending, then you would have been best advised to practice what you preached. How could I do differently?"

The men have closed the distance and are near now, Bolin putting two fingers to the edge of his fur cap in mock salute. The two unoccupied guards lay their hands on Emil's shoulders.

"Where are they taking me?"

Cardell steps closer, brushing away the guards' hands and grabbing Emil by the neck to hold him close, his lips next to his ear. He lowers his voice to a mere whisper.

"To the asylum, Emil. Now listen to me: you've escaped from such places in the past. I know that. When you get out, you will be safe. You will never be a threat to them again. Who would listen to an escaped fool raving about a conspiracy? Forget what has gone before. The life you want awaits you beyond a wall no thicker than your hand is wide. You can do it, Emil. Of nothing am I more certain."

Cardell squeezes his shoulder. Emil opens his mouth to reply, but closes it again, merely shaking the head that has been bent under the weight of the watchman's embrace. Anselm Bolin clears his throat self-consciously.

"It goes against the grain for me to interrupt your tender moment, gentlemen, but the cold troubles me and there remain matters to be resolved."

Cardell takes his eyes off Emil and offers the letter to Bolin, but withdraws it from the outstretched hand. Bolin jerks his head to his henchmen, and they bring forth the bound man. Bolin offers him to Cardell with open hands.

"As agreed."

The commodity is exchanged for the purchase sum. Bolin steps aside to examine what he has bought, chuckling in surprise at the odd name he reads until nodding his appreciation. He tears the sheet straight down the middle and then across, before turning to his four companions.

"One daler to each man who opens his mouth and doesn't open it again until it has all been swallowed."

None of them can afford to refuse. Like sacramental wafers, he places a scrap of paper onto four waiting tongues and stands stock-still until ink begins to stain the corners of their mouths.

"Good. That brings matters to a close. Well met, gentlemen. If I am not much mistaken, a carriage awaits us down by the Ship's Bridge to carry young Mr. Winge to his new lodgings. Mr. Cardell, it has been a pleasure of the kind that suffices for a lifetime. And so, farewell."

They disperse. The guards walk in pairs, chewing the cud, their chins black. One set goes back up the hill empty-handed, while the other walks either side of Emil Winge, down towards the water. Cardell takes from his belt the short length of rope he was given on the same day as he was the title of watchman, carefully so as not to disturb the flowers that have dried at his side. He makes a loop around Tycho Ceton's hands—the man's broken mouth stuffed with a bloodstained rag. All fingers and thumbs, he shapes the rope into a firm knot with the numb fingers of his right hand.

"Five bloody years I've been dragging this around, and I'll be damned if this isn't the first time I've had a use for it—and that's one more time than I ever thought I'd need it."

91

They have given him a cell of his own. There is straw scattered across the floor as if it were an inn or a sty. In the corner is a chipped earthenware pot, to be set down full by the hole in the door in exchange for a bowl of food, whatever swill is available. Oatmeal most often, augmented with lard congealing into tough lumps while waiting to be served. On Sunday there is salt herring, sharp on the palate and with an unquenchable thirst on its heels. The window is blocked with boards, leaving just a crack at the top—too high up to reach. The walls are covered in scrawls, carved or written using whatever ink the mother of invention had at hand: red, brown, or black. Some of it is legible, some isn't: dreams of retribution, of redress, of carnal desire and the anguish of enemies. None of it is of any use to him. By the angle of the light, he knows that his room faces west. If he could reach higher then he would be able to see all the way to the City-between-the-Bridges, the Quayside and the Ship's Bridge, with its teeth bared at the throat of the islands. The day is short, the night long—light never growing beyond murky. The back of a tiled stove arcs the wall adjoining the corridor beyond, its door beyond reach on the other side. He never feels it warm; the room is completely cold and at night he scrapes hay from the floor to tuck between his shirt and coat. Madness swirls in from all angles—it is never quiet. A chattering, howling, ranting, and raving chorus penetrates through the cracks between the floorboards above and below where others are shoved into cells no bigger than his own. Cries and whispers, laughter and prayer, pounding on the walls, groans of lust and pain, shattered stoneware. There is no escape route. They guard him closely, the wall is solid, there is a crossbar over the door—thick and invulnerable. The drop beyond the window is too high. The guards never speak to him.

Emil knows his fate was meant as a favor. Cardell couldn't have known. Emil ought to have told him while there was time, but the trust between them was forfeit and he saw no cause. Admittedly he escaped from the Oxenstiern in Uppsala, but not without help. His brother saved him that time. Back in the alley, the truth was on the tip of his tongue, but he was able to stop himself at the last moment. What has happened was done with the best of intentions. Why poison the gift he was given in good faith? He gave his silence in return.

Curled up in the corner he has chosen as his own, Emil Winge hugs his slender legs, his chin on his knees, and for the thousandth time he dwells upon his dilemma, reluctantly enchanted by its symmetry—as horrific as it is perfect. He is alone. There is no one who can help. Recently, he broke through the lock of an invisible prison and won a freedom he hadn't thought possible. Must he scale its inner walls again for a chance to escape from the prison hole where his body languishes? Can he? Can sheer will-power restore insight to ignorance? Is it an exchange worth its price? He doesn't know for sure.

Time presses its fingers to the scales. Soon he loses count of the days. Listlessly, he surveys the miserable piece of reality that is now his whole world, realizing that one of those chattering voices that never stops is his own. Then, one day, almost imperceptibly: a movement in the corner of his eye that disturbs the immobile shadows of the cell. A shift of light in the space that was only recently empty. He turns his head in its direction, feeling salty tears as his dry lips crack in triumph.

"Cecil?"

92

They trudge across the bridge to the north, through the Northern Isle, where the cold crackles around the dry-timbered houses and windows have been shuttered to better protect those crowded around the glow of the fire. Their soles shuffle around the Bog, whose marshy shore is trapped under ice and snow, and farther north, past the hill where the Observatory lies idle and the windmill scythes away the snowflakes with its swinging arms. Visibility is poor, few are outdoors, and still fewer defy the snowfall by raising their gaze to the odd couple. Those that do see nothing worth stopping for. A watchman with a prisoner in tow, surely some pimp or whoremonger. The only thing of note is their direction. Perhaps they are lost—and no wonder, given the drifts that have recast every familiar form.

At the Roslag customs booth they pass unhindered. Through the windows of the hut, he glimpses the officers sitting with their hunched backs to the fire with spirits to warm where the flames do not reach, rolling dice in a tin, too frozen and drunk to take any notice of anything else. Cardell follows the hill up into the woods, each new footstep uniquely visible, erased in just a few seconds behind their backs. His only waymarkers are trees and stones. He stops in a grove of trees, unsure whether this is the right one, until he hears the tinkling song of the streaming spring as water rises from the depths with a force too great to be stifled by the ice. He brushes the snow off a fallen branch.

"Sit."

He gets down on one knee to release Ceton's bindings, and pulls the rag out of his mouth, moist underneath a frozen crust. Ceton rubs his hands first, then his shoulders and arms. He wears only a shirt, and the hems of his breeches are unbuttoned around his knees, as if he has been abducted from the safety of his bed and given just moments to dress. He buttons up his shirt, turning up its collar, pulls his stockings higher up his calves, and wraps his arms around himself.

"And now?"

Cardell turns up the collar of his coat around his own neck and inserts his hand into a pocket.

"Now we sit here awhile."

The snow is falling more discriminately beneath the trees, filtered through the weave of dead branches. The short day is coming to a close. Behind the clouds, the sun tumbles over the edge of the world, plunging deeper and deeper, the final bleeding of a wound that must eventually close. It conjures darkness in its wake. Ceton shakes himself to relieve his tremors, his teeth chattering under his scarred cheek.

"So you are the last man standing. Who would have thought? I'm glad I got to see you push your friend into the abyss. Truly a deed worthy of a laurel wreath. I would like to hope that my own example has offered inspiration. You've come so far—cripple and all. From the first moment, I was certain the wood inside your skull was as solid as that in your left hand."

"I've had good teachers in recent years—more than one."

"Other than little Anna Stina? I wasted such time and attention on her, as if I were the father she never had. How did it work out for her? I took it as read that you would open your veins to her little fang, but now that I have seen how cold-blooded you are in sacrificing your minions, I suppose you probably wrung her neck. But only after you had taken what you had so long denied yourself, I hope."

Cardell takes out his tobacco pouch and inserts a lump inside his cheek, chews, and spits. Ceton casts his gaze down, shivers, and looks over his shoulder towards the deepening shadows.

"Forgive me. Let's talk about something else. The times, perhaps? The final year of the regency is drawing to a close. The Swedish estate will finally be passed on to its heirs. Soon we shall have a king again."

"One can only hope it goes better than last time."

"Do you think it will?"

Cardell shrugs.

"The lad knows the cost of war. A fistful of scrap poured into a dirty gun barrel sent his father to his death after two weeks of gangrene, and he wasn't even fourteen himself. Surely no one has greater cause to love peace than that boy."

"Jean-Jacques himself would be dumbfounded by your ideas of upbringing—nothing makes a man meek like moralizing the murder of his own father. But once again I jest. Well, the century is also drawing to a close."

"Not a year too soon."

"Do you think the next one will be better? Will the good years finally come?"

"At least it will be born with a decent advantage. This one has been war after war, each more meaningless than the last. Each step forward has spilled fresh blood. What can one hope for, except that suffering has bestowed erudition? They speak of new ideas, new order."

The grin on Tycho Ceton's face is scornful.

"I've heard about them. How beautifully they've been schooled by the French. But what then? Once the guillotine slows and the worst of the bloodlust is overcome? Should the liars compete for the favor of the mob, the shrewdest given the throne at a price? Even a king can be father to an honest son. Granted, the odds are lousy, but I'd rather take them than entrust the Crown to someone who sought it out with malice aforethought and defrauded the masses most skilfully in their ambition. And what would happen on that day when they free themselves from their bondage? Tell me how their time is then to be managed? They would ferment themselves into lofty self-conceit and capricious folly, consigning the city to damnation quicker than ever. Meager beacons of vanity, good for nothing except turning good timber to ash."

He pauses, shaking his head and pounding his arms against his chest.

"But perhaps it's all much the same. At any rate, there is no progress to be derived from numbers in a calendar. The truth is that a lifetime is not long enough to learn what has been in the past. No lessons arise from the suffering of others. Each new generation is a sowing of dragon's teeth. Nothing gets better—different, at most. Men such as you and I will always rise above the masses, equally strong and shrewd, equally bursting with hate. We will improve ourselves and forge new weapons to do more harm to each other than yesterday's warriors could have ever dreamed of, and what life is wasted along the way will hardly trouble us. We will dance around the atrocities until we have trodden a furrow deep enough to bury our entire species."

Ceton laughs.

"Shall I argue my case? Look at us now. Look at you and me. What does it matter whether I am right when you are the stronger? You're going to kill me."

"Strictly speaking, it'll be the cold that does that."

Ceton's voice takes on a bitterness in his reply.

"Surely you don't imagine there is anything to be gained from speaking of this? The worst go free—now as always. How could it be otherwise? That's what happens when the human essence is animated with enough power to put dreams within reach. What would the rich man's fortune be worth if he had to submit to laws made for the poor? You might as well designate the waves on the sea your enemy, or the falling snow. They sacrifice only what they can easily spare, and you accommodate them willingly. A victory so minute it isn't worth the name."

Cardell shrugs.

"Always something."

Ceton reflects for a moment, drumming his feet on the ground.

"You know, in a way, this is a moment I've been awaiting for a long time, albeit with mixed emotions. Nothing I've done or seen has given me any real knowledge. Finally, I will know."

Silence descends between them, and they sit there for a long time. Ceton shakes his head, causing his own snowfall onto his shoulders, and he chuckles in surprise.

"I'm not cold any longer. Look."

He holds out both hands in front of him in the falling flakes. They are pale, stone-still, untrembling, and he moves them up and down, letting them flow across the keyboard of an invisible spinet. As if in defiance, he loosens the collar of his shirt and raises an eyebrow at Cardell.

"Perhaps this isn't going as you expected."

Cardell spits into the darkness—a brown scar quickly healed.

"Let's wait a little longer."

They sit for a while longer until Ceton is beset by a sudden restlessness. His neck stiff, he shifts on the log to stare into the night—not down towards the hill from which they came, but through the trees behind him and to the side.

"Father . . . is he . . ."

Beneath the trees, the night stands empty, with no company save the rustling breeze that aimlessly dances across the fresh snow.

"This world is expiring around me. I can see into the next. But it's all black."

At last he falls still with his head bowed, tears of despair falling to leave shiny marks on the cloth of his breeches.

"There's no one. It's all empty. No one is coming for me."

....

Cardell remains in the same spot for a long time until the mist of breath from the slit cheek stops and the snow around Ceton's blue lips no longer melts. He leans in close, attempting to move the head atop stiff vertebrae; he taps the nail of his index finger against an open eye left cloudy by hoarfrost and hears a dull clink in reply. He resumes his former position, tunelessly whistling an old march. He makes an effort to conjure the image of the face that hasn't yet been born, wondering whether she will ever look upon it and glimpse a piece of who he was. He hopes not—he hopes the little one benefits from its mother's features. Then he takes off his coat.

Epilogue

SPRING 1796

From dry bark and thawed earth life breaks forth. The sun shows its mercy to new buds. The current of the forest spring has burst its former banks, swollen with meltwater that wants to go up and out, in a purling canter down the hill and away through the trees.

In the middle of the clearing, stones are stacked around charred twigs where the fire has played out its game of angles and space. Lisa Forlorn is sitting on a branch, her eyes closed. She is listening to the singing birds and the dance of the spring, eyes closed and her face turned upwards. The afternoon sun is too strong for her eyelids to obscure it—beneath them whirl will-o'-the-wisps and colors she cannot name. Now there are footsteps, a cautious drumroll against the ground, still distant, but nevertheless clear among the sticks and fallen leaves. Lisa cocks her head to one side, her best ear forward, and immediately knows much about the person approaching. Someone who knows their way here, seeking out this very clearing along the path that is still hidden. It is not the heavy stride of a man she can hear—the steps are neither clumsy nor assertive, the fragile twigs don't snap under their heels. But there is something else—something she cannot put into words. Closer and closer, and all that she has learned is in fiery rebellion against risk, but hope whispers its reply and she remains there with her eyes closed until the footsteps are joined by breathing and the new arrival stops at the edge of the clearing. She can hear that she has been seen—has surrendered helplessly—and all she can do is screw her eyes more tightly shut.

"He said you'd be here."

Lisa opens her eyes and replies.

"He came to me in the autumn, supported on a crutch, and asked me to wait for you here when spring came. He said he would send you here if he found you."

Her clothes are worn but clean, her hair braided, and her face pale. Her belly is big, although the rest of her is as lean as ever. Anna Stina Knapp is the same and she is not. If she had a mirror, Lisa might say the same about herself. A year has passed. It has left none of them unmarked. For a moment they are still, until Anna Stina puts a hand to her navel.

"You said that two children was too many—that one was hard enough. Can I come with you this time?"

Anna Stina doesn't want to wait for the answer, frightened by silence and doubt. Breathless, she continues.

"This forest is so full of memories. I don't want them to stand in the way of the future. I know what draws you back here. If you help me, won't you forget what has been, and give what love you have to the child that comes? You know that in return it shall be yours just as much as it is mine. Won't you show us the way?"

Anna Stina casts down her gaze, unable to prevent herself blushing with shame.

"I have nothing. I want you to know that. That which I stand and walk in. Everything else is mere burden."

She averts her eyes in the moment of gravity and waits, unable to hear the answer over the beating of her heart.

"Lisa, I didn't hear you."

"I said I needed to find myself a new name."

Anna Stina opens her eyes and sees a tear on each cheek—on the white one and on the red one. The sun has sunk low enough to spill through the crowns of the trees, warm and yellow, making each swarm of gnats a play of light, brushing gold leaf around the slightest twig. From a distance, the dull chime of a church bell: Hedvig Eleonora. Soon there comes a reply from Johannes. Beyond, at the very periphery of the senses, the sharper sound from towers in the City-between-the-Bridges. Anna Stina shivers and hugs herself.

"The day is already far gone, but I don't want to stay here."

"The stars will light our way. The sky will be clear tonight. I know the path—in shadow as in light."

Lisa hoists the knapsack that she always keeps packed to her shoulder, free and ready from one moment to the next. Fear germinates in Anna Stina, recently forgotten in the uncertainty of the moment. Hesitation teeters on tremorous knees, the inner resilience that has previously been so constant now faltering. The burden of an unknown future leans back onto the present like a top-heavy stack of pig iron. Her hands seek out the weight of her belly.

"Perhaps the road will prove difficult."

Lisa turns to her. A white gleam cleaves the port-wine stain.

"Are there any other roads worth taking?"

Their path crosses a flourish of young pink flowers. Hand seeks out hand. The first shy stars of the evening ignite above them, beautiful and indifferent. Distant. Just a few steps later they are lost to the green.

Acknowledgments

Thank you to Fredrik Backman for your years of friendship, company, support, and literary discussions of the kind that are the prerequisite for personal development.

Thanks to my publisher, Adam Dahlin, and my editor, Andreas Lundberg, for all your constructive discussions on language and dramaturgy, and particular thanks to the latter for your assiduous scrutiny of my linguistic vices.

Thank you Sergej Stern, my translator to Russian, for lending your watchful eye to a comprehensive read-through.

Thanks to my friend and agent, Federico Ambrosini, for your indefatigable work on my behalf both in Sweden and abroad, and to Marie Gyllenhammar for your deft management of my contacts with the outside world.

Thank you to Martin Ödman for reading and commenting on the manuscript.

Thank you to Stina Jackson for your collegial support, insights, and perspectives.

Thanks to Mickel and Cecil, Emil and Anna Stina, my imaginary friends since the age of seven. You have been there for me every time I've closed my eyes. With the passing of time, you have become real enough to me that the fact that the world you inhabit is not a pleasant one is something that troubles my conscience. One critic insightfully noted that each time I dipped you into a mire it was to allow you to rise from it under your own steam—and my goodness, you did.

Thank you to my wife and children for the life we have together.